Win

3

Thank you for sticking by my side through thick and thin, and always loving me for all my perfect imperfections.

This one's for you, baby.

Love, Meagan xoxo

Prologue   Alexis

Skilled in swiftness, he has come prepared for a fight.

Dressed like he is a fashion God thundering down from the sky in a fitted navy suit, this force of a man demanded the attention of the room when he entered, locking eyes with mine while two badged security officers from the building follow in from behind him to diligently close the door before taking their sturdy places to guard on either side. He is a very handsome clean-cut man in his late forties. Introducing himself in a clear authoritative voice while standing straight at the head of the table as Sean Perris, legal authority over anything regarding the estate of Ms. Rachel Butler. It was the most well improvised plan of attack that you only see in movies or hear about in conspiracy theories.

"The only one authorized to be here and partake in the reading of Ms. Butler's Last Will and Testament is solely, Ms. Alexis Paige Andrews. The rest of you are dismissed."

The punchline he delivered jolted my entire nervous system, however the shock I felt had nothing to do with me sitting here being named the sole executor to Rachel Butler's Will. It has more to do with the fact that Rachel and I have been like sisters since we were fourteen years old, she was my soulmate friend that I thought told me everything of importance, with this particular bit of being named as her voice after death without her mother's knowledge being one of those important things fumbling around in my brain as I try to figure out if... maybe she mentioned it and I have forgotten. But I keep coming up blank.

Another blank.

When I was called by Perris Attorneys at Law to attend this reading of Rachel's Will, I was only informed of the time and place of the meeting and to come alone due to privacy for the case. I cannot convince, even myself, that I am not naive. I owned that trait too many times I care to remember, but really my mantra moving forward was to just be happy and content due to the plate I've been given. So, I did as asked, and confusingly enough ended up here, being ushered in by a beautiful tall blonde woman, up into this high-rise meeting room, with Terrie Butler already sitting front and center of the table. Her fiery red hair up in a sleek bun, the ugliest shade of red, she was pinning her very pissed and confused look on a suited man next to her. Surprisingly enough, avoiding looking at me altogether.

Hate seethed inside of me as I passed her, trying to keep this professional and get it over with, whatever this was. I held my ground and confidently got comfortable in my chair, as the blonde usher interestingly sat down next to me. Quite possibly to be a buffer since it isn't a coincidence that Terrie and I were seated as far away from each other as possible at this large, lacquered mahogany table. And now this lawyer man is sweeping me up and claiming to be the only one here with any sort of dictation on how we are going to proceed with today's agenda., I fumble to find composure when I rock on my heels in my seat for a quick second, apparently too long of a second.

A high-pitched shriek in the tone that made the silence even more cruel, hissed across the boardroom, "What the fuck did you just say?"

Although, I do think that's exactly what I would have said too if that were me talking, but it's not. I tear my gaze from blue haze, for a hurried glance at the deceitful woman sitting on the other side. Terrie Butler's eye sockets look like they are going to pop out over top of her uplifted, very fake cheekbones, and I can't help it if that grosses me out enough to be the reason I can finally, halfway, come out of my stunned silence.

"I'd like to understand what you are telling me. How...I mean," my voice started breaking up as I try to speak out on my tornado of questions, "and when would Rachel do that?"

Mr. Perris didn't get the time to answer me because Terrie's furious eyes I am accustomed to dart over to meet mine for the first time here in this meeting, interrupting as she starts in with a squealy pitch, "This is nonsense! What are you even doing here at this meeting, as it was supposed to be private? We have Rachel's binding legal Will." She starts picking up the pieces of paper in front of her and slamming them back down in place as if we didn't see her documents there, to then go on in an even louder wretchedness, "I am Rachel's Manager! I have authority as the ONLY one by her side throughout any decision in legal or financial action. You cannot tell me ..."

"Mrs. Butler, please stop for a second," puffed the grey-haired lawyer she brought with her to this meeting. He wipes his hand over his eyebrows and winces as he grunts to her in a sharp tone, "It seems as though Mr. Perris here has every piece of proof needed to determine his statement's legitimacy. Ms. Rachel Butler's estate remains in the hands of its executor, to Ms. Alexis Andrews."

Terrie continues to bark at her lawyer in her matter of fact, condescending tone, "Michael, do you even hear yourself right now?"

"What the hell estate?" She emphasizes each letter and continues her rant by raising the volume, "Does anybody here even realize that Rachel's only estate is her condo she lived in that was purchased in my name, that she rented out from me, thank you very much. Her bank accounts were monitored and shared with signatures of mutual consent, mind you. If this is trailer trash coming up with some ludicrous scam someone has drawn up for her to get paws on my husband's wealth since her friend isn't here anymore to help her out with that, I can assure you it will be shut down faster than you can walk out of here!"

There she is, the Terrie Butler I know. Always using her manipulative punches that remind everyone of just how much she controls, because when you get sucked into a world with her, she holds the keys tight to her late husband's fortune he earned as a music producer. That fortune has cost me so much, but in the end, it was Rachel that suffered the indescribable loss. It is at this moment that I realize today may be Rachel settling the score.

Loud and firm, "Ms. Butler, I apologize but Probate is already one step ahead of you on this." It is Mr. Perris speaking, Rachel's personally appointed lawyer. He looks as confident as he sounds when he rounds the room, strutting back towards me smiling, pulling his suit jacket together with both hands near his abdomen. I can see why Rachel chose him to stand for her, handsome yes, but his energy is palpable in the room, and only screams power. Rachel may have felt weak within herself, but her choice in him seems purposeful.

"Ms. Rachel came to me privately 98 days before she suddenly passed away, making a clear binding request, in front of myself and two other witnesses, needing me to collaborate with her to create a specific will to conduct, written to protect what was hers, if in fact the unfortunate day of her death would come."

Terrie was about to speak but got cut off by Mr. Perris's voice aiming down towards me, "An unspeakable tragedy this must be for you. Rachel was way too young for us to be meeting this soon."

Then he lifts his head back up and states loudly, "But Rachel was also strong willed, smart, full of all the sense, and she has already arranged this meeting to be done on her own terms. So, before you even go there to try and say this won't hold up in the court of law because of her mental health history, don't. Believe me, these documents," he points to the packet Terrie's lawyer is currently sifting through in a panic, "are the only ones to hold up in a court of law. Period."

There was a quick pause before he went on, "Legally, I cannot discuss more with you regarding my client's decisions." Mr. Perris changing his tone to only slight compassion towards Terrie, "I know this may be difficult for you to come to terms with Ms. Butler, but I can assure you," his arm reaches around the back of my chair, and he grips the top edge looking down at me with tempered eyes, giving me a little hope that everything he is saying may truly be a part of Rachel's fairytale. With a sly grin, only I could see from being this close to him, he spits out, "The only concern Ms. Rachel Butler had, was putting her trust in me to not disclose any details of this matter with you," he points to Terrie then proceeds, "nor anyone in this office, besides Ms. Andrews."

I could feel the tension starting in my forehead, the storms clouding in my senses, radiating through me in the chair. First, how dare that woman act like she gave a shit about Rachel's best interests, assume Rachel wasn't smart or strong enough to make adult decisions regarding the worth and legacy she worked her ass off for. And second, it reminds me, that the person I need the most right now isn't here.

There was a sound of scuffling in the room. Terrie stood up hastily but before walking out the door, directing daggers with her eyes at me, she said,

"You don't deserve the platform Rachel gave you, the platform I gave to you. You came from nothing. The money and time I spent on you-"

With my arms crossed and displaying the most ruthless stare I can come up with, I snapped before she could finish, "The only thing you spent... Terrie, was every last nickel I ever made you, while you forced and operated me, on that platform!"

"You always were a manipulative manager over a mother, and Rachel knew it!" I tell her. Then continuing even louder, I shout, "Leave!"

"Like Rachel specifically stated in the end for everyone to truly get a hint of the shame you brought to your family. You don't have any business being here discussing what she would have wanted because, dammit, she already spoke, it's not you. It was never you, so get out."

I was somehow still coolly sitting in my chair, and I felt anything but still.

My heart was pounding in a deafening rage as the grief slammed back the memory of the day she died, shivering standing out in the rain in my workout clothes, watching the dozen EMT's rolling out her lifeless body on a stretcher. The rain was dropping down on the white sheet that covered her over top, while the distraught condo employees banded together to form a path for the stretcher to come through the front of the building into the ambulance. All I could do was curl up on the ground, tune out everything except the sound of the rainstorm, and lay lifeless too, while my door attendant held me tight singing me his prayers.

Whiplash.

Terrie's heels clicking and clacking through the halls snapped me back to reality, to my today, as I take the time to listen to her passing through the front office yelling about everyone getting fired until her voice faded and it went quiet, but only for a second.

The door to the office I was still seething in shut hard with a bang, jolting my focus to a now smiling Mr. Perris. Pulling out his briefcase, he got seated at the front of the table.

Refusing to have any self-doubt after a glorious moment, and hoping Rachel is proud, I follow suit and meander to the chair closest to join him, settling in with a sigh.

"Okay, I'm ready," and give him the most dazzling smile I have.

Hours later...

Holy Moly. Maybe I wasn't ready.

I'm a bit restless taking a sip of my first gin and tonic of the night, then another sip to try and chase the endless dry desert of thirst down. I'm waiting in a red leather booth camouflaging me with dim candle lighting, and abstract black and white artwork centering each table, at the back of Blanc Rose Lounge. This French themed hideout is usually somewhere I try to avoid, since it sways to the more romantic scene. Romance for me has been non-existent. I have had my fair share of dating and hookups in the past, but with work being so demanding, I gave up on the idea of love a long time ago. The only true intimacy I think I have ever felt, is with my vibrator. Tonight, I am going to try to see if this gin can take me there.

Blanc Rose Lounge happens to also be the closest place to my friend Jameson's current location right now as I have sent him an SOS to meet me here.

"Hey!" Jameson greets me as he slides into the booth, seating himself directly in front of me, putting his left hand on top of mine face down on the table, using his other hand to steal a sip of my drink. Some people may assume this was a passionate moment of greeting between the two of us, although not wrong in the sense of a moment of understanding, our relationship has always been purely platonic friends and work partners. This is Jameson letting me know he is present and ready to give me his full attention, and he also wants to try my drink.

"I got here as fast as I could, even tripped a lady in flip flops running out of an elevator. I managed to save the damsel in distress from falling with my wicked reflexes," his smirk lightens my mood. As I am sure whoever the damsel was wouldn't have minded the incident once she saw her prince charming up close. Jameson oozed typical rock star sex appeal with soft dark ringlets and a long lean muscular body, blessed with a sculpted square face toned in darker silk skin. His honest chestnut eyes looking sullen while he gives me his full attention. "Tell me everything."

Regardless of readiness, I start speaking, trying to make sense of it all, "Rachel went to a lawyer before she died to create a will and cut Terrie from having any power of her assets. I didn't know about anything like this, did you?"

His neck jerks, "Seriously, no way I didn't know."

"Sorry, let me finish...Rachel named me the executor of her will. She left me things, Jameson, massive things, and I'm confused and mad at her about it all right now. Exasperation in my voice, "She left me a house!"

He replies, "A house? Like not her condo?"

"No, her condo is owned by Terrie. Honestly, it's like Rachel hid something from us, something major. My name is on a deed for a house in upstate New York, purchased by none other than Rachel herself, and then she gifted the home into my name. Why would she buy a house and not tell us?"

The waiter comes over to bring me another Gin and Tonic and get Jameson's order. I take a big gulp and when we're alone again, he asks, "When did she purchase the house?"

"Like, the first week of January, four months before she died. It must have been winter break, where I thought she was at the beach house with Terrie. That is where they always go for the holidays. I guess she made a random house buying pit stop in a nice place called Paisley."

I take another big sip.

Look up and see a very disheveled Jameson staring at me.

After our pause, he seems to still be with me, so I keep on,

"Her lapses in judgment and episodes seemed like they were improving since moving out of Terrie's house. I didn't even know she was feeling that low that night, well, until it was way too late obviously. But apparently nobody saw it. Even the lawyers told me Rachel had proven to be in a healthy state of mind during all meetings discussing her plans."

Rachel was diagnosed at ten years old with depression and anxiety after her father passed away. Her mother treated her using her own rules of treatments and medicines. Privately hiring doctors to come in to avoid being seen, always trying to sweep the label away as if it might taint the reputation of the Butler namesake. But as Rachel grew older, the depression kept coming in waves, some larger than others, and panic attacks started taking over her restless body throughout her nights.

I explain to Jameson what Mr. Perris told me about this subject. About how Rachel made sure to have legal representation and witnesses appointed by her lawyer during all meetings and finalizations of this will. All her medical files were pulled for the lawyers, and a team collaborating with her, and reviewed on request of Rachel herself. She was adamant about there not being any sort of loophole standing to where someone, like Terrie, could appeal due to her mental health history. And then I hit him with another thing,

"Oh, and her daddy's trust fund he set up for her to access this year once she turned twenty-five."

"I'm not even sure she knew about the account since she doesn't have access to anything Terrie controls, now she's left it all to me." I roll my eyes and raise my voice, "What the hell was she thinking!"

Entering the rabbit hole shaking my head in disbelief, I ask before he has any chance to speak, "Can you imagine how pissed Terrie is right now realizing this?"

Responding with his eyes locked on mine, Jameson continues, "It was her way of giving you back what Terrie took from you. She was making it right."

My voice agitated, "No way did I ever earn even a smidge of all of this. And it wasn't hers to make right because it wasn't her that did me wrong. She did nothing but have my back and be the best friend she could possibly be for me while the both of us went through Terrie's grooming project. Rachel owes me NOTHING."

Then I really fluster, "Oh my gosh, I'm just so pissed off right now."

"Relax. Relax, Lex. Try not to go there," he says trying to calm me, "because you will never find out what you are looking for. What you know is this, Rachel knew her mother had signed rights to everything of hers, she knew the control Terrie had over her head, and yours. Hell! She's who took Rachel's sanity! It wasn't a life like she wanted, ever. She made it right for herself." He takes a gulp of his drink, marking his end to his steamed-up rant.

I can tell Jameson is serious and trying to be strong for me, for us, for Rachel. Grief is a terrible strain of evils, and with us just losing her last week, Jameson and I hold a burden of guilt on our shoulders nobody will ever understand. We were like the three misfits that created an unstoppable camaraderie, and we were known for holding each other together for a lot of years, keeping one another accountable for any actions that would stir the intention away from being our best selves. We didn't help Rachel in time. It is the both of us drinking more excessively now.

Jameson grips his glass firmly and stares into his drink like it holds all his secrets before he says softly, "This shouldn't be a shocking surprise to us, you know." He takes another long sip out of the short crystal glass until the ice clinks with emptiness. Showing me the sadness on his defeated looking face, he places his brown eyes on me and continues with his next thought, "You were eventually able to cut yourself off entirely from Terrie a couple years ago. She couldn't so much. Terrie's her mother, Rachel had more to lose, expectations to withhold, even if she wanted nothing to do with her. She considered you her family, and dammit, she was yours. So, she did a normal, professional function as an adult with a career and money and created a Will."

His voice grew louder through the scream of his finished thought, "Fuck Terrie! She will get what she deserves one day. Leave it at that."

And so, with Jameson's request, I tried to do just that for him. We told our waiter to keep the gin and tonic coming...quickly. We ordered, Truite en papillote to share, and quietly ate with only light conversation from then on.

He didn't need to know yet, all the questions left with me today that hold a different burden altogether. Because everything is still too fresh, I took this moment of quiet for him and for myself. He is right, Rachel was sick. If there were to be a blame on anyone who may have caused her to be in a pain you can't come back from, it was her mother, Terrie. That idea made us feel better about ourselves when we were already knee deep in our own pile of feeling like we didn't do enough to help her.

Does that make us better people?

Not so much, but we are going for happiness and contentment, remember?

Jameson and I paid the bill and took a short cab ride back to our condo building to end the night, splurging on the dinner and fare to try to make us happy.

Once I got inside, skipping anything more and heading straight to my bed, I tossed the large packet of paperwork to the side and pulled out the envelope left addressed to me.

Filed with the deed of the house, as the only other personal item she wanted to privately include, no eyes to see it but mine. Inside was a piece of writing Rachel wrote with purple gel pen, her words written to me in a song.

I barely got through the first paragraph before the tears were barreling out of my eyes. I couldn't handle it just yet, too tired, quickly sealing it back up in the envelope, and turning off my light.

11

Wings of Paisley

A piece of you
A piece of me
No witness to our sins
Never peace in hearts of thee
Lost in her head
Rather be dead

Fleeting this earth
Writhing, rolling, throat on fire
A can of waste
A can to taste
Knowing her was my last desire
Bury me next in Paisley
I found my wings in Paisley

Amidst the battle within her head
Came a demon topped in Red
Speaking tongues
A cry passed along
Away from her truth in Paisley

I found my wings in Paisley
First in your womb
Last all I see is your tomb
A solemn truth that was hid from my youth
Desperate to forgive
Secrets for me in Paisley
I found my wings in Paisley

A deal at a cost
She took and she lost
Her only truth lives in Paisley
His searching couldn't find
The memory she took in her mind
The day she went home to Paisley
I found my wings in Paisley

A sight to see
A buzzing bee
My only truth lives in Paisley
Fishing for the strength to come across
But the shadows from my dark

May make them fall apart
Not in on the secret, I don't want to bring you pain
So, I was happy to be a fly on the wall in Paisley
I found my wings in Paisley

Chapter 1   Alexis

Focusing my switchboard of a brain, I tuned into the loudest sound that could help push my body to keep moving forward. Drumming legato caught my attention, like a hard deep hum that rolls until it dips, in and out, in and out of the ceramic tiles, like a scratched disk skipping in a fast, even tempo, until it hushes, hitting the carpet. I managed to fit everything I could possibly need in this one giant bag I was rolling through the airport. I was proud of myself, I literally almost knocked down Jameson's door last night in my excitement to show him.

When his door finally flew open, plaid pajama pants and eyes wide in panic, when he blurted out asking, "What the hell, Lexi!"

Looking at me, then at my bag, and then back at me, while I stood there almost waiting for his pleased 'way to go,' instead he asked me, "What, did you get an earlier flight or something? Holy shit, are you leaving now?"

My face went from delighted to annoyed when I realized he had no idea why I was there, when I replied, "Jameson, I'm showing you how I fit everything in this bag, look, it zipped with the extender thing you told me about." I was bending down wiggling the zipper in demonstration. I swear if I weren't leaving today, he would have slammed the door in my face. He only appeased me a little when he gave me a 'good job.'

But then when he actually looked at my luggage bag on wheels, he raised his neat black eyebrows and said to me,

"You're kidding me right, Lexi this is twice the size of you..." Hands on his hips in his rant, he continued saying, "You cannot lug that heavy bag and pull Luna at the same time."

Like a true independent adult, I stuck my tongue out at him and rolled my luggage back into my condo's front door, only a few feet away from my best friend and neighbor.

On the day I first met Jameson, the bell couldn't have come fast enough. I was eleven, in fifth grade, and I hadn't slept much the night before since my parents had decided to stay over. I woke up to the sound of one of their monstrous fights involving screaming profanities and something breaking. I ran to my favorite hidden spot in a nearby park thinking I could get some relief from my stressful night. It was therapy for me. Pressing play on my headphones, I would dance. Drifting into a whirlpool of colors surrounding me, the feelings and shades of the rhythm will start to swirl, like a mood ring trying to choose the right one.

I remember running past the basketball courts to find my favorite small clearing off the path, but on that day, I wasn't alone or hidden. Jameson was sitting on the picnic table with his book bag next to his feet. Once he saw me standing there looking bewildered, he spoke to me right away.

"Hey, oh good, got ya right where I want you. My name's Jameson, and I've been sitting over there watching my brother play ball the last few days and I saw you here dancing. I couldn't come up with a way to introduce myself since you always have those things on your ears. Anyways, I want you to work with me."

Jameson had to have been born bossy. Once he gave me a chance to talk back, I found out about his dream of being on stage singing, preferably in a band, and how he wanted me to be his first bandmate. I remember laughing at him, telling him how I didn't know how to sing or play instruments, thinking it was best if he did his own thing. Instead of taking no for an answer, he decided he would bring me a song the next day and we would work together finding the best beat. It was a strange feeling, having someone see you, see a worth in you that nobody has ever tried to notice, not even yourself. He saw me for my dance, sharing a common love of the arts, the only type of love we felt, we were compatible in determination as he decided to make it his job to mold and perfect us to get us out of the slums one day. As we grew older and still hung out as best friends, there was never that chemistry to build anything more, it wasn't ever there to be anything more.

Jameson was the first and only person that had stepped up in front of my face and made me become his person, always convincing me it is because I needed him, but over the many years we both know he needed me too. It was like he reached out and grabbed me from the bottom of a pool and swam me up for air, then in a domino effect, I did the same thing for Rachel a couple of years later, and the three of us became a solid trio. Until Jameson and I blindly left the lifeguard stand one day, and drowning in her mental agony, Rachel took her breath of life away from us.

Grief in my heart.

Oh, the ache.

No peace in the hearts of thee

I've tried to convince Jameson in these last few months that I was capable of living on my own, too many hours away from him, starting up my own business, in a new town, with all new people. He has taken a selfish stance on the matter, staying unconvinced that moving will do me any good and it wasn't realistic for me. Picking myself off the ground and moving because Rachel and I had a dream of a new normal, and she found a desperate way to give that to me, while I am left shattered and alone, still wishing within the depths of my soul this was all a joke, and Rachel was still alive.

With no such luck, today, Jameson stood with me outside our building, waiting on a car to take me and my dog, Luna, to the airport. After having one last teary goodbye with my loving grey-haired doorman, Fergus, I turned to try to say goodbye to my only person left in my life that is considered my family. The words wouldn't come out, only muffled sounds through my tears. Jameson squeezed me tight and told me I always had a home with him. Then, I rolled down the window, despite the cool breeze, and waved him goodbye as the car drove me away, still so early the streetlights were highlighting the cityscapes of Boston.

When I checked in, and they made me pay an 'over the weight limit' fee, of a hundred bucks, which I thought was a bit overboard, but paid the dues anyways, deciding it was not going to ruin my day. I most definitely will not be telling Jameson about it. Besides that, annoyance, the flight was smooth, and I was feeling good about my journey. The airport noise grew louder coming up the elevator at the Arrivals terminal, buzzing with cheers and cries from friends and loved ones greeting my fellow passengers. Being alone has always been in front of my face, and I have learned not to let it bother me so much, but that's mostly because I had my friends. Now without them, I am orphaned again. There won't be anybody I know waiting for me to arrive.

My parents overdosed together on the same shared drugs that contained a deadly amount of fentanyl when I was only 17 years old and still attending my senior year of public school. I was an only child, living with parents addicted to methamphetamine and I started tuning into music blaring in a pair of headphones around my childhood apartment to drown out the noise of both the screams and the silence. My mother, Tereza, had moved here from the Czech Republic with her grandparents when she was seventeen, and got pregnant with me a year later. My father was raised by the slums off the poor Boston streets. Both worked slimy jobs for under the table cash, both made the pool halls their primary perch. My great grandparents mostly raised me as an infant and toddler but passed away before I was five. Left with just my junkie parents, I think the only way I survived as a child in their hands has got to be due to that government monthly stipend that surfaced in their bank account every month. Proof of my life to the Department of Family Services equaled food stamp money my mother could trade off for cash to feed her drug habit.

On the last day I remember seeing my mother Tereza alive, she was strung out laying naked on the couch with her backside facing the room just staring down the couch cushion. She had a thin blanket slinking off her body, and I remember walking closer to her about to pull it up to cover her. My mother's eyes had stopped sparkling altogether after her years of drug use. So like her normal state, she didn't even flinch when I hovered over to check for signs of breathing. Her lips were deep pink and parted wide showing off acne rashes around the corners of her mouth as I listened to her vibrating snores quietly escaping. Breathing, but she was so out of her mind on a normal basis, quite literally, and I said nothing when I turned and walked out. I didn't pursue any sort of loving relationship with my parents after a certain age because I knew better. Even then, I was too detached to care.

You can do this, Alexis.
A piece of you
A piece of me

Finding my way through baggage and pet pickup, I was grateful when an employee on a golf cart stopped and drove us to my new leased SUV I paid to have parked in the lot. All thanks to my new normal dream with Rachel, she left me a five-million-dollar bank account I will never get used to. One I don't want to get used to because, that was not the reason she wanted me to be here. A new normal meant blending in, suburban life with close friends and neighbors, a place to dance, to find new hobbies, possibly everlasting love... but above all, a new normal meant staying away from people like Terrie, avoiding the sharks that prey on the naïve and innocent. Freedom to follow your own rules and make your own mistakes. A life without a chain attached.

The acorns crunched underneath my tires as I slowed to a brake and pressed the button to park. My dog's boxy white head nudged against my right shoulder as her paws stood firmly on the center console. She was probably just as ready to get out of the car as I was. It has been 6 weeks since I was last here finalizing renovations. Charismatic from the outside, it is a round shape house lifted off the ground, with traditional red brick layering, and a wrap-around porch. Located in an aged neighborhood, the private lots give the feel of retreat from everyday living.
The closest neighboring house across the street that has the same sturdy red bricks as mine, seems to have occupants quite a bit older than me. Maybe I am profiling but seeing that the mailbox looks like a freshwater fish with a wide mouth, and there is a quilted flag in the shape of an apple, hanging off their front porch, I'm assuming they are older than sixty. I quickly stepped

out of my car and headed up the steps of the porch to my teal-colored front door, and with Luna beside me, we crossed the threshold in together.

It took Luna no time at all to race in with her toenails clicking along the hardwood floors, through the hallway, whizzing by me to jump on the couch in our new wide-open space. I only allow my heart to jolt once before I snap myself out of my head and smile at my charming new home. The ceilings were open, boasting natural wood beams enhanced with professional indirect lighting. In the kitchen, there were even tiny crystal specs in the ivory granite countertops popping out from the light, looking like a constellation of stars. Cherry cabinets and a Mediterranean palette throughout the house, with just a hint of fresh paint smell fluttering off the walls. I walk around the living room, stroking the edges along all my new loungers and chesterfields, the crème couch wraps around in the living room centering in on the stone stacked fireplace. Displayed luxuriously across the hardwoods, a giant mahogany fur rug on the floor, and matching fur pillows aligning the couch cushions bring texture to the room.

During my initial walkthrough the first-time visiting Paisley, one of the contractors who helped me decide on flooring, tried to convince me that his daughter, Sabine, was the only one in this town to hire for interior design. She was the friendliest face I had met in a terribly long time. Tall and thin with a straight posture, she has the body to be on a runway, and a personality that fit with my quirky one immediately.

Sabine is twenty-one years old, and still attending classes at a college nearby. I didn't know her ethics or street cred enough to believe she could do it professionally, and in a crazy small timeframe, but as she and her father stood in front of me, he pulled my heart strings by listing off all these numerous reasons why I should hire her, giving me nothing but glowing reviews. She hugged me when I agreed, the first happy endearing embrace I have felt since Rachel died. So, I tried to absorb as much as her glowing energy as I could and hired her to be my new assistant and dance studio employee, here in Paisley, NY.

Looking around, I will also be giving her a glowing review. Her personal touches like the aloe plant in the corner, and the multiple oil paintings of street dance on the walls, she somehow made this wide-open space feel like I was made to be here, even as a solo occupant, and not feel so…well…lonely.

After unloading my luggage out of my car, tagged with neon stickers cautioning the weight, I decided I needed some fresh air to help shut out the panic that is starting to simmer inside myself. Sporting my purple rain boots, Luna and I go explore the back side of my property. The property stretches with eight acres of woods and patches of fields, until you reach a side road leading into the old town of Paisley. The breeze picked up a cooler temperature as Luna and I walked at a brisk speed across the grass into the wooded cedars, trying to keep the house in view since I was uncertain of my way around.

There is that doubt again, go away.
Yes Lexi, you can manage this.
You are in control.

Luna, taking advantage of my sudden uptick in pace, started pulling my arm directing us into a patch of green leafy weeds, so I unclasped the least to let her run free. Always getting us into a bit of trouble, she is ignorant to whether I could break out in poison ivy rash, her nose down, hot on a scent. Considering all this land she has now to run around in, I think we are both going to like our new life in Paisley. A few feet ahead of me, Luna barks and snaps me out of my head.

I ask her in my best high pitch dog mom voice, "What is it?"

She stares back at me with a big slobbery grin and her whole backside swaying from side to side being so cute in her needy moment of happiness. I turn, "Come on, let's go back home so you don't spook me deeper in the forest."

Luna runs past me back towards the path we came in on, and we make it back home right as it starts getting darker outside.

After tidying up with pinot noir, I muster the energy to eat some peanut butter toast and bury myself in my bed covers. The master bedroom shares one of the same walls of windows off the backside of the house curving into a panoramic view of the wooded backyard. Also, I'm certain this can act as my bat cave since I splurged on custom black out curtains that can be set to open and close on a timer.

I feel like a queen bat in a treehouse, a fucking awesome treehouse at that.

When I awoke early the next morning, I decided to keep my exercise routine as normal as I could in a new place, wearing my hoodie and headphones. I start into my hour of yoga and Pilates. After showering and making sure Luna has gone potty outside, I texted Sabine.

Me: Leaving the house now, see you soon

It was the beginning of October, and the frigid air was already swirling around outside. The reds of leaves started poking out from the tops of the trees almost looking like hats, aligning, the town roads. The charming shops were mostly local named stores but noticing most of these shops were not yet opened. When I looked at the time and realized that it was in fact a quarter till nine, I couldn't help but be a bit surprised. The pace of life is a bit slowed down here as opposed to the speed of minutes I have been running through since we got our first gig. Needing to hear a familiar voice, I dial the person who usually needs my wake-up call. Jameson answered singing a tune to me, a beautiful voice with that roughness for jazzy blues and the edge for rock and roll. As his number one fan, I hummed along while I drove. Detailing my day helps his anxiety as Jameson likes to be fed his need to be sure about who, where, what, when. So after his morning solo, it's unsurprising Jameson asks, "I'm glad you got there okay. Are you heading to the studio today? Lots to do and I don't know how you are going to manage without me."

I tell him, "I'm going in to see it today, but first Sabine is meeting me nearby at a coffee shop in town to give me my keys. It appears I won't be giving up my caffeine intake after all."

He laughs out, "You thought country people don't drink coffee? I mean surely they do; it probably just tastes like motor oil."

I try to put on my most fake positive voice possible, "Don't knock small town coffee, I'm sure it tastes country fresh. And let's not forget the perks like shorter lines and simpler orders! I'm sure the customers around here will be smiling and polite, and not those, nose in their phone type, rude city slickers."

Just then the thought of Sergio's coffee stand back in Boston had me feeling that worry again. How could I move away from a daily hot cup of breakfast tea sifted to perfection? Sergio made sure my tea was always large, hot, and strong. Just like your men, Sergio would say to me in his strongest Italian accent when handing over my cup. Of course, I always had to respond, you're damn right!

There was another silence across the phone line.

I call out, "Jameson!"

Knowingly caught at being distracted, he replies in a quick breath, "Yeah?"

The night we lost her, Jameson's common flame he had blew out, holing up in his condo most evenings, barely showing any creative effort during group meets. Now months later of robotic movements, he has maintained a healthier rhythm in these last few weeks, showing more readiness to return to his new normal.

"You promised me mind blowing lyrics and a year we could celebrate. Write me a song, let me mix and choreograph and then together we can prove to ourselves we can still pour love into our art even without her here. I'm trying to find my happiness again and I can't fully commit to doing so if I know you aren't trying to do the same."

There was a long breathy pause until he spoke, "You're awfully bossy like a city girl. I am not sure Farmer Joes are going to be able to handle you." Jameson is skilled at deflecting and is a typical stubborn man of emotions.

"Ha! Who is to say I am even wanting to find a Farmer Joe? "

"You moved from a city filled with good looking people and successes that only dreams are made of to some diluted idea of normal happiness in a random town Rachel got you..."

The pause is heavy.

"That can only mean you dig coveralls and crocs. I'm sorry Lex, I just don't understand why you want this. You have guys lining up falling to their feet in lust for you and a career you could take to the next level here, it's called having your new normal life here."

"Okay, so you will send me a song?" I ask, copycatting his stance on deflecting to dig just a little deeper...

He replies, "I can't wait to see the look on that toothless hick when we take the stage together next time."

Our friendly arguments always have me smiling. Playfully I tell him, "Stop it..."

Toning his sass down, he says, "Knowing you are away finding your path isn't easy for me. I just want to be sure we will still be able to make music together, take the stage together the way it should be."

I tell him, "It's going to be a really good new chapter. I can feel it."

Now that I'm here, hopefully he will find his way.

Carla's Coffee Bistro is one of the storefronts found in the heart of downtown. Original buildings aging with grace, most of the stores boast their charm with wide window fronts along the clean streets. Not the one to try to parallel park, instead I circle around twice before finding a parking spot in a free lot. Stepping out, I quickly zip up my white puffy coat and make my way towards the shop that holds my tea destiny.

At 5'6, I have a lean muscular body frame with all my fat packed into my breasts and butt, yes, apparently God was having a guy's night when he made me. In my defense I have kept it up with challenging work for these 25 years.

Barely any warmth on my body, means cold winters are brutal, so I layer up. I spot Sabine getting out of her car just a few spots away, one hand on her face as the breeze blows her long ashy blonde hair all around. I toss up my own hood and wave to her.

"Alexis! It's so great to see you again! Oh my God, can you believe this wind?!" Sabine is in a navy blue peacoat with a belt tied in the middle, and her long lean legs hidden in wide legged jeans, and I can't help but feel under dressed for this coffee date. I am the one to launch into her for a hug hello, missing my new friend while I tied up my loose ends in Boston.

"Tell me you're here for good this time!" she says while giving me the warmest welcome back.

"Here for good," I reply soaking in that thought. "I haven't seen the studio complete yet, so I'm looking forward to today."

We walked together towards the café at a brisker pace, trying to find shelter inside, only when the sight of pure man goodness strutting across the street caught my eye.

If this is Farmer Joe, I could be into it.

He is tall and broad with messy hair blowing from the wind, just long enough to lightly cover his ears.

I tried not to be so obvious covered through my hood, but I took him in longer than one needed to, wearing a black leather jacket like it was made for him, hands in his pockets, yeah, he is definitely NOT a Farmer Joe.

Are you sure this is not Boston?

He struts confidently with conceit coming closer, closer...

Sabine's voice cheers, "This is Carla's!" She then stops abruptly, and I subtly run into her enough to make this moment so awkward.

"OH," is all I can bellow out quickly as I look up at the sign in blurry vision. Sabine opens the door and then, an arm covered in black leather reaches out from behind me and wraps his fingers around the entrance door, allowing Sabine to toss a smile back with a loud, "Thank you!"

Mr. Not a Farmer Joe sends her a quick courtesy nod, as I peer over my hood to see lips in a hard line under light scruff. Slightly turning, his eyes like Iceland catch mine for a quick second. Fire and Ice.

I glanced away so fast, I felt my eyelashes tangle with the fur on my hood's edge.

Keeping my cool moving forward, sandwiched in between Sabine and hotness, I start feeling the warmth as the heat from the cafe greets us. The menu written above the counter on a chocolate-colored chalkboard, the decor is simple but homey. Customers seated spaciously throughout.

My friend asks, "So, I've got to ask what you thought of your place when you walked in last night?" Sabine prompts me with a huge smile on her face awaiting my answer as we stand beside each other waiting in line.

Snapping out of my black leather thoughts, I tell Sabine, "I was floored how great it looks! I literally danced around with wine all night admiring the details in all the work. And my bed is huge! I cannot thank you enough for helping me through all of this."

"Heck ya girl, I made sure you came home California King style...within budget," she adds with a small laugh.

The employee greets us, "Hi there, what can I get for you?" The boy, no older than eighteen, had a red long sleeve t-shirt with a logo of a brown coffee cup steaming out the letters CARLAS. Sabine looked at me for the go ahead and placed her order of a hazelnut coffee. With my turn, "I'll have a large hot tea, please."

"You said a large tea, what kind of tea would you like?"

"Oh, um, I'll have just a plain breakfast tea, please." I bite my tongue before I tell him to hurry because I can't feel my nose.

"Okay, would you like lemon?"

Gosh, could this kid be any slower? Now I'm just getting irritated thinking of Jameson laughing at this. I need caffeine stat.

"No thanks."

"Alright..." the boy continues punching in my order to the register, and asks, "Honey?"

Confused, I reply, "Uh, yes?"

I look at the boy now with a little more glare to my eyes. He points to a jar in the shape of a bear sitting in my view, just in time for me to zip up my next comment that may not have proven a good first impression. The only thing I have ever eaten honey on is a piece of bread. "No honey for me, thanks, just plain. Please." I emphasized the last please.

The boy shakes his head and grins at me, "Sorry, it's just with all these options, I have to offer. Hey, you never know you might want to try something new one day and end up really liking it." His smile grows larger with more teeth as he looks at me. I know this boy is just trying to be sincere. So, I participate in this cute coffee shop kindness and muster up my biggest smile for the boy, "No problem, I totally get it. I assure you I like mine large, strong, and hot."

Holy crap!

Did I just say that aloud?

And yes, apparently kind of loud, because there was a grunt, choke like sound coming out from behind me. I glance to find Mr. Not Farmer Joe staring at his feet, hand reaching behind holding the back of his neck. I don't think he sees me squirm from looking at him as I quickly move out of the way, fast, and towards a back booth hoping to reclaim some color back in my face. I didn't even look back to watch the sexy man walk out. Not a very smooth first impression on my first male encounter in town.

Sabine slips into the booth with me and lays down her cup to take off her gloves, "I know you are probably anxious to get to your studio today, but I have a gift for you," placing the floral printed gift bag in front of me and scrunching her face nervously, she proceeds to say, "I want to say first that I hope I didn't overstep."

I give her a look of question and ask, "Not my keys?"

"Those are actually in there too, but there is something else. Just open it up."
I start pulling out the tissue paper until I come to a large, wrapped present, heavy to hold. Unwrapping, I pull out a large frame, decorated in pearls, and behind the glass is the song, Wings of Paisley, that Rachel had handwritten in purple gel pen.
The last time I flew in to meet with Sabine, I had pulled it out to read it over for the millionth time while we waited for the inspector to finish his report. She peeked over my shoulder, so I let her read it. Then, I made her keep it for me as an incentive to get back when I was actually here for good.

"Wow, Sabine, this is beautiful." My eyes are full of warm tears I urge to fight back.
Sabine warmly states, "I thought it would be something nice you could display somewhere private in your studio, like your Mixx room. And if you don't want it framed like that for anyone to see, you won't hurt my feelings by taking it out, and forgetting I ever did this. It's just, I have gotten to know how important this piece of you is, and I thought the frame would help it from not getting ruined."

Wiping the moisture from my eyes, I manage to say, "Thank you, really. Yes I am going to hang it. It will remind me of her in a somber way but that's okay. I saw that part in her that was raw and dark, and she was never afraid to confide in me that pain she always felt. These words were her strength when I wasn't there to know why."
I finish, "So, yeah, this is the best gift ever!"

In hiring Sabine, I gave her most of the truth about myself, that I am a dance choreographer from Boston, and I'm starting over from the tragic death of a friend. After we spent some time together with projects over phone calls and face chats, I felt good enough to share with her the identity of Rachel, who was a celebrity in her own right with her short career.
Being linked to the Butler name may cause me issues while building my business at the dance studio in my new hometown, so as taught since childhood, I like to be cautious. Sabine reacted like the good human being I hoped she was, following my lead in the conversation, and not asking me any personal details of the family. I appreciated her natural respect for me, and I'm not worried she will lead the rumor mill to defame me before I step into a grocery store in town.
Rachel had accomplishments some only get to dream about, dancing along stages amongst some of the most talented artists, but it was just being the daughter of the dead high profile music producer, B.B. Butler, who would get her the recognition. B.B. and Rachel were a close daddy daughter duo, a father known to always have stars in his eyes when Rachel was with him. The media ate it up all throughout Rachel's public childhood, and when Rachel was ten, and he was away on business, he died suddenly in a car accident, leaving Rachel with only Terrie.

Rachel always tried her best to keep her adamant loyalty to her father's legacy. Unfortunately, it came with many long years with Terrie always deepening the wound by rooting thoughts into Rachel's already sad and anxious head, convincing Rachel she was never going to be good enough in her father's eyes if she didn't work harder. Rachel told me she always felt like a caged animal with her hidden treatments and constant monitoring under Terrie's authority. She would say that one day she will find her freedom is a do-over. That was the beginning of our constant chatter for a future new normal.

Refusing to be without the lavish lifestyle he built with talent and arduous work, Terrie took advantage gaining recognition just in the last name by creating her own production company. She took notice of how well Rachel, and I worked together, and derived her selfish, lucrative plan, to use it to her own advantage.

 Once high school was over, that's when Terrie told us she was going to manage our careers. Anything we did went through her. She was the only source of income for us, the only source of our dance classes, the only source to all our electronic equipment. I was an orphan and a legal adult with nothing. Rachel was tied and I wasn't going to leave Rachel, so we signed contracts Terrie convinced us of.

Young and naïve, once she legally owned our talent, she squeezed us for every ounce of energy we had. Rachel's struggle with panic attacks got worse around this time, she was constantly worried with never being good enough for Terrie's impossible demands. I was just aiming to be something more than nothing and sticking with Rachel was all I became to know. I was also sleep deprived and weak from the nonstop work we were having to complete. My inner strength was much stronger than Rachel, and I tried to hold her tight in the days and nights, because I was there throughout all of it with her, at every lesson, workout, recital, weigh in, show, contest, every try out, we were signed up for it all together. That was the only way Rachel would take part, I would have to join.

Perfecting us both.

Sabine digs into my gift bag to pull out the second small, wrapped box.

Woo hoo

 Inside are my new keys to my studio and loft hung on a keychain next to a large picture charm of Chuck Norris. We drank down our liquid warmth and planned our upcoming weeks with work. Sabine is also finishing some of her college course classes, giving me extra time to spend on my own to settle in.

The idea of owning my very own dance studio had always been my main goal for myself growing up. Since putting it in my head as a teenager, I felt like if I didn't carry out this dream, I would drown in a life that wouldn't be mine to claim. Dancing became my source of power and freedom. I like to share the love of dance, always lost in rhythm on dance floors next to random sweaty bodies. Call me crazy, but as long as I'm not getting groped inappropriately, I will dance with anyone in a crowd, but never for anyone but myself.

But this one was created for me. So, as a leap of faith that my future holds the dreamy new normal Rachel and I intended, it was Chuck Norris who opened the door for me when I walked into my new studio today. Totaling the hot guy count I have seen in Paisley today to two.

Chapter 2   Declan

As the double automatic doors open, I managed to keep steady enough to not slop all down my trousers today. The fluorescent lighting overhead is a stark morning greeting as I approach the nurse's station in my typical Monday fashion, welcomed by Sydney peeking up at me from her black cat eye frames, she exclaims, "I don't know how I would be able to survive Mondays without you, Declan," and reaches for the beverage carrier holding the usual order of coffee favorites from Carla's.

"You over exaggerate," I say wryly, as I pick up the chained pen to print my name on the mandatory sign in list, right as another employee appears. I don't remember the petite blonde's name, but when I look at her all I can think about is her tedious drink order that annoys the shit out of me. This girl's customized drink has more modifications than my Ducati speed bike parked outside. That not being bad enough, I have to endure her ruthless come on every time I visit. She speaks bending across to pat her hand on mine while I'm writing,

"I still don't know how you manage all this on your bike," proceeding to bat her eyelashes a little too long at me, as her eyes linger over my body.

"I've seemed to have gotten a handle on it I suppose," I retorted, sounding uninterested to continue a flirty conversation. While sipping her drink she gets foam on her upper lip, only to look at me and swipe her tongue in a long deliberate stroke across. I'm not sure how bringing coffee has tipped the wrong impression to this one.

I step back from the desk, and with a smile and nod, I continue through to the patient corridor and stop at the familiar entranceway. The door is cracked, and I knock stepping into the room. I am greeted by Isabelle, one of the veteran nurses on staff I most admire.

"Hello Declan," she says in greeting.

"Good morning," I reply, removing my leather jacket, I reach for the inside pocket, to pull out a bag of trail mix and place it on her iPad that's laying on a side table in the room.

"Ooo,"

"I love Mondays," she cheers clapping her hands with her wide smile. Isabelle is not a coffee drinker, and once, I noticed her stash of trail mix, with raisins, flowing out of its bag next to her workstation and found out her love for the snack. In a feeling of not being able to help, Monday coffee and trail mix is my gift of appreciation for the healthcare team.

I step quietly over to the hospital bed draped in white thin sheets and place my hand in one the same size as my own. "Hello, brother," I voiced audibly in greeting. No matter how many visits, it still always feels terrible the way I have to watch my older brother rot on this hospital bed. Laying on his back with tubes encompassing his body, his irreversible vegetative state seeming to depress me more and more every time I see him. Daniel is twenty-eight, the eldest brother of David and I, with me being in the middle.

While I adjust Daniels pillows around his hips, Isabelle drifts around the room working and quietly notating in his health chart. Old enough to be my grandmother, Isabelle acquires a face of beauty with her Korean lineage and a heart of pure gold. She's a smart ass too.

"He seemed to have had some wild dreams that kept him restless a bit in the night," Isabelle says in her warm tone. She always somehow manages to give me an update on Daniel's state. Due to the likelihood of him not ever gaining consciousness again, it is kind of her to give me comfort with details that help me stay connected to him as a person, rather than a puppet to a machine.

Finding a seat on the stool, I speak to Daniel aloud, "I bet I would have liked to hear about those wild dreams!"

"I bet you would, too," Isabelle snorts, her aged mouth creasing as she smiles wide.

I've always felt unclear about what to do when I visit, usually I just like to sit with him quietly. Finding words to fill space and discussing deep feelings isn't something I'm good at. Repetitive beeps sound in the background, as I manage to come up with telling him a story about our little brother, David, who brought a date back to his place Saturday night, only to walk in finding dad in his underwear, shuffling around in the kitchen looking for a snack. David called me complaining, on and on, about how the girl took one look at Dad's beer gut and briefs and decided it was best to leave. David and my father both work in our family-owned boxing gym that has an apartment above that they live in. That's where I used to live as well, before I started renting a condo closer to work. My father has grown feebler in his years, and usually keeps to himself resting in his free time. But without my mother here anymore, he still needs to be house trained. Discussing my family when I talk to Daniel is always something I try to do.

I was born in the green hills of Northern Ireland, extending from generations of hard-working men and women trying to build a mountain with a molehill through their years of poverty. My brothers and I grew up in a small white concrete house in a quiet village right outside of Ballymena, Ireland. My mother and father worked in blue collared jobs living paycheck to paycheck, but it never felt like we went without. My parents were so in love it felt like that's all that mattered while we were young. We were always sent to school with something to eat and money never seemed to be an open worry in our house.

My father, Len, worked as an auto mechanic in a small garage in town. It sat next to an old gym run by a short, bald gentleman who was a longtime friend and mentor of my dad. He would let us wrestle around and practice our kicks and punches while waiting for my dad to finish work. We were young spectators of the ring, witnessing friendly competitions morphing into brute, bloody, intense fights, exposing us to the idea of focus and determination within the sport. Calculating every movement as I watched fight after fight of local leagues and sweaty bar patrons settling scores, it was mesmerizing to watch. Unlike David and I, Daniel was less invested in the sport even as a child, instead choosing to wait in the mechanic shop to read or draw waiting on my dad to finish.

My mother, Celia, had light brown curly hair and dark green eyes, with a fiery beauty that lit up a room. As a longtime secretarial employee at the hospital, she worked hours both days and nights, and devoted all the rest of her sleepy hours to creating a loving home.

Unfortunately, I do not have too many memories of my mother since she got sick and passed away when I was only seven, leaving my father with a broken heart, trying to take care of us the best he could. With help around town and our grandparents stepping in occasionally, we managed to run the household with 4 boys and not catch it on fire.

A few years after my mother's passing, my maternal grandparents also died within the same time of one another, leaving an unexpected inheritance of money from an insurance policy written to my father.

Possibilities until opportunity presented itself.

It's a vivid memory I have shortly after that time, when my dad sat all three of us down for dinner one night and made it feel like a formal family meeting.

He addressed us wearing corduroys and a collared shirt, which was unusually nice for him. I remember him saying with a sterner voice to his normal,

"Boys, I want to talk to you about somethin' important, so I need yer to listen carefully, my grandfather used to say, Anáil na beatha an t-athrú, which means, change is the breath of life, almost like a gift."

Six puzzled eyes stared back at him as he continued,

"I made a decision for us today that I think you are going to like, but there's going to be a lot of change for us with it. And I need to be sure you three understand how different it might begin to feel for all of us. But this is a challenge we shouldn't back down on, one that, I'm not going to back down on, and I'm sure there are going to be plenty of excitin' things, for all of us, along the way...as long as we keep our hearts open."

My father spoke to us that day with the first fire in his eyes since my mother passed, not the same flame that used to burn for her of course, a different kind. After all the years, I've realized that flame he had that night, was one for his three boys, burning for the opportunities he was trying to give us at a time he felt like giving up. A chance, a way off the path of the dull future, a way for us to survive.

A month later we moved here to Paisley, NY on an investment opportunity. With a lead from some Irish chatter and some opportunities for European investors in the market, Len bought a boxing gym. In the middle section of the main street, and named after my mother, CeCe's Gym, still stands proudly 17 years later. Once we arrived from Ireland, my father dedicated every waking hour he had, pouring himself into CeCe's. Back then he even worked extra hours as a mechanic, keeping our family and the gym afloat, until one day he was able to slow down once we were old enough to help take over.

Mondays have a way of brightening up by the time I drive from Daniel's long term care home to work. I make it into the club where I'm engulfed in the familiar smell of vanilla mixed with tobacco walking through the staff hallway towards my office. Echoes in the long-illuminated hall start getting louder as I round the corridor passing one of the security stations. I walked to the end and entered my key passcode to open the unmarked door.

"Well, well, well look who decided to show up?" Jokes Ronnie, then throws a red rubber football in the air towards me.

"Miss me, Sweetheart?" I croon as I'm lifting up, wrapping my fingers around the ball for the catch. Tossing it back and finding my green leather chair, I sit.

I do not hold a typical day to day, 9-5 job. I'm a co-owner of the nightclub, Swollen, located in a more Indie rock community right outside of Paisley. With the club in an old warehouse, the guys and I decided on an open concept for our business offices within the space. We have neon signs decorating the walls and a quarter of the space dedicated to our workout area. As the three owners of the building and nightclub, Dax, Ronnie, and I all set up our individual desk and computer equipment around the other three corners of the room.

Friends since youth, we started bonding as we played on the same recreational rugby team. Our friendship broke into a brotherhood when we all started after school training together in the ring at my family's boxing gym. Even though all three of us grew up quite different from each other, we were teenage boys all packed with angst and aggression, bonding with the same values of hard work and dedication. The sport became our obsession as we enjoyed living, breathing, watching, doing anything we could, sport related to boxing and martial arts. We went from good to good enough trying to perfect our skills in each match. And through the years, once we followed each other into the world of underground fights that held big payouts, we made a pact. Me being the finance guy in the group, I set up a financial goal with a solid three-year business plan for each of us to reach. Agreeing was the easy part as we shook on it, all our hands and knuckles were bruised and swollen, and that's how a detail became the name of the club three years later.

"Piles and Piles, numbers and numbers.." I grumble out loud as I try to organize the stacks of paper scattered throughout my desk.

Dax breaks the silence first, "Hey, Irish," the nickname referring to me, not the most original, but these were teenage Americans coming up with it, "did you see Ronnie actually chatting up that chick at the bar the other night?"

"Oh, Fuck off!" yells Ronnie.

"The one that looks like she'd slay him...he has no chance," I say, pushing to aggravate.

Dax laughs, and Ronnie pipes back," I remember it being Saturday night where I was working, and you two assholes sat at the bar drinking all night."

Then Ronnie adds, "She was Brady's friend, waiting for her to get off her shift from the bar. I wasn't hitting on her."

Dax quips, "And why the hell not?"

As the more sensible one in our group, Ronnie is generally quieter around women, as well as meticulous when it comes to who he takes home. I do recall Ronnie looking rather happy on Saturday night.

"She was hot," I add, even though I don't actually remember.

Ronnie rustled around in his chair annoyed, pretending to be looking at delivery orders. While still looking like he is studying the one, he says, "She was hot. I have better standards than you two idiots."

Considering I was preoccupied with a handsy, Lydia, on Saturday night, Ronnie isn't wrong. Thankfully, I was able to get rid of her before I got stupid enough to do anything I would regret. Been there, done that.

I shrug.

Dax says, "If Declan doesn't keep hooking up with these stage 3 clingers, I might have to agree that Ronnie is a better wingman."

I grimace at the reminder, and reply, "Ha, that broad has some serious problems."

I had run of the mill sex with Lydia a month ago, nothing I need to try out again. She knew my intentions prior to the hook up, and I try not to treat women poorly. I find it hard to attach any feelings when I get the chance, I'm just not a serious relationship guy, especially not with her.

"She keeps coming back to the bar like a stalker," I say only slightly serious, "I may have to tell security up front to not let her in."

Ronnie shakes his head, "you know all you need to do is come up with a way to pawn her off on Dax."

"Oh, heck no!" Dax retorts, "Plus, he's already tried."

This is true, I have. Lydia had been coming to the club regularly on weekends since that night, finding me every time. Dax has brushed her away for me a couple of those times now, but she doesn't seem to take a hint. The three of us usually always trying to keep our presence known around our staff and club goers, finding me isn't hard. Tackling the business and administrative aspects of ownership during day hours, we each have a preference on overseeing certain areas about the hands-on side of ownership. Fully staffed, and managers to report, we try to just step in where needed.

I like to spend more time with Security, leaning towards the fighter in me, finding myself better focused, and more controlled in that environment. Ronnie keeps behind the scenes of events and the bar area, while Dax oversees the entertainment and works the crowd, befriending our big spenders for the night making sure they have a good time.

Getting out my old manual calculator, I take the rest of the day to focus on managing spreadsheets. Hours later, with his dirty blonde hair covering his eyelids, Dax speaks out, "Okay, whenever you guys are ready to go over some marketing projections and upcoming profitable events we have to bid on, I have the main discussions in front of me."

"Ready," replied Ronnie, while I agree with a nod.

"Alright, I'll email you the meeting link really quick," Dax says, as he starts typing at the same time, he groans out the phrase, 'hold on,' but stretches the words in a long baritone voice. I enter the meeting room page Dax sent me so we can all have the visual bullet points and graphs in front of us.

Dax begins, "So, the first slide starts us on the calendar for events. As you can see we have some big holes throughout some of the holiday weekends but don't be alarmed," he lifts his arm and dramatically finger dives the keyboard sending us to the next slide, "These are the top 10 most profitable bids we have out there right now."

There were a lot of zeros displaying on this page, "Even if only one of these organizations picked us for their event, filling those nights up, the profit is unreal, not to mention, the big names alone boost our popularity..." Dax turns his head side to side, meeting each of our eyes with a cheesy, shit eating grin on his face.

He looks like he is pulling a classic Jim Carey move as he continues with his comedy act, hand gesturing proudly like he is 'making it rain' dollar bills, swiping his hands, then regrouping his straight stance to deliver the mic drop, "It doesn't make or break us, it will just bring growth to the club, Swollen swells and gives us headway to burst into Swollen babies!"

Cackles can be heard all around the room.

"Unreal dude," exclaims Ronnie, over on his corner, head shaking in laughter, "We better hope the only babies coming out of Swollen don't have our DNA." We all grumble in agreement with that thought simmering us back down to regain our professional cool. I can't help but think this is why I love my job. These guys are the very best lads I 've ever known. Being partners in business requires true gritty commitment. If my life were thought of as a thing, these two would portray my comic relief. The air I breathe in when they are around is much lighter, breaking up the clusters of pollution clouding in my lungs ever since...well ever since the accident happened. Stress invades my body like a takeover attack, those moments of terror booming through me.

I should have never let it happen.

Clenching my fists, I shift around in my chair as my body's natural response to shoo those thoughts away wins the battle this time. I refocus back on our meeting as we mastermind together a task list and prepare assignments for our team, we end the meeting per usual with a timeline of goals to reach. Dax exits us out of the online meeting room and prompts us with a different link to enter a second meeting room. This is the interesting shit. So, I sit up.

Dax, Ronnie, and I, acting like the teenagers we once were, only now, we are the grown successful businesspeople that still like to risk a good fight.

The Club is a warehouse, backed onto a grassy field sporting an old, abandoned barn. We have renovated the barn to now hold exclusive fight nights, at a hefty dollar.

There is always risk to your reward.

When we all grew more invested in the business startup for a possible nightclub/bar, we had to put our nonstop fighting addiction to rest. A light rest of course, nothing too drastic. But we realized fighting had a time limit for us and we needed to take better care and slow down the buzz in case of any problems. Fly under the radar so to speak. So, we built our firstborn, Swollen, who we treat as our baby with all the time we spend and the care we invest in this club. It's like three men and a baby, a good size baby, since Swollen, is responsible not just for feeding for the three of us, but also the dozens of employees we have on staff that devote their work to us.

After full participation in the second meeting, involving highlights from recent UFC, and absolutely nothing related to our work, we ended our man chat with plans to have a drink together at the bar on Saturday night instead of making rounds.

Taking advantage of the slower Monday in the office, I decided to take that extra time and head to my favorite local getaway.

Musty heat greets me entering the gym, recognizing some of the members there, I spot my brother David, inside the ring training a man on the shorter side, only reaching up to David's chest. David in height has two inches on my 6'1 frame, but I outweigh him in bulk. I suppose the height comes from our father's side, since he stands eyelevel to us. Sliding over to the weight area, I nod to the others while beginning warm up reps.

David steps over, his mass muscle bulging from his quadriceps, while his gloved hands sat on his cutting hips, "Let me help you out there, good to see yea. Did you see Daniel today?" He questions while stretching his other hand out, gesturing me to position myself on the bench to start my reps.

David, always a coach, stands behind me to assist, adjusting the weights for me as I start power lifts while I respond, "I saw him this morning before work. You?"

David speaks, "I haven't had a chance since a couple Fridays ago. Dad went yesterday, he only worked a day in the shop and two nights out here this week."

"I don't think we can ever expect any more than that."

David gives a sarcastic laugh and then tells me, "There is a rumor going on I think you should know about." Even from upside down I could tell it was exciting him.

"And what's that?" I ask, not trying to sound amused.

"There is some word spreading about a possible match up under the sea," that means an upcoming underground fight, "that apparently is not one to miss. I've had a couple guys in here talking quietly about it. Xander told me I needed to ask you."

"Oh yeah?" I say struggling, "I haven't heard of anything good like that, sounds like something to chew on."

David carries on saying, "I mean there is literally no concrete information on this, so it could be nothing," he turns his head to scan the room and continues, "Actually, Xander heard the only one that has any more details is a big-time bookie, from a city a couple hours away."

"I wouldn't put it past this just being a rumor to pump something else up, I take it there hasn't been a call out yet," pumping iron in between breaths I proceed stating, "probably why there hasn't been much information, if the fight isn't yet on the books."

David shrugs, "Feels like something might be coming."

It is not unusual for the chatter about a potential fight to be tight lipped until the players have confirmed. The clique in the boxing community is tight and you must earn your right in. The crews we mix with have a lot to win and lose, so we take it seriously. I fought my way through many rings and took plenty of beatings to earn my reputation. Running the gym gives David the insight from the streets, and even though David has stayed away from the underground, he knows from me to not run your mouth or start rumors, or you'll be sorry when you get caught betraying the wrong person. There are some major players with clout, one's part of gangs and mobs, international entrepreneurs who like to gamble, even some pro sports players, who you don't want to double cross. Earned respect gets you hierarchy, some more ruthless than others. One in particular person coming to mind who always makes my temper flare. I give my brother a warning,

"Keep your mouth shut tight if you hear anything more, we don't need any problems in here."

"Yeah, I damn well know that!" He snaps back to me.

As much trust I put in David, he is still my little brother. Looking out for him is a natural bias. I tell him, "Selling the fight blind boosts the interests, anticipating underdog favorites, to have sizeable side bets drop before the countdown begins. Usually, the tactic works on the guys trying to make a name for themselves, if only a seat at the match. I'll let you know if I hear anything," I say in the last lift, placing the weighted bar back to set. We dropped the conversation and headed to gear up and step into the ring for our friendly competition. I can focus better when I get a good couple of sessions in with David during the week, taking out some of my aggression that keeps building up.

Thoughts of today whizzed through my brain on my way home. My mind going from thinking about Daniel, the club, of that ass hidden underneath a marshmallow coat in the coffee shop this morning. Yet, forefront to it all right now is what David told me tonight about a fight I wouldn't want to miss. Intriguing as all get out, it feels like fighting is something I have put on the backburner recently, in all actuality my fighting has been drowning in dust on the side. Between Daniel and work, I've looked down while I've moved forward since the accident. Set on automatic, I've devoted most of my time to the Club, and it seems my care for anything else has run dry. If this rumor of a call out is real, the buzz in our club will catch the names first. It will not be long until my curiosity is cured and knowing I just might be in for an interesting upcoming week.

Chapter 3   Alexis

I spent a long time in my life hiding myself behind lies and secrets to save face to keep Rachel and I safe. When I decided to commit to moving here, it meant also committing to myself that I can move forward. Feeling like I have gotten a good start cleaning and setting up my studio inside, my excitement during the video chat was palpable through the screen. Showing off the lights blaring high on bright illuminating the space, Kel and Jameson, "Oooed," and "ahhhed," while I started from the front door, and walked them around my new workplace, carrying my phone out in front of my face. Peering through, looking like they were both trying to get that little extra screen closer, while I'm flaunting my equipment in the Mixx room to show them it all set up and in its glory.

Kel switches from friend mode to manager mode after my tour, saying, "Oh good, now that I know you are set up with everything in the history of electronics, I have a waiting list of clients ready for a consultation, whenever you're ready."

"Slowing down, Kel!" I reply, "Part-time number of consults to help keep me busy, remember?"

Continuing, "I have a million things to do here before I can even think about opening the nameless studio for business. Sabine cannot start here with me until her finals are over," I say picking up the whine in my voice now.

"Lexi, I know, I know. Hear me out, I have two important clients with needs, I need you to look at for me. Just the two, and then we can go from there."

"Fine, send them to me and I'll look them over, but not until next week."

Agreeing to the light work with Kel appeased enough to give me a smiling nod, Jameson sits next to her looking cheerful as we ended the conversation, not before sending me one of his dazzling winks.

I can't help but roll my eyes once out of view.

Annoyed that he seems to be more 'approving' of my old work habits, still not giving me the satisfaction, I want from him about my new journey.

I do not need his approval of my changes, but I do wish he would support me without thinking he knows better. I do not let that feeling slow me down because I usually divert the thoughts to Rachel, giving me the strength, I know she wanted me to have, here in Paisley, for some reason.

Writing down a to do list helps ease my thoughts, managing to think of items I need to order or pick up at the store.

Phone buzzing

Shortly after, an unknown number with a local area code called me.

"Hi, is this Lexi?" A female voice sounds chipper with her question.

"Yes, this is she," I reply as she continues, "Oh good! Hi, my name is Autumn. Your friend Kel just called me…"

You always feel pretty until you don't.

An hour later, I'm sitting at a hair salon in said Autumn's chair. Apparently during my FaceTime tour, Kel thought my hair needed some attention. She decided from miles and miles away to manage me, over exaggerating, probably overpaying for my hair appointment to be pronto.

That doesn't make her deserve of the word pampering, I thought to myself. It's managing to control the frizz she saw in zig zags, popping out on my normally straight hair. The salon is a narrow room with stylists filling stations along both sides of the brick wall.

Autumn greets me, looking flawless with her long dark auburn hair, iron straightened, flowing over her crop top sweater, and skinny jeans. I decided once I saw her, that maybe this wasn't such a terrible idea.

Leading me to my chair, she excitedly says, "I'm so happy your friend called me!"

"Yeah, me too," I say, since technically it's not really a lie anymore.

Zoning out, I watched Autumn float around her station to get us started, after reviewing my hair like a scientist, she feels certain that what she has figured out for my look will intensify my green eyes and stun the pants off my next prey. Wouldn't that be nice. It's been too long since I have gotten any, and by that, I mean since long before Rachel died.

Autumn rolls her cart of tools beside her, snapping me back to earth as she gets to work while chatting with me,

"Ok, so your friend actually told me when she called, that you are the owner of that new studio that has been under construction in town."

"With the glass windows? How cool is that?"

"It is very cool," I agree. "I've been dancing...since forever, so it's my dream dance studio. I am far from opening it for business just yet, I haven't even come up with a name!"

Plastering dark dye on my hair, seemingly sure of herself, she replies, "I'm sure you will come up with something, like a family name or a generic one for the phone book," smiling she adds, "So tell me, where did you move here from?"

I reply, "I have always lived in Massachusetts. I was recently living in a condo right in the center of Boston city life, busy and chaotic, a lot different than here."

She changes the subject to the topic of dating by asking, "Are you single or did you move here with someone?"

I reply, "Single---"

She questions me. "Gay?"

"No, I'm straight." I tell her to then add in question, "You?"

"Yeah, I'm single and straight too, just never seem to land the good men," she says with a sigh, then adding, "but I have a good group of friends here, guys and girls. Actually, I know a lot of my guy friends that would be happy to change that relationship status for you, I'm surprised you haven't been swept off your feet yet."

I pop out a flustered laugh and reply, "I'm not sure that's possible for me."

Autumn laughs with me, "I understand that all too well, but girl just look at you, how are you this lucky to have the body and the natural pouty sex face?"

Not letting me actually speak she continues on, "I'm assuming you are picky about your men in order to keep up with you, am I right?"

I looked at her through the mirror and gave her friendly sarcasm, while I took a breather.

"Dang, Autumn, I thought this was our first date?"

I then proceed by answering a partial truth about my not existent love life,

"I guess I just dated the wrong ones and eventually got too busy with work and just life stuff, nothing ever genuinely real, more so convenient. And you're right," pausing with a playful smile and adding, "they could never keep up."

We share a laugh and I continue saying, "It's hard to connect with someone who understands my need for dance. It does take a lot of time and hard work to keep up, so I have to put in lots of hours."

"Yes, men can be time consuming."

She gives me a tongue in cheek smile, then quirks, "I'm just trying to piece you together. There is no way, a girl who has a friend from far away calls, pretty much demanding--"

I interrupt, "She's a good friend."

---- "paying triple for" ---

Then I shriek, "Triple!"

Ghhhaaa I knew it!

"Yes, paying triple, with a great tip may I add. Anyways, AND you own your own brand-new studio," She is pointing at me through the mirror, scissors in her hand still very close to my head, "And you seem normal enough."

I can't help but think that is the nicest thing anyone has ever said to me. I'm normal enough. But this is the thing I was worried about. Explanation. I'm not sure she would still consider me normal enough. I try with starting with work,

"Kel is my friend who manages my clients, clients who will have a sound bite or a song and they need me to produce the steps for. Sometimes the entire dance or sometimes only a piece--"

Autumn nods at my general answer and asks, "So did you move here to keep doing that type of work or what's your thoughts with your studio?"

The observation is one I have also been struggling to find a balance for.

"My main focus and goal will be at least opening up the studio, but I will be working remotely on projects that I will keep my friends happy and a decent enough paycheck."

Two reasons that I realized aren't so great when starting off in my new normal plan, since letting go all the way isn't easy, for everyone.

"Well, I cannot wait for our second date," she says. Then, begins to open to me about moving here with a friend of hers she knew from college. Her friend, who wasn't there today, is a part time stylist in the salon and works at a nightclub. They live in a nearby apartment and have a cat named, Skipper.

Autumn was really quite great, attentive as a stylist and inviting to talk to as a peer. I'm not sure if I was happier with my newfound friend, or with who I saw when I looked in the mirror. Styled in beach waves passed my shoulders, brown a dark midnight, with one strand near my face glittering silver that peeks out.

"I weaved it in," Autumn says to me, catching my surprised reaction. Then she adds,

"I thought, you're already drop dead sexy, so we needed to add some flirty!"

Tossing my shiny tresses around with my fingertips, Autumn makes sure to exchange cell numbers and plan a night together soon. I was exiting the salon when I heard Autumn groan aloud behind me about my puffy coat's hood I had flung over my head, messing up the style.

I changed my mind about Kel deserving the word, 'pampered.' It was so nice, and I did indeed get pampered. I texted a selfie of my new look to Kel and Jameson, with the middle finger emoji next to a heart, then slipped my phone inside my pocket, driving home for the day with the rationalism of continuation of normal pampering.

Not expecting company when I arrive, I park to find a couple standing on my front porch. An older looking woman, with chin length orangey blonde hair, came barreling down the steps towards me before I could even close my car door. Oven mitts carrying a large casserole dish in her hands, and smiling from ear to ear while her husband stands still on the porch waiting, she hollers out, introducing herself,

"Oh, hello! I'm so glad you got here just in time!"

"I'm Margie, we live across the road, and that's my husband, Estel…"

Faster than she looks, I had to twirl Margie around, gently leading her back towards my front door as she continues speaking,

"I wanted to invite you to dinner but have not seen you here at a decent hour recently. I saw you getting in your car this morning and told Estel, 'That girl is too skinny.'"

Managing to control Luna's excitement as I lead my new chatty neighbors inside to the kitchen, it is my turn to introduce myself, "I'm Alexis, or Lexi. Wow, this smells amazing! Thank you so much."

Estel is a slightly husky, very tall older gentleman, with white sideburns under a linen cap. Bouncing his eyes all around the room, dazzled by the renovations inside, he speaks still looking all over, "Talk about an improvement! I can't believe this."

Margie completely ignores he said anything, instead her eyes don't leave me, "You live here alone?"

"Yes, but not completely, you met my dog, Luna." I say trying to lighten the conversation.

"Well, that does not make sense. Come on, I'd like you to come back over to our house and we can all eat a hot meal together." She has already started putting her mitts back on.

"I don't think that's necessary. I can just grab some plates here and we can eat on my table. Let me move some things…"

"Nonsense sweetie, I didn't make this for you to serve us, and besides you are here now and it's supper time."

Margie already had the dish back in her mitted hands. A compliant Estel already had the front door open doting on his quirky wife. Margie approved of my ten-minute request, and when I walked through their door, Estel led me to a mini fridge in his garage area. Already loving this man, I chose a cold Coors Light in an aluminum bottle while he grabs the same, unspoken words as he walks me into the dining room. Original to the house, the walls throughout the house were constructed in a blonde wood palette.

"Lovely," I say, sliding into a chair at the prepared table with plated China. Since Margie snapped my hand back when I tried helping her serve food, I start up a conversation, "How long have you lived in Paisley?"

"Oh, we've been here over 35 years. It's a great place," Estel says as he looks at his wife adoringly. She gives him a quick smile then turns back to me to press on, "Alexis, please tell us about yourself. That house! Carl lived here for so long, he swore up and down he was going to die there! We couldn't believe it when we started seeing moving trucks. How did you get him to sell?"

I ask sheepishly, "Get him to sell? What does that mean, it wasn't for sale?"

Margie just gives me an unexpected piece of knowledge. I feel silly now that I am sitting here, realizing my assumptions. I don't recall seeing any information of a seller on the papers Mr. Perris gave to me.

It was an honest question I asked next, "Wait, this Carl fellow was the last owner of my house?"

"Who was he?"

"And where did Carl go?"

Even Estel's normally cool face looked panicked. I figure I have to backtrack, so I tell them, "I was given the house from my friend, and she must have been the one to buy it from Carl. It was a surprise for me, as well, so I wasn't told any information about him. I'm from Boston, and I am starting a new dance studio near town."

Stunning them both into silence, an obviously shorter silence for Margie, who then says,

"Oh, well, that is news to us as well. We just assumed you were the one who persuaded him to sell."

Rachel.

It had to be Rachel about whom they were talking. How stupid of me for this to not cross my mind... my mind that feels ravaged lately. There is already a giant question mark lingering over me as to why Rachel chose to live in Paisley in the first place, but now it's like she had a one-track mind. Who sees a house they like, and persuades the owner out of it?

Looking at my new witnesses to my new mystery case, I ask,

"Did you meet the girl who did?"

"The one who convinced Carl to sell?"

"And what do you mean by convinced?"

I had so many questions now.

Obligingly, Estel takes a quick glance over at his wife and then to me to begin saying, "We probably have less information than you do about how and what happened regarding the switch of hands. But Carl himself was a longtime owner. He was a widower, his wife Jan passed away about six years ago, so he was living alone in that big house. But he was certainly attached to it, not letting anyone talk to him about why he needed to downsize. His family tried to get him to move closer to them in Florida, but he never budged."

Margie adds, "That man is as stubborn as a mule. He was having a hard enough time maintaining the yard, I couldn't imagine the filth he probably lived in," scrunching her nose as she speaks, "That makes me really happy that I tore it all up and had it redone. I wouldn't want to live in Carl's dirt."

Now it's me with the scrunched-up nose as I pick up my fork for another bite. At least my taste buds are exploding in joy, tasting this delicious food.

Estel proceeds to speak while Margie and I chew, "One day in January, moving trucks arrived. Then the house remained empty for months, until the next thing we know, there were groups of workers in and out fixing the place up."

Margie chimes in, "Carl was not too friendly, and we really only engaged with him if we ever saw him outside, so it wasn't surprising he left without the courtesy of telling his neighbors of the past 30 years."

Her annoyed sarcasm is thick while Margie explains her extra feelings towards her old neighbor. "Of course, when those moving trucks were here, I did go over to speak with one of the gentlemen. They assured me he wasn't dead. All they told me was that their destination was Florida. So, that is why we think he got an offer he couldn't refuse, and finally moved close to his daughter," Margie finishes, while giving me an extra spoonful of gravy she thought I was missing from my plate.

I blurt out, "She came from money!"

Realizing I slipped in past tense, I silently hoped they wouldn't notice.

Estel's tone perks up as he reveals, "Actually Alexis, which is another odd thing about his move. The moving trucks hired to clear out his house came after he had already disappeared, and the company was a large corporate one you use when you cross the country, expensive ones."

Hmm

Rachel had to convince this man to sell? This question irritating me, because this gift Rachel gave me, apparently comes with a giant puzzle.

"So, you're thinking he was approached by someone with an offer to buy?"

Estel puts his fork down before he takes a breath and presses on, "Honestly, that is just what the two of us could come up with that makes sense. Sometimes we do get a lot of offers from people in cities. They see our property and quieter community and want a part of it. Investors from out of state, but sometimes real part time owners just looking to escape. However, to get Carl to leave, that had to have been an offer nobody could refuse."

Paisley.

The Song.

Why?

Is there a Why?

"I'm sorry that must have been a shock for you both. But if it's any consolation, all of this is a major shock for me too," I admit.

Estel's eyebrows were sticking high on his head in surprised thought and Margie just smiled like all is well, while dropping another dinner roll on my plate. She breaks the silence and says finally,

"Well let's just say it's a happy surprise for all of us, because I think Estel and I can agree that we would much rather have you here than, Carl!"

I appreciated Margie's way of moving on from the subject. After all, it was my first time ever meeting them. We weren't going to share all our secrets.

However, I did learn that Margie is a retired high school teacher in town, and Estel works as a business consultant part time. I talked to them all about Sabine and how much she has done for me in just a short amount of time, praising her sounding like her father. The homemade chicken and rice was the comfort food a girl can only dream about. I did not want to linger after we ate, so I hurried to get going soon after. I had already predicted my fate as the neighbor of these two, with Margie sending me home with leftovers and a message loud and clear, "You must come over for dinner again on Friday night."

This time, I obliged knowing what my stomach was in for, and headed home for my bed. My new neighbors had introduced me to the feeling of being welcomed.

The next morning, I'm running around the house gathering laundry in a skimpy black lace thong and bra. I have officially run out of clean clothes. Basket in hand with socks toppling out the sides, I open the back door to send Luna out in the cold dark morning, shutting the door behind her quickly to block the cold air from getting inside, to continue on to stuff clothes in the washer.

Deciding on some hot tea with my morning yoga, I was in the middle of a headstand when my phone started ringing, snapping me down to my feet.

I answer to a panicked Margie, "Alexis! It's Margie! I'm sorry to be calling so early, but your dog got into my bees and ran off. She might have gotten stung. Estel's just getting his coat on now to go out back and take a look around."

My mind must have slipped, to not notice the time that went by without her return. Panicked, I throw on the first pair of leggings and a hoodie I can find out of my hamper, slip on my rain boots and run out the front door.

"Luna!"

"Looney, come here!"

I keep calling her name, loud and high, walking around the side into the back, treading towards the last area I took her on a walk. The leaves are a thick covering on the ground. The sound of them rustling in each gust of wind.

"Luna!"

I call, stopping silent to hear any sounds, then keep on. Minutes go by as I search through the vast woods. She is all I have here.

I have to find my dog.

I can't lose her too.

It's the bitter cold raindrops that stun me to a stop next. I look up in the sky through the barren trees to see the upcoming storm above.

Crap.

Total Crap.

I can't lose my dog.

Wishing my only clothing wasn't these thin pants and one measly hoodie, not to mention the pointless lace, I was starting to notice the freezing cold on my skin.

The rain started to come down harder.

Luna is my solid, sixty-pound white coated boxer, with floppy ears, and a short nubby tail. I was in the thick of my career when one of the occupants in the building abandoned Luna with Fergus at the door when she looked like 6 months old. When I walked through the lobby and spotted Fergus trying to plead with the dog to stop jumping, my curiosity sent me over to check out what was going on. While I was booming with excitement, petting, and playing with the cutest energy filled pup I had ever seen, Fergus took that moment to nonchalantly disappear leaving me with the leash and Luna. It was like fate knew how much I needed her, and so I decided to hold on tight to my surprise gift. My dog has been my companion through my hard nights and busy days, and I couldn't imagine not having her here with me.

A wave of panic comes, intensifying the chills in my body.

Crap Crap Crap

This isn't good.

"Luna!"

How do I get myself in these situations?

I'm lost in the woods and mother nature is not on my side.

Chapter 4   Declan

It wasn't really my plan to even be up this early in the morning let alone getting smacked in the face with freezing rain. Just what I needed after already getting no sleep last night, something else smacking into me. Thankfully I am covered by my full-face helmet and gloves, as I keep riding on my way to visit Daniel. I was not able to sleep last night because the guilt of not protecting my brother, the rage of not protecting my brother, the complete regret of not protecting my brother that night claws in my stomach, like a slow sharpened slice in each stab, and I couldn't breathe. I laid in my cold bed alone, exhausted, I even counted my sheep, and I. still. couldn't. breathe. So, instead of looking at his face on repeat in my mind, I thought maybe if I sat with him, it could calm my soul. However, changing course to find shelter, now it seems it is just adding a cold bucket of water on top of my soul's slices, since I'm getting drenched and in danger on these rural back roads. Squinting my eyes, as the sky opened up its cold wet fury, I couldn't see shit!

Mud was flinging everywhere while I was cutting a few corners, down a small side road with which I was only slightly familiar. These are the most rural, older parts of Paisley, populated few and further between most parts of this town, boasting more original buildings along the miles stretch of woodlands.

Adjusting the throttle, I drive slowly down the road until I see the shorter road tunnel ahead, light gray concrete and rounded on top, probably built in the 1920's, the tunnel is used as a local thru only. Easing the brake to a stop, the rumble of my exhaust bouncing loud echoes when I park it to the side. The hot air escapes once I pull off my helmet, chilling the back of my neck as I shake off and out the lingering drops of rain. Cursing in my idiotic impulsive decision that has left me stranded, I pull out my phone to call Ronnie for a possible rescue effort if this rain doesn't stop, only to be trapped in a tunnel while I'm still fighting for air. No bars on my phone indicating what I fear I already know, no cellular service.

It seems that waiting it out, counting my sheep, is the only option right now. Nothing but time on my hands, I can't stay still. I rotate from wandering around underneath, to sitting on the curb, to standing watching the rain drench the ground for over half an hour, adding another thirty studying the graffiti art and hardened bubble gum decorated along the walls from inside the tunnel. Many people claiming rights over the years as hideout passersby's, proving many love trysts drawing hearts and initials in sharpie or scraping with rocks. Every foot of space tattooed with intimate tunnel moments, wondering if I should permanently mark my lonely stay since nobody has ever claimed my initials in their heart.

Leaning on the wall, I was just getting nice and relaxed when the startling noise came out of nowhere.

A high shriek, "SHIYAT!"

I jerk around focusing on the sound and surprised what I see scrambling on the other end of the short tunnel. Or who I see. With her back to me, a girl stomps around in purple rain boots and what looks like a nightgown, oblivious of my presence behind her. I was not wanting to freak her out, so I go in for a gentle greeting to let her know I'm here. I smile and say,

"Good morning, beautiful, great day for a run, wouldn't you agree?"

Spinning around abruptly, her hands wrapping tightly around her middle, she faces me, a stunning face barely recognizable underneath what I now see is an oversized hoodie, all the way to her knees.

Her voice was shaky in her surprise when she shrieked, "Hi! Sorry, I didn't see you there. Wasn't thinking I would have company in..."

She pauses to take a breath, eyeballing the inside of the tunnel before her voice drifts off to finish saying, "...in this road room."

I can't see anything except for her inside of here in this moment as I reply, "It's more like an art gallery."

She gives me a sheepish smile and says through her teeth chatter, "Well, I wish it had heat, it is so cold. I hate the cold because it is so miserable, right? And the freezing rain....sheesh, those drops are like angry drums."

She then asks randomly, "Your name is not Joe is it?" while squirming around, taking small steps in place, and cradling her body inward.

Not exactly what I was expecting to come out of her mouth, she doesn't seem scared of me at all, so I find myself walking closer to her in small steps now.

She is petite, and her gray hoodie is drenched from the rain. I'm trying to assess her features to make sure she isn't close to hypothermia or a panic attack since she can't stop talking in between her short breaths. Now maybe her incessant talking has rubbed off on me, or maybe the lack of sleep, but my brows crease in concern as I say, "Are you crazy? If you had a shovel in your hand, I would assume you were burying a body. What are you doing out here like this?"

"No." She states firmer in her voice, yet she is still fidgeting around, "I'm not crazy, I was just looking for my dog!"

Taking her hand she swipes through her hair, bumping her hood down from off her head, revealing dark wet tresses falling around her face as she then states, "And I really don't like to be in the cold rain."

Taking slow steps, I start walking forward towards her, closing in the gap from stranger to friendly.

Air teases my lungs when she snaps her head up.

Her eyes of Emerald green boring into mine, like the vibrant hills of Ireland, their beauty whooshing into me in a smack. I'm forced to try and balance myself while still rolling down in her eyes.

Luckily, she started speaking again, "You haven't seen a white dog around here, have you?" There is worry dancing across her face while she adds, "I got turned all around looking for her and ended up getting a bomb from the sky dropped on me."

I react before I think, moving my body and stepping too close in front of her now, Staring down over her shorter stature. I pull off my gloves and throw them back towards my bike as I reach for her hands.

She didn't hesitate, almost giving them to me in a hurry the minute I took hold of them.

Suddenly it was her small, damp, cold, and my large and warm, capsuling together entirely in my palms. Her fair skin was reddened from the chilling and all I could do was rub them, trying to warm her up.

"Cripes you are cold," I say to her now that she has gone quiet, "And the answer is no, I haven't seen a dog…. I'm still trying to figure out where you came from to end up here…I'm guessing you don't have any phone service either?"

Looking up at me, she frowns, "No, I left it at home because I ran out in a hurry.. I wasn't planning to get lost, or better yet the wrath of Elsa! My neighbor called me to tell me she saw my dog in her yard getting swarmed by bees."

I don't think while I ask in question, "How did your dog find a swarm of bees in this weather?" Instead of words, her lips pierced together scrunching out while she breathes in a deep sigh, then huffs out the sounds of a motorboat in her agitation.

I can't help but find it cute.

Trying to calm her down from that awful thought of being swarmed by bees, I try to change the subject, saying,

"I'm Declan, by the way. Not Joe. Do I look like a Joe to you?"

I got a small smile out of her while she replies, "I'm Alexis. And no, you don't look like a Joe, sorry, I guess I was just nicknaming you."

Then she laughs saying, "And now that you know my name, I hope that means you're not here to kill me, because I'll freeze to death without you anyway so it's pointless."

Replying back, my hands still engulfing hers, I keep on our friendly conversation,

"No thanks. I'm not interested in murder today, but I am interested in how I already got a nickname."

She lets go of one of my hands to swipe her wet hair back out of her face, but then quickly locks it together back with mine. Wary of my hard focus on her, she says softly,

"You know, there are farms somewhere around here."

It took me a few seconds before I figured it out to react, "You think I look like a farmer?"

She starts laughing a bit shaking her head, looking at me responding, "No, I'm just surprised to see a man…here. Why are you here?"

I could tell her panic was starting up again in her possible embarrassment.

"I got caught in the rain on my way into town, and with a bike, I could get away with side roads, seems as though I'm just in the right place at the right time for you," as I finish saying this, I can't keep my eyes off of her lips now, fuller with a natural pink. I shift on my feet trying to push those thoughts away, needing to instead try to focus on getting this girl back home safe. However, even with her sopping wet mess, I can't NOT notice how attractive she is. Grinning at her during this crazy encounter, I ask, "Alexis, Are you okay?"

"Loaded question," she replies, then continues after a slight pause, "Yes, I'm fine. I just want to find my dog and make sure she is alright," adding in quickly, "What about you? Are you okay?"

I can't help but smile at this girl, looking like a sopping mess and worried about me, the straggler from under the tunnel.

"I will run you back home when the rain slows down. It shouldn't be too much longer. I'm sure your dog is waiting for you there."

I was trying to soften her worries about her pup, but I also had my own worries going on. One being how cold she looks.

"Also, I have no other way of saying this without making it weirder, but…"

I pause to be certain of my word choices to finish my thought,
"You are going to freeze to death in front of me if you don't take off that sopping wet blanket."
It wasn't not true, the sweatshirt looked like it was quadruple sizes too big for her, acting as a barrier to any heat. Even if it's a short sleeve shirt underneath, she would be better off than keeping it on.

She fidgets in response, blurting out some noises again and shifting on her feet until she finally replies, "Quite the predicament I'm in, I see."
I'm not following but luckily she keeps on speaking, "Well, that won't be happening. So, I better hope this storm moves quick. Greater my chances," ending with a smirk.

"Beautiful, you will have no chance in this heavy thin'," I say as I tug on it using our adjoined hands, "You'll turn into a melted Olaf. A pile of ice!"

Shrugging her shoulders like it's no big deal, she says, "If I could, I would, but I can't!"

"I'll give you my coat to wear, it's a million times dryer than yours," I say trying to convince her I'm not a creep trying to take her shirt off. Then also privately try to convince myself.
Alexis answers curtly, "Yes, but that's just it. This isn't a coat, per say, more like just a shirt."
Maybe I just started following and maybe I'm clearly mistaken, because I did not realize some people don't wear shirts under hoodies.
And also, maybe when the time is right, I can be an arrogant ass.
Clenching my teeth, I grit out, "Are you telling me you are naked underneath this mop?"
Fumbling with her words, she fires back, but not without another huff first, saying,
"I won't be telling you any such thing. Other than the fact that I will go out as a melted Olaf in black lace."
Shocked and more than pleased this girl can keep up with my humor, and since I can't help myself sometimes, I push further and ask, "Well, is it a matching set?"
She busts out laughing, embarrassment flooding her cheeks trying to shy away from me when she replies with thick sarcasm,
"So funny, I'm confident you have it all figured out."
"I'm confident you aren't from around here."
"Not at all. I just moved here. I can probably guide you once we get on a road I recognize."
I'm relieved she had no argument about me driving her home, seeing that she has no other choice. There was no way I could leave her out here alone in good conscious.
"That sounds like we may be taking a longer ride than needed but noted." She didn't elaborate so I kept pressing, "Where did you move here from?"
She gives me a short answer, "Boston."
I say like a rhetorical question, "So, you really don't know your way around?"
"No, I really don't." Her lips pout as she adds, "And honestly, I just got a new phone too, so I'm not even sure if I have a picture of her if I need to print out signs..."
Imagining this new hot city girl hanging pictures of her little white fluffy dog around town is the last thing I need smacked in my face.

Shifting my focus to eyeball the outside, I reply confidently,

"I don't think that will be necessary. Looks like the rain is about done, what do yer say we get you home to check back there? Dogs have good instincts, I'm sure you'll find her close to home."

Whipping her wet hair in a turnaround, cold swept over me instantly when she let go of my hands, taking away our matched warmth. I didn't blink watching Alexis as she made big gushing steps in her boots towards the outside of our shelter to go look up to the sky for herself. Taking in her surroundings now that the haze of the rain has simmered down, she seems curious but quieter in her assessment of the wooded area she came from.

All I can do is watch, swallowing spit while saying nothing.

She turns back towards me with glee on her face and finally says, "Well, ready to ride?"

I quirk a smile while she excitedly bounces herself back beside me so we can walk together over towards my bike. She was staring it down with bright wide eyes as she got closer, and I couldn't tell if she was still excited or changing to a nervous.

I ask. "Have you ever ridden on one?"

"No," she replies, still looking over it in serious thought.

"Come here, you have to wear this helmet," I tell her.

She tosses her damp hair behind her ears to allow me to place it down on her head, and she bobs up at me.

The helmet is way too large for her head, but it will do the trick for getting her back home, for now.

Joking, I tell her, "You look like a bobble head."

Causing her to laugh, a real honest laugh aloud, muffled under the helmet. I got us adjusted on the bike and walk us out of the tunnel onto the road to start it up. Her arms wrapping around me as soon as I sat down, I wondered how this was happening.

Starting the engine, I let it hum for a few minutes, then slowly take off back towards the highway leading us into town. Steering us, I listened to her directional commands as we drove, trying to ignore how nice it felt having her arms around me. We turn into an old desolate neighborhood, and she guides me towards a cul-de-sac and then down a long-wooded driveway.

I reach my hand out to help Alexis off once I turned off the engine. Not shy about taking it either, she grasps to hold it while kicking her legs over the bike, and before I know it, she darts towards her front porch.

Figuring out her dog's name through her calling, Alexis keeps yelling out in a squeaky worry, "Luna!"

"Luna!"

"Are you here?"

Following the path toward her, I take in the enormous round house in front of me. I don't really know what I was expecting, but it wasn't something like this.

I was snapped away from taking in my surroundings when another yell from afar jerks me around.

"Lexi! Over here, Luna is over here with us!"

It's an older woman standing on the end of her driveway across the street. Alexis appears from around the back and is about to run to her neighbor, but I stop her and shout, "Wait!"

She freezes looking at me while I continue, "You need to go inside right now and change before you go anywhere else. I'll go check on your dog and meet you over there."

I turned quick on my heal, I didn't want to give her time to argue with me. I knew she wasn't happy about my firm demand, but nevertheless, she gave me some more of her famous noises as I heard her opening her front door.

I make my way down to the road, meeting my eyes with a lady I do recognize from around town, but personally do not know. Her short, chubby stature and a smile wide as I step towards her, "Hello, I'm Declan, a ...friend, of Alexis." I didn't think the whole story was necessary just yet.

"Oh Goodness me, I am so happy to see Alexis back home! We were so worried about her when she didn't answer her phone!"

This woman seems to be close with Alexis, so I try to explain as best I can without Alexis here to do it.

"She got lost looking for her dog and forgot her phone. I helped her home," I was about to continue until a tall older gentleman stepped out carrying a leash. Pulling him in front must be Luna. A big dog with an all-white fur coat, slobbering on the sides of her jowls. I chuckle at the sight of quite a different animal than I had imagined for such a tiny person like Alexis, not giving me much time to breathe, the woman carries on, "OH! Her very own Prince Charming! I'm so glad you saved her, dear. I'm Margie and this is my husband, Estel."

We shake hands in greeting as I reply, "How do you do, it's good to meet you both."
The big dog of muscle bumps my leg to smell my feet, and get a pat on the head, while we were joined by Alexis.

Still leaving me guessing, Alexis makes her way towards us in a giant white puffy coat. I am quite certain now this is the same girl I saw at Carla's the other day, as I try to remember that morning. Margie greets her with a hug, as Alexis crouches down to throw her arms around her safe and sound, Luna.

Alexis giving her hugs and kisses and 'I love you's' on repeat, this lucky ass dog is just standing there gleefully happy taking in all the attention, like it didn't just leave its owner stranded in an ice storm.

Margie's voice speaks out, "She tipped my bee's a bit I guess when she was sniffing around. Estel found her here on the cul-de-sac, and he brought her in and gave her some sort of medicine that he said would help with the stings," pausing to look at her husband in question of the medicine.

Estel is given a chance to speak while directing his attention to Alexis still crooning over the dog, "I looked her over and only saw a couple of stings right around her neckline where her collar is. I think a couple on her paws too, but she seemed fine enough. I gave her a Benadryl capsule in a slice of cheese and that made her spirits rise," he says it all so smoothly while giving the spoiled dog a pat.

Alexis thanks them graciously and takes the leash from Estel, looking much drier now, it seems her worries have softened since she has her precious dog back. Alexis taking the first step towards her house but didn't get far.

Margie speaks out, "Alexis do not forget about dinner tomorrow night. I'm roasting a chicken."

44

The older woman, smelling like a sugar cookie, reaches over and grabs my arm pulling me in close to hers.

"And you my boy are also invited to come," she adds with the warmest smile. "I will set the table for four and have dinner at 6pm if that is alright with you."

Margie is staring at me with full force right now as I don't know how to answer this question, or if I even have a choice.

I try to be vague.

"I'll see what I can do."

Her persistence making me smile a little bigger than my usual.

"Yes you certainly will," just as she moves her gaze over to Alexis waiting on a response from her, who looks stunned in silence for the first time today. She finally looks at me, then back to Margie to ask, "Tomorrow? I thought you said Friday?"

Margie responds, "Oh no dear, you must have heard wrong, tomorrow sweetie!"

Her nose rosy, Alexis stands there for a moment just blinking at her, then throws a wave as she makes a bigger step towards her house and says, "Yeah, I'm not sure about, Declan here," pointing at me, another noise coming out of her mouth, along with, "Uhh..." finally ending with, "Sounds yummy, I will see you tomorrow."

Watching her, she peers over her shoulder at me, commanding me with her eyes to follow her. So, I do, I stride up next to Alexis and we walk down her driveway to my bike. Luna is pulling the leash towards the door as we come to a parting.

Alexis speaks first, "I'm really, really sorry, about all of my mess. Thanks for helping me, and not killing me."

"Yeah, I'm sure Margie over there would have had a search party out before I would get the chance to." I joke.

She laughs, "I bet you are right!" then she takes a step back and gives me a wave.

A wave.

So, I did what anyone would do.

I waved back.

She turned and went straight inside, shutting the teal door behind her as our last goodbye.

I got on my bike and left. Driving away from her house, I realize I didn't even get her phone number.

Feeling the motor roaring vibrations through my speed bike gives me a rush of endorphins, just what I needed right now to help work through the thoughts of my unexpected morning, thoughts of Alexis, thoughts of jealousy for a dog, thoughts I shouldn't be having because I might not ever see her again. I can't help but think, maybe I will bump into her at Carla's one day and say, 'Hey, remember me, the guy who held your hands under a bridge while stranded in a rainstorm.'

I don't know anything about her, we didn't actually speak about anything of personal detail. She could be someone's wife, that thought alone making me feel...feel what, I wonder. What is this feeling inside of me.

Disappointment?

Then I remembered touching her hands and rubbing my fingers all around hers trying to warm every crevice, there was no ring. I took notice. Regardless, whatever this is I'm feeling right now, I'm sure it will pass after I get some much-needed sleep.

Chapter 5   Alexis

After shutting the door behind me, I fled to the shower like my life depended on it. I couldn't stop for one second, I didn't want to, I couldn't even think straight. I stood underneath as the hot water spurt out down my body, stinging my skin like pin pricks causing shivers down my spine. I force my mind to the attention of the warmth of the water, reminding me just how much I prefer heat, and just how much I may have liked a certain somebody's warmth a little too much this morning.

I must have seemed like a complete moron looking like a drowned rat. I recognized Declan the minute I laid my sights on him, those icy blue eyes, that leather jacket, the waves of his hair a mess from his helmet, it was my Not Farmer Joe from the coffee shop. I'm pretty sure it was that realization that allowed me to let my guard down near him. Or throw my guard away depending on how you look at it.

Gahh, groaning, I just hope that when I thaw out, I can forget all of this ever happened. Occupying my time with very important things like, laying with Luna on the couch, sorting my clean clothes, I even tried meditating, it was no help. I couldn't stop going over and over and over my crazy morning. I felt so frozen, and I remember my anxious babbling to Declan, how the cold must have affected my brain cells to make me look like a loser.

Why would Rachel buy a house up North with me in mind?

Why not, Florida or Arizona? She knew I warped in the cold.

 It was that thought that finally allowed me to put my crazy train aside and remember what I was wanting to do today. I'm here in this house, in Paisley for a reason. It wasn't a drive by purchase, like I had guessed. With that in mind, I packed a few items and headed to my studio. I needed to clear my head and the best way I knew how to do that, was press play.

I ended up spending the rest of the night at the studio painting, only to also have returned early this morning for finishing touches. Thankfully, I had set myself an alarm reminding me about dinner at Estel and Margie's tonight, because I got caught up finishing the reception desk area. I had used a stencil to paint a cutesy diamond black and white design with pops of other colors mixed in.

 When I got pinged in reminder, I had to race home for a shower because I had paint all over myself. I tried scrubbing it off the best I could but I'm going to need a manicure afterwards, because I still have it all over my fingernails. Throwing on my thick knit pale pink sweater and my skinny jeans, I'm trying to rush as fast as I can, knowing I'm close to Margie's exact dinner time. I'm sure she will be calling me if I'm even one minute late.

I don't know if maybe the woman is having some forgetful moments because I could have bet she told me Friday for dinner. What a piece of work that Margie can be. And poor Declan, I didn't have a chance to give him a fair warning on Margie's...persistence, but then again, he didn't get any fair warnings yesterday.

Declan, oh gosh the memory of holding on to him creeps in.

I have to stop these schoolgirl thoughts, the last thing I need is more complications. That would be adding too much on my plate right now, I have work and Rachel and now these needy but kind neighbors always feeding me. I'm going to be in no physical shape to date, not even really knowing what dating even means, but maybe Autumn is right, and a girl's night is just what I need. I decide I should try to call her after dinner tonight to see if we can make plans for some time soon, not wanting to sound too desperate for a friend.

I'm grabbing the pack of Coors Light beer when my doorbell rings.

Ding Dong

I curse under my breath right when Luna comes hauling it at full speed around the corner barking her head off.

This is probably Margie even though I swear I have six more minutes!

I fail miserably trying to pull Luna back with her collar while opening the door, only to have Luna run and pounce over my bare feet, digging her toenails in my skin and tripping me.

Whoop!

Diving headfirst over the dog, it was a hard landing, but not the kind I expected.

"Whoa!"

"Hey! You alright?"

It's a soft, slightly accented, familiar voice I thought I wouldn't get the chance to hear again.

"Declan?" I squeal out, as he sets me back on my feet. I look to find him standing there looking like sin. His hair all a mess in fitted jeans, sporting a navy blazer.

"Were you expecting someone else?" He asks curiously.

"No, I wasn't. Maybe that's why I'm surprised." We are both standing in front of each other again, this time seems to be on purpose.

"What are you looking at me like that for?" He asks this with a cocky grin, pinching his eyebrows together. "I'm here for supper, did you forget?"

Luna is invading all of the extra space, sniffing Declan like a fresh new toy as I get a grip on my stunned scrambling face.

"Come in, I have to get shoes on." I say to him, turning to continue leading Declan inside, thankful I spent extra time cleaning this week since I wasn't expecting company.

"Hey girl, You are all sorts of trouble aren't yea." Declan is in my foyer crouching down next to Luna speaking to her in his own doggie voice, giving her big, long scratches around her neck, already finding her sweet spot. I take that time to throw on some winter boots and grab the pack of beer and my coat. Trying to manage it all, Declan strides right over to me, taking the case of beer out of my hand to hold, allowing me to put my coat on, and we start walking across the street for dinner.

"I see you've thawed out," he says lightly starting conversation.

"Yes, God yes, thankfully."

"Have you been over here before?" He asks, eyes on me the entire time besides gesturing to the house we are walking towards.

I respond honestly, "This is going to be my second time."

Declan nods with a smile but he doesn't keep speaking, so I fill in the words.

"I hope you came hungry because I don't think you will be disappointed; I won the food lotto in my new neighbor."

Declan replies, "I don't turn down food. They seem fond of you. I would have thought you were closer to them."

"So," he stops.

His abruptness rubbing off on me since I stopped with him, and we just looked at each other, both not saying anything. It is closer than a friendly encounter, his chin lowered as he looks at me, he finally breaks the tension and says, "I think I've seen you before at the coffee place in town."
Crap crap crap
I play dumb replying, "OH?"

My higher tilt at the end giving away my bad lying.
Declan looking rather intense as he stands over me.
He nods as we are still standing there in a moment of just looking at one another, a shorter moment than it could've been if it wasn't interrupted by Margie's loud voice, "You two better hurry in while the food is still hot!"

Margie yells holding her front door open, as she stands from inside with her eyes pinned on us. Declan is the first to break apart from our standing silence, as we head up Margie's walkway into her house.

Chapter 6   Declan

I was feeling uneasy about why I decided to come over here tonight to participate in Margie's dinner plans. It would have been easy for me to just ignore the pity invite and not show up, because that's what I knew was the best thing to do, but it wasn't what I ultimately wanted. I needed to see Alexis again. I tried not thinking about her ever since I waved goodbye last, but it seems useless, because I found myself leaving the Club early today to pick up a dessert that I ordered earlier this morning, planning for tonight's second chance to lay eyes on her.

I don't usually feel this pull with women.

I don't know what has taken over me, but this feels like battle of static energy, zapping me with commands; to make sure she is safe, to make sure she isn't running into someone else's arms when she is cold, I'm a selfish prick.

But now that I'm here, walking into a stranger's home, I have no regrets. Still feeling sucked in every time Alexis' green eyes meet mine.

Margie leads us into a room she has set up for dinner. It's a cozy room, the table is set for four just as Margie said. Except, her seating arrangement is like couples sitting across from each other, rather a seat on each end, and there are candles. I already knew Margie was a fast friend, but I fell for her harder when the aromas of her cooking hit my nostrils. Smells of rosemary and garlic, silver plated in the center on the table, fresh roasted chicken surrounded with stuffing and fresh vegetables. Saucers surrounding filled with side dishes and fresh cranberries.

Salivating, I stare at the pristine arrangement of the dinner table while I share my appreciation loud and clear, "Margie, you out did yourself here. This looks terrific! I have not eaten a meal like this in..," I crane my neck back trying to think of the last decent meal a woman cooked for me, probably Ronnie's mother, "it's been a long time. Thank you for having me."

Not quite sure how, but I was raised with some manners.

I was about to take a seat at the table when I looked around to notice that I was alone in the room. I scope out my surroundings to find Margie already back in the kitchen pouring a steaming pot of brown gravy into a floral China gravy boat. I'm thinking I must have licked my chops a little too long when I stepped into the dining room, seeing the buffet of food displayed had my eyes fixated on the delicious display.

I wasn't even sure if Margie heard me talking to her, until she comes barreling back through the doorway, holding the hot gravy boat to add to the table, and responding back in her chipper voice she says, "I'm so glad you rearranged whatever it was you had going on to be here with us tonight, dear. You've dressed up so nicely, surely you didn't dress up just for us," she says, not necessarily waiting for me to respond I suppose since she just runs back to the kitchen for something.

Then, I hear the sound of a door closing from down the hallway, and footsteps in the Kitchen. Alexis, walking back towards me with a sheepish smile on her face, holding two bottles of beer. She must have followed Estel to the apparent beer fridge when I handed him over Alexis' two-sided gift. Or three, as she hands me a bottle and walks in to take her seat.

Yep

I don't mind if I do, standing here a second longer to open my beer and watch how fucking fantastic Alexis looks from behind walking to her chair. Like always, wearing a sweater covering her so I'm undoubtingly left guessing again. However, this time I'm getting to sneak another peak to absolutely confirm I like what I see.

So far, I'm screwed.

I take a long swig and follow to the seat next to hers.

We passed around the food rotating counterclockwise, all of us heartily filling our plates up, and Margie crisscrossing over the table with spoonsful of anything she felt you needed extra of, to also add on to our already way too much food, plate.

Alexis starts with a question about our last encounter, "Margie, I was wondering what you meant about 'your bees' yesterday?"

Margie smiles while placing her napkin on her lap, "Oh, I was going to tell you about that tonight. I'm a beekeeper, so I have four beehives out in our backyard. I have been harvesting honey from them these days. Luna was just sniffing and some of them felt threatened enough to go after her."

Alexis's grinning, "Aha! Margie that is so neat, I want to see them someday...but without Luna, I'll have to look into building one of those doggie fences." She finishes with a bite of food off her fork.

"I would love to show you my bees, most people find me a bit looney having a beekeeping hobby, but it has always been one of those things I just can't seem to get enough of," only to change back to course to quickly reassure Alexis, "Luna did not harm a thing, don't you worry, We were more worried about what happened to you," looking at Alexis first then pinning her eyes back to me as she states, "but once we saw you on the back of a motorcycle holding on to this one here, turns out we didn't have to worry at all."

Alexis looking quite embarrassed seems to be guzzling her drink down, giving Estel a convenient moment of reprieve to fetch us all another round of drinks.

"Glad it turned out alright and everyone is safe," he says, trying discretely to cover for his wife's forwardness while getting up from the table, leaving Alexis and I to remain seated in an awkward silence across from only Margie.

Our drinks too empty to even pretend to sip.

"Where do you work, Declan, since you dress so sharp and drive that fancy bike?"

Another quite forward question I should be ready for from Margie as I don't think before I reply, "I work at a bar."

Margie grins at me with her thin lips and straight yellowed teeth,

"That sounds exciting, are you a bartender?"

Feeling like my part ownership status to a nightclub may be a bit presumptuous on the first meet, agreeing sounds truthful enough, "I sure am."

Alexis peering over listening, Margie keeps on, "You young folks and your jobs are a lot more fun now a days. You a bartender and Lexi here a dancer."

A dancer.

I can't help but wonder, what type of dancer? Is she a stripper?

As this thought is processing through my brain, I see Alexis touching the side of her forehead looking slightly embarrassed, not saying a word, allowing Margie to continue,

"Speaking of, Lexi, is that paint on your hands?"

Luck on her side, Estel brings in our drinks while Alexis confirms replying,

"Yes, I've been at the studio painting in the reception area, along with getting started on my other giant to do list."

Peering over to see Alexis, I ask, "Where is your studio?"

"It's in town," she replies quietly, "off a side road from the main street. A dance studio, I'm a choreographer to mixed genres of dance."

Not far from CeCe's, I know exactly the place she is talking about. Seems as though there is a lot more to this lost ballerina after all.

Estel says, "You two really don't know each other?"

I laugh while I take this moment to watch her squirm uncomfortably. I answer sarcastically, "Alexis practically threw herself on me, I had no choice."

Alexis squeaks out a noise in astonishment as I sit there trying not to smile too hard.

I look at her, her cheeks are recovering from a pink while she blurts out, "You found me in a weak moment, and I did NOT throw myself on you!"

Estel and I are laughing adoringly at her as she shakes her head to try to find her composure, but I don't want to stop just yet, "I bet you felt weaker than you should've with that giant soppy moo moo hanging off of you."

Her lips are parted from shock now, and I do my most obvious stare, checking out those lips more than anyone possibly could have with Estel and Margie watching us. Alexis noticed my lingering, shutting her mouth quickly and jerking her head away from me.

I try to recover from teasing her.

"I'm only kidding," I say as I softly bump her thigh with the back of my hand under the table, gesturing my apology.

Looking at Estel and Margie, it flew out of my mouth when I said,

"Really, she looked beautiful, even in her moo moo," I try not to pause for long, "..and no, we didn't know each other prior."

Estel says, "And here we are, life can be quite curious sometimes."

Alexis finds her voice, "I'm just happy you two know him now, in case you need to ID him in my disappearance." It's her turn to laugh now, and wouldn't you know it, she bumps my leg.

Seems I really might be screwed.

After our dinner, Margie gets up saying, "Declan brought us dessert from Nannies Bakery in town, let me go grab it with some new plates."

We all end up cleaning up after ourselves, placing the dirty dishes in the dishwasher before we sit back down for dessert. Something that I might have taken a little overboard.

"When did you bring dessert?" Alexis asks me as we are settling back down.

"Before I came over to get you." I speak.

Her face quizzical but appeased by my answer. Until she sees, "Here we go," Margie says while opening the box on the table, "Oh Declan, how cute."

Inside are a dozen crème filled donuts, custom designed with Olaf sitting on a lounge chair at the beach, in a black bikini.

Alexis whips both hands up to her mouth trying to cover her expression. Stating with a cocky grin, "I agree Margie, I think I out did myself with these!" Estel is looking over his wife's shoulder while they try to figure out why I would bring such a peculiar dessert.

Finally, Alexis turns to lightly push me on my upper arm, obviously taking the joke well, because her laughter is the only thing I can hear right now.

"How did I end up here with you guys?" She says as if joking, but then I see her wincing like she was thinking about something, only to try to recover from showing it.

"You're stuck with us now." Says Margie

"Margie, I'm a dancer, I cannot be fed like this all the time, or I'll be out of a job."

"Well, it seems as though you could use a few extra pounds on you, I don't know how you survive in this cold weather. Plus, your other half here is a big boy, he needs to eat." Lots of things come to mind about what I could say, but I don't in this company.

Alexis responds, "Oh yes, I'll make sure that's on my Declan duty list, 'send him to Margie's to be fed.'"

"I would like you to put that down for same time next week, please." Margie says to Alexis.

I can't help but laugh. Considering I walked into this night with strangers, having this good of a time was unforeseen. Alexis and I thanked our hosts and walked out into the dark evening towards her house. I wasn't sure where to park when I got here, so I decided to park on the curbside of the cul du sac.

Patting my stomach, I tell her as we start walking, "I don't think I'm going to be able to move tomorrow."

"Ha, I know what you mean. She is a mean cook."

"So, the dance studio," I say trying to push for something more in my short amount of time left.

"Yes, my dance studio, my new project," she replies as she gives me a wry smile and continues to say, "I guess this town needed one."

I ask. "That's what brought you here?"

Looking at me a bit more seriously, she replies, "I'm a complicated story. The gist is that I had a friend of mine, a very good friend, she died a little over six months ago and if you can believe it, left me a house. I moved here to try and start fresh."

There was a touch to her voice that sounded annoyed when she mentioned the house being left to her.

Alexis continued, "So, I took the time to get my crap together in Boston, tying up loose ends at work and finishing the projects that needed to be done. Built my studio here in the meantime, and now here I am."

"Is this what you want, then?"

I ask her to continue, "Here, with the new house and a dance studio. Is that you?"

"What you wanted?"

Coming up to where I've parked my bike, her arms crossed, she speaks softly, "I'm going to try to make it what I want."

I ask, "Do you live here alone?"

"No all my roommates are inside partying...Yes, I live here alone."

"Okay," is all I can manage as I think about if I should try my luck with another question. Looking at me with a frown, she asks.

"What's wrong, do you not like my bat cave?"

"It's just," I halfway reply as I swipe my hand through my hair to think, all I can come up with saying is another question.

"Are you a bat?"

She gives me a big smile, making me feel not quite so dumb, and answers, "Well I'm alone and I like to fly in the dark when no one is watching too, so, maybe I am."

"And you make squeaking noises." I add, finishing the night off with some more sarcasm points. Or flirting like a middle schooler. I don't give her long to think of a come back, because I continue my forwardness,

"What are you doing this weekend?"

She tries to fluster quietly, but I hear sounds from where I am. It's been since the first time I met her, the way I stand with her is close, almost intimate.

We are focused on each other now.

"I'm at my studio usually," she replied.

I cock her a smile, "Can I call you?"

"You can," she says back.

"Give me your phone," I say holding my hand out in front as she swings to her back pocket and places her cell in my palm. I text myself from her phone so that way we have each other's number, and hand it back to her. It was as smooth of an exchange as I could muster up at the moment, trying not to end with another wave.

"What do you do on weekends?" She asks.

"I'm usually working, but sometimes, I'm at the boxing gym in town. My brother and my dad run it."

"Mmm hmm I knew it. I saw those knuckles." Stating it gleefully like she got the answer correct. I hold up my hands in front of me now since it has become the topic of conversation.

"Yea, it's just a part of it I guess, I don't even feel it. This actually looks pretty good, usually it's a bit worse."

Alexis looks down and reaches out with her index finger to trace the healed scar on my knuckles, then she asks me, "Is this you, Declan?"

Her question similar to my own before, I stand as still as I can as she drops her hand and looks back up at me. Looking into my eyes like she is looking through me as she waits for my reply.

"Yes," my voice raspier than I intended.

"Okay, you know I'm an experienced bandage wrapper, so if you ever need first aid, you can just write that down on my 'Declan Duty' list," she says, somehow again, finding a way to make any sort of conversation easy.

We share our laughter as we stand there together.

"I'm really liking this list," I say playfully as she rolls her eyes at me.

"Well, I'm going in before anything else gets added. Goodnight, Declan. Maybe I'll talk to you soon," then she takes a step back. I don't move my legs.

Instead, I nod and say, "Yea, get in there, I don't want to worry of your wandering."

Setting forth, she gives me a small wave, goodbye.

So, I give her a small wave back.

I watch as Alexis turns and heads up to her bat cave and slips inside before I pull away.

Phone ringing

Back at my condo, I was too revved up to care whoever was calling me. Standing in the shower, cock in my hand, I stroke, and stroke, and stroke.

She's in front of me, dark waves covering each breast
Her green eyes staring at me as she is sauntering over

I stroke faster, thickening under my palm.

Her arms are around my neck as she straddles my waist
Those lips I've burned into my brain to remember, even the goosebumps lining her lips in the cold

One more stroke until cum shoots out of me.

Phone ringing

I just stand under the water, breath heavy, one arm leaning me up in the stall. Wondering why my phone is blowing up right now as I begrudgingly quicken my shower to dry off and answer. It's my brother, David. I answer annoyed asking, "Why are you calling me so many times?"

"Declan, geez, you're a hard man to get a hold of. I need to tell you something. Are you sitting down?"

Feeling my blood pressure rising, I snap at him, "What the bloody hell is going on, David?"

David's voice steady when he replies, "He's back. Vince is back in town."

"How do you know?" I ask, now sitting down on my bed.

"Boomer came into the gym tonight with another friend I didn't recognize, but a bigger dude."

"They each paid for the daily pass and stayed for about an hour before they started packing up, so I of course followed their Ass's to the door."

"Good," I respond, happy my brother stood his ground for our family gym.

David continues, "He asked me if you were working on your beer gut or if you still had any muscle left in ya."

My annoyance rumbles out and David gives a short chuckle before he proceeds to say, "he also asked me if you were working towards any fights, and all I said to him was that you were keeping up with your practice and training."

"What the hell does he care if I can keep up, he was never anywhere close to my level."

"He's just a nosy cocksucker. Anyway, are you listening to me?" David huffs out in question to try to keep me on the right track of mind.

I answer. "Yes, I'm listening."

"Boomer told me we should expect a visit from an old friend soon."

Chapter 7   Declan

My father put our names on the map when he opened the boxing gym here in Paisley. The boys from Ireland earned the reputation around town to be a bit wild and reckless to the public eye, but it was my name, Declan McQuade, that brought attention to the fighting world.

Daniel never pursued the sport like David, and I always had. He liked to watch the sport rather than actually take part. He was athletic and strong, but besides the casual family squabble in the ring at home, fighting didn't interest him. I, on the other hand, lived the sport of boxing. David a bit younger, was following in my path, pursuing the sport full time.

I remember throwing up in the morning before Daniel's accident. It was the early hours in that time of night, where you lay there awake in eerie silence, and that silence somehow becomes the loudest thing you can't stop listening to. It became so deafening to me, that I shot out of bed towards the bathroom to end up hugging the toilet. I couldn't stop vomiting, sweat pouring out of my blood rushed face. Everything in my life I had at that time, was right in front of me, and all my body was doing was trying to get rid of it.

The fight of my life was set for that night. I had trained and prepared for that moment for what felt like ever. My body grueling over the constant beatings, the pit of hunger in my stomach that didn't stop badgering me, the lack of sleep, and the beast that roared in my soul obsessed with the feeling of it all.

It had been the fight everyone wanted in on. The two rivals sparring for what mattered most, proof of who was better.

My biggest competitor in the fighting underworld, Vince Bordeaux, who is a year older than me, moved from New Jersey with his younger sister to the town a couple of years after I was out of high school. Both his parents are high ranking officers in the military, and signed indefinite long term overseas deployment contracts, forcing their decision to send Vince and his sister to live with their cousin, Pauley, and his family. Vince was more trained in martial arts growing up but stepped into a boxing ring after high school and started excessively training nearby, gaining a massive amount of muscle, trying to perfect his skills in boxing with a dream of becoming a professional UFC fighter. He was known for having a problem with controlling his temper and had an apparent rap sheet throughout his teenage years. Picking fights in and out of the ring is his specialty as ego and arrogance have always been Vince's best set of mastered skills. Even though he was older and bigger than me, we were paired competitors in amateur boxing leagues through the years, hating one another on site and never engaging on any kind of friendly personal relationship, but each of us earned title wins that gained us the recognition and invites into hushed fights with bigger purses outside the leagues.

Outweighing me, he strived for professional grade and had the muscle to back up his strength as he started tearing through matches being an unstoppable force in the underground fighting world. We had the odd run around town in social settings that always ended up in argumentative exchanges of some sort. Always a sneaky snake who would encourage anyone with money into making sizable bets on him to help his numbers and popularity rise, scamming paid fights by bullying lower level amateurs that were just there for the thrill to take him on in the ring and squeeze the pennies out of the unfair advantage.

While I was earning money doing accounting work on the side for Dax's father who owns a commercial real estate company, and taking on mid-grade fights, doing nothing but adding up to reach my goal of owning a nightclub, Vince ended up hiring an agent and started traveling around the country picking brawls he thought would boost the interest of UFC.

Fighting was my source of freedom, but it wasn't ever a career choice for me, I didn't want it to be. Instead, I became a co-owner when Ronnie, Dax, and I, bought Swollen. Since the start, the club has been a booming success. Vince reappeared in my life, calling me out on a fight against him in front of all my friends and family, while we were celebrating our one-year anniversary in business.

With my name attached as a nightclub owner, he knew my reputation was important for me to keep. My training had been put on the backburner and I wasn't at my best strength, which was Vince's plan all along, knowing I wouldn't back down, and striking when my focus had shifted. Still, I was more than eager to knock his teeth in.

The fight was set for the winner to take home fifteen thousand, and scheduled in Buffalo, NY two hours away, a month from his callout. I was never afraid of losing to Vince, winning had always been my only option, but that gets complicated when you are trying to run a business. I had a lot on the line, Daniel and I working to cover most expenses in the gym while David ran it with little help from my dad. Adding in a nightclub to run, losing would create a bad rep for both spots. But I wasn't going to lose.

Empty from spewing my guts out, I entered that illicit ring as the underdog with Vince the likely winner to big betters.

My reputation held strong, I won after a bloody fight, knocking Vince out with a right hook in the third round.

It was the three hours later that changed it all for me.

Daniel's Accident, two years ago

I was feeling high on the win, I tasted it with every drip of salty sweat from my top lip, cheered the victory throughout the night, like I was on top of the world. We started celebrating at a local rooftop pub near the hotel we were staying in. Both Daniel and David were with me, along with some of my closest friends including Dax and Ronnie.

An explosion of testosterone in the air filled with women and booze, we were sitting outside on these cushioned patio benches that had gas fireplaces lit all around the edges of the space. Not far into our celebration, I noticed Daniel sitting on a chair with a red headed girl looking rather cozy. Elated my win of the night could bring my brother some pussy, I ignored the pain from my wounds and instead reveled in my own thrown, watching girls dance all over me like a king. Not long after, Daniel winked at me, like giving me a silent solute, as the red head was leading him away from our celebrating group.

Commotion stirred in the stairwell of the rooftop about twenty minutes later. The sea of people all huddling to find out what was going on.

I then got a phone call from a panicked Daniel that changed the course for our night and the rest of my life.

"Declan, I, uh, I need you to come out here to the parking lot."

Not understanding what the hell was going on, it was the swarm that was following me that led me to conclude there was something wrong.

Outside, I found another large group of people surrounding Daniel's truck, and once I got closer and I saw who was standing in the middle of the chaos, surrounded by his cousins and team of friends, it was Vince, and in front of him was a dis shoveled Daniel, and a half naked redhead.

I parted through the people to get to the scene as my buddies held me back at the sight of my defeated opponent while I stepped in front of Daniel determined to shield him from the wrath of Vince's freshly beaten face.

"What the Fuck is going on here!"

Vince turns his two purple eyes on me and says, "Your Leprechaun brother was caught in his truck fucking my little sister you fucking piece of shit," then huffs, "And she is only seventeen!"

I could feel the wave of panic radiating off of my twenty-six-year-old, soft big brother from behind me when called out on the error of his ways, but he was my brother, my family, and one of my best friends, and I stuck up for him.

"What is your slutty little sister doing here in this bar then? You obviously need to take better care of your family instead of messing with mine."

The red head now a furious rage, set off trying to get as far away from this embarrassment as she could. Daniel reached for her gently to try to comfort her, but she only shoved him away and ran off in only pants and a bra.

Vince glares through me, as he screams out loud to Daniel, "You and me. In the ring, one hour. Grudge match with me to settle the score for fucking my sister. I will call it even."

The surprised group reaction was audible as I rebut back, "Not a fucking chance! That isn't a fair fight, and you know it."

Vince opens his arms wide and says, "Fighting fair would mean allowing your poor brother to stand up like a man in front of me and deal with the consequences himself."

Daniel steps around, shoulders next to me, and sticks his hand out to Vince. They shook on it in front of my very eyes.

I was livid, getting robbed of my celebratory night while Daniel had a mask of steel, and the crowd started making calls and setting up in the midst.

An hour later, after listening to Daniel try to explain how the minor sat on his lap and started flirting with him, swearing up and down on repeat that he didn't know she was Vince's sister nor that she was only seventeen, I was standing there in Daniel's corner trying to shake him to focus, slapping his cheeks, while David wrapped his wrists. I kept trying to remind him of all the techniques he was familiar with over his years of watching on the side and owning a family gym, that he could use to his advantage. Before he stepped in, the last thing I remember telling him was to just give it what he had, and then once it was over, his debt would be paid, and this would all be swept away from him.

We all knew he didn't stand a chance at winning.

Hell, Daniel even knew he didn't stand a chance.

A fight for accountability with a handshake that no real man can back down from.

Daniel had made it to the latter part of the first round, until Vince pinned him down and shot blow after blow to Daniel's face.

Struggling, Daniel kept trying to swing his arm out in his front trying to protect himself, although he was getting too weak from the beating, and couldn't manage getting back up on his feet.

With a face covered in blood, he mustered up enough energy for one last effort, lifting up on his left shoulder in quick movement, but turning his head at the same time. The referee was about to call it, but Vince already had his punch in motion, crushing his fist directly at Daniel's temple. Then, like a heartless beast, Vince cocked his arm back up after the whistle was blown and Daniel wasn't fighting anymore, only to drive it down for one last merciless blow to the back of Daniel's head.

When a fighter loses consciousness during a match, the opponent is declared winning by a TKO, technical knockout.

Daniel's body fell still.

And so did mine.

I stood there and watched the EMT's arrive and take him on the stretcher, it was all a blur. David shook me to get into the ambulance, as I stood there in despair, but I didn't feel like I could move, and David ended up riding along with Daniel without me. Ronnie and Dax lifted me up and threw me in the passenger seat of Ronnie's car, Ronnie drove following behind the ambulance while I remained impaired and entranced in the flashing red lights and siren.

The force of the trauma caused a brain bleed that swept through Daniel before he arrived in the emergency room.

The brother I knew, was gone.

That night changed my life forever. After the TKO was ruled an accident, Vince took his posse and left, staying as far away from here as he could. I have not seen him since but if Vince Bordeaux is back in town, there is only one reason, a fight. Perhaps the same rumored fight that David has been hearing about.

Chapter 8   Declan

Restlessness is a cruel feeling to have sitting next to Daniel, someone who didn't deserve to be turned off like a switch. He was too young and way too good to deserve such a cruel fate, one that changed everything I ever thought was important in life. After my phone call with David, the memory of that punch, constantly playing on repeat, reminding me about just how much damage can be done in every action. How if I only held my ground and sent Vince away instead of letting him bully Daniel into evening out a childish score. Even if I had to fight Vince again instead of allowing Daniel, I would have, but because I didn't do any of those things, I have been left with chaos, regret, guilt, so much sadness within me, that I can't seem to shake. I thought coming to see Daniel this afternoon would help me work through those things, but now all I feel is selfish. But, I had to come sit since I'm stuck feeling like a ticking noise is above me, and I'm not sure how to turn it off.

As minutes passed, unexpectedly, I start talking to Daniel about something unrelated to my chaos,

"I met a girl the other day. Actually, I was on my way to see you, mate," that thought making me chuckle, "I should have been sitting here with you, but I had to pull over on my bike in the freezing rain instead."

I stopped talking for a good minute. There was too much to say and I didn't know how, so I tried my best with saying,

"It's a good thing, too. You should have seen her…"

As I'm sitting there with only my own rhetoric, it reminded me of her, so I pulled out my phone.

ME: Do you have big plans watching Frozen tonight?

I sent the icebreaker text to Alexis, hopeful of a quick reply. I hadn't contacted her yet this weekend, which is probably best considering how derailed I have felt since I was given the message of Vince's return. I spent the day yesterday mostly taking my aggression out on the worn leather punching bag hanging inside our office corner. Ronnie and Dax calmly sipped on their coffees during my racket as if there was nothing going on around them, the raging sounds of my jabs to the bag like a melody to their ears as they continued to work. Our security team for the club has been briefed to be on the lookout for Vince or other known guys he usually has with him, prompted to page me if they get a visual or name on ID check. I am not afraid of Vince one fucking bit, he can enter the club and spend his money there all he wants, but he won't get the chance to catch me off guard ever again.

If Vince sets foot on my turf, we will be watching that ruthless numskull's every move, and I will be prepared for his intrusion this time.

Chime

Alexis: It's like you know me.
Me: Can I join you? I'll bring my hands.

Alexis: Come on, but only if you like a party. And I actually may need your hands, I'm in the studio along with many new friends currently fixing my broken heater if you can believe it.
Me: I'm bringing them to you now, but I am not sharing with your friends.
Alexis: I'm waiting.
Another ding
Alexis: And I don't share.

I basically flew out of the parking lot on my short way over to her studio. The things this girl can make me do in just a few short days of knowing her is bewildering. Her dance studio sits beside itself further up a long drive off of the main road. Recently completing construction, open to the outside, you can see through to the inside with her glass front windows.
Walking through the front door, I am greeted by a young girl holding up a measuring tape to the wall with a yellow pencil gripped in her mouth.
Seeing me standing there, she pulls the pencil out of her mouth as she asks, "Oh hi. Do you need something?"
"Hi. I'm wondering if Alexis is here?"
The girl standing tall with shoulders back looks at me skeptically questioning, "Are you one of the HVAC workers?"

"No," I reply, "I'm a friend."
Her eyes widen brighter now as she asks. "Wait, are you Jameson?"
With that, I can't help but now feel like I shouldn't be here. The ticking gets louder over me as I compose my next move. Shifting, I run my hand through my hair as I respond, "No, I'm Declan."
"Well Declan, give me a sec, last time I saw her she was in her Mixx room ordering wool socks on Amazon."
Putting her tape measure on the reception desk, the young girl starts leading me around the corner into the area with a vast open dance floor. I immediately spot Alexis peering up talking to a worker on a ladder. Dressed in a different oversized hoodie and leggings with giant puffy socks rolled up to her calf, she turns her head once she sees me here, and heads towards me.
"Hi, you must have been nearby!" Alexis says to me smiling, "I see you met, Sabine," gesturing to the girl, "she's my new everything."
"Oh yes, Declan caught me by surprise, he didn't seem like a worker," Sabine says her voice still questioning my identity.

"Not Jameson," I say starkly. It flew out of my mouth before I could think to stop it. What can I say, I'm a man that likes to know the details of things that pique my interest. Sabine stiffens as I mention her slip up.
Alexis still smiling showing no reaction, responds, "Yeah right, Jameson would have waltzed right in here without stopping to ask, plus he lives in Boston," stepping over adding, "Come on, let me show you around."
After notating in my brain, the questions, I have for her that I will put aside for now, I allow myself to relax. Alexis starts leading me through the different areas and rooms of her building, avoiding the random ladders and workers all around, explaining to me another couple of electricians showed up right before me to check on a wiring issue.

"This is what I call my Mixx room, it's basically my office."

Except her desk looks more like a switchboard, entering the inside room, there are multiple different sizes of turntables and speakers around with a desk that has three large computer monitors setup on top. The room was remarkable.

Alexis explains, "this is usually where I am when I'm here, I do a bit of work with mixing music and sound along with dance."

Looking at her with my eyebrows raised, I say,

"A bit? Holy shit, this is impressive," no doubt complimenting her awe-inspiring career.

Sabine pops her head in the room where we stand and says, "Hey Lexi, can I steal you for just a minute? One of the guys has a question."

Alexis floats out while I stand there still, just looking over all the equipment, and spot a frame laying on a stool next to me. I couldn't help myself, as out of place this looks in a room full of nothing but electronics, I had to pick it up and read the purple words as it seems like a written poem.

Never peace in hearts of thee

...

Lost in her head

Rather be dead

Each phrase a bite of tragic darkness, I can't help but read it through, into my second time I was interrupted.

I feel her before I look up to see her standing next to me looking down at the frame in my hands, she quietly states, "It's a song she wrote for me."

"You're friend?" I ask.

"Yes, my friend, Rachel," crossing her arms and continuing, "it's like she wanted to drive me crazy on purpose. We work in the music business, written songs and jotted down lyrics is a frequent thing we have always done," pausing, "...yet this...," she takes the frame out of my hands and holds it in front of her,

"This is just mean, like she wanted to give me something else to constantly remind me of her pain."

Looking at Alexis during this vulnerable moment, I can't help but feel understanding of the pain she seems to hold onto. Each of us robbed of someone in our lives and left here to feel tortured by their loss every day.

"I know this is none of my business, but this sounds like a story to me."

Alexis turns to me and asks, "What do you mean?"

"She was from here? She was obviously hurting about something and talking about it."

"That's the thing, she wasn't from here," she replies sounding defeated.

"I was with her almost every day of my life for the last ten years and felt pretty damn confident I would have known about this town if it meant anything to her or her father she loved.

Then, she gives this to me on purpose to only leave me to question everything I ever knew about her."

I watched as Alexis seemed to be wrestling with her thoughts, going down the well-acquainted slip into the abyss of the past memories with the person you need most in this moment.

I grab the frame from her hands and place it back on the stool where it was, then looking at her, I say, "It seems like she had some sort of attachment to Paisley."

As Alexis considers this staring at me, I reach down and grab one of her hands, wrapping my fingers around hers, "Do you want to get out of here for a bit, warm you up somehow, like," trying to come up with just that but, "get soup or something, or coffee, or.." clearly fumbling. Alexis finally puts me out of misery and replies,

"I don't need anyone else trying to feed me, but I do want to go for a ride."

"A ride?" I question. Already smiling because I've already lost my cool.

"Yes, on your bike," Alexis says in her assertive but cute kind of way.

"Yeah, I understood what you meant, but isn't that going to make you the opposite of warm? And we all know how you feel about that."

I'm stepping closer to her as she replies,

"You said you would share your warmth with me, but if you changed your mind, we could go get soup?"

I'm already pulling her along with me as I lead us back out into the massive dance floor area.

"Wait, wait, wait," she laughs out still holding onto my hand. I don't have shoes on!"

Letting go, she darts back behind her, passing the workers as she finds a pair of shoes that must be extra wide in order to fit her giant socks inside. I just stood there smiling, in my own moment not caring about the half a dozen other people in here watching. I wait for her as she walks back to me, covered from head to toe with layers, her face the only skin visible. Even so, she could still turn heads in the room, with a face of a natural sexy goddess, with gems in her eyes, charming those who look her way.

"Are you ready now, beautiful," I say as she tries to pass me on our way but not before I reach out on instinct and grab her gloved hand to hold it when we walk out the door, Sabine giving us an all knowing, mocking smile as we passed her.

Walking forward, Alexis grinned eyeing my black and silver whip, showing off her straight white teeth.

With a burst of spontaneity, I sweep in front of Alexis and skate my arm low, encompassing her small waist, slipping my other hand out of her fingers, and around her bottom, lifting her up to me.

She shrieks out the sound, "Eek," as she wraps her arms and legs around me.

Greedy swirls of desire rippling throughout us, holding each other tight, as I walk us in slow strides to my bike. Using all my inner strength trying not to devour her right here in this parking lot, I regretfully parked too close, her eyes peering up at mine while dropping her softly down on the seat. We didn't need words as I placed the oversize helmet on her head and hopped on, her arms enveloping my midsection to hold onto like they are made to be around me, while starting the engine.

We had nowhere to go and nowhere to be, so I took advantage of this moment and rode us along the countryside of Paisley and the outskirts of town. Leaves of autumn colors left few and far between on the barren trees as winter rears close. I paced us at a slower speed, driving using only one arm to steer, as my other has placed itself on top of hers. Appreciating sights along the ride, with Alexis strumming her fingertips over my middle in excitement when trying to get me to see what she sees, usually the cows grazing close to the barb wired fences. Passing local Apple Orchards, busy with mini vans bustling in and out of the parking lot, packed with families all filling their buckets full of ripe reds and greens. We rode relaxed like we had done it together a million times. She was carefree leaning into me, vibrations of the engine humming underneath us, as the early sun set between the evening's thick clouds.

An hour into our drive, traffic started picking up in town, with the Saturday night party goers beginning their nights out. Reluctantly, I pulled us back into her studio lot, now lit up in the night, you could see Sabine still tinkering around inside.

We broke apart stepping off the bike, both of us shaking off from sitting so long. I was about to take this moment and take her lips like I've wanted to do since I met her, but the night had other plans, getting interrupted by a gruff older man dressed in tan Carhartt coveralls.

"Ms. Andrews," the old guy bellows walking out the front door, "I am sorry to tell you, we may have a couple more hours here before we are done. I've got my son and some other guys heading up now if that's okay with you to keep working, which means we will try to be out of here by ten tonight."

Alexis nods to the man and replies, "Yes of course, I'm heading home in a minute to pick up my dog because I plan on staying over here tonight, anyways."

Uncomfortable at her statement, I shift on my feet as the man turns back inside and leaves us just outside the door alone again. "What do you mean you're staying here tonight?"

"In the middle of town," shaking my head I finish, "that doesn't seem like a good idea"

The thought of her being alone somewhere besides her bat cave bothers the crap out of me for some reason.

"I'm pretty good at taking care of myself even though I may not have given you that impression." Alexis replies back to me, amusement fluttering in her expression.

I refrain from telling her how I really feel, as I keep the rest of my thoughts quiet, her not needing to know how psycho I've become constantly concerned with her wellbeing. Sabine comes to view just inside from us now and that seems like my final cue to leave and get to the Club for the night, as I have drink plans with Ronnie and Dax.

Alexis steps back from me, saying, "Thanks for the ride, I needed to get away like that more than you know, but I guess I have to get back inside."

I take a deep breath as this isn't ending the way I was wanting, I tell Alexis, "I'm just at work tonight, so call me if you need anything, and I'll text you later, okay?"

Alexis smiles, tip toeing up to wrap her arms around me, hugging me tight. My arms around her, there is an unspoken passion between us, as we stand there in our embrace. She went inside, leaving me feeling elated, even though it was only a hug, I didn't get a wave this time. I am walking into the club meeting the guys at the bar when I realize, the ticking noise above me is gone.

"What's got you in such a good mood?" Ronnie chirps as I find a seat beside them.

Brady sporting lilac colored hair braided down in front of her, appears almost immediately, "Hey boss, whatcha having?"

Responding I say, "Snakebite on ice, please, Brady. How are you keeping?"

"Doing good," she responds while promptly working on my order telling me, "That sick band from Georgia is playing here tonight."

"Oh right, that is why Ronnie booked us off, he gets his socks off watching the chicks in cowboy boots."

Ronnie quips, "I just find it hilarious that these women come in here dressed like farmers because the band is from Georgia, but it's a fucking rock and roll band!"

We all laugh in agreement to Ronnie's strong opinion of what the band's fans wear. When it's just the three of us listening, Dax drops his playful tone and grabs me and Ronnie's attention stating, "I have a theory I want to share with you guys."

We both signal Dax to continue with his thoughts,

"I have a hard time believing Vince has anything to say to you on a personal level after everything that happened. We know he is in town now because you were told to 'expect a visit.' All of this right at the same time David hears about a major fight in the works..."

Dax sips his glass at his stopping point to make sure we are all following where he is taking this conversation.

"A warning to Declan." Ronnie confirms but keeps on, "But not a warning regarding just his return."

"You think he wants to fight me again?" I ask while processing this getting furiously tense.

"You think I'm the call out for this big mysterious fight?"

Vince knows the sight of him would set me off and sending me a warning of his return was possibly planned. Maybe I gave him the benefit of the doubt to not even think he would twist the knife of my brother's accident and plan a grudge match between me and him.

Dax nods his head and speaks as I chug my glass,

"I do, Declan, I think a fight that has personal grudge like Daniel's story attached to an already tight match up, that adds interests from all over."

Making money off my tragedy.

It's Ronnie's turn to say, "Which makes for huge payouts. Maybe he's back in town to call you out, Irish. And if he is?"

A rematch with Vince, the man who turned my brother Daniel off with a punch. A punch too strong, that shouldn't have been thrown that night in the first place.

Dax speaks, "I don't think you should give it to him, man," "There's too much involved now."

"All I know, is if it's a fight he wants, I'll gladly give it to him, but it will be on my terms."

Whatever those are.

I'm quiet while I discuss this further with my two best friends. Dax may be right, this idea already has my emotions involved talking about it, keeping my focus during another fight against Bordeaux may prove more difficult.

Dax using his goofy humor to change the mood, points to the front entry and says, "I already see your girls coming in swarms, Ronnie!" Egging him on as we all laugh watching the cowgirl groupies enter the dance floor. Brady comes over with refills as we watch and listen like we were guests rather than the owners. Just like clockwork, I feel an unwelcome touch as Lydia snakes her arms around my shoulders in greeting, along with the return of the ticking sound above me.

"Well hello boys! Glad to see you're letting loose tonight." Lydia says as she sneaks close up next to me.

66

Ronnie rolled his eyes and Dax raised his high as they both took big sips of their drinks. Even Brady gave Lydia the obvious shade trying to help me out by saying in the most sarcastic tone, "Oh Lydia, I am LOVING your pink cowgirl boots."

The three of us guys all look down, and sure enough, Lydia is wearing hideous barbie pink boots that must match her bright pink bandana around her neck. Lydia ignores Brady and lays her sights on me, her hands still caressing my back, "Declan, how about a drink? Or a dance?"

Dax couldn't help himself, laughing he says, "Declan go dancing, yeah right, Barbie, not in a million years."

Lydia snipping back, "Dax stop being mean, he might want to one day."

Dryly, I tell her, "I don't step foot on the dance floor for any reason."

Laughter is erupted amongst our group as more friends and acquaintances start piling around us.

Dax continues, "Barbie, you could be choking in the middle of that crowd, and Declan here would take his time to find someone else to come rescue you."

Lydia laughing along, not taking the social cues from all of us. She continues focusing on only me again,

"Well, how about a drink then?"

"How about not, I'm actually on my way out of here tonight." I say this as I stand from my chair and pull out my wallet. Throwing a $100 bill down for Brady, I grab my jacket and pull it on.

"Oh, come on!" Ronnie puffs at me.

"I have somewhere else I need to be." I add.

Ronnie asks, "Like where?"

I decide with the people around to throw him a wink, leaving both he and Dax staring back at me in disbelief, as I walk away. Unfortunately, while trying to make a swift exit, Lydia takes this time to follow me through the doors to the outside. I have found that ignoring people is the best way to get my point across, except Lydia doesn't get it.

"Declan, I'm ok with a quiet night in, if that's something you are up for tonight," gesturing an invite to sleep with me.

Feeling pissed that she already tainted my warm spot for Alexis, I decline firmly, "No Lydia, that is never going to happen between us. You go back in, have a good night."

I walked faster than she could even keep up with if she tried. On my bike, I rode to the place I knew would be what I needed.

Parking, I pull out my phone to text.

Me: Baby, if you're still here, open the front door.

Standing there in the parking lot, I waited for a reply from the one person I can't get off my mind.

Chapter 9   Alexis

The heater was blasting so high I had to take off my layers. There was a total of six men from the heating and air company working inside with me tonight until around 10:30pm when they finally got all units working and left.

 Luna and I were trying to get comfortable as we are spending our first night in my bed in the upper loft of my studio. Trying to sleep and actually sleeping are always battling within me when I lay down. Tonight, I'm finding it especially difficult since all I can think about, is a certain demanding, solid, disheveled haired, funny man that is seriously messing with my brain. I didn't really think Declan was going to contact me after dinner at the neighbor's house the other night. I don't know what comes over me when I'm with him, but he says things, or doesn't say anything at all, and every second feels more and more intense. He read Rachel's song and had insight about it that opened up an idea I hadn't thought to look for, an attachment to Paisley of some sort. I don't even know where to begin if I plan to join Rachel's scavenger hunt.

 My phone lights up from the floor, attached to the charger on the other side of my room. I'm so cozy in my covers, the last thing I need to add to my train of thoughts is Kel talking work or Jameson drunk dialing me. But as I stare at it, I realize how alone I am, and if I can't get up to see who needs me out of the handful of people who have my number, I'm a terrible person. So, since I am not a terrible person, I got out of bed and picked it up. Maybe my eyes need to adjust to the sudden light from the phone shocking them, because it sounds like Declan is telling me he is here, right now, outside my door. I look down at myself, looking slutty in my spaghetti strap silk nightgown that stops mid-thigh.

Am I going to open the door dressed like this? I think about it, I've been dressed like a gorilla every time I have seen him before.

 In the text, he called me 'baby.'

Besides how much he makes my vagina throb, there is so much I don't know about him, only assumptions off of what he has shared so far. A sexy, mysterious, and broody man that works at a bar and rides a motorcycle, he doesn't come off like a serious relationship type of guy, but maybe that is exactly what I need right now. He makes me feel so connected to the moment, which is what this is, another moment I get with Declan.

Looking at my phone again, I text him back.

ME: Be there in a sec
... I am so doing this.

Already feeling the goosebumps rising on my arms from the chill as I make my way to the front door in the dark. Unlocking it, I open it up only to be blasted with cold wind. I don't see him...until I do, walking towards me from the back of the parking lot.

 Even though I know he picked up his pace when he noticed my bare skin, it feels like I'm in slow motion watching him take each confident step towards me. His expression a hard line looking composed until I follow his eyes taking me in to find the edge of need in him. His arms are slinking over my silk fabric before he crosses the threshold inside, his large thick hands slowly grazing below my waist until he grabs underneath me full palm to lift me up. Our bodies like magnets as we connect like a force, Declan's hands all over my ass as I wrap around him, squeezing my thighs close to his core. I can feel his heart pumping fast through his jacket.

Buthump
Buthump

"Alexis," he says my name in a growly whisper as he just holds me, killing me with anticipation. His ferocious eyes try to lock with mine but distracted, as they keep grazing over every inch of my exposed body, heating me with desire. He carries me in his arms, finding the reception desk in the dark and sitting me down. Using the desk's height to his advantage, I part my legs as he steps in between.

His erection bulging against my inner thigh, as we come to a stop, face to face, his blue eyes filled with lust as he says my name again, trying to complete his sentence this time, "Alexis, baby…"
He reaches up to the side of my face, my breath hitching when he leans in to kiss me. Like a full body experience, our lips devoured one another, tongues meeting for the first time and exploring in a game of tag.
Tasting of whisky, while trailing his fingertips along my low waistline, Declan started to unravel in front of me, groaning in my mouth when my fingers slide under his jacket along his covered chest. My nipples hard pressed against him barely covered in my silk teddy, as he begins trailing slow teasing kisses just below my jaw line, and back up to my mouth, my fingers trailed up to slide through his hair.
He shifts on his feet, slowing his pace kissing my lips but keeping a tight hold on me. Fighting his control, he moves his mouth back to whisper, "I've been wanting to kiss these lips the moment I laid my eyes on you."
He kisses me again and again, his lips so soft against mine.
"If your married, I'll beat the shit out of him," still not letting me talk as his mouth covers mine over and over again, while I kiss him back harder in hopes to answer his question.
His normal composure fighting within him, I was in absolute bliss while he kept stopping every now and then to give me his growly thoughts, making me feel desired.
"I'm not waving to you ever again," he groans out while continuing his kissing me. I had never felt so turned on and at the same time my happiness a goofy smile when I ravage him back. Staying tuned, relishing in his honest confessions during our passionate embrace.
Opening his eyes and looking into mine he says,
"I'm sorry,"
"I didn't mean to wake you, but I had to see you," he brings both hands up, cupping my face, staring into me while lightly nipping my lip.
It is so hot in here.
"Then you finally decide to ditch the damn hoodie," kissing me again with his throaty growl that makes my insides tingle.

Carrying on as we smile and kiss and smile, Declan never pushes any further than our touchy feely make out session. I have never sensed anything like it, this wave of desire dueling in our mouths.

Slowing my sultriness down to a speaking level, I pull away to whisper over his lips, "You definitely heat me up."

Declan quickly exclaims, "Oh, Thank Christ!" claiming my mouth once more in a stronger pull sending shivers through me, his hands rub down my bare arms before slowing to say, "I can't even stand it when your cold. I have never hated a temperature so much in my life until I met you," as he pulls his mouth away further from me.

I give him a shy laugh as I cling on to him, both of us trying to catch our breath.

He asks, "You have Luna?"

Responding, I say, "Yes, she is sleeping in my bed upstairs."

"What kind of guard dog do you have?" he asks in disbelief.

Protecting Luna's reputation, I retort, "I was quiet when I snuck out of the room to come down here."

Smiling and shaking his head at me, Declan steps back and holds my hands helping me off the desk. Pulling me into him close again, he leans down to give me another kiss, this one a gentle brush, then he states, "I need you to add something to your Declan Duty list."

"Oh really?" I say sarcastically to him back.
"You sure are demanding."

"Yes, I am," he says sternly back but then quirks a corner smile and tells me, "I need you to make sure to lock this door the second I step out."

"Why do you say it like that? I thought this was a safe enough town."

Walking me the short distance through the dark reception area to the door, Declan stops and says, "You should always use caution wherever you are, but I want to be sure you lock your door to protect you, from me, coming back in here for you." He smiles and kisses me again,

"Go back to bed, Alexis, stay warm."

He stood there outside the door until he heard the lock click. Then I waved to him through the glass door, he ran his hand through his hair and waved back to me, before turning away.

Back upstairs to find Luna sprawled out on her side, her head on a pillow like a human, I crawl into my bed. All I can do is touch my fingers to my lips and stare at the ceiling.

In the morning, I sleep in past 9am for the first time in a very long time. No complaints coming from next to me, as my dog patiently waits for me to move. And moving is something I better start doing if I want to ever open this studio, with a goal in mind of starting youth classes hopefully by the Spring. Sabine is meeting me here today to run some errands, mostly personal, but I think it will be a good way for us to get to know each other better.

Putting on my sports bra and boy shorts, I try out my new surround sound speakers for the first time by myself in here. Since this is feeling like it should be a celebrated moment, I decide on a track that was one of me and Rachel's favorites.

Christina Aguilera – Candyman

The jazzy rhythm has a speed that warms up my blood, each step a quick staccato.

The song reminding me of when Rachel performed it at the Hard Rock Hotel during a birthday dinner for one of the Wahlberg's. Terrie booked the gig telling us the money was not even the best part. Yet, I don't ever remember her telling us what the best part even was. It was our usual contract for the show. I wrote the script and Rachel performed. I was kept in the shadows while Rachel was in the limelight.

My name was hidden, Rachel Butler's name was plastered all around.

Neither of us better off, we held each other together.

I recall all the days and nights it took me to write out that dance performance for a solo artist with a remix sound added. Then I had to teach it to Rachel step by step until she mastered it, and our hard work played out on stage. It was impressive if I do say so myself, I remember ogling her dance and sing, looking like perfection with her blonde curls we hair sprayed for 15 minutes straight. I stood next to the cocktail table and had the unfortunate smell of shrimp rippling through my nose. I was trying not to be too weird as I kept skirting down every so often to get away from the stench. I like seafood, but nothing about raw shrimp appeals to me. The reason probably stems from the required lunches Terrie enforced during our low caloric diets, including small cut up pieces of raw shrimp around the plate to make it appear like more than it was, with an arugula salad as the side. If we didn't eat it, there was nothing else in the house and our money was her money.

My steps speed up faster with the next few songs as I try to bounce, twirl, leap, jump, even some low break dancing, to dodge the past that tries to haunt me. Sweat trickling down the back of my ponytail to my neck tickling me to swipe it away, a reminder of the shivers that ran through my body last night while Declan held me close. Another new memory now encrypted in my brain, a damn good one.

Sabine meets me at the studio in the afternoon in a break from her studying. We walk into town together, counting the extra steps for the day a win. I have learned quite a bit about Sabine since getting to know her, one being her knowledge of dance that surprised me. I should have known by her straight stance that she had a dance background, growing up taking ballet classes as a younger child. Other personal details about her like how her education took precedence during high school and she studied her way to graduate early at the top of her class. Her proud father is from Colombia, South America, and Sabine is the first female to graduate high school in his family. Beyond her book intelligence, Sabine is a hard working, mature, flirty 21-year-old girl who likes to make time for fun too.

As Sabine and I walk down the streets peering in and out of the shops we continue our friendly chit chat, Sabine states, "So, Declan McQuade has set his sights on you, I see?"

My eyes widen as I fluster, "I don't think it's like that. We are friends," I say as there is no other possible label needed, adding in question, "I didn't think you knew who he was?"

"I didn't!" she says with a smile, "I literally had no idea until he told me his first name. I had never actually seen his face before, I've heard of him. It's his brother I know, David, who runs the boxing gym down the road, that guy is so hot when he pumps iron."

"Who?! Declan or David?"

"Probably BOTH!" she says laughing, "But I'm talking about David being my eye candy, don't worry, I won't swoon over your guy."

I laugh at her as we keep walking, "I am not worried, you weirdo, swoon away. Anyways, how do you know his brother than?" continuing with our conversation.

"I actually have never really met him," Sabine replies, "more like, I have seen him around town and purposely walk by just to get an eyeful, sometimes. Do not tell anybody this either, this should be private employee information."

I give her my promise of good faith as I ask, "So, you like the older guys, then?"

"He's only 24!" Sabine huffs out, "Besides, it isn't like he will ever know my existence. He is this big popular guy and I've always been the book worm."

"The world works in mysterious ways." I say as we pass a few other shoppers down the path, "Why don't you ever try to run into him since you know where he always is?"

Sabine shrieks trying not to be too loud on the street, "Ya Right! Like how? Plus, he is not going to be the least bit interested in me, he seems to have no problems finding women," giving me a quirky smile while she slows her pace in front of a small clothing boutique shop.

"Sabine, shut the hell up!" I tell her knowing the unworthy feeling all too well as I try to convince her the best I know how by telling her, "You will have no problem getting his attention if that is what you want, because he won't be able to look away." I end my positive reinforcement rant while stepping in.

The inside of the store had an array of clothing scattered among racks as well as shoes and jewelry along the walls. Besides my love of comfort clothes during my me time, my closet is mostly filled with assortments of dresses and jumpsuits, fancy and sexy, taking up the majority of the hangers. I am a sucker for sparkle and bling when I go out and my two best friends knew my soft spot, always having Rachel and Jameson bringing me random purchases to dress me up whenever they got a chance, since they assumed I was incapable of knowing when to show off my body. Sabine and I were in and out of the dressing rooms, trying on our outfits and modeling before one another, judging the look of the fit. We laughed at some of the ridiculous fabric that was so thin, if you went out into the sunlight you would look naked. It was fun having a girlfriend for the day, both of us coming out with bags full as I treated to her dismay. Sabine is going to be around me a lot with work, so I want to make sure she is included in the important things in my life too. As we carried on, I decided to bring up the subject of my small circle of tight knit friends.

"I wanted to introduce you to Kel and Jameson on FaceTime one day if that is OK with you? Kel, the band manager, will end up having your number on speed dial and Jameson just always thinks he knows better for me, so he will be calling always for reasons unknown."

Sabine responds, "Absolutely. They sound great."

"Kel was originally hired by my former employer to manage me and Rachel," trying to explain small details of my twisted past that paved the way to my present, "But Rachel and I had a falling out with that former employer, so, Kel worked with the two of us to get back on our feet, and in the meantime, I introduced her to my friend Jameson's band. She ended up swooping them up under her wing and that created a rippling effect of success for the three of us." Then I add, "Jameson's band is called, MartaBeat."

Sabine stops and turns to ask, "Wait, your Jameson is, 'Jam Fresh' from MartaBeat?"

"Gah, yes, one in the same. MartaBeat local to Boston, plays both mixed versions of cover songs as well as their own written songs. I've been the ghost choreographer and DJ for them since they started up."

Sabine swoons, "You have hot guys all around you!"

Making me laugh just thinking about Jameson and his tacky nickname from eleventh grade when he showed up to school after summer vacation and puberty transformed the normally geeky skinny Jameson into a tall and toned stunner. We all joked about his 'Fresh' new look. JamFresh.

I continue on in my explanation, "Anyways, when I decided to move here permanently, Kel and I agreed on work projects primarily only through the band. But knowing her, she will also be sending proposals from other clients of hers who may offer a good bit for me to do things like, map out a dance for them, or sometimes even coaching their performers."

I pause before I keep on, "Really though, that was my busy work life in Boston that I'm trying to avoid now that I'm here. I don't want or need those projects to be my primary agenda anymore and both Kel and Jameson are having a hard time with that."

Sabine nodded and smiled thoughtfully in understanding, finally saying, "I'm so happy to work with you, Lexi."

I nudge my new friend, Sabine, and reply, "I am so happy to work with you too AND WORK OUT with you, because we are walking to the gym.

Sabine croaks, "Are you crazy, I can't go in there. I can't even box!"

"NO, not that gym," I say clarifying before panic gets both of us, "The big athletic club that just opened. I'm signing up under the company so anyone who works with us can be part of the membership."

"That sounds great," Sabine replies, "how many more employees were you thinking you needed at the studio?"

"I am going to put feelers out for someone else once we get off the ground running." I finish saying.

We get to the gym which looks oddly big in comparison to the rest of the buildings in town.

"I heard this has a pool!" Sabine says as we walk inside.

There wasn't much this gym didn't have. Sabine and I got a tour from a man named Connor, who was pleasant enough, but he pushed personal trainers on the two of us close to twenty times.

Also, Connor is one of the personal trainers as well.

I was in cardio heaven when I saw all the equipment they had, even the treadmills on the balcony looked good to me, planning to people watch the entire time I ran. Even though Terrie forced workouts on us, I never held a grudge. Fitness has always been part of my life because it makes me feel good. The personal trainers that would come in and work with us were valuable in my journey towards a healthier lifestyle, after all, I was not born into anything healthy.

Sabine and I registered for our gym pass and left feeling energized, even though we didn't actually work out yet.

On our walk back, I pulled out my phone to see I had a missed text message from my night owl.

Declan: I want to kiss you again

His message making me smile, grabbed Sabine's attention.

"Oh, did you get a message from someone important?" She croons side eye to me and I can't help but admit telling her, "It's from Declan."

"Uh huh," she says all knowing, "You know that coworker privacy thing goes both ways, you can talk to me if you ever need someone."

"Thanks Sabine, I just don't really know how to feel. We kissed last night." I feel weight come off my shoulders as I accept her offer and tell her about Declan. After all, it gets lonely, and I trust Sabine.

She seeks for my thoughts, "Can't you feel happy and excited?"

"I feel those things, but that doesn't come easy for me sometimes, so I question it more I guess." Admitting my feelings. "I don't think I can handle any more hurt in my life," shocking even myself as I give her this forward truth.

Sabine turns to me, standing like a stoic statue, without any pity in her voice says, "Putting yourself out there is going to be scary no matter who it's with. I think for now, you can't close the doors that just opened for you, especially if it involves a door to Declan McQuade," her message loud and clear.

"You aren't wrong." I say as a matter of fact, giving her an appreciative smile.
We made it back to the studio and Sabine went home while I gathered my items from my sleepover to take back with me to my bat cave.
Before I drive home, I text my new guy.

Me: When and Where?

Chapter 10   Declan

I must have lost my mind, finding myself scrolling through security feed from the past week to make sure there was no signs of Vince entering the club without us knowing. My anger against him rising out of me more and more this week while I think over my ultimate decision. There would be nothing I want more than getting another chance to knockout Vince Bordeaux in the ring, but it would take a lot of work and extensive practice, hours of training to get prepared for a match like that. I feel like a beast being dragged out of his cell for the first time and waiting for someone to tell me to warm up, Since I haven't stepped into a fight since Daniel's accident.

"Find anything?" a deep voice behind me asks from the security booth as I sit in his chair and sift through images on the computer. Al is one of our head bouncers on the Swollen team, and a loyal friend to me as well.

"Not a damn thing," I tell him as I huff out and close myself out of my search. Already knowing my security detail didn't miss anything, I needed to check again myself to help my rattled uncertainty.

Pushing thirty, Al has brown skin and a long dark goatee he calls his tailback beard, which he also thinks is his finest trait in picking up women. Taller than me and pushing 300 pounds, he has proven his worth here dedicating himself to the safety team night after night. He also is good for gossip, which is why it is driving me crazy that even he hasn't heard of anything yet of Vince's return.

Al feeling my stress, reminds me, "You have a radio on you at all times, boss. If he comes here, I will be on him like a germ in a bounce castle."

"Thanks for that, seems like you have it all taken care of while you plan children's birthday parties."

"Hey, it was the first thing I thought of. Besides, Lawrence asked me for this specific Hulk Mania castle that I can't find anywhere."

Turning around, Al is on his phone scrolling to find his six-year-old son's requested inflatable. He seems to think this is more stressful than my obvious Grudge Match dilemma, even though without a doubt this man will find a damn Hulk Mania castle.

Looking up, he asks me, "Will you be working with me at the door for some of Ladies night on Saturday," playfully wiggling his eyebrows up and down at the topic, adding, "it's always my favorite night of the month."

"You know I never miss," I tell him as I stand up to head out, but before I could, Al asks.
 "So you're not hittin' it with Lydia then?"

Standing there with my hands on my hips, I retort back with a quick, "Hell no."
"Why would you assume that?"

"I saw her follow you out the other night, and then when you came in on Sunday morning you looked all cheery, like you got laid," Al replies with a laugh.

"No, Lydia followed me out and I told her it was never going to happen again. Actually, I was leaving to see someone else I've been talking to."

Remembering how Saturday night played out, I know exactly why Al would have guessed this about me. That was the night I left the club to see Alexis.

Al pipes up in interest and asks, "Oh yeah?"

"Anyone I would know?"

"No, I don't think so, she's new here."

Al has always been in my relationship business, or my casual hookup business, since he watches us all so closely. He is also used to helping me, Dax, and Ronnie, avoid some of the drama that comes along with owning a club and hooking up with women. Not knowing just what to say about my status with Alexis, I kept it vague.

Al wanted more so he kept questioning, "And? You going to show me a picture so I can keep an eye out?"

"No, it's not serious like that. She doesn't even know I work here."

Al gives me a skeptical look and chuckles, "You mean she doesn't know you own the club?"

"No." I reply shortly.

"Okay, well like most of those girls, I'm sure she will show up here one day to scope out whatever drama she heard about you to get more of your attention, and then you will be calling my name to kick her out."

Grinning at him, I say, "She isn't my girlfriend. Don't get ahead of yourself, there."

"They never are," laughing in disbelief, Al finishes, "See you, Saturday."

Not sharing details of myself to Alexis isn't on purpose. We haven't gotten to know those details of each other and I'm not sure how she is going to feel when she finds out about my fighting hobby outside the gym or my attachment to a nightclub. I don't think my boxing scares her, because she didn't act like she was bothered when telling her I fought in the gym, she just touched me in comfort and quirked a joke.

As far as talking about my job, that one is up for debate, because I'm not opened to speaking about my private self when it comes to hook ups. But that is all I've known is hook ups,

and I can feel that Alexis already means far more than that to me, but I'm not sure how to define it.

Either way, just the thought of everything possibly going wrong with Alexis pisses me off now because everything has been going so right. This girl is an infuriating temptress and has had me tied in knots. I knew when I texted Alexis on Saturday night at her studio that my desire for her was high. Hell, that is what made me leave the club and drive straight to her. I needed her to know I wanted her, enough waving.

I am not sure what I ever really expected her to look like underneath her giant coats and sweaters, well I had ideas, but when she walked out in that striptease worthy nightgown, I lost my sense of composure. Small in my arms, kissing her felt like we were made for one another. Nerve endings exploding as I relished in every kiss, suck, and nip we gave back and forth while our bodies spoke volumes in their own language. There was nothing but time, no rushing into anything more because we didn't need to. Never have I been so satisfied with a make out session before, like lighting a new candle wick, an unexpected crackle that leads to a flame, burning with our reaction, and I don't want to blow it out.

I wanted to take her right there on that desk and with the way she pressed against me, I think she wanted it too, but somehow the need to indulge in the moment came over me. Why rush the most beautiful gift I've been given, handed over in an ice storm, mine to protect. That was the only thought that allowed me to slow it down and I'm not sure if I am going to be capable of having that control again.

I haven't taken a girl on a date in quite a few years. I haven't needed to. I get what I need, when I need it, and I certainly don't have the time to put into a relationship. So, I surprised myself when I texted Alexis that I was coming to get her tonight.

Like the goddess, Amphitrite, pulling me in, circling me with a fast-paced flow of river current, I keep swirling.

Honestly, walking up to her door has me feeling a little nervous. Living in a condo near the club, it's about twenty minutes to get to Alexis' round house in Paisley, and even the bike ride didn't vibrate the nerves away.

God, I think Vince has gotten in my head, I need to get it together.

Taking a breath to regain my cool, I ring her doorbell. Luna's barks are right on cue tonight, high yelps screeching out of the dog's lungs on the other side of the door, then I could hear Alexis trying to calm her down with her noisy hushes.

Shh Shh Hush Luna

Without tripping forward this time, Alexis opens the door jolting a shock down my spine the first second I see her.

Flashing red for danger.

Enter with caution

I'm walking into the ring.

Be confident.

Keep up your defenses.

Give yourself 30 seconds to read her first.

Dressed in tight black jeans ripped in the knees and a plain white tee that hugs her big tits so nicely, even teasing me with hints of her white lace bra outline, her dark hair styled down in waves, losing all my trained wisdom, I launch at her as soon as she has me step inside.

I didn't even say anything in greeting.

Caging her in around the closed door, her green eyes dilating, our hands already wrapping around each other bodies like we are starved for touch. Holding my arms around her back to catch the brunt when I slam her up against the door. Her mouth seizing mine and we are finally kissing again, tasting her sweet hint of strawberry, starved. I groan in her mouth, licking her tongue seductively, appreciating every stroke in our entanglement. My hands run down the sides of her and around her small waistline discovering all of her sensitive spots, wiring details in my brain from her body's responses.

She slows to a quick stop to look at me, almost questioning, then swiftly she hops up, as I growl in her ear, catching her ass as she hangs off me, our way, mine to hold.

Placing her hands to the sides of my face, her natural full lips parting as she reaches for my mouth again, seducing me like a dirty tease, as she places light slower sucks on my lips.

God Damn this girl can work her mouth.

My cock that has been semi all day thinking about her, is now hard as a steel pipe, hard to miss, she rubs against my pipe at the same time my fingertips underneath her ass are centering in closer to her, lightly grazing over the thin fabric that covers her folds. Her green eyes closed in her bliss, only to open in between her suckles in our kisses.

I hear my coach yelling at me to pace myself.

She gasps for air, her chest heaving as she tries to talk, "Oh my god," her perfect breasts bouncing up and down so close to me with her deep chested breaths, growling in appreciation, I can only stare as she continues, "You just may kill me after all."

"Baby, trust me, it's not killing you that I want to do," in case she didn't get the hint with the bulge between her legs, I add, "but before you kill me..."

I try to focus on my breath count to allow myself to loosen my hold of her, allowing her back down to stand. It wasn't easy to relax myself enough to settle my lusty haze, and I am going to notate this as an accomplishment for having the control to stop before I explode in my pants. Adjusting myself, I say, "Let me at least take you out, first."

"Take me out?" she asks, "I thought you were just coming over to kiss me?"

Alexis sounding serious as she pouts a bit when I let her go fully, pulling her shirt back down from my mauling.

Pace yourself.

"I'm nowhere near done kissing you," I tell her while she walks us forward into her living area, Luna at our feet who just witnessed the whole show.

The inside of her place is remodeled, new like her, fresh and bright in whites and crèmes throughout her large square footage. It is slick and clean with a homey feel, fireplace lit and a seating area with enough spots for multiple family members to comfortably sit. The room reminded me of my home when I was a young child in Ireland, when there was a woman still in the house. Always had the wood burning stove on and the living room was our sanctuary.

"Where are you taking me?" She questions as she walks out of the room into another hall, on the hunt for something.

"Out, you'll see." I say as I keep peering around. She comes back out with her puffy white coat in hand.

"Your place is nice," I tell her as I begin slowly walking over towards her, realizing I can't keep my hands off as I help her slither inside her big coat.

"Thanks, it's quiet."

"Yea, well maybe you should host a raging party." I say sarcastically as I wait for her to put her shoes on.

Alexis coming back with, "Oh yea, with all the people I know, maybe Margie can bring the food."

I assure her, "I'll be there, that's really all you need, even though I'm sure Margie would insist on bringing the food." We have a flirty laugh as I lift her up when we get outside, walking her to my bike.

"Declan, I'm going to get used to you carrying me everywhere. Maybe that should be part of your Alexis duty list," the glint in her eyes cute as she proudly smiles at herself for her remark.

"Done." I say as I get her on her spot and pull out her helmet.

Yes, her helmet, the one I bought yesterday just for her to ride with me. A girly one, some would possibly say it is the Barbie pink. I won't tell Dax or Ronnie.

Alexis cheerful in her mockery, "What! Aw cute, I get to use the old backup chick helmet," she says as I put it over her head.

"No back up chick. I just thought I'd keep up my good marks on keeping you alive."

"Thanks, I was more worried about head lice. Will you pick the bugs out of my head if your backup chick left lice in here?" Her girly laugh is loud even under the cover while she enjoys her own sense of humor.

I just smile and shake my head as I start the roar of the engine, waiting until she is hugged tight against me in her warm spot, her arms like my seatbelt, and we ride out.

Chapter 11   Alexis

I never realized how freeing it feels to ride on a motorcycle. Maybe it's the driver that I hold onto that keeps me from worry, maybe it's the rubber tires racing underneath me that draws my focus to the sounds, whatever it is, I am feeling a hint of both, happy and content, when I am on this bike.

Not anticipating an actual date, I am going to try my best to just relax and enjoy a night out. Like a normal person would. And Sabine is right, a night out with a guy like Declan, whew, Maybe I should wonder if Rachel had something to do with this too.

Here is a new house, and a hot new guy to kiss!

Dirty, Dirty man. This better not be a dirty joke.

Trust your gut, Alexis.

Declan holds my hand and keeps his eyes more focused on me, rather than where he is going, as we walk towards what looks to be a dive bar. It's a corner building with murals covering the entirety of the brick, guitars and flowers in psychedelic chaos of blues and pinks shadowed in black and white. It seems like a popular hotspot with circles of friends littered in front. Declan leads us inside where I immediately hear the woof of the speakers blaring with some side static. We are greeted by a hostess stand with two girls with matching pink eyeshadow and high floppy ponytails and led by another matched ponytail worker, through the center of the room. The bar crowded along the wall and a small stage a few feet off the ground by the side. Florescent lighting, mostly pink, shining down bright enough to make the entire place feel like we are in a pink fog.

Speaking loudly over the welcomed blaring music, Declan says,"It's called Ripley's, probably the coolest spot in Paisley."

Ripley's was cool, a fun artsy vibe that was nice to see in this quieter town. We walk into a darker corner that has pink leather sofas surrounding tables for seating, with a great view of the stage.

Declan asks the hostess as we take our seats beside each other on a sofa, "Do you mind getting us one of your checkers mats, please?"

She obliges with an eyeful of flirt and walks away, leaving Declan and I alone together.

"I didn't take you as this much fun!" I say amused.

"I'm not," he says with a chuckle, "I used to come here a lot when I was quite a bit younger, but I have not been here recently."

I reply, "Living on the wild side," adding, "it's great! Will they have karaoke there then?" I point to the stage that currently only has music equipment occupying its space.

Declan explains, "There should be a local band starting here soon, they usually have jam nights during weekdays with all sorts of different groups and artists."

Just then, our waitress comes over, double ponytail action,"Hi guys, welcome into Ripley's," she says sweetly with the name TALIA on her nametag. She lays a small mat in front of Declan and unravels it on top of the table, turning out to be a carpeted checkers board. Along with walking back with stacks of plastic red and black to pile on top. My eyes watching her to my surprise.

Peering up at Declan, I ask, "We are going to play Checkers?"

He gives me a boyish grin and replies, "Yes, it's one of the best kept secrets here. I hope you're ready."

I tried to look confident, even though I really only had played a few times, but he seems giddy in anticipation for this board game, so I wanted to rise to the challenge.

I tell Declan, "You do realize I am a dancer right? Taking calculated steps is kind of my thing?"

Declan's face lights up as he looks at me and replies, "You do realize I am a fighter right? Boxing in a ring taking calculated steps is actually my thing," his smile bright.

"Game on, Tyson." I say, just as Talia comes back over to take our order. "What can I get for you two tonight?"

The drink menu was in my hand as I lean into Declan questioning in silence on what type of drink to order on this casual first date.

Declan sees my plunder and whispers to me softly, "Order whatever you want."

I do, "I'll take a gin and tonic please, with lime."

Declan orders next, "I'll just have Crown Royal rye over ice, please," he says as he hands over our menus to the waitress. We start setting up our game for battle of the better checkers player. Our drinks come and we decide not to order food. Alcohol and checkers at a quirky bar kind of night.

It's pretty perfect.

"So, how do you know about this," I say gesturing to the game.

"It is an old local secret I thought I'd share with you, being new here and all." He laughs as he continues, "I used to come here to chill out and play with my brother."

"Is he a worthy opponent? I need to know what I'm up against." I ask trying to lightly start a conversation. Something flickers across Declan's face as he answers, "Yeah, but I was always the reigning champion."

Biting my lip in a smile, not believing how cute this big strong confident man is right now over a classic board game, I tease, "Yea right, I'm sure your brother tells a different story."

That same flicker waved through his facial features, and I couldn't figure out exactly what it was, because he was too quick to snap it away, as he says to me, "Probably. Do you have siblings?"

"No, no siblings, just really close friends that were my family growing up. You have one brother?" I ask him this remembering Sabine telling me about his younger brother that runs the boxing gym in town, but not bringing that up as I wait to hear from Declan.

"I have two brothers, I'm in the middle. It is my older brother, Daniel, who used to play with me up here," changing the subject back to me, "Are you one of those only children who were spoiled all their lives?" he asks me lightly.

Light is how I'm keeping it tonight, because there is no need to ruin this time I have with Declan with all the ghosts of my past.

"I am most definitely not the spoiled type," adding in a bit of the truth, "both of my parents are passed away, I'm more independent than you take me for," crooning my neck to him in my playfulness as I set up my red discs on my end of the checker's board.

He gives me a thoughtful smile saying,

"Hmm. My mum died when I was young too, we were living in Ireland. That's where I'm originally from," adding, "We will see how well you're managing life on your own depending how well you perform in this game," as he nods to me to make my first move.

I do, as we start sending out our first line of defense in each of our dozen red and black discs, with the obvious first outs in the beginning, still even score.

"So, you moved here with your dad and brothers then?"

"Yes when I was 10, my dad bought the gym and we have been here ever since."

"How old does that make you now, Declan? I've been kissing you with no age or last name."

"I'm 27, and my full name is Declan Wesley McQuade, and while you're telling me your last name," Looking across at me now as we have moved away to play the game, he grins a stupid wide grin saying, "King me!"

Gahh

I moan as I place the 2nd tier on his black disc.

"Alexis Andrews, I'm 25 and from the Boston area always. Now, KING ME!" I leapt a bit out of my seat with my happy comeback. We play back and forth as the band arrives on stage for tonight's performance. Ripley's was full of happy patrons of all age groups, mostly college goers, busting out fancy cotton candy topped cocktails from the bar, and some groupies forming a crowd, ready to dance. We sipped on our drinks like old gentlemen playing a game of checkers.

Declan chimes up as he gets closer to his mark on the board, giving me a scandalous smile as he asks, "Are we setting a wager?"

Squinting at him, I ask. "What kind of wager were you thinking?"

"Friendly enough," his smile grew, "If I win, you kiss me again and you have to flash me later."

Rrrr

The sound coming from my throat and my face reddening in a nervous panic, I accept his challenge, "Deal, but if I win, you have to dance with me over there," I say pointing to the group in front of the stage.

Declan rebuts, "No deal, I don't dance, I won't do it."

My eyes widen as horror is shown on my face. "Declan Wesley McQuade, are you backing down from the challenge?"

He looks at me hard, his thick ashy brown eyebrows furrowing over his sparkling blue eyes while he thinks over my obvious jab, even bringing his fingertips to his chin during his moment of pause.

Breaking from his pondering, Declan declares, "Fine. You have a deal."

We each still had a chance of winning, but the odds were definitely against me when his black jumped over another one of my reds. Taking some bigger gulps of my drink while he looks cooler than Kool-Aid across from me, I try to distract him, "tell me about your boxing."

Peering up from his concentration to the board, he replies, "Boxing's just always been a part of my life, I suppose. I had boxed in youth leagues, but I started training more seriously when I was a teenager. Two of my really good friends and I would just box and fight after school all night. We were all pretty good, always in the gym together, and it got us noticed by underground scouts that started sponsoring us for some higher-level fights. I've slowed down to just practice now that I work at the bar," He finishes saying as he takes a swig of his rye.

I was glad to hear him open up to me about himself and his growing up, but I could tell it made him on edge. It gave me more insight to this mysterious man that has shown up out of nowhere. I ended up putting two more tops on his black checkers as I start rolling down a losing slope in our game.

In a friendly tone, I state, "That's a neat story, you must be good," then ask, "And those underground fights? Is your body too old to perform anymore or are you still going strong?" Understanding what it is like to dedicate yourself to a sport, I try to ask in a way he knows I'm not bothered by his confession. Knowing it isn't society's term of right, but I also danced and performed in underground, illegal challenges and tournaments. It is one of the things I credit for keeping my spirit alive while under Terrie's wing.

Declan meets my eyes with a small, tight smile, "I can still perform if I need to," he says dryly, "King me."

Gahh

I do and it is not long after that he reigns King of the game.

His victory is contagious as we laughed and lightly chatted until it was time to go. He paid the bill and we stacked up our checkers. Putting his arms around me as we walk out, Ripley's got livelier as the night went on, causing Declan's over six-foot mass of iron to block me when he leads us through the swarms. Right before the door, a couple of men at the bar drinking must have noticed us walking through, as the one with a beastly figure and a shaved head stops Declan in greeting.

"Irish!"

"What the hell are you doing here?" he asks as his eyes turn over towards me, and his stare moves up and down my body in a noticeable nod of approval, not impressing my current date as Declan takes another step to block me more while saying coldly, "Good to see you, we were just leaving, Boomer."

"Yea well maybe I'll be seeing you around more if you are ruffing it down in these parts of town."

The man, Boomer, places a snarky smile on his face as Declan returns a short, "Maybe," And moves us past the two men to get us through the door. Walking to the bike, still holding me close, he says trying to make light of that awkward encounter, "I have a feeling I'm going to have to make you put your hoodies back on when we go out."

I cannot help but laugh out loud at him. He gets us on the bike, safety helmets on, as we ride back to my house.

Declan lifts me off but doesn't move his feet when I start walking toward my door, our linked hands stopping me as I realize he isn't following.

"Declan, are you ok?" I ask him as I face him. He pulls me in to his chest, looking down, he starts kissing me. It is a slow and passionate kiss, unlike our frenzies we usually partake in. Light stubble around his mouth brushes me gently as his lips move in a slow caress.

Lifting my chin with his fingers, his eyes opening, Declan peers down at me to say, "I'm going to say goodnight to you from here because I can't walk you to that door."
Looking up at him and seeing the blaze in his blues, I all knowingly understand what he is trying to tell me, but I like to press his cool.
I put on my displeased face and return, "But what if I freeze to death on my way there by myself?"

Instead of joking with me back, he remains more serious this time when he replies, "I won't ever let you freeze ever again if I can help it. But I know I lose all my control with you when I walk through that door," his lips meet mine again as he indulges in between his thoughts, "Like a real first date, I just want to end tonight with my good conscious. But don't you worry, I will be back to claim what I won fair and square from you very, very soon."
We kissed in his sweet truth, and I couldn't help but appreciate his patience.
Finally letting me go, I walk in as he waits in his firm position, watching.
The night started out assuming to be a hook up, then he took me out almost casually, then it became a date, and now it becomes a little bit more with being labeled as, 'our first date'. If there is one thing for certain I can say about what happens when I am with Declan McQuade, is that things start moving fast.

Chapter 12   Declan

"Darling I just told you, not but 20 minutes ago, Your ID is fake, and I cannot let you through this door." Al tries his hardest to nicely send this underage girl on her way, but she is not letting it go. Appearing to be over intoxicated, this pixie of a girl is spitting fire at the front door to Swollen tonight, as her just as young-looking boyfriend tries to hold her back.
"I am NOT a LIAR Sir! You are the Motherfucker that needs to leave! YOU are the LIAR!"

Other club goers that are waiting in line start getting annoyed with this hold up, causing more yelling back and forth to the inebriated minor, until a woman pulled a scared straight moment on the girl, getting up in her face and telling her to go home to mommy. Luckily for Al, the ones in line were the ultimate heroes at kicking the intrusion away. Leaving me to my reasoning for coming out here.

I'm working tonight and I couldn't concentrate, because Alexis hasn't left my mind since I took her out last night, taunting me about holding back to claim my prize. Trying to be a decent man for her is downright killing me.

Ripley's was the only place I could think of to take Alexis to, only second guessing it when the thoughts of Daniel were rolled out with the checkers mat. Yet somehow, Alexis turned those avoided memories back into good ones again for me.
A new worthy opponent.
I may be screwed.

And now, here I am standing with Al at security check in trying to think about something other than the anticipation on seeing her at tomorrow night's dinner with Estel and Margie.
"How is the Hulk castle coming along?" I ask him as he checks the ID's held out to him with his flashlight for entry.
"Man, come to find out, Lawrence tells me he saw the castle at another kid's birthday party a couple months back. So now, I have to find out the name of that kid and hunt down the mom or dad to find out where to find this fucking thing," disbelief rolling off him as he tells me about the update on his dad mission. He knows I don't really give a shit, and he can read me like a book. I start helping Al out with the assembly line of people while we spoke.
"So," Al says to me in a side eye, "something's up with you tonight."
I agree too quickly, "Yeah, you could say that."
His side eye grows harder, "You heard something?"
"No, I haven't, I think it's messing with my head."
"Is that all that's messing with your head? Or are we also...just talking about nothing serious right now?"
Bingo! This guy knows things enough that I should write him a recommendation letter to join the FBI. I give him the all knowing look instead of any words, causing his big belly laugh to start

quaking up. A couple of women passing through take long ogling looks at us, flirting with conversation. Al and I have to smile and nod then turn away to get rid of them.

Continuing, Al asks, "Am I going to get a name or a picture, yet?"

"Not going to happen," I say as he continues to laugh at me. There is no way I'm divulging any details on her, but it is nice to just know that someone else kind of knows. Even if that someone is Al, and he probably does know more without me telling him. I for some reason wish he did have better intel than me, then maybe he could help me figure out what the hell I'm doing. The thoughts of Alexis that haven't relented all day, the image stitched in my brain speaking to me in a swirl of somersaults.

Al laughed at me pretty much the rest of the time I spent with him. It was worth it though, because just that comradery helped calm me down as the night grew darker. While the lines slowed outside, I followed the crowd inside, nodding to a few familiar faces along the way when I spot Ronnie talking to a woman at the bar in his Batman t-shirt. He was standing behind with Brady and the other bartenders, with a clipboard in his hand. Brady has her lilac locks up in a messy bun tonight, with straws sticking out of the top. Once I was closer, I noticed him fidgeting around not acting his usual cool while speaking to the girl seated by herself on the end of the bar. I can't help but understand how a girl can make you feel unsteady because I know that feeling all too well right now.

I stride up where they are standing, Brady is quick to slide down and reveal, "Hey Declan, this is my good friend and roommate, Autumn," smiling and looking over to greet the familiar face, I realize this is the girl Ronnie has been ogling that I said will slay him. Sitting tall, she has long dark hair with red highlights that match her ruby red lips.

With a corner smile in my realization, I greet her with a handshake, "Hi there, I'm Declan. Nice meeting you."

Shaking my hand in return, she says her name, "Autumn," and smiles politely back at me.

Ronnie sees me saying, "Irish, I didn't know you were still here?"

"I'm not sure I will be for too much longer tonight," I add as I mosey around to see what's needed, which is likely nothing because we run a damn good ship around here.

Brady was flipping around bottles of liquor and pouring her orders while taking this time to remind us, "So, you guys remember I'm off for Ladies night on Saturday?"

"Yes, we got the shifts covered, all the male bartenders offered to work so we are fully staffed behind here on Saturday." Ronnie charms as he and I bend underneath the counters to pull out the emptied beer kegs needing replacements.

"Nobody wants to miss Ladies Night," Brady exclaims.

Another one of our bartenders, Tham, carries out a full keg from the back room and hands it to me to swap out the empty. Tham is a favorite amongst the older women who sit at the bar, always creating his own cocktail recipes and upselling them, boasting it was made specifically with them in mind.

The cougars love Tham.

Tham bellows over to his coworker and friend. "Oh, Brady, are you going to be here pouring your own drinks again?"

Autumn, starts laughing as she stands up from her seat, her purse on her shoulder, when Brady throws a maraschino cherry at Tham and yells,

"You better pour my extra, extra shots in my drink I order then, Tham!"

Tham exclaims, "Four extra shots in one drink is way too much!"

It's Autumn's turn to say out to Tham, "I'm glad I have you on my side, because somebody needs to help me slow her down."

Smiling with her bright red lips, Autumn adds, "Brady, I'm going home, I'll see you guys on Saturday."

"Oh, and Hey by the way, I have a new friend I'm going to ask to join us!"

"Woohoo," screams Tham, "the more the merrier!"

Ronnie and I agreeing with Tham in a laugh, Brady responding back to Autumn, "The man eater?"

Autumn laughs as she starts stepping back saying, "YES, you guys just wait," eyeballing me and Tham first and quickly grazing over Ronnie, "She is the hottest chick I have ever met, single, mysterious, she would be a reason for me to give up my love of a penis," her eyes seemingly serious with her wide red sarcastic smile.

Brady is laughing harder now as she pours another clear drink, stating back, "Shut Up on your girl crush, don't give up on men just yet," Autumn throws up a wave and walks out. I watch as Ronnie stares at the back of Autumn, running his hand through his dark wavy hair in his moment of nerves, while Brady, oblivious to Ronnie's crush, walks to the other end of the bar to take an order.

"Maybe you will do better on Saturday," I tease my good friend who seems to be riding on the same boat as me, "All in due time, and speaking of time, I'm out of it," sending my shipmate a slap on the shoulder to comfort. "See you tomorrow."

There was an old tale I was told growing up, something about when the mouse steals a cookie once, he gets a pass, but when the mouse steals a cookie twice, there's the warning shot you've been caught...that tale reminds me of my position right now, me being the mouse. Ronnie rips out before I can turn, "Where are you off to in a hurry again?"

Standing there tall with his hands in his pockets, Ronnie, 27, has always played the responsible father figure in our trio. I happen to have an honest relationship with this father.

"I'm going to head home, maybe make a pit stop first." I say looking at him straight in the eye now.

Ronnie pulls my arm to lead me away from the bar, walking towards our staff wing leading to our offices.

"Is everything alright, Declan? I am hoping you are implying your pit stop may be a woman, but we all know your life has been grabbing you by the balls lately. So, if you are in trouble or something, I'm here..."

I had to interrupt Ronnie before he could continue, "You're right about the female, bud, no need to worry further."

He gives me a look of disbelief, keeping a hold on the sterner look questioning, "Not Lydia?"

"Hell no, why does everyone keep thinking that? It was one lousy time so long ago," I say getting mildly angry.

"It was like a month ago and I'm actually happy you've cleared that up for me. She's a nut job."

"Fucking right she is!" I say back in our moment of agreement.

"So, who is she?"

"She is new to the area and weirdly enough, we went on a date last night."

Ronnie's look of disbelief is wavering in his face again as he keeps asking, "Whoa. Ok, well, I'm not sure when you've had time to meet someone to know you like her enough to take her out," pausing and ending with, "I've been with you like, every day."

"It's really recent. Her name is Alexis, she just moved here from Boston. I don't know too much about her but...I know I like hanging out with her." I voice it finally like I'm admitting to someone about my feelings for this girl who has me twisted up inside all week. Although I appreciate my friend's concern about my usual somber bitterness, because he has been with me through the hardest times in my life, I am thankful this conversation didn't go in that direction this time. Ronnie smiles wide now, his deep side dimple poking through, a sure sign of his happy relief.

"Tomorrow, I get more details, but for now since I'm a damn good friend, I'll let you go so you can make it to your Cinderella before she turns into a pumpkin," looking at his watch and giving me a nod.

I didn't actually have any plans to see Alexis tonight. I blame it on the extra frostbite against my skin that led me out of my way to drive by Alexis' studio, anticipating to just be able to see it closed up and keep going back on my way home to bed. The distance from the turn acts as her only camouflage to the blaring bright lights shining through the windows as I drive up to the parking lot. Somehow, fate has us colliding once again.. My surprise in awe like opening a jewelry box, Alexis' silhouette moves and sways with featherweight glides as she tosses around the dance floor. I pull into the furthest corner to lean on my bike to watch, stare, possibly grow a beard.

Sexy dark hair flying around her face, with her pace quickening, a priceless vision through a distant reflection off of the mirrors surrounding the room. Enjoying my own private show, convincing myself that this is for my eyes only, watching her closer now, realizing the body on my muse.

Holy Shit.

I really am screwed.

Looking tantalizingly bare in underwear and some sort of shorter top cut off midriff, her legs a golden shimmer. All I see is her skin, a tightened frame of perfection that has been hidden under giant piles of cotton.

Clearly a creeper, engrossed by this part of her, but I can't take my eyes off. The way she moves is bewitching me like a seductive chant, luring me into her world, taking my lungs and stealing my air until I hunt my siren down and force her powers to fill them back up in a massive gust. The boom of her speakers thundering out as the song speeds up, intensifying her stretching steps high and low, until she ends head bowed to a pointed step. I watch as she ties her dark hair up on her head and walks out of the dance floor into what is probably her Mixx room.

Chime

My phone buzzes in my pocket, knocking me out of my trance to read.

Alexis: Do you like what you see out there?

Shit, realizing I've been caught in my creeping, I give my honest confession.

Me: Baby, I am so into what I see it's driving me mad.

While I wait for her response, I start walking towards the front door now when I see her come back into view. Still in her underwear and top, she walks closer to the dance floor view window. With nothing but a few feet and a thick sheet of glass, my siren stood there staring through to me, finding my eyes until our blue and green were locked together. I wasn't prepared for the night at all, let alone this minute being taken over by pure sorcery watching her every move through the window.

Alexis gives me a seductive smile that makes my knees wobble, then, she does something completely unexpected. Slowly reaching down, Alexis grabs the bottom hem of her short shirt, pulling it up, and tosses it off over her head, flashing me the glorious view of her full round tits that sit up perfectly over her tight abdomen.

It took me a minute...

..or two.

I stared at her, determined to mold this in my brain and enjoy every second of my checkers win, the rush of aroused thrill running through my body and all into my dick.

She could probably hear the howl that reverberated out of me, feel my mouth salivating while she allowed me to ogle.

And ogle I did, fiercely, until she cut me off to cover her face with one of her hands while reaching for her shirt, and to my dismay, put it back on. She then points to the door where I immediately followed as she unlocks and opens it up for me.

Self control must have rejoined my body for a second, Closing the door behind me, I lock it and turn to my siren.

I regroup before I start to advance on her this time, now that I've been blessed with a sight that should be riding on golden dragons in the sky, my worthiness has been made lesser than, I speak nervously, "HI."

"Hi," she replies back quietly.

"Don't go shy on me now," I say as I step forward closer to her, shifting the focus away from my own not cool and onto her, a jerk move, but I'm trying to flirt. She gives me more silence while her body language is bursting with need when I pull her in close to me.

No questions asked while she decides it's time to ditch my coat, using her hands to glide in delicate warmth over top of my shirt to help me throw the leather off and over to the side. Clinging to me around my neck, she lifts up her chin to get my sure affirmative before lifting herself off the ground to straddle my waist, eyes on me the whole time provoking me more.

"Do you think you are confident enough to know what I want right now?" Her question slaying me as I plunge my mouth to hers hard, throwing my restraint for needing her out the window. We tangle and glide our bodies together as she stops in between kissing me to give me orders, "upstairs," as I kick off my shoes and hold her while I scramble.

"Around the corner, find it now," neediness projecting in her as she grinds down on me, crazy pounding coming out of my chest as I lead us to her bed up in the loft.

I lay her down softly, staying over top of her in my ravishing as I reach to pull off her shirt, this time being able to touch. Moaning in my mouth as I grind my unyielding pelvis in between her legs, my cock begging to be let out, she takes my shirt off me.

Bare chests meeting for the first-time sending arousing sensations through our middle to tighten our nips. Shifting my gaze to my own fingertips, I slowly skim down from her neck to the peaks of her breast as I watch the goosebumps of pleasure beg for me.

"You are so sexy," I muffle out in confession, as I feast my mouth down to kiss and suck all around her breasts, not leaving one left out as she starts flustering in guttural sounds. Her skin so smooth under my calloused hands as I trail down her defined stomach to her panty line. Bringing my face back to her mouth, I kiss her until I stop to just look in her eyes, wanting her full focus and attention before I make my next move.

I speak over my thudding heart, "Baby, tell me I'm on the right track of what you want."

Alexis's tone not wavering, "Declan, you are all I want right now, please don't stop."

Thanking my lucky stars because it would take an army to get me to stop right now, anyways, I kept ravishing her and my need sent my hand south, my finger budding against her slick pussy. I used a slow pace while circling at her entrance, pooling warmth, using just my middle finger.

She unzips my jeans.

I curse breathlessly, "Shit."

Feeling like this is anticipation at its finest, I am trying to catch my breath in my arousal but teetering to remain in control as I begin fingering her slickness in and out, in and out.

I want her so bad, but Alexis has turned out to be in a category all on her own, that has settled into me quickly, making me want to enjoy every round I get to spend with her. Her tight, supple, and wet, adding up the reasons I can't stop, and I need more of her.

Alexis sits up on an elbow, her eyes searing in lust as she lowers to grasp her hand around my dick, hushed noises of exasperation fall out of her mouth while she explores my girth in her hold.

Psshit

"What do they feed you in Ireland?" she whispers almost to herself as she stretches her torso slightly over to reach her arm down my full length.

Her words beef up my ego, and also have a truth as I start adding another finger in my strokes in pure determination. "Do you like this," I ask her while I try to not be too rough with her extremely tight tantalizingly wet pussy.

Her breathy answer of a simple, "Yes," builds up my crazed attraction with both our mouths parted in ecstasy from the feelings of pleasure that just our fingers can bring. I kiss her lips hard, pushing my fingers deeper, and at the same time, her soft grip starts pumping my dick, harder and harder.

Panting in heavy pants, need sizzles in our kisses and red blooded looks until we can't take it any longer.

Like a clamp trapping me in, she writhed in her orgasm around my fingers.

"Declan!"

Her crying my name in her release being the call that tips me over the edge.

Falling

Falling

Shooting warm spurts of cum out onto her bare stomach, slipping into her belly button, I bury my face in the crook of her neck as we sink into this realm with each other.

She huffs out a laugh in her pinched pink cheeks, turning her face to nuzzle me, she says, "I didn't think I was going to see you."

I lifted my head up so our foreheads were touching to speak to her next.

"I didn't think you would be up this late, I just left work and I saw your lights on, so I had to stalk you," smiling at her beautiful face whilst noticing the tiny freckles along her cheeks.

"I'm glad you did," her confession earnest. I don't know how I managed to complete a sentence, but I had to confess, "Alexis, I knew you were a dancer, but my grasp of how beautiful you would be in the moment where you dance when you don't think anyone is watching you, I obviously knew nothing."

And I am usually pretty confident in what I know."

Shy taking a compliment, Alexis replies a soft, "Thanks, I wasn't planning on performing a private show."

I grin and say, "I found a lucky ticket."

I give her a kiss with my nice line, then tone down my cheese when I get a grip on my surroundings and ask, "Why are you up here tonight this late? And where is Luna?"

"She's at home, I have to drive back tonight. I was just here to try to...." she pauses in her train of thought, "calm down I guess. I had a bit of a day."

I'm sitting up beside her as she lays under me, gluing my attention to her, "Tell me." I demand. Alexis gives me a sweet look, and replies with a question instead,

"Do you want to shower?"

I waited, assuming she was going to open up about why she was needing to dance off her apparent long day, but she didn't. She just held my gaze, unfaltering, as I nodded to agree, and lifted her into the bathroom.

The steam of the hot shower didn't compare to the hotness of the female body standing before me. Kissing her all over nonstop, I contain my obsessiveness momentarily to wash her body, as I try to ask about her day, "Talk to me, why are you up here this late?"

Cutely crinkling her nose, she says, "I had a late work call, it just got me feeling anxious is all." She gives me a short smile and continues, "I needed to get away from the silence afterwards, so I came here."

"That's not telling me anything," I say plainly, "explain the phone call to me."

As she sounded out a few 'huffs,' here and there, I couldn't help but notice how much I was anticipating her answer, needing to know more about her.

Needing her to allow me to know her, to trust me.

Alexis starts, "I was on a Facetime call talking with Jameson, earlier."

I couldn't help but have a tinge of jealousy as she mentioned this other guy's name I've heard before, when Sabine mistook me for him. I composed myself enough to not interrupt and just get what she gives me.

"Jameson is my best friend that plays in a band I work with. Anyways, he isn't happy I moved here, and he keeps trying to persuade me to go back to Boston, but he doesn't know about the song Rachel wrote."

"Rachel, your friend that...died, right?" I ask.

"Yes, Rachel...she killed herself in April. We were all very close, and I haven't been able to tell him about the song she left me, because he hasn't been taking losing her too well. I'm sorry, I really don't think we should be talking about this while we are naked in the shower."

Holding her face in between my palms, I see the sadness in her eyes, the reason she is here in Paisley couldn't be easy on her, especially seeming pretty alone.

I try to persuade her to keep opening up, telling her, "Alexis, I want to know everything about you, please keep talking," kissing her lips to help seal my true words.

"I was called into a reading of the Will for Rachel, where I met a lawyer that she had secretly personally appointed to help carry out her, end of life business. Her mother also managed us since we were teenagers, after my parents died..." she pauses during, giving me a second to keep up. I have to wrap around her to kiss her more, selfishly trying to convince her to keep talking to me, and she eventually does.

"Rachel struggled with manic depression which put her in these highs and lows. Then this past April, she killed herself. Nobody saw it coming, myself included."

Alexis looked composed in her pause while in the meantime, she took a bar of soap and started lathering my skin. I kept silently waiting, enjoying her hands all over my body, giving her the moment to eventually muster up the strength to continue, "Let's just say her mother is a witch, and Rachel went behind her back to name, me, the executer of her will, leaving me the house, the song, too much money, but it leaves me with a big gaping hole of a puzzle as well. I assume the song was written when she was here in January, when she purchased the house, which was not even on the market by the way. It was bought in a private transaction. So, with that, it proves she plotted her suicide for months, something must have triggered her to come to Paisley and write about wanting to be buried here."

I ask, "And you are left to figure out why?"

"Yep, it seems that way. I just assumed those words were for her, about her, by her, as a sendoff note to me in an apology or something to hold onto from her. How stupid am I?"

"I've never kept things from Jameson, which makes it especially difficult, because he can be a lot, but I don't want to put him in this position like me, because it changes everything we thought, or assumed was wrong, and there are still no answers for why."

I insert, "You're not stupid. You couldn't have changed the outcome, being thrown into all of this is not your fault. She obviously loved and trusted you enough to leave it for you to keep for her."

Deciding this is the best time to suds her up in shampoo, I also have to ask, "Just to be sure, when you say this Jameson is a lot..."

She cuts me off, "Not what you think, he is a lot like my very overprotective brother, we are friends... and he is all I have left."

Firmly, I said, "Well you are not going anywhere," I position us under the hot water while I take my time kissing her, "And, I'm going to help you figure out how Rachel found her wings in Paisley. I'm here with you now."

Alexis gets up on her tiptoes, squishing her body to me to give me a full kiss on the lips, smiles and says, "Okay good, because there is something else I had in mind for right here, in this shower," pushing herself back to get a better view of me, her seductive eyes trail down my body, and back up.

"Tell me," I moved in on her with more intensity, my mouth on hers, ready and willing for her command.

She said two words, "Hold me."

I had picked her up before she even finished taking a breath, causing her to squeal in delight. Settling into me, our sexes so close, as our minds and eyes flutter for approvals.

My demand all I can muster up, "Tell me, Alexis, tell me what you want from me, anything."

Our energy already making plans as Alexis voices our fate,

"There is nothing I want more right now, than to have you inside me, like this. I want to be with you...like this."

The head of my dick poked at her entrance, pleading to be allowed in, while I curse in a grumble realizing I don't have a condom.

"It's not right what you do to me," I say in my childish complaint.

Carrying on, "But baby," kissing on to tops of her shoulder, "I don't have a condom..."

Her sigh audible, then she replies, "Okay, you're right, I've never done it without one before...and I don't want to make you do something you don't want to do..but I'm clean and on birth control in case you wanted to know."

I have been informed that women are confusing to men, but I haven't been acquainted with this type of thing before. Still, when you are with a woman, who you are feeling completely upside down about, already in an unknown territory, and she says things to you that aren't completely clear during a naked shower a thrust away, the need to understand her mind is necessary.

Brief in a breath, "I'm clean as well, and you are fucking insane if you think I don't want to do this with you." Finding a way to make sure I am making myself extra clear during this very important conversation, I reach down rubbing my hard dick against her slick and say, "This right here is what you do to me every time I get near you, I want you... only you, Alexis."

Alexis adds, "Just be careful, I'm not sure you will fit."

Gearing her up for the ride, our bodies were unhinged, her ruling over me with her short teasing licks and light sucking on my neck, all the way down from behind the back of my ear, leaving me writhing in pure sensual torture. As the steam builds up around us in the shower, the water drops are hot until they become boiled reaching our skin. Alexis using her hand and helping guide my dick in, but stopping with just the head fitting in, her fist around me shielding me to thrust any further, while she teases bounces on top.

Impatience took over in our hungry desires as she settles down firmer on my cock.

Easing in her tight warmth, I groan under the spray only halfway inside her, "You're so tight," I curl my fingers to her clit and start stroking in hopes to alleviate some of the pressure of her pussy stretching to harbor me inside.

Reacting to my every touch, my grip firm under her ass grinding her down on me, Alexis cries out, "Oh my god, it feels too good, please don't stop!"

As she takes more of me, her pleas of ecstasy cause her to jump off the deep end, and all I can do is stare at her soaking wet through my blazing eyes. I felt the blasting lava against my solid torpedo, the direct heat coursing through my body, as Alexis slowly leans herself back to regain her balance from her orgasm. Her superior strength from all of her dancing makes her even more of a vixen, stretching far enough that I have the view of my dick stroking in and out of her tight wet pinked pussy.

She is like a gift that keeps on giving and I couldn't stop rumbling my pleased hyper satisfied moans, filling the shower stall, loudly. I watched her pussy suck my length all the way in, water slapping around us in hurried strikes. The most spectacular view, as I fucked her hard, the sound of water slapping.

Slapping.
Slapping.

I roar, "It's too good!"

Alexis then screams out an obscene amount of noises as we cum together, bringing her mouth to my neck, as sounds vibrate off my skin, our body's weakening as the orgasm steals all we have to offer, taking us out of this world while holding each other tight, like this.

Just like this.

Chapter 13   Alexis

I was nothing but a wet log as Declan carried me out of the shower. He managed to find towels and wrapped one around my backside. He put his arm overtop to protect me as I eased down off of this glorious man cock. Totally exposed, we playfully scrambled around, getting redressed as we floated in a foreign flutter of exhilaration. His intensity didn't waver, Declan has seared through me with his stares and glances, always watching me like I'm the only thing in front of him, every time he is with me. Some might think that gravitational pull he holds on to me would be too much, too demanding, too confident, too soon, but not me. Instead, I feel necessary to someone when he looks at me. I revel in all of his dominant glory, completely at ease like it's necessary for my own health as well.

While Declan was sitting on the end of my bed putting his socks back on his feet, I slipped into the bathroom. Looking at my reflection in the mirror, I smile gleefully back at my splotchy overheated face of contentment.

How did I get so damn bold? Maybe it's the fresh Paisley air that has me unleashing the need within me.

I have never looked into eyes during an orgasm, my first set being Declan's Icelandic blue waves crashing in his bliss, the most captivating sight I have ever seen, and I'm not sure how I'm ever going to be able to look away. Wondering how much longer I have until the well-known feeling of unworthiness creeps inside me, I grab my toiletry bag while gathering my things to take back home tonight, not anticipating the longer hours spent here at the studio.

I tried sending a brush through my hair that was on the border line of nesting. Makeup free, I have no idea how it is possible a Thor wants to look at my face so much.

I walked out of the bathroom and into my quiet bedroom. Declan was not up here, so I made my way with my things downstairs. Dropping my bag in the front to walk through a now dark dance room, I make my way to my Mixx room to get my purse, the sound of the silence beginning to worry me when I begin to realize I can't find Declan.

"Declan?" I call out into the dark wide space, the echoes loud enough to hear within the building.

Still silence.

No response as I start looking around almost like I'm playing a game of hide and seek, panic starting to course through me.

He isn't here. I run back upstairs and check once more, only to come up with the same conclusion.

Declan is gone. He already left.

My heart was pounding in my chest as I was fighting with myself to not get too overwhelmed, forcing my legs to walk, grab my bag and open my door. Locking it up while the wind chills my ears and cold damp hair, I turned and there he was.

I jumped at the sight of him. His voice alleviating my panic,

"Hey, it's just me," he takes my bag off my shoulder and says, "You were fast, I just turned your heater on in your car, so it may not be warm enough yet."

What is chivalry? Obviously a trait that is new for me that I need to remember about before I determine the worst.

"Oh." I said, flustering still a bit. "Uh, thanks!"

"What's wrong?" He asks furrowing his brows.

My irrational panic doesn't have to be discussed, right?

"Nothing, sorry, you just spooked me coming out of the dark." I told him trying to brush it off, "Where did you park?"

"Over in my designated lookout corner," he replies, gesturing far back in the lot, I cannot even see his bike.

"You're lookout corner?"

Declan not allowing me to walk without him surrounding me somehow, now holding me close to help block the wind, my own personal shield as we walk.

"Yes, I've decided to claim that parking spot. I may even bring a bottle of spray paint up a bit later," he says kindly.

"You are being Silly," I said to him.

He comes back with, "You don't think I will? Baby, you're going to learn how serious I am soon enough. Speaking of which," we reach my black Acura as he opens the door and cages around me, as he continues his thought, "I don't like leaving you like this."

It threw me off, making me feel a bit unsure of where this was going, so I asked him, "What do you mean by that?"

Declan replies, "About how tonight happened is all, now I am here saying goodbye to you. It just feels off."

Now I was really unsure. It sounded like he was nervous when he spoke, like maybe he was regretful.

"Off.." I mutter, questioning in my confusion.

His awareness cluing into my confused vibe, he says sternly, "Yes, Alexis. Off," his hand comes up to my face, laying his thumb on my cheek, "The last thing I want to do right now is watch you drive away from me. I know that's how tonight goes, I guess, but I don't want to get cut short of time with you anymore."

"Where do you even live, Declan?" I know that may have not been the best response back, it just came out since it is something I've always wondered. When he leaves here, where does he go? I just had sex with him and now the unknowns are buzzing in.

"I live in a condo about ten minutes outside Paisley, it's closer to where I work."

He gives me just enough to settle me a bit but not enough to make sure for my next question that comes blurting out, "By yourself?"

Declan's lips curve up in a smile, "You're cute when you get nervous," he states while progressing to answer, "Yes, I live by myself. I used to live above the boxing gym in town with my dad and brother but moved out when...I got my job. Honestly, I sleep in my condo but I'm rarely there, always more so at work or in town. Late nights like tonight, I'll go sleep on my dad's couch, wake up and workout in the morning. Tomorrow night I will come get you for dinner at Estel and Margie's."

Okay, so he is planning on seeing me again. Thank goodness. Not everyone is going to disappoint you, Alexis. I need to chill.

Planting a big smile on my face, I tell him, "You better come hungry because Margie hollered across the street to me today while I was getting in my car, that she was cooking prime rib for my hungry man."

Like a kid in the candy store, Declan's face of pure joy is priceless. Deciding this is the best time to wiggle my way onto my seat, he brings my seat belt strap around like I'm the kid this time. Leaning in he places a hard, sweet kiss on my lips before whispering his driver safety demands to me for my ride home.

Lights on.

Windshield defroster on high.

Drive slow in case deer come across the road in the night.

Call or text as soon as I get home to let him know.

I squeeze his hand, give him a kiss, and say goodnight, and he shuts my door.

I went to bed with a grin on my face and a very happy vagina, all because my thoughts were focused on my night with Declan. Yet somehow, evil always tries to make its way in because I awoke in the night from the sound of my own cries, scaring me upright in bed. I wiped the tears trickling down off of my chin, trying to calm my nausea enough to not have to throw up. My nightmares have placed themselves on repeat since Rachel's death. Tonight's being trapped on a collapsing stage and trying to run to safety. It's the vision of Rachel in front of me as we run barefooted in our dresses, and pinned up hair, and I am always trying to catch up to her, but I never can. Although it is customary for me to have had nightmares since childhood, I have always been able to manage well enough that they don't wake me up most of the time. In these ones, I can't hear her voice, and she never replies or responds, making me crazy. I'm stuck in this collapse, shouting at the top of my lungs, fear coursing through me that shakes me awake.

Then, I'm left in uncontrollable hysterics.

All by myself.

It's like I'm invisible.

A Ghost.

Invisibility was my most solid trait growing up, the older I got and the friendships along the way helped me progress to a more grounded social acceptance and a healthier self-acceptance. The dreams always stemmed from that deceptive idea of loneliness, being a part but still never wholly there.

Yet the ones with me running after Rachel have become so enraging to me that she will not tell me the answers, I can't go back to sleep afterwards.

I turned on my nightstand light to look at the time, 04:24am. It was like the only thing I could think of to shake my dream, try to catch up.

So, here I am at the 5am opening of the gym, running on the treadmill with my earbuds in blasting my old school hip-hop playlist. Trying to distract myself by watching the lower-level early risers piling into the popular cycling and Zumba classes. It seems the invisibility thing doesn't come in handy when you need it the most, my peripheral vision determining a giant man has started up the machine directly beside me, as I up my pace. Although it is unlikely to be a problem, it just seems annoying since the gym is empty enough during this morning time, to find more than plenty of unoccupied options of your choice of machine. Like the other ten on both sides of me that are also empty, but nope.

I tried not to let my new workout neighbor distract me, but he turned his pace up to a high like mine and synced up steps with me as well, doing what I was worried about and throwing me off. I pushed to the next level, amping up my mind and finding the one thought that had me able to stabilize, Declan's naked body in the shower. The man was perfection from head to toe, like his smooth chest and defined set of abs that came from a serious amount of aggression and work. But the part that reigns king on Declan is his King Cobra Cock, earning every right to rule over me, dominating my needs and desires in our entanglement of pure pleasure.

My vagina is stirring while I run and reminisce, planting a grin on my face that was apparently noticeable to my too close to my property line kind of neighbor.

"If you were mine to put that smile on your face last night, I know for certain you wouldn't be having to take out your extra energy on that treadmill this early in the morning," a snare like voice invaded loud enough for me to hear over my music.

What the actual hell.

I do not bother to take my earphones out nor adjust my music, while I look over at the copycat who has again synced up with my faster speed.

He clearly has no manners.

Beef may be a thing in Paisley because I notice this dude is big, sporting those unnatural, too large size arms with veins bulging. He looks close to my age, with a faded old gray t shirt that had ripped off sleeves.

Deciding on insulting him back, I retort, "You must do your best with the company of mediocre stamina."

"Feisty, is actually my favorite kind of company," he replies swiftly, his breathing still even during this intense pace of the treadmill, seeming so easy to keep up with me.

Going with my next plan of ignoring him, being the worst kind of company, as I try to focus on anything else, peering over to the Zumba class currently in mid workout filled with tennis skirts on middle aged women.

"Feisty and plays hard to get," he keeps on, "That's fine I like a challenge, I didn't think this fucking town was capable of having such beautiful women."

Still portraying the 'I'm invisible' act, I keep running and keep my mouth shut. Even though there are a bazillion things I want to say to this arrogant piece of muscle, I hold it in, praying for the hint for him to leave me alone becomes a flashing sign in front of his face.

He says as a matter of fact, "You are an athlete of some sort...let me see if I can take a guess,"

Not my lucky morning, maybe I should have stayed home drowning in my nightmares instead.

He starts his list of inferences of me like it's charming, apparently thinking every woman should fall to his feet, kind of man.

"You run fast with the intention of a quick release of your tension, not because it makes you happy, so I would say no to both running and soccer. Now it's your sculpted middle that implies you use all of your body muscles frequently. You are extremely fit, with feminine features like small wrists and ankles and definitely not broad like those butch babes, so it's a no to swimming or hockey."

Urggg.
I'm groaning out loud at this point trying to shut him out.
Of course, he gives me a cocky laugh while he keeps pushing my buttons, "But my oh my," he whistles forcing me to crack by glaring at him in my run now.
He is as giant as I assumed, solid muscle, and a short faded blonde haircut that shows off his mild cauliflower ears. He turns to me and doesn't even meet my eyes, only intrusive ogling while he continues, "It is those luscious curves on your petite body that suggest..."

I interrupt him before I have to hear anymore, "I do not give a shit about your assessment and would appreciate it if you would go the fuck away!"

"Well, you see, I can't do that. No, no, you see this is my treadmill I use every morning, and an obvious good luck charm," his snake eyes winking at me, "let me know if you need any help managing that vulgar mouth of yours."

"My vulgar mouth?!" I scream back while I start slowing my speed to a stop. My time on this treadmill is over, I grab my bottle of water and step off. As I am walking away from this guy, he backtracks adding some flirtatious tone,"Come on, Feisty, I was only trying to talk to you."
"Not a chance, dickhead!" I yelled back as I walk fast heading for the stairs to get as far away from him as possible. Seems like I am still running away.

My whirlwind continues.
I found solace in the hot sauna before I got back home to work on Kel's emailed projects. One she marked as urgent, being a request from a director named, 'Maya Gueterra,' for some fashion show. Reading through the details, Ms. Gueterra's request is for a private meeting with me at my studio here in Paisley. What kind of major project has Kel gotten me into? This question has me calling her to find out.
Kel answers cheerfully, "Well if it isn't the most popular name around lately."
"What the hell does that mean! Kel, I just skimmed that one email and..."
She cut me off, "Alexis, that one email? Did you not read it?" Now her cheerful has become exasperated as she continues giving me shit before I can even speak, "I mean holy crap, the lead director for the Eastern Region Lingerie Fashion show hosted by one of the biggest brands, SheerMe, has specifically requested you to meet with her at your new place!"
Kel, how did this even come about? I don't understand how she knew about my studio location?"

"She reached out to me about your work on a critical dance performance piece and I told her you were not available, like you wanted me to. She was pissed! I told her about your move and opening of the studio. She must have found out your address on her own. Lexi, they will not speak of any details before an NDA is signed! How freaking awesome is this!"
"It sounds like a huge thing, Kel, I'm not sure I can do that without Rachel here anymore."

"Lexi, you need to at least hear what she has to offer you. Her coming all the way from NYC to meet at your studio, even. An opportunity like this doesn't happen unless they have done their research, and Maya Gueterra wants you. I will fly in and meet her with you."

I take my time before I reply to Kel, "I will email her back to set up a time and let you know. I want you here, and I also want Sabine present, she will need to know."

Kel cheerful again, "Just make sure Sabine knows she will have to sign the privacy consents. Explain it in detail to make sure she understands the rules."

"I will definitely do that, but Kel, this will out my name in the industry so I will have to use a pseudo name."

Keeping the motto to stay hidden in the shadows has been drilled into me since we started working, allowing me to keep my name out of any type of gossip and more importantly, allowing me a normal life and not one, as Rachel and I would say, being an instrument in someone else's show.

Kel replies, "I've already thought of that. Lexi, I don't know why you want to keep hiding from how amazing your work is. Terri isn't in control anymore, you can literally sign your name proudly on all of your work now for everyone to know who they should give credit to and receive the high paycheck in your private account."

Reminding me of how Terri manipulated me into thinking she was spreading my personal work around for me to gain recognition in the industry and land projects, while continuing my life as Rachel's side kick. Instead, she hid from both Rachel and I what she was really doing, which was selling my private work as her own or in Rachel's name, to big names, and not telling me, stealing the glory and all the money. I was too young and naïve to quite understand, always being told nobody was interested and even if it was sold, the money I earned was never enough after all the expenses. Terri would give me only enough cash to buy me my bus tickets.

"I'll hear out the proposal first before I decide. And Kel, does Terri know about Maya looking for me?"

"Not yet. I can't wait, she will be so pissed!"

I laugh with Kel because that thought does satisfy me in so many ways.

"I need to change the subject before we hang up. I want to ask you a private personal question," stating before I lose my courage.

I hear her 'uh huh' me before I continue, "Do you think you could find out Rachel's whereabouts between the week of last New Year's Eve and the first week of January from this past year for me?"

Kel replied in her friend voice, "I guess I could look back in our calendars and private messages to see, but I'm pretty sure that she was in the Hamptons with Terrie for the mandatory holiday party attendances Terrie always made her do."

Trusting Kel isn't the problem, I just don't want to make any suggestions into my inquiry on Rachel's Paisley song just yet. "I would appreciate it if you could dig and let me know if there was anything out of the ordinary she was talking about doing that week, I'm trying to settle some ideas and memories I have since she died."

Could I sound anymore vague? I tried to sound convincing.

Kel finishes, "Of course. Also, don't forget to call me as soon as you hear anything back from the director," with a big kissy sound before hanging up.

I send Ms. Gueterra a reply, agreeing on the future meeting at my studio to hear her out, and for her to decide on when, giving her the opportunity to arrange travel.

Leaving me to nap until dinner, there cannot be anything else added to this day besides dreaming of Declan.

101

Chapter 14   Declan

It started snowing this afternoon forcing me to change vehicles and drive my old truck I park at CeCe's instead. Enjoying the heat blasting on my face instead of cold wind, I'm in said truck and on its way to find a girl.

I called and texted Alexis a couple hours ago and she still hasn't responded, and I also may have driven passed her studio to see it empty. Since I wanted to spend extra time with her before our dinner, I came just a couple hours early, to know for certain she isn't out in the snow. Not like a stalker, more just a little concerned and early on arrival.

Sigh

This girl makes me all kinds of crazy, grabbing me by the balls, I just want more and more of her.

The black Acura sits parked in Alexis's driveway layered with the fresh sheet of white snow looking untouched. Along with the first layer on her driveway. I am bothered about how she thinks she can manage everything on her own, this house, the studio, this life, shoveling this driveway. She has all of this responsibility on her two tiny shoulders, it is understandable her friends back home may be concerned on her single-handed giant leap. Then again, Alexis is a lot mightier than she looks, and sports an inner shell I would like to crack as well. She goes with the flow no problem, but she isn't as open about things like most girls I've ever been around. Alexis is a bit more private and closed off. She doesn't blow up my phone or ask me any questions that may or may not be too personal or invasive. I always thought that having low maintenance is ideal in what I wanted in a relationship, and that is great with anyone else but not with Alexis. The one girl I meet that I really like, I can't tell if she is about to bag me up and throw me out, the more and more I get to know her the more and more out of my league she becomes.

And that idea causes me to do insane things like, I don't know, hunt her down because she hasn't answered me at all today. So, I slow my crazy and texted her again once I pulled up and waited in my truck for a reply, but ten minutes later and incessant amount of knocking, I ended up opening the unlocked door. I was walking through her house, calling her name out, all while giving my new dog friend some back scratches. Her phone and laptop are left on the living room table, lighting up an alert with seven missed calls on her cell screen, me being only two of them, maybe three.

There in a dark bedroom, shades down shutting out any daylight, lies an angel's sleeping face with dark hair splayed on her pillow, laying underneath a pile of white fluffy bedcovers.

I just watched her sleep there still and beautiful for a minute before Luna decided to jump on the bed and make herself a spot, so I followed the dog's lead. Whispering to her that it was me, hoping not to scare her, I slip in beside Alexis laying on her side, under the covers and pull her small body in close to me for more warmth. Nuzzling her, smelling her fragrant shampoo from her hair, I feel an ease in my chest that lately has felt nothing but relentless thudding. Here like this, I fell fast asleep next to my angel.

When I awake, it's from the light tender strokes along the side of my stubbly cheek. My eyes still closed and too tired to open, my angel starts whispering softly to me, "Baby, it's time to get up, we have to go to dinner."

"I really want to know if you have ever seen Riverdance...cliché question maybe since you're sort of Irish."

I hear her mumble a bit more until she finds a new tactic and starts pressing her lips to mine. I kiss back the best I can in my dreamy state but still cannot open my eyes.

"I think I can smell the prime rib from here," she takes a big audible inhale through her nose and keeps on, "Wow, can you smell that big piece of meat?"

"Baby, I really, really want some of that big juicy piece of Irish meat." I hear her start giggling, trying not to be too loud, but obviously gleeful with herself.

It's that delightful sound that makes my voice box sound out again, "You can have my meat whenever you want, baby," I bark out with a grin, only to have her lips reach mine again and again.

Finally, my eyes open to the sight of the most beautiful green eyes I have ever seen, looking back at me.

I squeeze her closer while she breaks her lips from mine and says, "Declan, your salami is going to have to wait, we have 5 minutes to make it on time for prime beef."

"So, are you saying you will want some of my salami later?" I tease still not moving.

"Are you kidding, absofreakinlutely, but beef first," giving me a bright smile while getting off the bed. Fuck if she isn't half dressed in a tank top and those tighter than tight rope booty shorts that cut into her ass cheeks just right, my salami at attention with no concept of time, it only knows what he wants and likes, and he more than wants and likes what he sees in front of him.

I don't hide my aroused grumble, hoping her sultry side glance turns into her jumping my bones, as I watch her continue getting herself ready adding layers and layers...and yea, another layer over top.

Still, I am pretty sure it's the all knowing of what is underneath that makes her look hotter and hotter with each layer...literally and figuratively. Hope of extra time came to a complete stop after Alexis walks out of the room when she finished getting ready, leaving me to scramble off the bed onto my feet and run out following behind her.

"You got over here early," Alexis states as she waits for me by her front door to walk out, while I've slipped beside her still in the middle of throwing my shirt back over my head. I give her my most innocent look hoping she will take that instead of making me explain my insane neediness. Working like a charm as her own face softens to show a happy smile, without words as well, her show of approval of my invasion.

Grabbing her hand to walk beside her across the way, Alexis noticing the surprise afternoon snowfall for the first time since her nap, stating, "It snowed! Look how pretty everything looks! Declan what are you driving?"

Being sheepish, I quip, "You must have been tired, Alexis, to be able to sleep through and wake up to this. Did you have a long night?"

She keeps her eyes on her feet, shaking her head, embarrassed of my smart-ass comment since we both know she was with me late last night. Tugging her hand, I tell her, "I've had to put away the bike for the winter," pointing to my truck I say, "She'll at least give us heat inside."

In her aha moment she says, "Maybe that's why I didn't hear you, I can usually hear the sound of your bike coming, I wasn't expecting truck muffler noise, you were tricking me."

"I don't get how you have super sound powers." I say, adding it to the list of powers she possesses over me. Estel, dressed in a nice orange half zip sweater and khakis, was waiting for us with the door open, hollering to us as we approached, "I don't think I'll need the fridge anymore," pointing towards his feet at the open case of beer on the deck, "Grab yourself a bottle and get on in here."

The two of us reach down at the same time to pick up our own bottle, I'm about to grab hers out of her hand to open it for her but she beats me to it, twisting off the cap with experience. Maybe I should start coming to terms with the fact that Alexis may not be as sweet and innocent as I imagine, and possibly telling her about my shared ownership in Swollen may not be the usual domino effect disaster. I'm fearful about her not approving of my club/work lifestyle I have, causing problems for us in the long run. Especially now that we are sleeping together, which I mean fuck yea that is definitely going to continue so I'm hopeful she fits with all parts of my life at this point, but still hesitant to let her in on all my shit. It's going too well. The table was set up in Margie's typical spread of delicate dishes with the centerpiece of prime rib, looking like juicy perfection as Estel gets started on slicing slabs of beef.

Margie starts us with opening conversation, "How wonderful you two could make it tonight in the snow, Declan I see you got to Lexi's house quite early this afternoon, you should have just called me and we could have eaten sooner if you were hungry," she says straight faced about to take a bite, feeling odd that the attention has drawn to my obvious stalker tendencies, I brush my hand through my hair taking way too long to answer, until finally my pal, Estel gives me a save with piping in. "Well, I'm sure he didn't want to get caught in the snowstorm is all," while throwing me a wink.

He probably could have done a bit better for me, but grateful enough to give me time to let me answer, "Actually, Margie, I think you are right," I sit up in my chair confidently saying, "I have been feeling quite starved all day, maybe it was my hunger rumbling about within me that had me driving over here early," deciding to stick a fork full of beef, potatoes, and horseradish, in my suggestive mouth.

Alexis starts speaking but is cut off by Margie, whom is directing her attention towards her now, "Lexi, remind me, I will have to start sending over more leftovers if poor Declan isn't getting proper nutrition."

I stop breathing to keep from laughing so hard I choke. Meanwhile, Alexis also looks like she is going to choke.

With not a clue, Margie keeps forward and asks me, "Now I recognize you from town Declan, you boys live in that boxing gym in town, right? I can't imagine too much cooking going on over there."

Shit.

Of course, Margie would know about our family being local here for so many years and the gym downtown. Strange unsettling forming in my stomach in panic they know about Daniel, as I try to navigate answering, "Mostly only liquid dinners coming out of there," giving her a genuine smile, as it is now Margie's turn to look like she is going to choke. This dinner is going well enough so far.

Alexis is next to change the direction of the questioning, looking to Estel and Margie and asking, "Do you have any children?"

Margie lays down her fork and Estel takes a long pull of his beer, suggesting more uncomfortable reactions. I do not know this couple one lick either, so it is a friendly enough question.

Margie is the one who answers, "We have a daughter, Laura."

"Had," Estel says hard.

Margie looks over at him in annoyance and keeps explaining, "Yes, had. Laura was our only child, the love of our lives, but she passed away 25 years ago, while she was only twenty."

Alexis was sinking down in her chair as she spoke, "I am so sorry to hear that, that's so young, did she like to spend time with you in the kitchen?"

Margie answers, "Laura was always wanting to help me cook when she was young. I can remember the first time she made us a dinner all on her own for our anniversary. She was only 12 and spent hours making a giant mess on the countertops, the stress causing her to be flustered all day long, I almost told her she didn't need to, but I didn't want to hurt her feelings. Laura was quite a sensitive girl. However, that day she didn't quit what she started, and that night she gave us each a handwritten invitation to attend dinner on the kitchen table at six pm."

Estel chimes in with his part of the memory, "She had the whole table set up for us with the candles and everything," sporting a huge smile on his face looking at his wife. All of us give a small chuckle as Margie continues saying, "She served us shake and bake pork chops with egg noodles on the side and salad with fresh cucumbers from the garden."

Estel again adds, "It was nasty, but we ended up eating every bite for Laura's sake. She was quite proud of herself that night."

Margie adding, "I'm pretty sure she didn't dip the chops in egg before the crumbs. Anyways, she actually didn't end up liking cooking much as she grew up. Laura wanted to be a singer."

"Aw," sighs Alexis.

Estel brags, "Yes, she was quiet as a mouse, but could belt out the tunes."

You can tell how much they adored their daughter, Laura, by the way they spoke about her, I'm sure Estel and Margie would have made excellent parents, and their heartache is seen in their eyes as they tell past memories. Yet for now the reason behind their daughter's death remains unknown to Alexis and I. Knowing Margie, she will let us know if she is ever ready to talk about that sore spot they hold onto, but for now, she passed on discussing it further.

Alexis speaks up and says, "She sounds like she was lovely."

"Oh yes," Margie agrees, "losing someone you love is one of the hardest things in life, and I am going to sound like an old bat when I tell you this but I want you to know, the only thing that got me through each day is this man right here," patting Estel on the arm.

Estel now doe eyed to his wife continuing, "We got through together. Love is strong enough to perform miracles sometimes, and it was our love for each other, and for Laura, which allowed us to move forward."

"Speaking of moving forward!" Margie suddenly exclaims, surprising us all out of our deep thoughts, "Lexi you won't believe what we got in the mail today."

She was out of her chair and bringing back an envelope a second later and handing it to Alexis, who is looking quite confused as she pulls out the letter. I'm taking in all of Alexis now trying to read what she is thinking while she reads through this mysterious exciting note.

"It's from Carl," Margie states, "The old crab had to get the last word in," rolling her eyes as she sits back down and continues to eat her dinner.

Alexis finally looks up, over to me, giving me a small smile and divulging the contents secrets, "Carl was the man who owned the house before Rachel bought it," her greens still looking at me, so I'm included in this story and how it involves her.

Snickering, Alexis says, "The only thing he said was that he wanted to let Margie know he was alive and well...." she pauses while looking over to Margie who is still blatantly rolling her eyes and Estel laughing quietly to himself even now, all while Alexis keeps snickering and holding one hand over her mouth now trying to control her laughter. Her making me start laughing, for who knows why, she finally looked back to me and said, "Carl wanted her to know he is all fine in Florida, living in his daughter's pool house. That's really it, because he knew Margie would be, 'likely to report a missing persons case,' if she never found his whereabouts..."

All of us are chuckling with each other now as Margie states in a huff, "He must be ill if he thinks I cared that much."

Contagious laughter is heard among us now, even from Margie herself. Like a true budding family around the dinner table.

Margie cackles out her end thought to Alexis, "He left his new phone number on the bottom, and I thought that could possibly help you reach him to get those answers you were looking for."

Wiping away a tear with her sleeve, "Thank you very much," Alexis states earnestly, "I will call him, hopefully get him when he is in a good mood too, so he doesn't hang up on me or something."

I run my hand on top of her thighs and get a chance to say, "I'll call with you if you want."

Alexis gives me a small smile, then looks across to our hosts and says, "I'm not sure if you would even be familiar with..." she pauses in a breath and when she recoups, she continues,

"Rachel, who bought the house from Carl in January, committed suicide in April, and left me the house in her will. Her name was Rachel Butler, she was the daughter of a well-known music producer, B.B Butler, whom died in that car accident when Rachel was still really young..."

My thoughts scrambled in my mind to piece together the who is who, with the confession of her friend's identity. B.B. Butler's name I am familiar with, forming a company that pumped out hot 80's and 90's rock and rollers in the prime of his career until his tragic death, leaving quite a legacy to his family. Yet, I have no real recollection regarding the personal family details, only their status. It would be Dax that would have knowledge of the industry like that. What this does tell me, is that Alexis comes from something much bigger than I anticipated.

I keep rubbing Alexis' thigh, hidden underneath the table, as she fidgets around in her openness.

Estel answers her first, "B.B. Butler's name was famous in our house when Laura was a teenager, but that's all I really know or remember of his name, only because of the singers or bands our daughter listened to and told us about at the time."

Margie's nose crinkles, "I don't recall that name one bit," she grumbles in an aggravated tone towards Estel, then looks back towards us smoothing out her wrinkled face to show her adoring grandmother like look before she says to Alexis, "How truly horrible that is, and for you Lexi. That must have been so tragic, this all just happening so quickly, and now here you are. Were your families close?"

Her face a stoic mask while answering Margie, Alexis replies, "I met Rachel a couple years after her dad's accident in a dance class. We became fast friends and were inseparable from then on, like sisters slash coworkers. It wasn't as easy of a life for her as the media makes it out to be,"

Adding in that to defend Rachel's honor, "maybe I shouldn't be telling you this but what the hell...it's not public knowledge of the house or anything here regarding Rachel Butler in Paisley. There is only a handful of us that are aware, and I would like it to stay that way if I can help it, keeping the media storm and her mother at bay and out of my life."

Coming out in my raspy breath, "Baby," is all I can muster up saying while lightly squeezing her thigh making the wide eyes shift to me with my big mouth term of endearment as my only response, outing my more than friends nickname I gave to Alexis. She brings her hand on my leg now, more discreet than I could be, and gives me a playful smile to help me through my lack of words.

"You have our word, Lexi," Estel says to her, "we would never say anything that could potentially harm you, and I think all of us can say we appreciate you opening up to us."

Margie and I both nod in agreement while looking into the big green eyes that have been witness to much bigger, much more difficult things in life than one would think.

Alexis states smiling, "Thanks, it feels actually quite nice to be able to admit that out loud," turning her attention to me as she adds, "now you can be with me when I call Carl to figure out what Rachel offered him to keep quiet," creating a much bigger picture of the puzzle that was indeed left for Alexis to solve.

I give her a smile just as Margie gently pounds her fist to the table, "Aha, I knew it had to be something good to lug Carl out of that house so fast! Greedy man likely took more than his fair share from that young girl," giving us all another loud cackle around the table.

Conversation lightened up after Alexis stowed the letter from Carl in her pocket while we finished up dinner. After dessert, a homemade apple pie with a lace top crust, Estel and I stood to enjoy another beer together out on the porch while Margie shoed us boys away, while she and Lexi chatted together cleaning up in the kitchen.

Estel asks me, "Do you know if Lexi has any family around?"

Replying back, I say, "Not that I know of her parents have passed away and there seems to be only a few friends she talks about."

"That's what I thought," Estel says as he stands facing her house drinking his beer in deep thought, as I copy him swigging more of my own. Still studying across the street, he continues,"Well, my boy. She is going to just have to be a part of us now. I don't understand how a girl as special as her ends up alone here with us," he says while shaking his head in disbelief still in thought, "She comes and goes at all hours, worrying me sick, reminding me what it's like having a daughter around. I know Margie has swooped her up like her own, so she has family now." He keeps still before finishing, "She doesn't deserve anymore heartache, Declan. Neither do you. I know you are a good man; you just need to be a careful one."

My heart started pounding in my chest with his underlying message for me, like getting the 'you better treat her well' talk, how a father would give permission to date his daughter.
"I plan on it, Sir, I don't know if I'm what she needs, but I damn sure am going to try." I say in my honest confession.
He gives me a wide grin and starts telling me, "I was on a lousy date with another woman in a diner the first time I saw Margie and couldn't take my eyes off her. She sat alone in a booth and ordered a full stack of pancakes. Meanwhile my date ordered some over expensive fruit bowl for her breakfast, irritating the crap out of me. I ended up ditching my date when her friends showed up uninvited and scooted into the booth across from Margie. She got up and I thought she ran off, only to come right back with a wrapped silverware from the host stand, handed it over to me and started talking like we had the plan all along. I knew then she was the one."
Estel walks over to me with a bright laugh and gives me an encouraging pat on the back right as Alexis and Margie appear in the entryway.

I was feeling faint at the thought of what a serious relationship entails during our guy chat, but when Alexis steps back out with a wide smile sporting her winter hat topped with a fuzzy pom pom, I feel my chest puff out in confidence and pride when I see her, overcoming my worries for now.

Chapter 15   Alexis

We had only made it past the fish mailbox before Declan had his hands on me, lunging out like he was starved while being polite through dinner. Planting kisses on the side and back of my neck while his arms wrapped around my front as we slowly walk towards my house. God, he made me feel so good. Every swipe of his lips on me sent shivers down my spine, leaning into him anticipating all the feels he gives me with each touch.

Nearing the steps to the porch, I asked, "Are you coming in?"

Declan stops, giving me a look like it was a dumb question with his now glazed over eyes. He doesn't say anything, just gives me his cheesy grin as he steps back from me, walking backwards towards his truck. I was about to stop him once he opened his driver's side door, but he leaned in and sprang back out carrying a duffle bag in hand, and still his cocky grin that I want to just eat up.

"So, you are coming in AND you are planning on staying over?" I ask not being able to hold in my giddiness as he smacks my butt on our way up the steps.

Playfully Declan stated, "You're stuck with me now, princess."

"Oh Goodie, I've got lots of shelves I need help hanging up, you'll do for the job."

That got me another butt slap as we made our way inside.

Despite never wanting to take his hands off me, Declan took my shelf hanging seriously and wanted to get it done as soon as he put his bag down. He went on the hunt for tools, grumbling when all he could find a hammer, while I poured some wine for me and whiskey for him. I made sure to have my liquor cabinet stocked full since I was assuming for it to be a cold lonely winter, which started warming up as soon as I met Declan.

After he also took the time to start the fire in my fireplace, he gathered the contents of the shelf project in the living room as he got to work, and I sat and watched. He sorted out all the pieces first, putting all the nails and clips in their designated groups. While he was busy organizing, he asks, "Do you want to call Carl tonight?"

Looking at him sitting there on my living room floor looking like he belongs here, the two of us surrounded by warmth, I decided to not ruin the moment.

"Not tonight. We will be way too busy," quirking my eyebrows at him while taking a smooth sip of my wine. He turned his eyes away from me quickly with a big huffy breath, pretending to ignore my come on and focus his attention back on his shelves, only to have to shift some more before he stands up, holding his hand out to me he says, "Come show me where these need to go."

Once he marked the spot with a pencil, I held onto the shelf itself to keep it straight while he nailed them up hanging in no time, poking fun at me about the height I needed them placed in to be able to reach, as he was almost eye level.

We walked back into the kitchen when we were finished, taking sips of our drinks on the counter. Declan tosses the hammer down in a corner junk drawer and stomps over towards me, picking me up off my feet and sitting me on the kitchen island. He takes a slow excruciatingly long sip while searing me with his sex eyes. I just look at him seductively back thinking game on, my anticipation making me needy as I put my hand on his hips to pull him closer towards me, my legs caging him to me. Besides his king cobra showing me, he is ready for action, Declan remains standing face to face with me, looking me all over with this stern and quizzical expression, like he is reading me.

Instead of his usual overzealous touching, both his giant hands rest laying flat on the counter at my sides. Becoming more agitated with the lack of attention, making my body squirm in response like I'm going through withdrawals, I frown at him and ask, "Why are you not touching me?"

Coolly he replies, "I'm giving you a minute."

Not comprehending what made him think I needed any more minutes, my frown verges on irritation responding back, "I still don't understand why," trying to make myself look more serious by crossing my arms.

His pale pink lips didn't even curve in response, only to reason with me saying, "Because Alexis, when I start touching you, this time I am not going to stop."

Okay, my vagina just felt its own solo dance performance, rippling angst and pleasure through me. Hot in every temperature, I reach down to take off my hoodie, only to have Declan's ninja like reflexes, grab a gentle hold to my wrists as his eyebrows dip in a perturbed reaction, "What do you think you are doing?"

"What? I'm hot and just wanted to take off my sweatshirt."

Declan's ninja hands now grabbing in a fistful of the bottom of my sweatshirt, his voice a stern gruff warning, "No, you don't get to do that tonight," finally close enough to kiss me, his breathy question my prelude, "Are you ready?"

There is only one accurate answer to him. "Yes."

Ripped over my head in an instant, and another, and another, until the only top on me is just my bra barely covering my full breasts, my chest heavily panting in front of him, wanting. His eyes glued on me as he unclasps my bra and pulls it off of me, and I feel it, everywhere, before he moves further, his carnal desire emerging from his inner depths.

Strong.

Ruthless.

Hungry.

I sit here like bait while he prepares for his next strike. I'm his for the taking, yet I've never felt so alive and free before in my life. Jaw ticking, his thumb a swipe away from the button on my jeans, before he swoops me into his arms, and kisses me all the way to the bedroom.

"You taste so good," I blurt out in a breath, as our tongues join in rhythm.

Declan speaks his own language when he kisses me, always grunting and moaning in my mouth, more than when he speaks in words. It's not even like he cares either, he is too entranced in our passion.

A new mixed version of his hungry song with every move I make or any new detail of my body he sees.

I love his noise.

I could wear my soundproof headphones and listen to this on repeat.

And it's only the Intro.

He doesn't just lay me on the bed either.

No.

This man uses his strength in a detail.

Standing before the bed, Declan bends his knees, low enough that my landing is a flawless meeting of the runway, keeping our mouths tight together until I'm at a stop.

He is the pilot, and I am the plane.

Grazing down my body with his mouth, it becomes a slow like departure, kissing every inch of my skin. Still knees bent as he unbuttons my jeans and pulls them off each leg, removing one more layer until I'm bared to him.

Bared to his all-consuming blue eyes like I've never been exposed for anyone else. I lay there in front of him weightless, with every goose bump on my body popping up to show my need for him. My blood pumping fast and strong, my body wanting to be seized like it has waited too long for this moment in life to feel completely desired.

In a precise movement, he plucks up my hips and drops his hungry mouth to my core, immediately lapping me with his tongue. Not leaving any part of me cold being his specialty, Declan uses one arm to rub up my torso with splayed hands, reaching up to grab on my breasts while I writhe in pleasure watching him devour his face in my pussy. For a better view, I sit leaning up on my elbows.

"MMmm baby..." I moan as he eats me alive, licking and sucking, over and over.

Declan grunts and groans in his feast like a horny maniac, and I am met with a heat wave within minutes that is so fierce, there is nothing holding me back. I start cumming all over his tongue, his feast not stopping as he overindulges.

"Holy sweet baby Jesus!" I yell out, thanking the gods of release.

There is no time to waste as he moves back over me, and we throw off his clothes. Straddling in between me, Declan places a soft sweet kiss on my lips, gifting me the taste of myself.

He groans aloud in admission in a thicker Irish accent than his usual, "I have never needed somethin' so much in my entire life."

So, with that, I sucked on his lower lip until it popped in sound, while I use my lower body to guide his king cobra inside of me.

It is worth every bite, as he starts driving into my pussy, hard and deep, over and over, and over again.

Stretching my legs around his hips, around his neck high above me, back so far behind my head that my legs lie flat on the mattress, toes hitting the pillow.

We were in torturous pleasure while time stood still. Fleshy thrusts met me to my core, each of us screaming our moans of bliss out loud, our songs becoming a duet as we both come at the same time, his cobra spewing me with venom.

Aftershock is a real thing.

A real fucking thing.

My hand curved through the strands of his damp hair as he lays his head on my chest, we stayed connected as our sexes ripple in the aftershocks of lethal sensation. I use none of my own strength while he lifted me up to our way, putting his lips on mine while he slowly pulls out of me, his extra inches loitering until I'm draining in a pooled encore.

Still holding me up, walking down the hall, "we need to hydrate," Declan says to my lips, "you are a wicked woman."

"I am so so happy we speak the same hydration language," I say kissing his cheek.

He questions in exasperation, "Hydration language? Is that what you think we speak? Hydration language?" chuckling while opening the fridge for bottles of water, grabbing us four and closing the door, huffing out, "I guess that's one way to look at it."

Needy, I grab a bottle out of his hands and twist it open to quickly chug it down before I dry up. His astonished eyes, "we are going to have to talk about why you know how to open bottles so fast," he says, tossing the top in the garbage can and walking us back to the bedroom.
"I'm just really thirsty when you're with me," I say now touching his collarbone and across his biceps, learning his defined lines in his muscles and smooth chest.
"I'm not buying your flattery," he says back to me as he brings us back onto the bed.
I kiss the tip of his nose.
"Well, you don't have to because I just gave it to you, freely," I say with an innocent smile, while we lie down snuggled up, face to face with one another.
Chummy he says, "Well, I do like when you give me things freely," he moves my hair out of my face and behind my ear, leading him to say, "Tell me about the sparkle in your hair."
"Does it make me look flirty?" "My new hairdresser told me I needed flirtier," I reply thinking about when I got my hair done with Autumn. Also reminding me to place a mental note to give her a call to hang out soon.
Responding dryly, Declan states, "I like it, but I don't think I want to know why your hairdresser thought you would need more flirty."
"I guess she thought I was a boring single loner."
His hooded eyes go wide now as he retorts back, "You are absolutely none of those things, neither boring nor a loner, and you certainly are not fucking single anymore."
"You and your words," responding while not trying to even comprehend what being tied to someone would even feel like, besides a friend anyway. A different type of partnership I have never experienced by myself or anyone close to me. Margie and Estel being the loveliest older married couple I have ever met.
Trying not to get too caught up in my thoughts, I start kissing him on the lips, drifting into my swirl of happy.
Through our smooches, he says, "I mean it," still kissing me, "Don't make me cut that strand off your head."
I laugh at his teasing claims, giving me more kisses only to provoke me to throw my leg over his waist. I sit up on top with the view of this Irish sex God laying underneath me. Straddling Declan, the lips of my wet pussy sliding over his erection while I simultaneously tease him with my mouth on his neck, sucking lightly, and kissing him around his ears, stirring the fire within him.
Both pairs of my lips stirring a need within us.
Declan groaning into the sky, "Baby, how do you make me feel so good?"
Gripping his massive erection, I ease Declan's dick inside me.
His calloused hands follow the path of my ribs across my sides to my back, my body hunched over on top of him, his fingertips loosely crawl down my spine as I tingle with every sensation.
Grabbing firm hands on my ass cheeks, Declan declares, "So damn good."

Erotic words make me so hot, slowing my kisses down to a breath next to his neck, being overcome with stimulation. The deeper his king cobra slides in, my eyes shut tighter with the 'oh' shape on my face, throwing out being discreet and becoming completely exposed.

I feel like I was made to take a ride on Declan. I wanted to spend all of my tickets, watching and listening to his throat and mouth for every swallow and hitched breath, every rumble of pleasure, I create my own dance on top of his dick, my tempo fast and strong while he pinches my nipples and rubs my clit with his thumb, he moans my name loudly,

"Alexis!"

"Holy! Ride it, baby!"

His words a cry while his eyelids slink up, as he watches my near collapse into a million pieces.

Screaming and mumbling all the things, I ride out an orgasmic wave, rolling in caps of white, sliding in and out of my massive amount of wetness, like we used a whole bottle of lube.

His thrusts become a frenzy taking over, his hands pushing down on my hips, crashing into me with his tidal wave following shortly behind.

True to his word, Declan didn't stop touching me all night. We sang in our pleasure, holding tight in each other's arms in between acting out our primitive needs. Always giving and receiving random kisses, touches, sucks.

Raw, and sweet, and dirty.

Declan cradled me in his arms when we eventually fell asleep late in the night.

Chapter 16   Alexis

A sight to see

My need to pee woke me up. I wasn't wanting to move from safety, like a snail in a shell, warm and cozy, buried inside for the next week so don't bother me, yet I have to move because of the inconvenient overflow of my bladder. I do feel like jelly, and I am slow, but the urge is too great to ignore, especially also feeling like everything down there is extra sensitive, after it's rough night. My rough, fabulous night with Declan.

 Squirming myself out of his spooning hold around me wasn't easy. I had to lift his arm off of me, heavier than I expected, his fingers grazing across my back as I roll out. Freed and bare naked, the cold stings me as I dart to the bathroom, leaping over littered clothes scattered amongst the floor.

I cleaned myself up a bit before I returned in bed to get nestled in my shell, lifting his arm back up again, using both my hands, like opening the door to climb in, laying his defined forearm back over me as he squeezes me in tight against him, sated and asleep. Declan's eyes were closed, and his lips shut together in a slight pout while I took my time watching his handsome sleepy face, using slight touches of my fingertips in my curiosity over an old scar that runs thin across his left brow, trying not to wake him. His jaw jerks in a back and forth motion every now and then during breaths, his skin clear and smooth, short brown waves a mess, he is a masterpiece. What I felt like was hours after, I woke up again, this time with a different needy urge, as my shell decided breakfast was blowing my mind with his mouth in between my legs. The strokes of his tongue feel soft and long, using his healing powers on my tenderness in each lick and caress, along with glorious suction around my clit tipping me over the edge. I joined the birds in their morning song with my outcry of pleasure.

"Good morning, beautiful," he croons in my ear as I lay there like the slug I've become, trying to manage to give him the best smile I can in my euphoric haze, making his grin even more big, ready after starting his day, and mine.

I tell him, "Declan, I'm not going to be any help to Sabine today feeling like this, you are bad for business." He gives me a big sloppy kiss, "Your phone has been ringing out in the kitchen since early this morning, I think you should get it," he says to me with too much energy as I try to move.

"It's probably just work calls," I tell him in no rush to the kitchen, only to saunter over to him and lead him into the shower with me, he follows with no hesitation.

 "He is shoveling your driveway?" Jameson's tone in my ear sounded in utter disbelief as I am peeking out my window trying not to be too obvious watching Declan outside in the snow.

"Yes! I don't even know where he found a shovel!" I tell him in my giant surprised smile that looks so dopey, that I'm glad nobody can see me right now.

 Once we were clean and toweled dry from the shower, Declan and I ate eggs on avocado toast together on the couch, while flirting throughout the morning until we decided, mostly Declan decided, we needed to go to the hardware store today before we parted to leave for work. He wasn't wrong about my phone ringing so many times that it probably sounded important to someone who hasn't met Jameson before. I wasn't wrong about it being over exaggerated no rush work calls, because besides the two calls from Kel, and a text from Sabine, it was Jameson's number highlighting the 13 other missed calls on my cell.

"I can't believe, wait a minute, who am I kidding, yes I can," he laughs while his thoughts roll out in mish mash after telling him I had a guy sleep over. As close as we are, he knows my sex life hasn't been so great, just as I know his sex life is like having multiple hook ups at face value. However, I didn't give him any gritty details of my night. I just returned his call once Declan went out to start his truck, and apparently, since I own a house now, shovel the snow... something I didn't even think about figuring into my new house lifestyle.

Jameson keeps on, "Damn, I'm happy for you, Lex. Feel sorry for the poor guy shoveling your snow, though. You are going to break his little country heart."

"There is nothing little about him," I jab, continuing, "And don't say that. I may be..."

"Emotionally unavailable?" he interrupts with more of a list.

"Get bored easily?"

"Make him lose his jollies when he sees you grinding with whomever in your own world on the dance floor, having a good time? I remember that happening at least twice."

I stop his rant and retort back, "Okay, I hear you, Jameson, but that doesn't have to be me anymore. Maybe I can be different now, feel again. I do like him," admitting only a pinprick of what I am feeling for Declan in this moment, a feeling I'm not sure I would even allow myself to believe let alone, convince Jameson of.

"I'm sure you do, just be careful and don't run into the first person's arms you find in Paisley and become too attached. You just got there, you need to be careful, and you have a ton of fucking work to do. I can't believe you didn't tell me about Maya Gueterra emailing you. What's the follow up plan with her?"

Still creeping on Declan with no shame, watching him cross the street handling that big shovel is worth an Emmy all on its own. The Declan I get to have after a sleepover is dressed in his casualwear, making it look so damn good I want him to sleepover more often. Also, I'm thinking I may have to buy him a pair of those pants in every shade. I watch him start shoveling Estel and Margie's driveway like the gentleman he is, making my panties wet all over again.

"Lexi!" Jameson shouts

Ahh

Crap, I've been daydreaming so deep in my head that I must have forgotten I was on the phone with Jameson. I scramble away from the window to try and navigate my brain to work mode. "Yeah, I'm here, I'm here."

"She wants to meet with me. I guess she is going to be the one directing the SheerMe Fashion show coming up during the holidays, which is right around the corner, so I'm not sure why she has hunted me down on such short notice. They pick a new location to host it every year, and it is an invite only exclusive guest list, but they don't send out the invitations, until like, a couple weeks before, or something."

"I've heard that too, they make it illusive to the public until they decide on a bid from a unique space to host it. So, she wants you to write and perform something on stage?"

My nerves are tingling more with the idea of possibly having to perform for the first time without Rachel in the forefront.

"Jameson, I don't know what all she needs from me, but I'm not saying yes if it is something over the top. I don't know if I can handle being in that type of lifestyle anymore, and I'm not going to be performing without you either, so there is that. I feel comfortable with our Live concert nights with MartaBeat, and of course I love to dance in my studio, but I don't want to be living from booked calendar events night after night."

"I've heard all of your rules, but this is such a big opportunity that you need to make the time for it. Don't get me wrong, I'm not letting you quit the work you do for the band, but this break is one of those reasons we work as hard as we do, literally next level shit, Lexi!"

Jameson always motivated me and pushed me, because he had a dream to make it big in a band one day, and that included me. I've had years of hard practice and playing the role of more is better, it's grueling hours on your mind and your body, and although I will never stop dancing, I can choose to stop a future that would ultimately lead me into a pack of wolves.

"I'll let you know when I know. I have to go in a second, tell me about the new drummer you need me to see."

Jameson says, "Did you watch the videos I sent you, this guy is bad ass."

"I haven't had a chance yet, what does Tyler and Slaw think of him?" Two of MartaBeat's band members have been with Jameson since they started, and out of three others, one being a drummer who needs surgery on his leg and will be out for some time recovering.

He replies, "They said he seemed solid, but they don't have an ear like you do. Just listen and call me when you do, please," his request being the reason he called me so many times. Jameson likes things his way, usually on his timetable, and I have always been able to take it in stride.

Now that I am away from him in Paisley, my timetable feels like it has just begun, so I am in no rush, especially if it involves looking at Declan.

Once Declan was finally done with his newfound chore, he buckled me in the middle of the front seat, that way I was right against him while we drove to the store in town. It wasn't like being able to wrap my arms around him but having the heat and still being able to touch him is not so bad either.

Declan thought it would be better if we had a written list for the store, steering and flopping around on the side of his door, he tosses me a paper and pen, and tells me, "You write it down, while I drive," then he begins his list out loud for me that was a mile long, and took both the front, and back of the sheet of paper.

"Bits, what are bits?" I ask as we roll into the parking lot.

"You know, little bits," he gestures, showing me with his thumb and index finger at an inch length like it tells me what he is talking about."

"No Declan, I have no idea what bits are!"

"The bits are for the drill. You know, for drilling a hole in something."

"So, we need a drill and it's bits." I confirm as I jump out of the truck.

"Precisely," he responds while grabbing a hold of my hand to walk in.

"What holes were you thinking about drilling into?" I ask him seriously without thinking about how it sounded until it was already out there.

He did not miss it, his smile showing teeth almost proudly while looking at me to respond, "I can think of a couple..." after his short pause and an eye roll from me, he says, "Yep, now I'm thinking about them again," as he yanks me in close while we start to cruise the aisles.

The shopping trip total added up to be a lot, since I threw in more than the list worth of tools into the cart, with Declan almost keeling over as I kept adding extras. Something has come over me, maybe it's the fact I own a house now and want to make sure I have everything ever needed in the history of home ownership, but I have the money on hand for the first time in my life and I am going to swipe away. Sticking in my card before they even scanned everything, that way he didn't try to be chivalrous and go broke for my home hardware. It made him uncomfortable to watch me do it, but we didn't comment about the prices once it was over, discussing finances seems too far off the radar for us right now. I feel like I know Declan, but at the same time, I don't know anything about Declan. So, I'm trying to find the possibility of those being the same for now within my mind. Until we reach that point of conversation in this relationship we have been building, I'll wait for him to let me in. No rush, remember.

Like a true smaller world than Boston, Declan and I were walking out of the store when a male voice screamed out over the parking lot.

"Deck!"

Turning us around, Declan's face softened as the man looking like the younger version of him, with darker features, steps towards us.

"It's just my brother," he explains to me softly, almost like he was relieved it wasn't someone else, "Hey David, what brings you out of the coffin?"

His brother displayed the same power, tall and muscular, with almond shaped blue eyes instead of Declan's more hooded. David's left eye catches your attention, with a big green spot sparkling like a gem in his blue iris. Sabine has good taste, quite like mine actually, and it just makes for a much easier friendship.

"I didn't think to find you here either, but I spotted the truck. I was just picking up groceries at the gas station since the old man has eaten everything, and low and behold here you are."

I may have winced when he said it, my childhood rummaging for food and always in the gas stations are a memory I like to forget.

Declan introduces me to his brother saying, "This is Alexis, don't be weird," making me bust a quick laugh when David holds out his hand to greet me.

David's hand massive around mine as he meets my eyes and gives me a friendly squeeze hello.

"Hi there, I'm David, it is so nice to meet you, Alexis," he croons and asks, "Are you the reason he's been on my couch recently, then?"

"I said don't make it weird," Declan pops out giving David a hard look.

Trying to not embarrass myself or Declan, I keep quiet with just a friendly smile towards meeting his brother, a family member, feeling out of my comfort zone when it comes to this sort of thing.

David outwardly much friendlier to Declan's broody, gives his brother a goofy smile saying, "Will I be seeing you tomorrow night then?"

"You know I'll be working."

"Oh yea, lots of check ins to be had I suppose" David giving him an apparent jab, but I am not fully aware of what they are talking about, so I just listen.

"David, I'll call you later, I'm going to run Alexis home now and unload all this before we have to go into work," rushing us away for nothing to rush to.

"Oh, do you two work together?" David turned to me when he prompted his question, but I couldn't respond faster than Declan's, "No!"

Once his harsh one worded answer was complete and we were both looking at him now in wonderment of his abruptness, I decided to take the reins of this uncomfortable moment, "I'm in the dance studio around from the main street. Sabine Woodberry works with me." Uncool, I added that last unnecessary bit of information, but what the hell. She isn't here to be mortified of my slip.

"I know exactly where that is, huh, I was wondering about that place. Although, I don't recognize the name of your friend, I guess this isn't that small of a town."

Declan quick to stop us from any more continuation, "Alright little brother, I love you, we are leaving," he lightly guides me away. I make sure to throw up a big wave to David while walking back, which got me an eyeful from Declan.

Declan made me get in the truck and stay warm while he loaded the cart of our items, organizing like he is playing Tetris. I like that he bosses me around to do nothing sometimes, it's nice having genuinely kind gestures every once in a while, and for me, it's been a long while. While he was busy, I reached down and saw my phone has missed messages. I must have put it on silent after talking with Jameson. My first message is from Sabine, telling me she won't be able to make it into the studio until later on this afternoon, so I make sure to let her know how much I am liking that idea too. And the second message is from the girl who transformed my hair, Autumn.

Autumn: Lexi! I want to extend an invite for going out this weekend.

I was about to text her back but decided to wait until later since Declan was getting into the truck. I did what I told myself I would and kept on the quieter side for the ride back to my house. We were playful but we didn't speak of his family or anything of importance after running into his brother, David. I knew something changed in Declan's temperament, like he was bothered, and I wasn't wanting to be any bother added in his life. Both of us tired from lack of sleep, not knowing any other way to keep calm, I just leaned on Declan and relished in his warmth as we drove.

With the later afternoon upon us, "So, I'll be working all this weekend," Declan states as he stands with me by his truck, about to detach.

"Alright, yea, I guess the weekends are your busy times, huh?"

Settling a new look on his face, "Yea, they are but, you have this little handy thing," swooping in to grab my cell phone I had left in the seat of the truck, "If you keep this at least near you during the day, people like to communicate better this way."

"Ha, funny," I reply, "I never really grew up with one, so I'm not used to carrying it around."

Playfully, Declan says, "Ok, maybe, but really who didn't grow up with a cellphone?"

"Me, I guess," as he is looking into my soul for answers I refuse to allow anyone to find.

"I don't get that. You have a room dedicated to electronics. All I'm asking is for you to try not to drive me mad and answer your phone when I call, or better yet, call me. Text me, pretend you like me."

"Okay, I'll try to be better at the whole cell phone thing."

His eyes squinting a bit more in his soul searching, but my guard has been placed. I realized Declan wasn't wanting or allowing me to see something about himself today, maybe he feels embarrassed about being caught with me in town, this being the second time he has acted so short, the first being the other night with the guy, Boomer, at Ripley's. Since he is the type that likes and requires order, it has me wondering now if I may have been dumped into his happy organized life, me carrying my own pile of pieces from my own chaos sitting in his world, but in his sorted pile outside from the rest. Ever since I moved here to Paisley, my normally closed off self feels safe enough to open up faster than I ever had, especially with Declan. It seems he is helping sort my pieces while he keeps me far from seeing his.

Dangling in muddy waters, I seek to my uncanny ability to separate from my heart and know when to jump down from a few clouds, and lie to myself about how high I felt up there to pretend my emotions were not gaining too much control. I nail the act with years of practice, not wanting to set myself up for disappointment. When you have only been handed a piece of the pot, because until the handler is ready to give you anymore, it's still only a small piece, you are not walking away with the whole. It has never been the whole for me, I'm still an orphan, so I don't set myself up for disappointment.

"Hey, are you okay? I'm just leaving for work, babe, not for good. Why are you looking at me like that?"

"I was thinking about how cold I'm going to be tonight."

Even though I don't even really know what 'work' means for him, I know no matter what there is a connection between us. He has been nothing but good to me, and I'm not willing to let him go, so I'll try to convince myself to stay strong enough for now to allow him to take and hold onto some of my vulnerability, hoping that he doesn't get tired of me yet and want to put me back into the lost and found.

Oh no, I feel the sting.

I reach around his neck and give Declan the kiss we both needed from each other in this moment, a deep and sensual reminder of our endless attraction with our lips doing the speaking for us and giving away all our answers, the kind of kiss you don't give or share without the promise of a follow up one.

Later that afternoon while I was in my bathroom grooming, tweezing, shaving, and waxing, I got a phone call from Kel, that added weight to my pile I was already struggling to carry.

"Do not freak out, but Maya Gueterra is coming to see you tomorrow afternoon! She has rearranged a flight and will be in Paisley tomorrow by two in the afternoon, the email is in your inbox."

"You are kidding me right now?" I scream into the phone in question, "What about you?"

"I am sorry Lex, but you know this is too short of notice for me to fly in."

"Well, what about me? Does she not assume I have anything else I will be doing?"

"Do you?" Kel asks me suspiciously, her tone knowing there isn't anything serious enough to be in the way.

The only thing I want to be doing, is Declan, but that definitely doesn't get me off the hook. "No, but she is lucky because I've been super slammed lately," I say this while I'm using my other hand to lather my legs in white foam.

Kel replies, "Just look at your email and I will set time aside for Jameson and me to call in to listen in with you tomorrow. Also, that is the reason I called today, but not the reason I tried calling you yesterday when you never answered me back. I did some digging you asked me to do about Rachel."

I unconsciously turned my wrist guiding my razor off course and dropped it into the sink, causing the crashing sound of the plastic hitting the porcelain. My face pressing hard against my ear while all I can ask is, "And?"

"And, I couldn't find anything on my phone or emails out of the ordinary that week, but there was a date on my calendar, Dec.14th, and it was a lunch date I had with Rachel. I remember she was asking me all about how to get a passport, since Terrie and her were at odds about something she wanted to do that was set to take place in Canada."

"She wanted to see Prince Edward Island in Canada, because we had watched the Anne of Green Gables marathon and talked about visiting." Remembering that so clearly when she found out she couldn't go because she didn't have a passport and couldn't get into the country. It wasn't really something you would normally feel tipped over the edge about, but Rachel's tipping over was much more of a jump than most, her mania rupturing from the idea of having to ask Terrie for her documents, it made her furious.

Kel continues, "Yes, that got her so adamant about getting herself a passport."

"But she never got it." I say in memory of the past.

"No, but I do remember myself explaining to her that since she was born in New York where Terrie and B.B. were living, she had to call their state's system to get a certified birth certificate to send in with her passport application. Do you think maybe she was considering running away or something?"

My mind was racing in circles down memory lane as I tried to grab all of my memories of this conversation I had almost a year ago with Rachel. There was the story about Terrie giving birth to Rachel early when she was by herself in the home, and they had to rush her to the hospital to make sure she was healthy. B.B. had nicknamed Rachel his 'surprise angel,' because they were trying for years to have a baby and she ended up being born when he was out of state working at the time. I wasn't sure this had any links to the information I was trying to find out about her ties with Paisley.

"I really do not think that was her intention. It was just another situation she felt out of reach about, and Terrie didn't help give her anything she needed to start the application because there was no way she would let Rachel out of her sight, let alone out of the country."

"Maybe," Kel continues adding, "but she didn't let that passport thing go for quite a few weeks, and I saw a text message in those weeks you were originally asking me about, but it was me texting her asking if she ever got the application done. And her response was that she got everything she needed and decided against it."

"Really, I didn't know she even went that far with it." I said feeling another blow of not knowing.

Kel finishes her thoughts with another, "Do you think she decided against it because she knew about her wanting to end it?"

I can't play stupid with someone who knows the details in our lives. Kel was handed all the details, but it just wasn't solved in front of her to know.

"I do think she made the decision to end it, I just don't know when."

"Well, she told me she put her passport documents in your bag of sealed documents you keep in your speaker safe," Kel said. So, at least we know she was pursuing a future in December, wanting to go meet her Gilbert."

"My speaker was moved with the trucks into my studio, so I will have to check. She always did sneak some of her own things in there." I say chucking, adding, "thanks for letting me know Kel."

After I read the email from Ms. Gueterra and knew my day tomorrow was going to be hard, harder than I had planned when I moved here, harder because it was already interfering with my new normal plans of possibility, because I had to tell Autumn I couldn't make time to hang out tomorrow night, and that was hard.

Chapter 17   Declan

"Please do not tell me you have come all this way JUST to make sure I'm not hot for your girl," David wailed as he joins my dad and I in their apartment living room. I came in for a nap before going into work and ended up watching the recaps on the sports channel sitting on the end of the couch with my father's feet on my thighs. My dad didn't think he should sit up when I came in either, already laid out, taking up the entire chesterfield, he greeted me with a big smile on his face, like Cheshire the cat lounging around for the visit. At least I have some manners instilled by my mother.

Giving my biggest big brother glare, I say to David, "You better not be looking even a half a second too long at my girl."

Hootin' and Howlin' in their amusement, because me having a girl out during the day is rare...to never, and I got caught with that rarity who has taken me over like crazy, leaving me here in our family home, to get goosed by my Pop and brother.

"How the hell did you land the new hot dancer in town?" David cries out, leaving me to glare at him again in response, "I beg your pardon! Watch your mouth little brother, and keep it shut when it comes to Alexis, you wouldn't believe me if I told you." My dad, Len, lays there with thick gray hair a few inches long, his blue eyes like mine, with a shirtless chest with long gray hairs down the middle, definitely not like mine.

"Oh, Alexis, is it? Please tell us Declan," croons my dad, "my heart can't handle the suspense," laying it on thick putting his hand on his heart, making me cave.

"I haven't known her but for like, two weeks. I ran into her, in town one day, and we have been seeing each other since."

David says, "You looked like a good ol' fashioned couple coming out of the store pushing your cart."

"We went to a store, no big deal!"

I tell it loud but clearly a lie as it's my dad next to say, "But you like her?" His side grin profound as a father would look at his son who has hearts in his eyes.

It's not even a question.

Voicing loudly in my playful temper, "Yes I like her, of course I do!"

If only they knew I just had the hottest night of my life.

I leaned into the couch corner and listened as more sounds of amusement rang from their chuckles. Alexis has worked her way in my heart enough for me to know that I'm standing on shaky grounds, and who better witness to my soul being taken over, than my family. Also, the hottest grounds I've ever set foot on, because there is nothing as beautiful as Alexis. Waking up next to her was like being mesmerized by the rising sun, bright and warm, with it being only her that my eyes can see.

David asks me, "You acted pretty rudely when I met her, what had you on edge?"

I reply, "I was just thrown off, not expecting to see anyone, sorry."

His playful toned down as he asks, "Are you uptight about running into Vince?"

My dad, Len, interrupts, "This isn't that small of a town."

It's the first time I really thought about why I acted so short. Why I didn't want to be open about myself in that moment and closed the door quick in David's face. Vince's name is not brought up much between the three of us that are left still grieving Daniel daily.

With the knowledge of Vince laying low around town, we have a silent understanding that it makes us on edge.

There is stinging in my ears while I manage to tell them the truer reason why I cut David off from talking about my work.

"She doesn't know about the Club yet. Or anything like that."

It's dad that pops up, "What do ya mean, son?"

Their eyes on me making me feel like I've done something wrong when I reply, "I haven't told her about Swollen, or Daniel, or Vince. She thinks I'm a bartender."

There was a silence stretching louder than the laughs from before, while I sunk into my seat a bit more. I raise my voice in defense to continue, "I haven't really known her long, it just hasn't come up!"

My brother David asks, "So then why does she think you're just a bartender?"

Stuck in my chair, my guilty conscience decided to tell my tale, leaving out our private parts. I told them all about how I met Alexis under the bridge on the way to see Daniel. They both sat and listened in stunned silence, as I described that cold morning, detailing her dog, as well as her neighbors, Estel and Margie. I also make sure to do a lot of bragging about eating dinner over there, rubbing in how delicious the food is. That's when I told them about answering that I was a bartender when asked of my profession. A grumble of understanding around the room as I explain my actions, until the parts where I say I may have avoided the topic throughout our time together since, and even today, all I said was that I've got to go to work. Maybe I'm digging a hole, but I feel so on top right now, that I don't know how to address it with her, or if I even want to.

David's first thoughts when I was done speaking were honest, "If she knew about Vince she would know about Daniel, so I get you aren't ready to share that. But your job, man? That's such a simple fix, you just tell her about it when you see her next time."

I nodded in understanding because I'm seeing this loud and clear in my face at the moment, but slow lived as my dad chimes in, "That was sad what happened to that couple's daughter."

Turning my head quick at his nonchalant piece of information, I meet his eyes to ask, "You knew about Estel and Margie's daughter?"

"It happened several years before we moved here, they had a young daughter who committed suicide when she wasn't but your age. That Margie woman told me about it when she came to drop off some casseroles after Daniel's accident."

My dad's admission jabs me, "Why do I not remember this?" I ask him in disbelief just as David also adds, "And why don't I remember those casseroles?" both out eyes on the old man now.

He stirs pulling himself upright more as he confesses, "I wasn't gonna let you boys get your paws on those dishes, I hid them in the freezer downstairs knowing you wouldn't look twice at 'em!"

My father has a point since the kitchen area in the gym is on an, enter if must, type of protocol. The fridge and freezer hold our water bottles and ice packs, as well as still bearing witness to all the old drink explosion tragedies, sticky inside, that haven't been cleaned up yet.

"You're a mad man!" David touts back.

Giving my pop the grace for hiding Margie's food since it is just that good, I would have likely done the same. I focus our attention back on my dad's first confession,

"What do you know about it, dad?"

He rubs his chin before he starts, "The both of them, Estel and Marg, they came over with their dishes just like all the others from town showing their support, and they were suppose to just leave the food downstairs with whomever, that way I didn't have to face anyone," he sighs before he proceeds, "I think it was, Xander, who came upstairs to knock on my door, told me there was a lady downstairs that had food and wanted to see me. He had already tried blowing her off, but the woman was relentless."

Len continues, "I ended up going down there and the woman pulled me over to the side and gave me this massive hug, I remember feeling odd with her husband standing right there. Anyways, they had heard in town about Daniel, who was still in a coma then, and gave us their well wishes and then they both told the story how they lost their daughter unexpectedly, by a suicide. She had gone off to the city, I guess, and never came back alive. Nice people."

I add, "They are very good people." The thought of how my dad met Margie, I can't help but laugh, just imagining how her persistence would have taken a hold of my father that day without him knowing, searing her kindness in him. Both she and Estel seem to have a knack for that.

The idea of the how horrible that must have been for my new dinner friends makes me cringe, but worse for me now, is the guilt I am feeling knowing they had likely known who I was all along, or about my brother, Daniel, anyways. My wires crisscrossing remembering Estel's words to me.

"She doesn't deserve anymore heartache, Declan. Neither do you. I know you are a good man, you just need to be a careful one."

A careful one, does Estel think I would physically hurt Alexis?

Because I'm a boxer? Or maybe because it was my victorious fight that ended up getting my brother dropped in the ring later that night.

David breaks my thoughts, "So when am I going to get invited to the next meal?"

My dad following up right after demanding the same, "I think it should be me that gets to go."

I got my phone out to text my girl while tuning out the both of them squabbling over who deserves Margie's food more.

Me: I can't stop thinking about you

I decided that my brother David is right, when I see Alexis next, I will have to clear up my job title, because she hasn't given me any reason to not be honest and move forward. Move forward, something I am not sure the meaning behind. I do know she drives me wild, and I like her too much to let my insecurities drive her away from me.

I got to whack David around in CeCe's before getting to Swollen, he can thank Alexis for why I was so light on my feet today. My kicks on point, and my adrenaline running high, anticipating on a message from her back.

With the hum of the stage speakers coming through the walls, Ronnie, Dax, and I, had sat through two interviews and a meeting with a new possible human resources agency, and I was still waiting for Alexis to respond. I was trying to play it cool and accept it as a challenge because, I fucking love a good challenge, except I was not cool and tried my luck to strike out again.

Me: Please tell me you haven't forgotten about me already.

A few seconds later my phone starts to ring and it's her. Looking up at my friends, who are nose deep in their own screens, I start getting out of my chair before I've answered her call to step out for privacy, but my brash move to talk privately caught Ronnie and Dax's attention. My phone still ringing, when I hear Dax say, "Someone so important this late and we can't hear?" My finger was hovering to press the green, but I wasn't but halfway across the expanded room, leaving me too near to just keep walking out. So, I say hastily, "Yeah it's your mother," as the joke makes the both of them laugh hard enough to distract my sped up steps. I got out of the office and around to a private corner and my phone had already stopped ringing. Feeling like an idiot on the missed call, I had to call her back to finally hear her voice. I blurt out before the call may have even been connected, "You remembered me."

Her words smooth like butter, "You're not that easy to forget Declan Wesley McQuade. I had my headphones on because I told Sabine she could study her French."

I was smiling wide for the corner I was standing in while I replied, "Should I ask?"

Alexis tells me, "She has a final exam in her French class coming up, so she had the audio practice streaming through the overhead speakers so the whole studio was able to listen and learn, parle vous France, but I had my ears on five minutes in."

I ask. "Your ears?"

"Yes, my headphones. I've worn them probably more than I've not in my life, so Jameson started calling them 'my ears,' and that's just what I say now. Anyways..." her speedy change of topic proceeds, "You had time to talk on a Friday night, sounds like a slow bar."

Her comment a question as I grind my teeth down to reply, "You're bad for business." There was a short silence burning between us when I say to her, "I'm not good at this, Alexis."

She responds sweetly, "I think you're pretty good."

I go in for my move, "I'm going to try to see you tomorrow, but I have to be back into work by the late afternoon. Do you want to have lunch?"

Only to be shut down when Alexis replies with her noisy, "Ahh", then, "I can't I'm sorry. I literally just had something for work come up for tomorrow. I have someone coming to meet with me about getting help on a possible performance piece."

I'm going long, "Okay, baby, Sunday then?"

"Sunday should be great," she said, finalizing my plan to see her then and speak with her then about my Club. Somersaults in my stomach as I drag what's left of my ego back into the office, to all knowingly sit through more laughter at my girl problems.

Chapter 18   Alexis

The pressure was building in my chest, thumping hard and fast, making me start flailing around the studio like a baby bird, waiting for the short notice arrival of Maya Gueterra this afternoon. Sabine and I are here waiting like the chickens, being fed to the wolves, because something or someone convinced me it is worth hearing the offer. I clued into my naïve brain that this may not have been something I was ready for, rather just a door from my past I shouldn't have cracked open when my new normal brain wanted to dig in my heels and daydream about Declan instead.

"Do you hear that knocking?" I ask Sabine as we are in the Mixx room going through past videos of performances Maya Gueterra directed. Sabine scrunches her eyebrows in concern while we both give each other a look of fear that she is here two hours early. Sabine leaps out of her chair and runs to the front, while I stay in the room and listen for the voices.

After she unlocked the door, there were faint sounds of chatter that did not sound like anyone Sabine was allowing inside, because the door closed and locked again before she came back to tell me, "It was a girl asking for a job!" Sabine gripes as she sits back in her chair, "Did you put that add out for someone?"

I reply with a relieved smile, "No, I sure didn't. Maybe she just saw it driving through town and thought she would inquire."

"I guess," Sabine says, "She was quite annoying, wouldn't take my no for an answer and demanded to see the owner. She wouldn't tell me her name. She just told me she would come back again."

"That is annoying," I reply, "and definitely already a 'no' for the nonexistent job."

Sabine says, "Lexi, I just thought about something. Rachel's song," she points to the spot on the wall where I have hung up, Wings of Paisley, in my Mixx room.

"Good Save," I tell her as I stand up to take it down. I hung it up with the intention of none other than Sabine and me, and Declan, to be in here to see it. Ms. Gueterra will be adamant about touring in here, not to mention the horror if Jameson or Kel noticed it through the phone screen in the middle of this meeting. I take the steps up to my loft and all I can do is smell Declan. I haven't been able to stop thinking about him, even harder to sleep, my bed was cold without him last night, and I can't stand how much I need Rachel here to talk to about it with me. I need Rachel to tell me I'm going to be ok and to remind me I am going to be good at being normal. I need her to tell me that I'm not just running into the first person's arms I find in Paisley, quite literally, because it's easy, and convenient.

Rachel was a better cheerleader for me than she was for herself. She would always tell me when I started getting jittery, *"Lexi baby, don't you be like me. You are too in your beautiful head right now and that's not you. You are much stronger than that. You are capable of fulfilling your own dreams one day, as long as you remember to choose it yourself."*

How much I wish my best friend was here to tell me that I'm right about how Declan looks at me differently than anyone I have ever known, like I am his, like he sees all of me. I wish Rach would tell me it's not a joke, and it really can feel this good this soon. I touched her words over

the glass frame, dancing my fingertips along her path, following behind her, tracing each word, each curly letter, wishing I could erase them all for her, wishing I didn't let her go.
I heard it then, frozen with my eyes still staring at Rachel's song, a voice growled nearby, outside. An angry disappointed tone I was familiar with, but a male voice I was not, so close to my studio it echoed through the loft in a quiet whisper. Placing the frame underneath my bed, my curiosity sends me to the window, which has those same blackout curtains as my house, needing a remote to open up. By the time I could look, there was nothing, my parking lot empty. The wind dancing through the main streets maybe, the beast howling loud enough I could hear.
Before I went back downstairs to wait, I chose to send a message.

Me: When you are about to enter the ring, what do you think about?

Declan: That depends on who is in the ring with me.

Me: What if it's a wolf?

Declan: Then I don't think about it. I would bring it down as fast as possible, knock its teeth out with one punch, avoid the bite.

Me: How do you know for sure that particular wolf will bite?

Declan: When the wolf entered the ring, it sealed its fate.
He gives me orgasms and pep talks without even trying.

Me: What did you do without me today?

Declan: You were with me the entire time, you never left my mind.

Me: Always the charmer.

Declan: You're my charm. I slept in, had a good workout, passed your studio in the morning and saw your car, and I'm driving into work here in a minute.

Alexis: You didn't come in?

Declan: You told me you were busy.

Alexis: I'm always busy.

Declan. Noted.

Alexis: Have a good night tonight. I'll be wishing you big Saturday night tippers.

Declan: You're the only tip I want.

Alexis: Always words.

Silencing my phone and slipping it in my back pocket, I thought about Declan's words while heading back down to see Sabine.
"Sorry, I texted Declan," I say as I enter back inside the Mixx room to sit next to her.
She gives me a rueful smile stating, "Lexi, there is nothing to be sorry about."
I took a big breath before I spoke, "Sabine, I want to make sure I can keep it that way, there is something personal I'd like to talk to you about before our meeting," her face looking more serious as she gives me a nod and a pat on my knee to continue.
"When I was young, I would dance in this clearing to get away from my apartment. I grew up really poor, with useless parents, and all I had was my music and dance, to get away. Jameson was poor like I was and adamant about making it big one day. Whether or not he actually wanted that lifestyle, I have my doubts, but that is what he has strived for ever since he was a kid. Then there was Rachel, born into the world of money and fame, her father set her up financially to make sure she could have every opportunity she ever wanted in her reach. Her choice got taken away for her while she was only 10 years old, when her father died, and her mother went from bad to worse. I hadn't met Rachel then yet, but from what she told me, she was upside-down in sadness and her mother only ever constantly tried to fix her like a problem. Then when I met Rachel, I was only 14 and still living in filthy hell. When we were paired up in a dance class, we collided our hells together...and she basically took me in. I have somehow always been a positive person considering my atmosphere, so I became her shoulder through her pain, and she became mine."

I paused to see if Sabine was following my story because I had a point I was trying to get to but couldn't without the background first. Her face still with a kind smile in her understanding, she said, "keep talking."
Loving my new friend that made this so much easier for me, I spoke my truth, "Some of Rachel's mothers demands of us were borderline abusive, but at the time, I didn't see it so much. I had already lived in a world where I ate out of a can, pretty much, every night. My dad was a trucker and literally never home, and my mother was technically a waitress, plus an under the table stripper, and who knows what else. Luckily, they left me alone most of the time."
"You were neglected." Sabine states taking away the possibility for it to be a question.
"Really, I sometimes wondered if they lived somewhere else and just kept me fed like a house pet," I say shrugging it off since this is old news to me, "but it paved the way for my life with Rachel."
I continue on, "Since I had nothing already, besides my friends, her mom, Terrie, convinced me to naively sign up for that world as Rachel's ghostwriter, making me the nameless friend in our partnership. I was placed in the eye of the storm, forced to see through it all but somehow end up never being seen, if that makes any sense."

I give a little chuckle, "Yet, we were a really good team, and we did have some amazing experiences, but experiences we didn't necessarily ask to be a part of."

With courage, I took the time to explain a scenario that played out when we were 18 that came to my mind while trying to explain myself. Rachel's mother signed Rachel up for a photoshoot that she thought would help boost her daughter's portfolio. Terrie built up the idea of being in front of the camera with so much excitement, convincing us it would be like playing dress up all day, like she was doing us a huge favor. I think even Rachel believed her, because we were looking forward to the fun day. When we were driven to this Malibu looking estate, we were only told then, that it was a topless shoot of her striking dance poses in the pool. Terrie and a crew of photographers were there, mostly men. When the cameraman noticed me and asked Terrie if he could shoot both Rachel and I together, topless and posing, I was stripped of my shirt. It wasn't a question if it benefited her, and she was good at stealing shirts off of people's backs.

I exclaim, "I couldn't believe it, it was mortifying, but my topless picture remains in Rachel Butler's portfolio, and I now have the legal rights to them since she died."

Sabine's normally stoic eyes flickered with emotion as I spoke, so I gave her a bigger smile in hopes to give light to only a smidge of our dark.

She asks, "Why would her mother want that for her own daughter?"

"I wouldn't know the answer to that question, and I don't think Rachel ever got her answer or not either. I split ties with her mother as my manager a few years ago and hadn't spoken to her since. My point in telling you all of this is because all three of us felt like we had no other choice but to live the dream, and I do not want to throw you into something that forces you to sign NDA's and work under a tortuous timeline for someone who expects perfection if you don't see yourself happy there. I wanted the two of us to partner up and open a local dance studio for lovers of the same. This whole Maya Gueterra job is big, she is one of those contacts that can put your name and face out there, and working with her will open opportunities, and doors, that could be exciting. If we blow her away, she could get you into a modeling career, or something if you wanted it. I just know that is not what you saw for yourself when you agreed to work with me, so you need to be sure you want to do this."

I'm almost crying sitting in my dark room only filled with light from the computer screen and power chords.

Sabine gets a chance to say, "You just told me all of that because you are worried about ME?"

Wiping my eyes so no tears fall out, I take a breath to stay strong while I tell her, "I lost my best friend because of the demands and expectations constantly in her face that she couldn't withstand. I don't want to go through that hell of a life ever again, and I certainly do not want to be the reason you fall into that hell."

She hugged me before she said any words. "But Lexi, why are you even having this meeting with a project that involves lingerie and being Live on stage, if you feel so strongly about not wanting to be a part of it anymore?"

My answer, "If I have to take on a challenge like this, one last time, to prove to myself and others, that I am still worthy of my own skills even without Rachel here anymore, I will. I feel confident in my work and of course depending on if I will even agree to the challenge, it won't change the course I had planned for my new normal here, I won't let it."

Sabine states, "And you are worried that I will let it change me."

"Yes." I reply, "Unfortunately working with me can have a door to the dreams some people will do anything for to reach, and maybe I should have told you that when we met."

It's Sabine's turn to speak her truth back to me now as we step onto a higher level of friendship in this moment. Still turned in our chairs facing one another, She replies,

"I don't have any words about what you went through, besides how much I wish I could throw a chair at that Terrie woman. But to be honest, you telling me this, only makes me want to work together on it even more, as a last hoorah or something." She chuckles with a smile and continues to say, "You inspire me Alexis. I want to learn from you. I've only known books and brains, and construction from my father, because my mother left us years ago. I can trust you, and I want you to trust me too. I'm not going anywhere, this studio here with you is where I will want to be. Consider me the uncool little sister that is eager to see all of her cool big sister's stuff."

Our honest conversation changed something in the air between Sabine and me. Maybe it was the fact that I opened up about a time when all I knew how to do was stay closed shut. We came together in the present, united for this Studio, and it seems that both of us were in need of a friend.

I said to Sabine, "Come on, it's time to go get transformed into the hottest girls of the town. You will not believe the outfits I brought for us to wear."

"I hope she can hook us up with some free lingerie," Sabine laughs out as we make it up to the loft.

"Oh, me too!" It was an exciting thought since now I would have someone to wear lingerie for, I am sure Declan would be ok with it.

A black town car that pulled right up to the studio front door right at 2:00pm. The driver got out and opened the back door for her to step out. I would guess she was in her fifties, which probably means her early sixties since she is looking as polished as ever, Maya Gueterra had a short chin length black bob with a long black coat that hung to her ankles with black heeled boots. Another female came around from the other side in a black and yellow suit ensemble. Sabine opened the door for them in greeting, and the two ladies stepped in, Maya's eyes directed straight at me, "Alexis Andrews, what a pleasure meeting you."

She walks over to me and rather than a handshake, she reaches out and lays her hand on my arm in greeting while I reply, "Welcome to Paisley Ms. Gueterra, the pleasure is all ours. This is my assistant, Sabine Woodberry."

Maya did the same arm touch to greet Sabine as well, then we showed her and her assistant, Marianna, into the main dance floor area where the four of us stood in front of one another. Sabine took out the IPAD and was about to call Kel and Jameson like we had planned, but Maya stopped her before she got the chance.

"Please let us speak privately first, it won't take long," Ms. Gueterra demanded in a kind demeanor.

"As fate would have had it, a bidding location is local to you, and I need both of you to help me. I found you on purpose, Ms. Andrews, and it seems you didn't want to be found. The SheerMe show is in a bit of a bind with needing a new choreographer for portions including the models and dancers, but I will explain all that in a moment. First off, I know you haven't had an easy year, and I want to extend my deepest sympathies with the news of the passing of Ms. Rachel Butler."

Even though her mentioning Rachel's death caught me off guard and was a bit confusing, I held my shoulders tall in front of this woman as I replied, "Thank you, Ms. Gueterra. It hasn't been easy losing Rachel, but that isn't the reason I am not wanting to be found, I am purposefully stepping back."

Her reaction was a smile, that got wider and wider, leaving the three of us entranced in watching it keep growing until it's a dazzling white straight smile that finally speaks after that painfully awkward reaction, "I also came here to your studio to meet with you face to face on purpose, Ms. Andrews," her arms folded in front of her as she steps around the room, "I didn't think you would give me the answer I was looking for right away, but you just did."

She stopped speaking again as we all just followed her around the room as if she was bringing us on her own tour of the studio. It was another awkward moment where I realized she wasn't going to keep talking without me responding so I ask the obvious, "And what answer might that be, Ms. Gueterra?"

"If by a step back, as you would call it, even though it is anything but a step back, you mean moved to become a dance teacher and still consult throughout your time, you are certainly under compensating for the hard worker you still are. I know all too well that you have already been through being undercompensated in your career."

Her knowledge of my breakaway with Terrie has me swallow hard while she keeps on saying, "Which is the answer. You aren't here because you lost yourself after Ms. Butler died. You are here to move forward, and that is the headspace I needed to make sure of. It is quite beautiful in here," she is looking up in the ceiling like she is at an art gallery while talking, sentences flowing out of her mouth until she pauses again to let you know it's your turn to speak. The IPAD ringing in Sabine's hands as we hold off on answering it.

It made me cringe to have to say it, but I was trying to have a bit of a fight in this peculiar, pleasant standoff.

"Then maybe you need to know I don't need money as an incentive."

"I can see that, but I also know what I see in front of me, and hiding you is not going to be easy for long if that is what you were intending," she says smoothly.

"If you think I am hiding you are mistaken. My worth isn't less than because the big dogs will only see me working in a small town studio and assume I am wasting my skills. I don't need the stage or money or people that feel like they know better for me to tell me I'm not living enough for them. I don't have to commit to nationally streamed projects. The only absolute certainty I have for myself lies within me and my choices."

"I agree with you, but it's not the media circus you are hiding from now is it? Rather a, who, you are hiding from Ms. Alexis? You can tell yourself all day long that you want to avoid any media tension for privacy, but we all know as a choreographer you can remain behind the scenes enough to where you aren't getting run over by fans all day long."

I snap, "What's your point?"

The iPad has begun ringing again and Sabine silences it quickly

"I don't want to complicate things in your life, Ms. Andrews," Ms. Gueterra says in her most gentle tone, her eyes on me, "That is why I did my research on you, probably more research than I should have because you intrigued me, and I have the resources. If I wanted to tweet out your name and tag an old video of you performing right now, that would make you lose your privacy for an uncomfortable few month of your life, since you hold no social media presence. I could...but that isn't what you are worried about. She doesn't know where you are and it is the possibility of facing and proving your worth to her in the same circles, am I right?"

"Is this a joke? Why are you so invested in my life?"

"I knew B.B. on a personal and professional level for years. Everyone in the industry tried to keep it quiet but all those who ran in his same circles would tell you marrying her was the worst mistake of his life. Even he knew., but he had a little girl to think about."

My heart was thumping out of my chest during her endless speech that she must have had prepared, looking still and sleek, this was more than just an offer, this visit has a personal agenda.

She sees me trying to breathe and returns to her story,"Terrie Butler has been trying to squirm her way into my life for years, always demanding me to take on Rachel for certain sets I was working on. She felt like I owed it to B.B. to use my position to get Rachel the parts in the shows or better yet sending sound samples and demo's to share with my contacts throughout the industry."

Looking at me, she saw something I didn't, something I couldn't, and she cared enough personally to take notice.

"My sounds."

"Yes, Alexis, your sounds, your breakdowns on moves, your talent was sent to me in email attachments and overnight delivery thumb drives from Terrie's office in Rachel's name."

"And I had no idea, because I didn't care enough to even listen or look because it had Terrie Butler's name attached to it. I made a personal decision long ago to stay away when Terrie started squeezing herself into a business she never belonged in, reaping all the rewards B.B.'s hard work ever made her. When I got news of Rachel's passing, I couldn't believe B.B.'s beautiful blonde angel baby took her life, but that's why I finally took the time and looked over the years of work sent in we kept. Something I should have probably done a long time ago as a favor for an old friend, but I thought I was doing the right thing for his daughter to not get her involved in my problems with Terrie. As it turns out, I ended up over examining Rachel's life and found you, I built my own assessment of Terrie's meddling in your involvement." She stops to take a breath and walk towards me, laying her hand on my arm in that weird sort of gesture she likes to do, "Your life is none of my business, but what is my business is your talent, I found years of videos of your dancing and found myself awestruck of this hidden girl on the screen, I couldn't look away, that doesn't happen to me often."

It was a tough truth to hear, a surprising twist to the reason the famous director is here. I look over to Sabine who looks pale, her eyes bouncing around, and Marianna pretending to work on her tablet.

I'm not interested in being used as a pawn to stick it to Terrie Butler somehow," my anger making me bolder since this just got really tense in here, "She has taken enough from me and all I want is for her to stay the hell away."

She nods at me sweetly, and I wasn't sure what I was supposed to think anymore,

"Alexis, I'm not asking for that nor am I interested in the woman either. I agree with you a thousand percent that she is to stay out of our work, if you agree to work with me, but I wanted to be honest about my ties to the family up front with you first before we discussed business."

"I appreciate that, all of that. I still want my name off the record."

Maya replies softly, "Of course. You know in working with me, I will use all my resources to keep your privacy at bay if that is what you prefer."

"I do prefer it. I will not be able to work with you unless I know for sure, my name, email, phone number, addresses, all of it needs to be as tight lipped as possible because I don't plan on ever doing a show like this ever again, meaning you don't share my contact even if your industry friends ask for it. I'm proud of my studio and that is my work now, and I don't want the outside attention."

"Done." She says is so quick, I decided to push my luck further, "As you can trust Sabine and I as well with this on such short notice, and I'll request for us both to not have to sign an NDA, as a courtesy to my personal situation anyways, I don't want to be shut up on paper."

"SheerMe is known for the silence and privacy to the show, Ms. Andrews. All the details of performances and show entertainment remain under lock and key, committing to a new version year after year for our guests. The NDA's are to make sure there will be no leaks to the press on any details for the brand to keep from losing value. I'll agree since I know for certain you'd avoid any publicity, and the show is about to send out the invitations as soon as I sign you and the Club that will be hosting."

It really did feel like she did all of her homework about me. Like she was ready for all of my nerve-wracking requests and demands and prepared to shut down all of my fears. Maya and I gesture to Sabine to answer this time when the IPAD starts ringing again, I can only imagine the craze Jameson is in with the call being declined so any times. Regardless, Sabine answers the call to a well-groomed Jameson and Kel. I noticed Sabine's face turn a shade of red when she laid her eyes on Jameson for the first time, or JamFresh, as she would say. She quickly mustered up a polite smile and turned the camera towards me as they waved and kept quiet, while Ms. Gueterra spoke her apologies for the delayed call with Kel and Jameson present and started speaking like the conversation beforehand never happened, which I appreciated as it was a lot of information to take in.

The air was thick, and I could even feel the tension through the screen as Jameson was probably drawing blood, biting his lip so hard to keep from telling me what to say. If it weren't for the noise from his leg shaking while he sits there impatiently, I would have thought Sabine had placed the video call on silent.

With her skin bronzing under the studio lights above, she explained the main part of the show needing our live stage performance, "Starter, the curtain-raiser, you will open the show on stage with the first round of the models being introduced on the runway, leading a group of other dancers SheerMe will provide for you to perform with. You do this for me, I let you take the reins of your dance, using or revamping any of your past pieces that you already created, that way it is familiar enough in the short time frame and I already know I approve."

"You want me to dance on stage with a group to a new hot version of a track I create and play it over the speakers during the live intro?"

"No, I had something else in mind for the music, I would be honored if you would consider adding MartaBeat, that way Mr. JamFresh over there can create the magic on stage with you."

She and I both look towards the screen as she said it to see a very gleeful Jameson wailing, "Woohoo!" I can't help but roll my eyes at him in pure joy. It's what we wanted, to perform together. That just took so much pressure away from me and made this more exciting. It all sounded too good to be true, but I still tried to hold my ground.

"And the rest of the show?"

Maya replies, "SheerMe is elusive, I can only talk about the work I need specifically from you."

I smile wide, "Luckily for me, I shine in the dark."

Chapter 19   Declan

Slap
Slap

David's voice is smooth like a coach when he says, "Try it again, this time aim more towards hitting direct at my wrist."

My little brother met me at Swollen to get some practice in at the office before having to manage the chaos of Ladies night, tonight. David is more patient than any man I know, except when it comes to his food. Other than his stomach, he takes boxing very seriously dedicating his life to the gym, and acts as one of the head coaches, along with Xander and Willis.

Slap

"Again, your parry will knock me more off balance for that control you want in my hand, if you stretch your arm just a bit further down to jab it out of the way."

Slap

"Good, let's do it with the gloves on now, and see if you can do it exactly like that but I am going to throw more force at you this time."

I nod while I step back to my desk to get my favorite pair of gloves out of my drawer. I remember stuffing them into my backpack, like a favorite teddy bear, the day we moved from Ireland to here. Old red leather, smelling like years of wear and tear, but fit my hands perfect, like magic gloves that morph only for me into this unstoppable force once I put them on.

Given to me as my only Christmas gift from Santa, it was the last Christmas we had with my mother alive when I was seven. Our small home had me and Daniel in a shared room with a queen mattress laying flat on the floor with no frame. I remember waking up that Christmas morning and leaping over, Daniel, accidentally kneeing in the balls, trying to rush to look under the tree. It was the one of the most exciting moments of my life when I laid my eyes on them for the first time, they were a used pair, still too large for my hands, from the gym next to my dad's mechanic shop, but still had that stiffness to them that indicated the gloves had many more punches left in them. When we moved from Ireland, I got in so much trouble from my dad for not packing them away with the rest of my checked luggage because I basically carried a skunk in my carryon for the hours on end of travel, leaving us all feeling faintly ill once we got here.

They are still going strong for me today as my favorite pair to practice in, especially if it's practicing some defense parries and blocks with David, because he hates when I wear them always complaining they smell like roadkill, giving me an advantage on him.

My little brother looking anything, but little was standing there in just his blue boxing shorts showing off the power in his legs, waiting on the mat for my return. Dax and Ronnie also gloving up to practice, the four of us were all in shorts, putting in some time on the mats in our office.

"Oh God no, not those ones," David says to me when he sees me putting on my gloves.

Dax covered in ink on his upper body, also notices my glove choice of the day as he says, "You better wash your hands really good before you touch your girl tonight, or she might just get rid of you because you stink so badly."

All of us in the know that I have become attached to a certain female now, these three have been razzing me any chance they get, out of pure jealousy of course. Quirking a smile at my friend, I reply, "Your mom likes my stench."

Laughs rumble out as we all get into position to do some defense drills together.

David asks me, "Why are you even working here tonight instead of hanging out with Alexis?"

My answer is easier said than done, "I'll see her tomorrow and we haven't been together long enough for you to worry about how I spend my time with her."

Being the owners, we are mostly needed handling the workload throughout the weekdays, keeping up with all the details that allow for successful, lucrative nights that can run strong on cruise control, all positions filled without needing our help. We all stay within the grounds no matter if there is actual work or not during nightlife, by choice, reaping the rewards of our hard work, time, and money.

Ronnie asks, "Why don't you tell her to come up here, we can meet her and have a drink at the bar with everyone."

"You wish," I say thinking about how out of control I feel with the idea of Alexis being ogled by not only my good friends, but by the public in a club, like I want to keep her all to myself. I just found her, and I'm not ready to share her time with other people yet.

"Don't hide her from us," Dax says with a smug grin on his face.

"He is going to have to," David replies with a smile, creating a storm in me while he keeps saying, "You couldn't miss her in a crowd."

Ronnie pipes in, "Shit really, Declan? You found yourself a vixen," his breaths fast as he and Dax rotate punches and deflects.

I reply cockily while I knock David's strike away, "I think you three need to get you some tonight so you can keep up with me in the ring. When you feel good, you are going to perform better."

"I'm sure she has friends," Dax says as matter of fact.

Replying honestly, "I'm not sure who she has. Other than me and the girl she works with, she talks about one guy friend a lot."

Ronnie asks suspiciously, "A guy?"

Just as Dax yells out, "I am certainly not interested in her gay boyfriend."

I say, "A friend she knows in Boston, some band kid, she told me they are just friends."

"Shit, this keeps getting better and better. I don't see you handling that well at all." Ronnie states.

I haven't really had the time to think through the feelings I have regarding Alexis' close friendship with the guy, Jameson, whom she considers her family. All of these somersault feelings I am dealing with for the first time are still so new that I haven't been able to add them all up and look further into it just yet.

Spiking my fear of jealousy, I divert the attention off of me, "Better than you are doing, Ronnie."

David laughs out loud causing Ronnie to step over and lightheartedly punch his side to knock him off balance, as David represents everyone's little brother around this room, even though he is in his prime fit shape, strong enough to take out any of us. Luckily the phone ringing in the room grabbed our attention and knocked it off of discussing women. The ringing was from Dax's business cell, and in one smooth move, he swiftly threw off his boxing gloves to run across the room to pick up, prompting our odd number to take a break stretching out. A few minutes later, Dax returns with news from his call.

Clapping his hands as he struts back over towards us, "You guys ready to hear this? That was a call from New York City, we are in the top bid for a women's lingerie Fashion show to take place here, in Swollen, December twentieth!"

Our excited eyes wide throughout the room, as Dax continues to tell us about this major opportunity that could tip us to be able to expand the club further.

"Fucking models and shit?" David asks in disbelief, all of us dreaming about the show rather than the actual business incentive.

Dax's happy expression on his face shows his answer as he continues to tell us, "The lady on the phone said we are waiting on an affirmative from another one of the director's choices over the show who is locally positioned here. This is so awesome, apparently someone will be here tonight to visit and make the call, check the place out to make sure it's suitable for their needs, which fuck, we know that shouldn't be a problem. They said they will let us know by tomorrow."

"So, the choice falls in the hands of a local model?" I ask trying to wrap my brain around whom it is we need to look out for tonight.

Dax replies shrugging, "I thought the show would already be in full swing practice mode by now, with the talents already picked, so this has got to be the snag that put our little town on the map, but seriously, I'm not planning on letting this slow down my night off I had planned after I tap out of work mode. It's Ladies Night, let's just try not to piss anybody off and make sure everyone is having a good time."

This unexpected visitor being the person with all the power we need to choose our club for the biggest event of our lives, forcing us to make sure tonight runs like a smooth electric guitar, all of our heads in the game as we discuss the plans for ourselves tonight, besides hanging out at the bar and slowly sipping drinks. Considering I don't give a crap about it being Ladies night, I was unconsciously planning on leaving early and going to see Alexis. With this news of the possibility of hosting a national live event, which would normally cause me to get really pumped up, probably turn it up later in the evening with my friends, however even right now, the only place I want to be is wherever Alexis is.

Securing head checks around the perimeter, Al makes sure to leave us all with our walkie talkies turned up high for tonight, as we prepare to open our doors for the local crowd hunkering together outside the walls anticipating another one of our well-organized Ladies nights. We started having these events from the start, but less frequently, and we were always told we needed to have more of them since they were so popular, always drawing in an explosive crowd of singles fueled with adrenaline. We have worked hard throughout the three years of owning Swollen, creating and maintaining new contacts in the party industry that bring new entertainment ideas, always changing it up with different themes and experiences for the paying partygoers.

Tonight, we have a DJ lit up on a pedestal on stage, cranking out electronic dance and current singles, accompanied by some female pole dancers in the late hours. Tham came up with the special pink cocktail being featured for the night, being served in plastic cups shaped as a pair of big breasts, a sure favorite amongst our crowd tonight. In lieu of it being October and breast cancer awareness month, we will share a portion of our sales of the specialty drink with the local women's hospital, our company philosophy firm on giving back to the community. Our servers and bartenders throughout the club are mostly male tonight, all dressed up in uniformed attire with pink bowties. Dax ordered us three owners matching pink ties to dressing up with tonight, leaving me griping since I don't usually dress formal enough for a tie. Feeling choked, I paired the tie with a black long sleeve button down and jeans. Before I try to put my phone down for the evening, I pull it out to see I actually have a missed text message from Alexis.

Alexis: It seems as though work has me dancing probably through the night, so maybe a good nap tomorrow?

Her message being the breath I needed for the night, knowing she is working in her studio and still thinking about me, and her sleep.

Me: No rest for the wicked
Me: I know how to hydrate you to keep you awake

"I'm still wondering why you don't just call her and have her and the chick she works with come up here, escort her in the front door or something to woo her, that way it smooths over the whole... job thing," David peers over my shoulder to make me wonder again why I ever opened my big mouth.

"You know David, what are you doing with your dick these days since the last I heard your girl bailed on you and dad in the kitchen? Maybe that should be more important to ya," I challenge back as he and I walk to the bar to start our evening. David will be able to drink himself stupid and I'm going to have to make chatty rounds all night, when there are many other rounds of things I would rather be doing with a girl named Alexis.

David remarks back, "Ok Asshole, definitely not my girl, I think Dad might have saved me on that one actually, I'm literally around sweaty men all day and night and you, you are around this," his hand out directed towards the heart of the club, the DJ has a full crowd on the dance floor in motion and the bar is packed with just as many men as there are women here for tonight's Ladies night. It is the outfits of this themed night that shine out to us overall, some people we even have to turn away at the door to cover up more before entering. "I think I'm doing it wrong," David adds with his tone full of playfulness with an edge of serious.

My gut stopped us in our tracks before we were having to navigate deep through the crowd, grabbing my little brother's shoulder hard, I leaned in close so he could hear me clearly over the music, "Don't you say that. You should be proud of yourself for making a good honest living doing what you were meant to do. Plus, you can always come take a night off with your big brother for some of those sweaty women, they are always here."

I say this as I'm pointing to the dance floor, never sure I'm good at saying the right things. Our eyes meet in a gentle understanding, and we continue our way towards Ronnie and Dax, currently busy perched at the far end of the bar.

"Yeah, well not all of us get to bump into the kind of women like you apparently can, let's just hope you can keep her," he finishes sending me a wink and leading us through the crowd, always better at chatting along the way.

Meanwhile at the bar, "On the count of three," Tham rolls his countdown backwards instead while Ronnie, Dax, and I, each take a shot of fireball to start the night off, "3, 2, 1, shots, shots, shots!"

Pouring liquid fire down my throat eased my tension until we got buzzed, literally, our walkie talkies were all ringing up on Alert from Al causing our early celebratory kick off to pause.

"What the hell," Ronnie grumbles out while I unclasp the device from my belt loop to find out the issue my head of security has out front.

Beeping as I hold down the trigger of my Walkie-talkie responding to Al's alert, "What's the problem, Al?"

Beep

"We got a situation, boss," Al says as we wait through his paused call to finish, "Vince Bordeaux is trying to come through the door, he has a group with him."

The fireball must have burned my throat enough I lost my voice, crippled in a moment, blinded by the color red, the sound of his name bringing the images of that night back to me. The last time I saw his face, he stood in his corner of the ring with his posse looking smug while they wheeled out Daniel on the stretcher. I couldn't move then, and now my body is against me shutting down at the sound of his name, ironically with David by my side tonight also looking pissed.

Ronnie says looking at me saying, "Shit, how do you want to handle this, out of all the nights he shows up now," disbelief rolling off his tongue.

Beep

Al's voice booms through, "He says he doesn't want problems, just to enjoy the night."
"His word is as worthless to me," I reply to Ronnie.
Then beeping back to Al to ask, "Who is with him?"

Beep

"Boomer, Nick T, and about five women." He replies.
I was looking in front of myself to my friends for confirmation on how we were about to proceed, mirroring the same question playing out in our minds, not finding anything but 3 men that have turned on their fighter faces, angry but stoic, looking to me for the lead decision.

"Go ahead," is all I can say back to Al, while I indicate to Tham that I need another fireball.

Chapter 20   Alexis

As a dancer living in my alternate reality growing up, I was raised by all the quotes in the world promoting the words of confidence and bravery. Be confident in yourself they said. Be brave, reach for the stars. All of those can be erased now since I have had the pleasure meeting Maya Gueterra, because her presence in a room spells out both of those things you strive to be to the full maximum capacity. Be like Maya Gueterra. She has trained and perfected the ability to lock down her confidence and bravery in front of people, creating an illusion with her powers, and the way it comes through you is like a breeze that blows while you are sitting on the beach, feeling good since you are there underneath the sun relaxing. I can't help but think about what the breeze is going to feel like when I get off the damn beach and move somewhere else.
Every detail of her needs was spoken to me with that soft beachy breeze, like she was giving me a gift, the sweet exciting tone she used, dark determined eyes softened by her long-extended eyelashes, her direct demands for me were even sparkling clear that all I could do was drink them down. I felt her breeze come over me today, but I must have been sitting on a beach, because I didn't feel the chill until after she left. I'm standing in front of the mirrored wall of my dance studio, feeling cold and half naked, while my eyes are staring straight at Sabine beside me.
The best part of Maya's breeze, she did leave Sabine and I all the lingerie we could ever imagine, but also branded it onto us since we were teaming up to promote SheerMe until my life returns on Christmas morning.

Jameson shouts from the speakers overhead, "Holy shit," calling us back on FaceTime after our meeting and the departure of Mrs. Maya Gueterra, "You babes are the most scandalous duo I have ever seen in my life! This is so dope, and you aren't even done up for the actual show yet. I think I am going to only wear the boxer briefs on stage."
His smile was a contagious nonstop fit, he was shining like I hadn't seen him shine in such a long time, and I could actually say I had something to do with it.
"Thanks," I reply still shaking myself, "you don't think maybe...I don't know...we might stick out?"
Sabine snorts out her laughter so loud, that it is all I could do with her, laugh like this is all so freaking funny.
 Jameson responds dryly, "Oh, you are definitely going to stick out, but I think that is the point. You two are like the bunnies giving a room full of hound dogs the chance to sniff you."
          Sabine says, "I think it will be fun, I have never done something like this before."

"Wear Lingerie? Or go dancing at a club? OR" ...I'm pausing for dramatic effect while I play dumb placing my finger to my closed mouth, hmming in thought mode, "are you saying you have never gone dancing in a club dressed in THE LINGERIE!"

          Sabine answers, "I have never done any of these things, I told you I was a nerd!"
Jameson answers, "It's not that bad!"

"For you, you are the guy staring at us right now"

"Well yeah," he replies with a shrug, "but you are promoting the fashion show you are about to be choreographing for once you sign those damn papers."

I scream back to him, "I needed to at least sleep on it, Jameson, something you are not good at ever seeming to do!"

Standing in my defense as our friendship bickering continues, "All of this is so much and, now, this dress up, and going to this Swollen Club, this was not necessarily on my agenda when I moved, or ever."

Right before she left, Maya came up with an idea that Sabine and I should not only go visit Swollen tonight, that we should also sport the free lingerie she had in our sizes conveniently with her.

Sabine interjects, "Think about it like we are having a celebratory girl's night! And we are proud of our bodies and want to show them off!"

"Yes," Jameson agrees, "just like that! Yes, thank you Sabine for being in my corner on this."

"Well don't go too far, I am on Lexi's side about taking time to let the whole entirety of the offer sink in. It is a ton of mental and physical work for the next two months."

I add in, "Two months of putting my studio on the backburner."

"Yes," Sabine nods like she is making a mental list out loud while Jameson piddles in his Kitchen, snacking, making me jealous since I was squeezing to death in my attire, "two months of managing group practices streaming through the screen until they all arrive in town, Two weeks prior to the show."

"Two months of dieting,"

"Two months of teaching me how to dance as your backup,"

"Two months of hot foot soaks..."

"Yay," Jameson fake cheers.

"Only for two months!" Sabine adds.

Urg

"Maybe we shouldn't go over the list right now," I say as my nerves are stirring up, "Tonight, let's do what Maya wanted, go to this nightclub to dance our asses off, and think the terms through, drinks on her."

Was I so naïve to not notice how I may have been breezed again!

Damnit

Looking back in the mirror at ourselves, Sabine saying matter of fact, "We do look pretty good. I don't mind the leather."

Jameson shouts with a mouthful of cereal, "Have fun tonight ladies, call me if you need me. You better let me know as soon as the ink meets the paper tomorrow, Alexis, I'll be filling mine out tonight."

Jameson ended the call before I could even say goodbye. Hopefully he has somewhere to be tonight too, and he isn't holing up in his condo eating cereal and playing Nintendo.

Sabine turns to me and says, "That just happened."

"I can't believe her connection to Rachel's dad, it's all actually kind of cool."

"Off the record, you are leaning towards actually taking this job, right?"

I reply, "Off the record, it's a 'we.' We are taking this job."

Smiling and Leather looks damn good on Sabine. Showing off her thin shoulders and neck with hair styled up in a messy ponytail, she radiates sex appeal in a strapless cranberry leather corset top that dips in a V on her flat stomach, boobs pushed up to perfection and a matching mini skirt. Her heels strapped up to her knees, showing off her long lean legs as I look up to her beside me. Other than looking quite a bit shorter than her, I show off the same vast amount of skin minus the leather. Straps so thin, I am in a neon yellow sheer mesh lace bustier plunging down to my naval, my breasts sit up full hidden by weaves of lace around the chest. I was not willing to show my open butt cheeks, so I paired it with tight black lace shorts to help at least cover most with tall heels.

"Ok, our ride should be pulling into the place, here in just a couple of minutes," Sabine says, staring at her phone in one hand and bending over on the other side trying to get her shoe to fit, "And I also just got an email…" she pauses to gather herself up straight before she proceeds, "Marianna just sent me an email letting me know that she has reached out to one of the owners of the club, Dax Morgan, letting him know we are visiting tonight, as authorized she didn't give out our names, she said if we have any questions, he will be present within Swollen tonight for anything we need. Then it just gives me this Dax guy's cell number and email."

"Wow, they work fast."

"Hell, yes they do, I can already tell this Marianna chick is going to run me ragged."

"I think we will both be rag dolls for Christmas morning."

We both giggle as the car stops us in front of the club's entrance. Bigger and sleeker than I thought possible to have this close to Paisley, Swollen, is a warehouse stretching far down the parking lot, brightened up with blue and white florescent lights streaming around the roofline, and an entranceway that blasts the shine to the inside.

"Wait, damn, if you go nameless, does that mean we have to wait in line, versus getting escorted right in? Because it is so cold that it may make you want to change that idea, altogether," Sabine cries out as we run out into the cold air and head towards the front door.

Brrr

Grunting out all of my noises for the cold, I reply, "Gosh you are so right, let's just hope that these bouncers like what they see."

Walking up, we literally had a man in security step out to acknowledge us to come right through instead of waiting in line.

Plus one for the Lingerie!

"Good evening, ladies," the heavy gentleman says as he eyes our bodies, a trade for skipping the line, I suppose. "ID's please."

Sabine and I give each other a look before we both simultaneously reach into our bras to pull out our driver's licenses for the bouncer to flash his light quicker than he could have even read the dates and points us in towards the pink ballooned archway.

"Ladies night," I say to Sabine as I am gathering the themed details as we walk in, as well as some dirty looks. My hair was hung down tonight, making me feel a little less naked, and possibly help cover my face from the jealous females around. We did look like a pair of Babes, but I was here with a plan in mind, drink and dance with Sabine and go home to bed before I get to finally see Declan again tomorrow.

Chapter 21   Declan

I was after only one thing and that was punching out my rage, ripping the fucking tie off in one hard pull, freeing the veins in my neck for pumping up my blood in a thick, even, tank full, leaving plenty on reserve, storming through the doors of my office towards the punching bag. The heat of the fire within me was set ablaze, losing my control, navigating to the closest place I could attempt to bring it back again. There was too much pressure to wait on Vince coming to face me, it wasn't right, and it's not what I was going to allow to happen. I needed to face this my way, and with eyes all over him in the center floor, I have nothing but time to figure out how I am going to approach him tonight. However, first I need to cipher through the emotions that attacked me once I knew for sure I was going to be seeing his face again whether I want to or not.

Ba thump

Ba thump

Ba thump

I am feeling so revved up, sweat is already trickling down my forehead to drip off my eyebrows.

Ba thump

Ba thump

Ba thump

Unsteady but quick, I reach to strike the bag blow after blow, placing the image of a face I have tried to erase so many times, not ever needing the reminder to who ruined Daniel with one shameless, vile, immoral punch.

My walkie talkie is still clipped onto me, Al voicing out Vince's tracked steps aloud for us all to hear in our group.

Beep

Left side sitting at table O11 ordering drinks

He appears to be staying far away from the main bar where you are

Beep

Ronnie's voice booms through now as I catch my breath and listen.

10 4 buddy, I want an update on his every move

The door to the office opened to a pissed off David.

"What are you running up here for?" he screamed it at me before the door even shut behind him.

"I needed a minute." I say shortly as I start to begin feeling a bit more grounded, but David is not letting me off the hook.

"I can't see how you think you can take on a fight with him when you explode every time his name is mentioned," his voice still loud and firm, "Damnit Declan, why didn't you talk to me about it if it's eating you alive!"

I scream back, "He practically murdered our brother!"

David and I stood in front of each other, breaths hard to catch as I try to focus in on the spot of green in David's eye, a piece of my mother's gentleness that softens him, and me. Regaining composure, I state, "All I needed was a minute. He is walking into my house for the first time since that night, drinking my drinks, still smiling like it never happened, and I am not allowed to touch him..." seething again in my confession.

"Why not? Why can't you lay a big punch in his face right now if that will help you gain control before he calls you out for a fight you can't afford to lose, Declan?" David's eyes staring into mine, as I say the only thing that comes to mind, "You know I can't do that in the Club. Especially with someone here tonight to book us for that show."

"Bullshit!" David replies, stunning me a bit while I grow impatient with him. I say, "Watch it."

"No, you watch it," he barks back, "I was there too Declan. I watched it happen with my own eyes too, imprinted in my soul just like yours," his voice was still raised but he remained cool while he spoke, "Both of us want nothing more than to go punch his face in right now. I won't start anything in respect for you and your club. But you won't go do it either, and I think it's because you're afraid you won't stop."

Eyes locked together as he reads me, my worst nightmare is tilting me off axis and interfering with my control board. All those hours of practice and training that add up to years of my life aren't going to help me, as David is right, I don't think I will be able to stop punching him once I get the upper hand.

My silence is my brother's answer as he continues, "And in a scheduled fight, what then? Are you going to be able to even step in a ring with him again?"
"I am not backing down from a fight with him. Period."
Beep
"Irish you coming back"

Ronnie's voice over the mic giving us the interference we needed to regroup.
David throws his chin up in a nod of truce, telling me, "Put your clothes back on. He isn't anywhere near where we are sitting at the bar. We can handle this together if we need to."
I washed myself off in the sink, ran my head under the cold tap to cool me off, got dressed, and walked back to the bar with David by my side again for the second time tonight, but ditching the tie.
 Back at the bar, my friends are locked in tight with other familiar friends and faces including Brady and Autumn, all dressed up in tight short dresses. Tham sees me coming and has a whiskey over ice next to another fireball shot on the bar as soon as I reach it.

"My man is back," croons Ronnie as I swallow the liquid down.
"I'm good, just needed a breather," I say as I say my hellos to the others around. Brady, who now has darker purple hair than before, screams in delight when she sees David, giving him a big hug saying, "I'm so happy to see you making it out tonight, I already saw some of your fan girls over there asking me where you were."

"Leave 'em there, I haven't even had a drink yet," David replies while I shove down a shot to him.

Brady has always been like the mother hen of our group in the Club, always looking out for our best interests and keeps her eyes and ears out for us at all times, which is a loyalty in itself.
Beep
"Moving to the dance floor now"

The bar hustling, we were all gathering around in a circular group standing together, buzzed, loud, and crowding in tighter. Brady and Autumn have brought three other girls from the salon with them, and there are also a couple guys here from CeCe's gym, Xander and Clay, ordering their drinks and floating to and from the dance floor. Dax says to me, "Don't look now but Lydia is entering the room."

Keeping my eyes on Dax, I say, "She knows better than to come find me tonight, I had to be pretty firm the last time she followed me out."

Brady sticks her nose in and says, "That won't stop her, she's dumber than a brick."

"What are we talking about," her friend Autumn turned back in towards us from talking to others, everyone so close there is no privacy.

Ronnie beside me is delighted to see this catch Autumn's attention, it is almost like I am giving him a wingman move here as he pokes fun at me to speak to his crush, "Declan has a regular Saturday night stage five clinger."

She smiles at my friend in a way I think he actually has a chance, then turns her face to me to reply, "I had one of those once, good luck with that."

Ronnie asks her something, but I didn't hear because Lydia has gotten her arm in between me and David, who is beside me not paying attention, so it gives her the space to squeeze in beside me.

Damnit

Lydia is not something else I want to have to deal with tonight, but it's clear I don't have a choice since her fingertips are already on my arm, and David finally turns to see my predicament.

He gives me a look right as Lydia says to me, "Hi Deck! Why aren't you wearing a tie?" Her question so annoying, that I just stood here ignoring her trying not to throw out an insult and moved my arm away. She reacted by scrunching up her face, causing her to look like a bird with her long beak.

Thinking I got saved by my friend, Dax chimes out loud, "Who the hell is that?" his chin lifted high peering over my shoulder.

Lydia puts her hand back on my arm and scolds my name in a whisper, while Xander and Dax simultaneously mutter a "wow," Dax adding, "it's like watching the parting of the Red Sea."

Clay, the youngest one in our mix speaks out, "I would love to part her sea."

I'm trying to turn and tell Lydia to get her hands off of me at the same time David stretches his arm across Lydia to grab my arm and yank me close to him, lightly pushing Lydia out from between us as fast as she weaseled her way in, like popping a pimple, the infection is gone now. Irritated as all get out, I step out looking at David's weird expression, while I hear Dax call to Tham to step over for service and Autumn now scream out loud, "My Maneater!"

Xander pipes in, "You know her? Fuck yeah!"

I finally get the chance to look past all the faces until I see. I felt my exhale slow, and once my lungs were deflated, everything in my body, every single part of my being, was focused on the girl shimmering in green in an outfit that has already made my cock twitch at a glance. The goddess of my dreams showing no mercy in her enchanting beauty. My girl. She doesn't see me, giving a polite smile as she glides through the crowd heading towards the bar, towards me. Autumn launches out in front of me shouting, "Lexi, how are you here?"

I'm looking hard wondering what the hell Alexis is wearing, growing angry watching all the men and women gaping at her glorious body. Looking up at Autumn, Alexis smiles and speaks but I am again bothered by the unwanted Lydia, during what couldn't be worse timing, as I contemplate calling Al to escort her out, she says to me, "Declan what's your problem?"
I ignore Lydia and end up calling out, "Alexis!"

She was still talking to Autumn and now Brady and hadn't noticed me until she heard me. Looking up, we locked eyes and stopped in our tracks, her mystified expression upon her face sends spine chilling down my back, while the clutter of people kept swiveling around us. I'm standing here with a drink in my hand with a good buzz until it all comes back to me, and I am beginning to realize how this looks.
"Declan?" She says my name in question, the same look I'm getting from a few other faces near me in wonderment.
I ask the obvious. "What are you doing here?"
"I'm here dancing," is all she says back to me while blinking.
"You told me you were working."
"I am working. Sabine is waiting for me on the dance floor."
"That's not working, why are you dressed like this?" I say now in question as my brain is on autopilot. I had never seen this type of sudden anger expressed in her now, making me shift uncomfortably while I wait for her to speak.

Her eyes wavering to meet mine, glancing to David, back to me, as she doesn't smile when she says, "So this is where you work, huh? It has really nicely graded dance flooring that helps with the resistance of your feet."
"Yes, this is where I work," I say adding gruffly, "Is that another reason why you're here?" My memory connecting her relationship with Autumn now has me guessing if she has known things about me all along, slowly drowning in what I do best and jump to conclusions, forecasting the threatening doom that multiplies forcing my instincts to protect myself.

Her face still perfection as she just gives me a quizzical look before being sidetracked by Ronnie's smooth entry, "Why, thank you very much," smiling at her in all our cloud of confusion like the compliment was really for him, stepping in to possibly help me out as I keep adding fuel to this fire. Ignoring me, she turns to him and asks, "Did you have something to do with that dance floor?"
He answers, "I may have had a lot to do with it. I'm Ronnie," he holds out his hand to her in greeting and she shakes it replying, "Nice to meet you, my name is Alexis or just Lexi is fine, you are friends with Autumn then?"
Stumping his cool face and I can't help but find that funny, I may have even laughed out a bit, blaming the fireball. Alexis blinks over to me, then back to Ronnie, while Autumn responds for us all, "Ronnie is actually one of the owners of this club, we know each other because my room mate, Brady," she puts her arm around Brady as the girls smile in their introductions, then adds telling Alexis, "Brady bartends here," turning towards to Ronnie beside her, "Lexi here runs a dance studio in Paisley," Autumn finishes, summing up all the intertwined webbing of the town. I can't do anything but stand here and watch as Alexis gets introduced to my best friend by someone other than myself.

Ronnie shoots a look to me with a quick smug smile as I try to step forward, only to have Lydia yell my name out from behind me again.

My nerves were quaking as I looked at Lydia and shouted at her, "Get the fuck away from me!" My reaction causing chaos to erupt, as Lydia finally takes the hint and storms away, all of us shifting around to let her through to leave. Not caring, I follow her opened path around to the side of Alexis who has skimmed her way forward, away from me, right when my speaker from my walkie talkie sounds out.

Beep

Right dancefloor

Cursing under my breath at the update on Vince while I follow Alexis to the bar, I listen as she orders two gin and tonics with Tham, then snag her side to pull her in close to my front, her face forward with an unreadable expression, her strand of silver taunting me with its sparkle. "Alexis, I'm sorry, can we go talk please," my words a quiet plea to her side as I took in the smell of her perfume and my hands holding her waist firm, all I can do is stare at the side of her face. She finally turns my way, her emeralds shimmering in neon when they meet mine, while Tham places two cocktails in front of her topped with slices of lime. She grabs the two drinks and twists around pulling away from me, and I can't stop talking, my knees are shaking in panic, my need for her all I can render, ignoring the people all around us I keep on, "Baby, please, where are you going?"

"I've got to run back to Sabine, or she is going to think I got kidnapped, can we walk and talk if that's okay?" She says it with her little steps getting further ahead, making me respond saying, "Can you find her and then come right back?"

"No, I told you I am working so if you want to talk, I'll be on the dance floor."

"I can't go on the dance floor," I reply back quickly since there are arms rubbing all over me following her through this crowd.

She questions me, "Can't or won't?"

"Does it matter?" I reply.

"I don't know Declan, I guess that depends on how bad you want to talk to me," shimmying her small frame through the last few feet before entering into the sea of dancers being lit up, I stop to watch the curve of her ass as the last of her I see.

"Fuck!" I shout in my anger while turning back around on my heel and head back to the bar. Dax walking up to me, "I thought you were about to go in for a minute there, I had to come make sure, so that is the girl your seeing?"

"Yes, but now it's complicated," I say walking back up to my group, gesturing to Tham to pour me another drink while I think and drink. Xander and Clay moved down the bar and Brady leads Autumn away to the dance floor, leaving me with just the guys surrounding me.

David being the first to say, "Well, I think that went well."

"Just great!" I shout back sarcastically. Ronnie snipping in, "Hey calm down, this isn't the greatest night to blow shit up, what did she say?"

"She had to rush back to her friend on the dance floor," saying this like it should sound like everyone should understand why that would make me crazy. But instead, David yells, "Well go out there and talk to her then!"

Temper flaring, my fog has silenced the noise around me. I separate myself to try to find her in my mind, needing to see the girl capable of cracking me open.

"Can someone tell me why this turned into a big problem?" Ronnie asks, his eyes squared on me.

"She thought I was a bartender," switching my brain into recovery mode, I grab my walkie talkie, "Al, I need an update now!"

"Okay first off, go tell her you're the owner. Bam, problem solved," Ronnie says.

Beep

My heart feels like it dropped down with my last beat thumping harder fueling me, as the overhead speaker's blast through the club with an Imagine Dragons song that isn't helping me focus on this walkie talkie.

"Still on the dancefloor, Boss"

"I need to know who is surrounding him," I shout.

Beep
"Uh, hold on."

Another voice comes through the line, *"Boomer and lots of females."*
Pissed off, I scream through the mic, "What females? I need details."

Ronnie butts in, "Alright I'm going to just go out there myself, we can't be causing a scene like this."

Beep
"Blonde girl that arrived in the same group as him
And...
Approaching another set of women, I'm not sure if he knows, blonde and brunette."

I throw my arm up, "I've got this," stalking past them, I throw my hand through my hair a couple times as I weave in and out of the dancers to hunt down my siren. It wasn't hard to find her, the electricity too strong to miss as I catch a glimpse of her across the crowd.

Watching her every move while I weave my way in and out of the crowd toward her. Her body oscillates up and down to the beat, flawless, the sexiest vision added to my Club. I was in a trance until I see my demons attack her from the other side, the face of pure beauty meeting the ugliest part of me before I was ready, before I knew how much she mattered, before I could get to her in time, his hands snaked down the side of her body. Appearing angry, she looked back to see him and tried to pull herself away with her friend helping her, but when he leaned into Alexis to tell her something in her ear, too close, and while I watched her flinch in fear, I saw red.

At my breaking point, I come up in surprise from around her back, leaning my weight on my front foot for my body to cover her while I barrel myself in the side of Vince, grabbing her body away from him in one solid swipe, pressing myself tight against her listening to her rapid breaths and cries while I pick her up, her legs diving into place against me.

She shrieked, "What the hell are you doing?" Her arms tightening around me, giving me the means I needed, breathing her in, our way, and my heart beats steadier in the matter of seconds, giving me the momentum to turn to face him holding her in my arms.

I was steady when I set my sights on him, Vince Bordeaux bulging out of a tight satin button up with his smug look, even though the energy from our connected glares is crackling with tension feeling like fragments of our past started exploding over our feet,

Vince yells out, "You ok there, Feisty?"

"She's doing a hell of a lot better now that she's gotten the fuck away from you," I yell out while I turn from the scene of club goers back towards the bar with her friend, Sabine appearing to have had a few drinks already tonight trailing in her corset by my side, in bewildered silence, as I lead us out of this crowded arena. Alexis is my light, being tricked by my dark in front of my eyes, and protecting her, whisking her away, is the only thing I can do right now.

Keeping close in her hold around me with her head on my shoulder, Alexis starts making agitated sounds that reverberate through our connected chests while I find a safe area, far away from him, to set her down.

"Declan works here?" Sabine questions to Alexis once we get out of the noisier section of the club as I answer her for myself, "Yes, Declan does."

I walk up to a wall of muscle leaning on the bar, gaping at us as we reach back to my friends. Our friends, apparently. David was about to say something to me until he looked beside me at Sabine and back to Alexis who I was still holding, fixed back on Sabine and not her eyes.

I place Alexis down and Dax says to her in a huge grin, "He just went out on the dance floor for you, do you even realize the power in your possession right now" like it was the most exciting thing about his night.

I made a mistake putting her down as the ogling eyes were all around getting a piece. I grab onto her hands, and speak, "We need to talk, it can't be out there with him."

"Somebody better start talking because I was just getting a good buzz until Rambo started dancing with us."

"Rambo?" David asks Sabine.

But she ignored him instead, saying, "Well shit here he comes now."

Sure enough, stepping towards us in his typical arrogant way, with three other husky men trailing behind him, not looking twice at anyone and only putting his eyes on Alexis as he approaches, Ronnie being the first to step in front of Vince and ask, "You've come far enough, I thought you weren't here to cause any trouble tonight?"

I let go of Alexis and guided her behind me watching out as Vince gives Ronnie a quick cocky smile, then took it back just as quick, returning to his thin lips in a straight line, stating, "Look the whole gang is all here, I've been wanting to get us all back together again, I didn't know it would be quite as exciting as this," pausing to add, "Feisty, if you need a helping hand, all you have to do is ask."

Alexis speaks out to Vince, "Piss off! I don't know why you want to cause trouble everywhere you go.

I snap at her in question. "How the hell do you know him?"

While David steps beside Ronnie, Dax stays close to Alexis, Sabine, and I. Alexis then looks at me while seemingly working on her own raging anger within herself, "He is just some jerk from the gym."

Vince makes a step forward to her, but was blocked, by David and Ronnie, spitting out,

"Feisty is my gym partner."

"No, I am not!" Alexis screams back to him, causing him to rumble out a low laugh, while Sabine darts her tiny frame through Ronnie and David in one beat, getting herself in Vince's face and somehow in a gentle tone say, "I don't know who you are but you need to back the fuck off," David reaches around her waist to pull her back while she keeps on, "you are spoiling a really good buzz I had going on!"

"Aw, Feisty has a feisty friend too," Vince lightly blurts out across all our heads, just as Al and his team show up in a fierce force surrounding Vince and his friends, causing a giant scene on one of the most popular nights.

I taste the sulfur in my mouth when I look at Vince and say, "I heard you were looking for me, Bordeaux! Well, you found me, in my club of all the places, imagine that, now what the fuck do you want?"

His smug keeps on as he starts laughing harder looking between me and the security team beside him, "You always do seem to get in the middle of things that don't involve you, Irish."

"Tisk, Tisk," I thought you would have learned your lesson by now to not butt into other people's business, this should prove quite interesting to watch for me, then."

I pounce in front of Vince, who is hard and cool, and scream my bloody rage in his face, buckling my arms straight down in front, "The only thing you are about to be watching is another knock out from my fist into your face, you piece of shit!"

I keep on in my boiled rage, "What's wrong?"

I spit at him, "Do'ya need my fist to help you gain exposure again? I'll beat the ever-living shit out of you again any day of the week."

Vince touts back, "Simmer down Irish, you aren't worth the time or money for another fight to anybody. You're like a secondhand fighter now that you've become a lazy businessman, you lost your seat."

Ronnie interjects, "You have five seconds to cut to the chase before I throw you out of here myself."

David, Ronnie, and I stand tall in front of Vince, the security team using their own bodies as a barrier to block the view from the onlookers in the crowd. I thought I knew what was coming to me, another fight I would have to train and strengthen for to put an end to this constant battle and give him the grudge match people deserve to see. Life turns the lights out on me sometimes.

Vince's eyes are searing into mine, "I hope you have taught your younger brother how to fight better."

Then he turns his head to David and speaks out a nightmare only my worst enemy would lay on me.

But isn't this who I am standing with, my worst enemy?

"Little Irish," his incisor teeth crooked in his smile, while I snap.

Pushing Vince as hard as I can away from the front of my brother, stalking and roaring, "DON'T YOU DARE!"

Our aggression thrown around in elbows as the team buckles him down and Ronnie and Dax come around to hold me back while David stands there with s smirk on his face saying, "I've been waiting a long time for this."

"No, David!" I shout at my little brother like we were the only ones in the house that he was about to torch, yelling out my cries of panic, to try and stop from having to watch another one of my brothers shake hands with this devil. But fate can be cruel because it was too late. David was the first hand to reach out, grinning with a face of pure happiness, as Vince returned the same right back, sealing a deal of a future Grudge Match against each other.

Chapter 22   Alexis

All I want to do is take these shoes off, and this itchy fabric off, and go home to my sweats, and my dog, and for now, that is as far as I'm going to stretch myself, because I've already been plowed over enough tonight. Instead, I'm trying to connect some dots in my brain while standing next to one of the large speakers, in an unauthorized zone of the Club's side stage near the DJ, letting the vibrations literally rattle through me. My tongue is tingling from both the alcohol and the speaker's noise. Sabine has perched herself across from me, leaning on the wall sipping on her cocktail while she scream chats back and forth with me. She is mostly laughing hysterically every few minutes and then chatty the other part of the time, but I can't hear a word she is saying, which is why I think she is laughing so much.

I couldn't sit at the bar with people staring me down any longer, and the last thing I wanted to do was sit in a sea of people's words, comments, and opinions, so when the blockade of giant men started pushing everyone back, I ran and Sabine followed, keeping me entertained through it all as she has come out of her shell once the liquor hit her, swearing this is her first time being drunk in a bar. A memorable night as one of her firsts for her I'm sure. She somehow stepped in for Rachel tonight, gutting me at just that description my mind has drawn out, but really thankful I have found a person in Paisley who stood by my side through every weak moment I felt in Declan's obvious world, I would be lost without her. Instead, I'm pretty sure I am lost with her hiding out. When I saw Declan tonight, not behind a bar, I panicked in sheer shock of not only seeing him, but he wasn't even behind a bar, rather socializing.

Then there was that girl.

Breathe

I thought I was mad. I was more so embarrassed feeling like an outcast standing in front of Declan, obviously not meant to be a part of his night, his lie stinging me. I've decided it's best to tune it all out and try vibrating the overwhelming feelings out with more powerful levels of volume that help numb it all. I'm wondering if this second storm between us was meant to pop in, this time we aren't shielded under a bridge.

It's been about half an hour since we escaped, walking over to Sabine feeling able to think a bit better, she gives me one of her happy smiles, some loose strands of her blonde hair from her up do have fallen across her neck, the pink in her cheeks makes her glow warm, and all I can do is reach out to hug her. She throws her arms around me, and I sink my face into her naked bony flesh across her shoulder. I don't cry. I can't cry over anything that isn't about Rachel anymore.

"Do you want to leave? I can call a cab and we can sneak through the other side to get out of here," she whispers to me while she plays with my hair, my weakness during a comforting hold.

"I think that is a good idea," I answer back, pulling back and looking into her blue eyes I ask, "Why do you think Declan pulled me away from that guy so fast?"

"That Vince guy was the one you were telling me about from the gym, did you tell Declan about him too?"

"No," is all I can say while she continues helping me talk this through for the first time,

"So, you bumped into Declan when you left to go get drinks?" I nod my yes as she gives me a look of understanding how this may be turning out, but she keeps focused saying, "You deserve answers from him, and this is going to be awkward when he finds out you are going to be working in here preparing for the show."

"Shit!" I scream, forgetting all about the real reason I was even here tonight, I will be the new choreographer for SheerMe's show that will be taking place at Swollen, Declan's workplace. Just then, someone found us in our hideout, the other blonde guy that was with Declan tonight.

"Hey girls, what are you doing back here?"

He approaches us with a stern look on his face.

I reply saying, "Hi, we were just finding some peace."

"Look, I'm sorry about all of that earlier, but you can't be in staff quarters so it's time to find peace somewhere else." He says it to us acting like he doesn't recognize who we are, like we are just regular partygoers breaking the rules.

"Excuse me?" Sabine questions his rudeness.

I pipe in before he can respond in anger, "We weren't trying to piss anyone off by being back here. Where is Declan and who are you, anyway?"

He replies, "It looks like you have done a good job already helping piss him off tonight." The easy going I saw on this man earlier, the one who looked at me in awe after Declan grabbed me out of the dance floor, this guy has turned into a broody, stinging me with his words and forcing me to react.

"Are you kidding me right now? I have nothing to do with whatever argument you and your boxing buddies have going on!"

"You come into Declan's work dressed like that," he exclaims eyeing our lingerie outfits, "and decide to grind on the dancefloor with your fucking gym partner?"

Sabine screams, "Whoa, hang on, buddy!"

Finding my calmest demeanor deep, deep, deep, within my inner depths, I respond, "I'm not sure how you may have been led to that sort of idiotic delusion, but whoever you are, you have no right to come pick a fight and boss us around after what just happened out there."

"Actually I do, I'm Dax, I own this place, and this is not the night to cause anymore trouble," he says stretching out his hand to me, giving me a second to remind myself I am not a coward, which is what it would look like if I refused to shake this man's hand.

So, using my mature professional rationality, and to his surprise, I reach out and shake his hand in return speaking, "I'm Alexis, nice to formally meet you, Dax Morgan."

"Funny he tells me nothing about you, but you know my full name."

I give him a big fake smile, still shaking his hand and reply, "Oh no, don't flatter yourself, He didn't tell me anything about you either."

Dax lets go of my hand; all of our faces still angry as we all start walking back towards the bar area we came from.

His stride fast but Sabine and I keep up, Dax still seething, "So you researched the club, figured out he was an owner and not a bartender, and decided to come confront him about it?"

"Declan is an owner?" The question coming out of my mouth before I could think about it, my mind spinning now in this new information on my mysterious prince. Sabine gives me a look mirroring my 'holy shit' reaction as the now cynical Dax laughs out as if that is his answer for me, like I had known, that idea causing this easygoing friend to change the script.

"Anyways, I just got you a ride out front, it's probably best if you head out of here tonight," he says as we round the corner and through the bar patrons to reach the familiar group of faces, including Declan sitting at the bar, empty shot glasses in front of him. He is slouched on his elbow, but when he sees me, his eyes a deep blue of sadness look away, shading me.

Ronnie turns and gives me a wide look of surprise, "Hey, we thought you left."

I reply, "No, but it seems like now we are getting kicked out," I manage a rude smile for him as he looks to Dax and then back to me to respond, "Listen, it's just a really bad night for everyone, including a business deal we've been working on that is based on how tonight runs in front of some important people, which as you can probably tell, it couldn't get much worse for us."

Declan stumbles up behind Ronnie stating, "Alexis, please... I'll talk to you later."

My heart on fire, melting in my anger, bitter and sad, I am not going to hide who I am in my new normal. I deserve more respect than this in my new town, from Declan, and if this is my initiation into this world, I'm going to take it with some dignity. Sabine tightens her lips beside me as I look at Dax and give him a smug chuckle, then to Ronnie, blurring out Declan from the background I question,

"A big business deal, huh?"

"And you think my personal agenda with Declan is why I'm here tonight?"

Ronnie gives me a confused pissed look and bites back, "This is about business, sweetheart, it's nothing personal. But if you care at all for this man here, you'll do him the favor and leave."

"Well, I think I'm going to do all of us a favor tonight and excuse all of you guys for your fucking ignorant arrogance," I say turning my stares at them all in front of me and land my sights on Declan when I tell him loudly, "I have been nothing but honest with you and I would never come hunt you down like a moron. This happens to be about business for us as well," pinning my eyes back on Ronnie, "I'm Alexis Andrews, the new choreographer for the SheerMe show wanting to take place in your club this year."

Dropped mouths and the sounds of exasperations were the background noise Declan's solo cry as I hear him grumble loudly as he slumps down Ronnie's back. Taking this moment, I don't even wait through their shocked silence as I grab Sabine's arm and start storming out.

Sabine turns back around to shout, "And that's why we are dancing in lingerie you idiots!"

Her delighted laughter bringing out mine as we run out the front doors to be beat with cold wind.

"We just threw the last punches of the night in a group of hot asshole boxers, how fucking awesome are we right now?"

Sabine trying to see the best of our horrible night, as she adds, "I think we knocked them out, I wish I could have taken a picture of their faces," laughing some more as she pulls her phone out of her chest and starts scrolling for a ride. It's freezing, we are wearing nothing but our heals and this lingerie trying to get as far away from this Club as fast as possible, the chill helping us pick up the speed in our steps.

"Shit, ok it looks like there is a ride available in four minutes, hope we don't freeze to death."

"It wouldn't be the worst thing that could happen to me right now," I say my breath in the air, my nipples a solid peak in their chill, adding my worry, "Declan looked miserable."

"He had a rough night, but it sounded to me like they are fighting rivals, and you just got caught in the middle of it. That was fucking rude of him to assume you were there to call him out for not being a bartender, though."

Looking at her as we find our stopping point to huddle down on the curb together, I say, "I don't know why, but I trusted Declan. I don't know why he felt so angry about me being there, yet he has given me nothing about himself in return. I thought I was going to just give him the time, but I don't think that's a smart thing to do anymore. Especially now that work is involved. Maybe this was all just meant to be," the sadness in my voice trailing in the bitter wind. It's the worst ending of my happy new normal I thought I was in the midst of, but another somber reality hit me to remind me I'm still alone and I was never enough.

"I think you need to give yourself some time to think more about it, unfortunately, tonight isn't going to end with anymore answers," Sabine says still trying to keep making me feel better, "Did you see David? God, that guy is so damn hot."

Laughing I answer, "Yes, and I think you are absolutely crazy if you think he didn't notice you tonight!"

"When he put his arms around me for those 2.5 seconds, it was magical," she says in a dreamy state, making me even more sad and jealous my Declan is not really mine.

He was never mine to begin with.

Chapter 23   Alexis

I have cried so much throughout the night, telling myself over and over again that it was because I missed Rachel. Then my hurt turned to anger and blame, these tears, and this pain, this is all her fault. The night Rachel convinced me to go without her to that Spin class in my old part of town, which was her fault. She signed the both of us up for the class a month prior, telling me we needed to go because one of my old favorite teachers from high school was leading it. Only to tell me that night she couldn't go because her baby toe was bothering her, but I had to because she had paid for the class and already had a ride waiting. That night, that lie, that was her fault, and that is why I have cried so much tonight.

That night, I came home from that Spin class to her dead body underneath a sheet. That memory of that day is the reason I must have been crying so much, it is her fault. She did this to me, it was her choices she made for me that left me now constantly heartbroken, and in so much pain. There were so many times throughout Rachel's life, when she would be experiencing one of her low episodes that would cause her to lay around for days in her sad silence, resisting all the helping hands that always reached for her, including mine and Jameson's, turning down all the offers we could give to make her pain go away. Now that she is gone, my body is feeling its own version of PTSD, it is her fault I've been left with a share of her earthly suffering.

My conscience is trying hard to convince me otherwise, like it has a loyalty to Rachel somehow and it wants to go against what I want, and stick up for her, and try to convince me that these tears are not all her fault. Nightmares of her begging me to go without her, turn into nightmares of her begging me to realize who my tears are really for, the man that stumbled down in pain, the only warmth I have ever felt all over in one touch cursed in his own demons and made me look like the unworthy fool.

Go home, get away from me, you don't deserve to know what everyone else here obviously knows, I just screwed your brains out, but you don't deserve to dance here. You don't deserve my eye contact any more, you aren't even going to get one last touch.

Sabine is on my couch in my living room, deciding she couldn't go home since she still lives with her father, and he would be furious if he saw her being 'a drunk slut.' She was so pleased with herself sinking into the couch she had chosen. She got comfy and was sound asleep before I locked up, probably dreaming about David.

Awake and drained, I went for a second hot shower to clean off the night, thinking I could scrub it all away with my loofa, only to cry more tears down the drain with the bubbles.

Misery and no company. Until I did, a knock on the bathroom door had me jolt myself upright and dry away my tears.

"Lexi, I'm sorry to bother you, but your neighbor, Margie, is out front asking to see you," Sabine calls out from behind the door. I dressed in a hurry, knowing Sabine was likely getting an earful from Margie while waiting for me, and found the two of them standing near my kitchen counter. Margie looked put together this early Sunday morning, wearing a long thick coat over her casual shirt and slacks, while Sabine looked a bit of a mess in my loaner oversize sweats.

"Good morning Alexis," Margie cries out and comes over to place her cold hands on either side of my face asking, "I wanted to come see if you wanted to join me to check on my bees this morning?

"Oh, thank you Margie but I'm sorry, I can't. Sabine and I were up quite late last night, and I don't think I'm feeling up for much of anything today," I say as Margie's eyeballs are fluttering all over my face, studying it with a frown.

"You look sick, Lexi," the back of her hand lands on my forehead as she continues to voice her concerns, "Your eyes are so red, honey, are you alright?"

I take a hold of her hand and manage to rummage up a smile to tell her a partial truth, "I just didn't sleep too well is all. Sabine and I are about to sign our lives away this morning because we are taking on a really big job for a choreographing and performance piece, so I was a bit stressed out."

Margie's face of concern didn't waver as she said, "Will that interrupt any of our dinner nights?"

"I am still going to need to be nourished during the week, but my portion intake has got to be cut down or I will have to end up cancelling." Margie finally gives me another sweet smile while she starts heading back towards the front door.

She says, "Alright, if you need anything at all let us know, I will see you for sure on Thursday evening," then she walks out through the door, leaving me to be strung again by the thought of Declan and how I'm going to have to explain to Margie why he won't be joining us for dinners anymore.

Closing the door in that reminder, I'm left to turn back to see a cheerful Sabine smiling to say, "Good morning Sunshine, are you ready to sign, because your phone that you insisted on not checking and leaving on silent is sitting on the coffee table with a lot of missed calls from Jameson."

"I'm ready to sign, and you know that's normal for him, right?"

Sabine cheers and jumps high in the air, terribly happy this early after our wreckage of a night, then chuckles stating, "Jameson is sexy as sin, but impatient as all get out."

I laugh thinking at her honest judgement based off just a relationship from a screen, one that has much truth behind it, especially since he feels like he has no boundaries when it comes to me, always barreling through when he needs me at once. Rachel used to tell me I babied him too much, but it has never bothered me the way others have always assumed. Bothersome yes, but it is the past behind the scenes of it that I allow for him and myself to have a mutual understanding, which erases the mindset of boundaries when it comes to reaching out to one another with any immediate needs. We both grew up in a poor, lonely, dark world and when you find someone loyal you can call in a tough spot, we would use his long-distance ranged walkie talkies, to reach between our apartments back and forth, a bit of static but clear enough to hear. He would practice singing to me some nights over the walkie talkies, I think I was almost forced to listen back then, he always talked to himself out loud in between songs, correcting his verses and repeating the melodies until he felt like he sang the whole song well enough to go to bed. Always trying to perfect what he does since we were kids, with nobody pushing him to do it, or critiquing his every move, but himself.

While I turn on my kettle to heat water up for tea, Sabine joins me in the kitchen to eat some breakfast before we sign our official contracts.

"Lexi, I have to ask, why are you and Jameson not together as a couple?"

I laugh out at her question, bringing me my first real smile in many hours as I tell her, "No, Jameson is my friend, and he isn't the one for me. I don't feel any desire to jump his bones."

"But have you ever jumped his bones?"

I stir my teabag all around while I give her my poker face look that I have distinctly created for this specific question I've been asked too many times to count in my friendship with Jameson. The suspense causing her to break out of her seat, "Come on!"

"It's a no!" I cheer out, while she gives me a face of dislike, then I add another cheer, "but I have definitely seen it! Honestly, our relationship was so fragile to each of us, and it's like that sexual attraction part was never a thing between us."

Sabine replied, "That is boring. But I will say, I would think you were a total liar if you were about to tell me you have never seen it!" Her face grows a bit more serious, and she says, "Maybe you should at least check your phone to see if Declan reached out to you before we sign these papers, we had a pretty terrible night. Hold on," she swivels out of her chair, "I'm going to get it for you right now," she says as she picks it up and brings it over to me.

I feel nauseous with this, and she sees it in my face.

Whiplash

I open up to a screen of notifications and say, "I have five, only five, missed calls from," scrolling through trying to be brave as I read aloud, "Jameson called me...all four of those times, and I have a one from Declan."

My heart skipped a beat when I played my last sentence on rewind.

Sabine asks, "Holy crap, are you going to call him back?"

"No," I say unclearly staring at my phone details to finish telling her, "The call was from last night, but the time says 11:48pm, and we were still there then, weren't we?"

Sabine already hunting on her phone replies, "Yes, we were. I didn't get the ride until 12:51am. So, that would have put us by the speakers."

I give her a skeptical look when I ask, "Do you think he was trying to find me and kick me out?" Wishing it was an angry feeling that was crippling me now, it hurts to even think, I'm sad and disappointed.

Always trying to be positive, Sabine replies, "Or maybe that fight ended faster than we thought, and he was just looking for you?"

"Why would he do that? He wouldn't even look at me and it was only about thirty minutes later?"

"Maybe you should call him and find out." I don't answer her because my mind seems to have not come up with one yet. I was a definite 'no' a second ago and now this magical device has given me a message out of its universe and switched my thoughts to default mode. I missed him already, I had that ache in my stomach that felt like pins.

I confess to Sabine my honest worry, "I want to sign this SheerMe contract before I throw up and avoid it altogether."

I was proud of my signature on the line today, and after a bit of celebrating with laughs on FaceTime with Kel and Jameson, and keeping our mouths shut about what happened at Swollen last night, I had to apply some of my beauty strips for my puffy eyes after Sabine went home, leaving me to take my Sunday nap by myself.

It was Rachel's fault that I woke up in a dizzy, scattered mess and fell out of my bed, leaving me with only a bruised ego, because the first thing that popped into my head when I opened my eyes on the floor, was the memory of checking for Rachel's documents for her passport in my speaker at my studio. I packed my overnight bag and my dog, and we made it in, right before the last bit of evening glow. When I dropped off my stuff upstairs in the loft and Luna got snuggled in the pillows, I remembered to pick up the frame from underneath my bed and take it down with me back to my Mixx room. I found my secret speaker that is really a safe and opened it up.

Sure enough, it was like opening up a treasure box, another piece of Rachel's puzzle. Neatly clipped together was her paper passport paperwork, but also, placed underneath her papers is her old childhood jewelry box that I've only heard Rachel talk about, and never actually seen. Holding it up, remembering the story of her father, B.B., giving this to her for her birthday when she was a little girl. He had come into her bedroom at the end of the night, to read her a story, and brought out this jewelry box for her as a surprise gift, telling Rachel it was special, like a magical box that only worked when she used her powers, as his shining star, telling her to keep it safe no matter what. A handcrafted box painted navy blue and covered in white shimmering stars, and the dancing ballerina that goes round and round to the melody in her circle, is dressed in costume as a Queen Bee.

As the story of the jewelry box went, Terrie had spotted Rachel playing with one of the pins from inside, and freaked out, demanding to know where she got them, telling her they were dangerous. Rachel lied and told her she found the pins in her daddy's bedroom, then went running to hide the box underneath her pillows for safe keeping. That's where the box was kept away from Terrie for many years, with the help from one particular maid's teenage daughter, Vienna, who had formed a special bond to Rachel while spending time in the house, waiting for her mother to finish work. Rachel used to tell me that she had to act like a persistent brat when demanding to the cleaning staff that Vienna, who wasn't even a worker, was the only one who was allowed to make her bed. She said Vienna always did it for her, keeping her loyal secret and tucking the box as far back under the pillows as she could.

Another low blow for Rachel when her father passed away, her mother firing all the familiar staff once she had the authority, never being able to see Vienna again, or the jewelry box she took with her for safe keeping when she left for good.

I opened it up to seek the tiny dancer, and to my surprise, there is a sticky note stuck with tape underneath the lid with more written words in purple ink.

If I made you a jewelry box, it would be you dancing inside.
If I had to pick one song, it would be Billy Joel's, "Just the Way You Are."
I will always be with you, fluttering around beside you dancing, wearing my new pair of wings I found in Paisley.

More stingers attack my soul, and I blame my Queen.

I am trying to organize whatever I could of Rachel's that I had, scrambling all of the pieces of her puzzle and sorting them out in front of me to see if there is a starting point here. Trying to figure out if I can find the first piece. All I had of her, besides my memories and what she has fortuned to me, are laying right in front of me. I was forbidden to enter Rachel's condo the day it happened, Terrie taking everything from inside and not allowing me or Jameson to even look for one last time. Her secretly leaving me this personal possession was purposeful, I was right where she wanted me to be, I know it, and I can feel that she knows it too in my teardrops now, every one of them shedding a different memory of our time together, a portal to connect with her soul.

My own small soul thumping out to take back control of ownership, stepping away from the puzzle and stripping down to my favorite bra with support, switching on the overhead lights of the dance floor and adding in a strobe light for effect, I scrolled to find the famous song to blast on repeat. Needing to move and create, I press record on my video camera, and wait for the swirl to pick me up. Warming up in a slow rocking of my shoulders, I tried to close my eyes and focus on the sounds I could hear other than the song burning me. My heartbeat thumping, the sound of my breaths, catching right at the loop of the 'J', before it reverses back up, missing while trying to connect in a controlled circle, loud and enhanced by the still, a thundering wave. I only see my movements from the inside out, tossing around capturing the colors and throwing them in steps on the floor. Fast, slow, jerky, confused in a world of greens and blues.

Writhing, rolling, throat on fire
A can of waste
A can to taste
Knowing her was my last desire

Rachel knew I would listen, I always did. I'm trying to hear what she is saying, and why it matters so much, and why she didn't just tell me instead of this puzzle.
Slowing down from my tears, my heart skipped at a different beat when my ears centered in on a new sound over the speakers. Another familiar rumble that I have obviously become partial to, because as it picks up and gets closer, I can't help but stay fixated in place.
Declan's motorcycle.
The snow is melted on the roads, only leaving dirty slush on the sides. I dance in a soft slow movement while I try to absorb his arrival. I can't help but wonder if he came back now that his Club is set for the show, a mutual working relationship we will have to agree to. In this little time of knowing him, I let him in too deep, because even with my lack of sleep and constant tears today, I can still feel him watching me. His power too much for my weak body, I can't help but stumble over to cradle my body, falling on my butt in exhaustion, heartbroken over Declan. This isn't Rachel's fault.
I hear the pounding on my front door now, and I can't move. The show, Rachel's pieces, her song for me, Declan is here, and there is no way I can move anymore today. Positioned ready for a tornado drill, head down and my legs are frozen.
My body has a word for me right now, 'done.'

The pounding gets louder and louder and faster and faster until I hear Luna start barking from upstairs, running down. Billy Joel blasting over while the chaos inside my studio erupts, the chaos inside of me erupts.

I hear him screaming my name, always my full first name with a lilt from his slight accent, I even think I feel his warmth, but I still can't move.

"Alexis!" he cries it out in a scared panic, "Alexis!"

My shell, on his knee's inches next to me now, laying his hands on my hunched over shoulders as he speaks over the back of my head, his breath hot,

"Please, baby…"

"Please!"

"Are you Okay?"

His thumbs move back and forth in tender digs with his hand's soft grip, and I'm soaking it in trying to not believe this may be my last warm touch.

I hear him mutter something and then leave my side quickly, sending a breeze smelling like my man goodness to chill me when he blasts away.

A minute felt like two. And two minutes has been pure torture in my cradled madness, but silence finally falls still in the room, and my shell has come back to me again. This time he comes over to swoop me in his arms.

I turned my solemn face away as I curled into him, his body encasing me once again as we start moving, I squeeze him tighter with each step up.

Don't let me go

Don't let me go

With my legs using mutant strength wrapped around his waist, he lays his knee on the bed, keeping me attached exactly the way I am, guiding us onto my bed, together, holding on, breath on breath. He reaches his fingers to start pushing my hair back from my face, my nerves keeping my eyes closed holding in my tears.

"I'm here whether you want me to be or not. So…" his voice cracked a bit in his words causing a slight pause before he continues, "Alexis I'm not trying to scare you, I have no intention of ever hurting you, I swear, but if you are scared of me now, I'll leave."

I knew I heard him correctly, but it still took me a second to process the meaning behind his words, his question, his apology, his plea. It caused me to open my eyes. Blurring with the moisture and light, I wipe away my tears with my hand as he also strokes his thumbs over my cheeks. The most handsome face in front of me also looking stained in sadness and worry, as our eyes meet in their moment of truth.

"You hurt me," I muster up to say plainly to him, his eyes warm with emotion looking into me like they always have.

"I didn't think about how stupid it was of me to not tell you about my part in owning the club. I was planning on telling you today during our nap we missed."

I pipe in to clear that up, "you missed," causing a small smile to come out of him.

Declan replies, "I missed because I've been recovering on my office floor all day." "I've been an idiot in my life for more times I care to remember, and last night might have topped the cake," "but, baby," the splash of pain in his eyes as he continues to say, "when I saw you with Vince, I lost my bloody mind. I am really sorry you had to see that. I'm so sorry I scared you."

"Would you stop saying that! It was like, a second, and then I knew it was you," I reply, rejecting his apology about scaring me and feeling even worse that he hasn't really apologized for the display of pure humiliation.

His hand stopped stroking my forehead as he squints his eyes to me and asks, "Come again?"

"I was a bit drunk, so it took me a longer second to realize it was you that had grabbed me away."

Again, giving me an unreadable expression, he says, "Okay well that's good, but I'm trying to tell you I am sorry you had to see that part of me, that mad, angry aggression that made you run away."

"Run away?" My irritation in my questioning,

"Pushed away?"

"Kicked out?"

"I wouldn't quite say I ran away," I finish ending my rant for now. Moving closer above me, he says, "I didn't know that happened until this morning and I'm sorry and I'll get to that, but wait,"

"Are you maybe saying I didn't scare you away?" "Because the last thing I want is for you to be afraid of me over my boxing."

"No, you don't scare me. Your boxing has nothing to do with why I left. Realizing I am again the one giving away answers, I revert replying, "What does any of that matter, now?"

"Scare me or not, it still doesn't change the fact that you lied about working when you were out with other girls and friends. I know we hardly know each other, and I am not asking you to tell me anything, but you made me look like a complete fool last night. I know nothing about you but lies."

He pulls me in a squeeze, we are attaching as much as we can while we can, "It was stupid of me not to tell you that I own Swollen with my best friends, Dax and Ronnie. I am most definitely not a bartender, and I'm sorry I wasn't honest about it. It was a big night and we let our female staff have off too, so that's why I felt like I had to be there to watch over things. I did a fantastic job didn't I? I should have told you about it and maybe all of this wouldn't have ever happened."

Blues sinking into my soul as he continues his honesty, "That girl, her name is Lydia, and before I knew you existed I had lousy sex with her once, a couple months ago, that's all.

My chest aches in the thought of his feeling towards someone else, I ask, "But you still see her?"

"No, not like that, if you think I am that stupid, maybe I have a lot longer to go than I thought to get you back," he said chuckling a bit and adding, "you are the only one I want. She means nothing to me, and I kept telling her that, and repeating myself over again, that we had no relationship and she needed to leave me alone, but she never did. And last night when I saw you, she was trying to talk to me again and I lost my cool."

I had to ask, "Is that the truth?"

"Yes. I won't lie to you about that. I won't be dishonest to you." He strokes his thumb down my cheek, warm and soft, while we approach filling in holes from our night, colliding together to redraw a different picture than the one we both saw before.

Gently pulling back, he asks, "Will you tell me how you know him?"

"Who?"

"Vince, the guy you were dancing with, he acted like he knew you."

Once I thought about the confrontation before we were pushed back last night, it was easy to figure out that Declan and Vince had a fighting history.

"He hit on me at the gym the other day, he was really rude but that's it because I walked away." Declan growls with lips hard pressed. His outward jealousy making me hot for him instead of pissing me off, so I keep talking, "Then he came up to me while I was dancing to try to talk me up again, I guess, then you were there," and since we are giving out truth serum I add, " and I don't know why you hate him so much but I could have handled it myself if you would have let me. I don't see faces on the dance floor."

A new shade of blue looks into me, "I want you to be safe and stay away from him, did he know you knew me?"

"No, why would I know you knew him if you've never told me?"

He takes a deep breath when he says, "I thought you heard from all the people talking about it," looking at me harder now to make sure I'm not lying to him.

He keeps on, "I thought your hairdresser friend might have figured out from Brady what was going on and told you about my history with him, I figured I scared you in my rage and thought that's why you ran away?"

"I ran away to the speakers because I was mad and confused and trying to get away, so I didn't have to talk to anybody. Then I was kicked out."

"You love a good speaker," he jokes sweetly, to then switch to curses under his breath.

Connecting his blues to my greens, he says, "I just assumed. I'm sorry for that."

Then he adds lifting my chin, "Baby, there is a story to tell. But first, I think you need to drink some water," reaching up, he turns on the table lamp to bring a new glow to the room. He's off the bed in a single movement, my eyes are forced to watch while he gets up and jogs down the stairs. I'm not moving my sights off the doorframe. To my delight, he is shirtless when he comes back up, his serious expression turns to a smirk as he opens the top of the water bottle and hands it to me.

"Drink up. You are dehydrated."

Chapter 24   Declan

Luck of the Irish. That is the only possibility. I'm beyond lucky for this miracle given to me of lying next to Alexis right now, the only way I can hold on and find the calm within me. Battered, wounded, on no solid ground until I reached her. "Why did you come here tonight?"

"For you," I reply, "because I spent a miserable number of hours stalling trying to figure out how to make things right between us again, with no answers except for needing to see you." My confession came out raw and real, and faster than it should have, but it was my truth in more ways than one. Besides my dick seeking for her all day because I dream of our sex, the misery that accompanied me for most of my night the with the thought of never seeing her again stood forefront to it all. I'm old enough to realize when I feel something different, and it took control. She was the reason I shifted myself into focus after hours of drunk talking, cycling through Ronnie and Dax's versions of the night that involved Alexis, a pretty ugly picture that had me exploding in anger at everyone around me. Now with that anger still fresh with just the thought of not being able to fix it with her and saying my goodbyes for good, has my nerves tingling throughout my gut in unease.

"But are you only wanting to make things right because of finding out I'll be working in the show?"

My anger rose in the assumption I didn't even bother to think twice about since it wasn't my first concern.

"I don't give a shit about the show right now. I only care about you and me."

"Okay," she whispers softly, touching my chest, her green irises sparkling in thought as she changes the dim mood and asks, "Where did your shirt go?"

"I had to find the switches for your damn strobe lights because they were making me hot and dizzy."

Alexis gives a squeak and grins, "You messed with my controls?" Teasing me with her hands finally touching my body nudging closer into me, my excitement shown with my own hands not holding back anymore as I tell her, "Good thing I'm a bit familiar with stage lighting, I only tried six or seven other switches before I found the right one."

Gahh

"And I picked your lock coming in the front door, but it shouldn't have damaged anything," impressed with my quick entry with a credit card, I give her my cheesy grin and she returns one back, even with her tired haze.

"Drink all of it," I push in a whisper as I try to help her regain her strength and help try to wash away her worries. Her green eyes glossy and her hair a mess, her lips have a swell to them that make them perk out more, trouble for me as I become swept away in her beauty while she just stares at me in silence and takes her sips. I can't help but want her, it's too hard not to. I am always hard for this girl.

"You were just unexpected," I try to open my mouth, about to try to explain to her my past with Vince, but she stops me before I get the chance.

"Shh, no," she says to me softly, "don't you dare tell me!" "I don't want you to feel obligated to talk to me about things you aren't ready to share."

"I wasn't trying to hide things from you on purpose. I'm a guy who likes order and likes to be prepared, then I meet you, and everything with you has moved so quickly that I wasn't prepared."

She smiles at me playfully, and decides to remind us both, "No, you weren't prepared! I could be that crazy chick that tricks the Club owner into having my babies!"

I shake my head at her for basically calling me out on my lack of condom fumble the first time we had sex in the shower, then I reply, "I can't say I regret that miss, actually,"

"Your crazy will just have to be stuck with my crazy. The joke's on you, I'd like to see my strapping boys try to fit in that snug Lil pouch there," poking her hard abs as her panicked filled face helps alleviate my own that I was trying to hide from. Even though once I said it, it didn't feel that crazy.

She states, "Maybe we should double up protection," giving me this strange look.

I reply, "I would do anything if it meant I could have you."

Now, just the thought of not being able to fix it, saying my goodbyes to her for good, has my nerves tingling, causing me to sit up.

Her face falls, "You're leaving, where are you going?"

Looking down to her, I say, "I was going to drive back to my place."

She replies, "The roads are probably not safe enough to drive on," popping out a smile and adding in quickly, "And you look tired."

I can't help but touch her face, stroke down her cheekbone to her jaw, and just lay here with her in the silent thought, while we figure out together if miracles exist and she may give me a second chance. It's true that I have never had this undeniable need to be with someone before. I always stayed focused on myself, always working or training on a strict schedule, and didn't want to spend any little extra time I had on a relationship. Yet, when I look at her, I have nothing but time.

Addicted.

It's why I am here now. Being with her helps tame my worries and bitterness, she sees past my muscle I've layered to shield myself; she makes me feel a harmony I didn't know existed when we are together. Needing the extra luck, I cross my toes and whisper to her, "I am not staying unless you tell me to."

"Leaving seems quite irresponsible," she replies back, still not budging on her lack of telling me if she feels even a smidge the same way I do, making me feel even more concerned about how unworthy I may be to my gift.

Cupping her face and whispering to her gently, I plea, "I know I really fucked things up, but I really do not want to lose you..."

She opens her mouth and whispers, "Please, don't go."

"No," I reply, "I'm not going anywhere. I'm too tired and the roads are slippery," quirking a smile at her and sealing this night as a luck of the Irish miracle. She didn't need to know that there was no way I was going anywhere if I still had a chance. Leaning in keeping my eyes open, I graze my top lip to hers and stop to breathe her in, shocked by the amount of electricity her little body can still possess over me by just her lips, just the fact she allows me to take my time, take my pauses, taunting me with her silent instructions. Her hand slips up and she gently pushes my face down on hers, swiping my lips with her tongue, kissing me with complete care and tenderness. A kiss I can't go without anymore, tied up to her in a way I have never been wound, knowing I was stepping into the ring with her with the intentions on claiming my trophy, and not leaving without it again. Dealt a path that took people I love away from me without any say so in the matter, powerless, I have a choice to try and let someone stay in my life this time, Alexis is worth my chance. Even at a time in my life when things are rocking on this unpredictable teeter totter, she gives me something to look forward to. Her tired body going limp in my arms while I takeover tender kisses all over her face, not stopping until she's almost asleep, kissing her salty cheeks and the lids of her eyes, mollifying both of our worries while enjoying every second I get to soak her in. With one last bit of her strength to kiss me back, goodnight, holding her close, we both crashed to our sleep.

The morning sun was shining through the window, blocked by the curtain and split up in rays blasting out the sides. Sprawled out on my back, it felt like waking up from one of the best sleeps ever, then remembering it's Monday. Feeling around for her woke me upright, realizing the heavy weight on my side is Luna, and Alexis wasn't here. I checked my phone in a panic for the time, but it was only 7:30am, with two missed calls from David that I'm still ignoring for now, even though it would be ideal to swing in for a change of clothes, I still can't do it. What he sealed is a cruel reality for me, and the thought of something happening to him too, all I ever strived for when I was young and growing up was to be able to protect my family. First my mother passes away from a cruel cancer, my father sinks in heartbreak, Daniel's days are ticking in his vegetative state, and now David going into this match with Vince, I feel like the biggest failure, losing them one by one to leave me alone in misery.
Me and a dog on Monday morning, I'm about to lose this too.
Pulling myself together, I had made the decision on what I was going to do today before I fell asleep last night. I go ahead and jump in the shower to at least feel clean since having to wear the same pair of pants, before I head downstairs to find Alexis in quite the predicament.
Stepping in quick beside her, "What is all of this stuff?" I ask, lifting the giant box out of her hands while she has the door propped open with her legs spread, almost doing the splits, to act as a doorstop.
"Apparently, anything and everything Maya Gueterra feels I need in order to start my day," she replies back while bending down to pick up another package.
"I heard a truck, so I came downstairs, and it was this mail carrier that had me sign for the package…he unloaded the entire truck!"
Chuckling at her, while stacking the boxes and plastic wrapped gift baskets in her front reception, right now feels like an, in your face moment, reminding me that our relationship is also going to entail a working one, and as little and quiet of a person she can be outwardly, Alexis is also way more well known for her work than I would have ever imagined.
I caught my eye on a basket, "does this woman also think you need a pair of teddy bears in matching underwear?"
"A teddy in a teddy?" She asks, now having me puzzled in looking to see her analogy for the couple of bears, one in a bra and underwear and the other in boxers with the SheerMe logo. I reply with a bit of distaste in my tone, "No, not even a teddy in a teddy."
"It's like see through underwear teddy."

Gleaming up at me in my state of wonderment, she comes over and looks at it from the side and swoons, Awe, Luna will like them."

My girl's got a bark and a bite, "You're going to feed your bears to your dog?"

"What good is a teddy if he isn't wearing a teddy?" she asks me, serious look on her face, making me smile for sticking up for my underline jealous rant. I throw the teddy basket down and swing her into me, taking her mouth in one swoop starved for attention. Letting me have it, she melts into me, and I can smell her freshly clean sent and see her damp hair. "You had a shower before the boxes?"

Apprehensive she admits, "I actually went for a run at five and then came back and had a shower and then, I heard the trucks outside."

Blinking, she gives me a cheery smile to help soothe the ache that she has let me sleep for over two hours while she starts her day.

Maybe I am a lazy businessman.

Huh.

Alexis tells me, "I didn't want to wake you up because you were sleeping so well."

Just then another van comes up the lot to park in front. Stepping out is a casual middle-aged woman carrying the biggest green leafy potted plant, screaming out, "You must be Lexington!"

Peering over, Alexis, or by what she is now being called, Lexington, turns a shade of pink as she replies back, "That's me," not glancing up at me, just proceeding to take the plant from the woman's hand.

"That friend of yours was very sure this arrangement would suit you, he said you would especially love the cattails!"

I step in right beside the two chatting and grab the plant out of Alexis's hands to carry it inside. It's a white concrete base with a variety of greenery and plants potted and arranged together with different shapes, lengths, and textures you would see biking through a trail. feathers, the cattails, some fuzzy puff balls, I'm thinking maybe this can be her new reception decoration. Alexis replies, "I'm sorry about him, I hope he didn't drive you too crazy."

"He was a doll," this lady swoons, now peeking over realizing I'm also standing there as my jealousy is now starting to ping, but to my dismay, she keeps telling Alexis, "He was just very adamant about wanting the video on to be able to see all of the options in the shop," again, giving me another side eye as I try not to look like this is bothersome. It feels very bothersome.

A huff of noises comes out of Alexis before she responds, "Yep, he likes handpicking to make sure they are up to par," chuckling and then adding, "I'll let him know how perfect it turned out."

I run in to find my shirt I had thrown in the Mixx room folded neatly on top of a speaker, everything she had out scattered around last night is put away and the room is neat. Coming back

to the front, Alexis is standing in front of her new greenery, she looks over to me and gives me a small smile, "It's a dumb joke Jameson likes to do for celebrating 'big wins,' he customizes bush arrangements instead of flowers. Then it becomes all about the bush and what's in the bush, and the textures of the bush, and he gets the kicks out of talking to florists about their bushes all day."

I can't help but smirk a bit of a smile at the humor of this guy friend of hers that is already on my radar to keep wary of when it comes to their relationship. I absolutely ask in a way I'm throwing a claim, "Do you even like bushes? Last I checked, you most definitely didn't? But I'd be happy to check again to find out."

She walks over and pretends to punch me in the stomach replying, "No, I don't like bushes, and that's not really why he sends them, he doesn't know about that part of me like you do."

I can take a bigger breath now as she continues, "he likes to tell everyone he found me in the bushes when we were like 10, and now he says I still hide behind the bush, and then there is just the thing about the word, 'bush,' he likes," ending with an eye roll.

I ask her plainly, "Who is Lexington?"

"Lexington is my pseudo nickname I go by so my name is off the records. I try to avoid the spotlight as much as I can."

"And this show has you in the spotlight?" I ask now in question since I haven't gotten any details yet to focus on.

Giving me a small laugh, she cries, "I'll be performing live on stage with Jameson and his band, MartaBeat. Have you heard of them?"

"I recognize the name, but then again, I've given up on knowing specific names. That's more up the alley for something Dax or Brady would know," I tell her honestly as I start trying to think straight for the first time since Saturday night and comprehend her role in the SheerMe show. "Wait..."

I toss the blame on growing up without my mother as my reason for fumbling so much in front of women, as she patiently waits for me to wrap my head around it. I give my last huff and say, "You are going to be dancing in underwear Live on stage?"

She only gives me her answer by the look in her eyes. I take really deep breaths and lean my head into her hand she places on my face, finding my voice I say plainly, "I guess I only thought about you dancing in here, I just never realized how popular you are."

She replies, "I'm not, Rachel was the popular one."

"Maybe we have a different idea of popularity," I tell her plainly after her quick underestimation of her own self-worth.

Looking harder at me she starts shaking her head to reply, "No, Declan I think we have the same idea about popularity. I'm not the type of person that fits in the popular crowd. This is why I was so happy to move here, so I can have my dance and my life back. I could do this type of work when I had Rachel here to do it with me, and Jameson swears I am meant to be on stage, but..."

Alexis takes one of my hands and covers it up with both of hers, lifting her eyes to me, she continues saying, "I think I made a really big mistake. This is all too much," darting her eyes around her stacked boxes, she starts to breathe erratically. "I didn't want to sign up for all of this."

I wasn't sure what else to do, so I picked her up and she fell curling into my neck. I didn't understand what made her so upset, and everything about us is new territory. I was cursing myself for not realizing her worries about taking on the choreographing job.

"Baby, doing this show doesn't change you, it's just a moment where you can master a certain skill," I say in a gentle sigh while stroking her back, "and even once the show is complete, you will still own that skill and possess that power to move forward in your studio, if that is where you want to be."

She wasn't crying, but I wasn't sure if I was saying the right words, so I kept quiet until she spoke out, "I think I really do like to hide behind a bush."

"We all do sometimes." I reply in understanding as I take this time to ask her, "Were you placed in that bush, or did you go in there to hide willingly?"

"Both. The bush protects me."

She was building me an equation that had multiple parts that I was trying to understand. Our bodies were still but her heartbeat was not, thumping in her downplayed reality of what happened to her that has made her so nervous and fearful.

"You are not alone, Alexis. Rachel is still here watching over you, and I'm here to protect you now."

My luck of words proves worthy as she rewards me, shutting my mouth up as she claims me with hers. Her heartrate slowed down to a beat back to normal and her breaths were even in my hold now, and since I was feeling emboldened to try committing to my promise of standing by her, I decided now was my time to ask, "Alexis, will you come out with me somewhere for a bit, I'm wanting to show you something."

Looking abashed, she asks, "Sure, like, right now?" "Do I need anything?"

"Yes, right now if you can," I tell her, setting her back down to her feet.

She answers my vague command using a more questionable tone when she asks, "Did you even bring my helmet?"

"Of course," I tell her evenly.

It doesn't take us long to get to the first stop on this show and tell, and when we arrive at Carla's Café off the main street, "Familiar?" Let's run in here, I have a quick pickup, do you want anything?"

Glancing at me through her helmet as we get off, she says, "No, I'm good thanks, but I'm a bit confused."

"I know, just trust me, okay?"

She nods as I open the door for her to walk inside, this time she is walking in beside me. Her eyes were dancing around the café and back at me, sporting a bit of a blush on her cheeks, biting her bottom lip to maybe hold back her thoughts, while I hold her hand. I decide to send her in another direction by asking, "How good are your balancing skills?"

She gave me a look that meant business right as we approached the counter to see Lewis working in his normal contagious smile, "Oh hey, Mr. McQuade, we weren't sure if you were making it in today or not. Would you like us to go ahead and prepare the usual order to go?"

"Yes, please," I say to Lewis. Nudging to Alexis beside me, I make sure to ask, "Are you sure you don't want anything?"

She gives me a warm smile and then to Lewis shaking her head and replying, "no, thanks."

The bag containing the drinks was placed on Alexis's lap as she still managed to slip her hands around my waist, I swear she even grazed more below my belt, giving me a nice distraction to my thoughts on where we were heading. I couldn't hide our destination once we parked in front of 'Paisley's Long-Term Health and Rehabilitation,' I knew there was no turning back, this story is also my story, everything she may have assumed or thought about me, might be different after this visit. My hands were clamming up in the silence once I cut off the engine, the paper bag spill free as her hands let go of me and we pull apart.

"Please tell me you didn't just go from a bartender to a Club owner, to a delivery driver," she says lightheartedly.

"Only on Monday mornings, babe," I reply forcing a smile while strapping our helmets to the bike and opening a small compartment to grab for my stash of trail mix before we head in. When I finally stop to see her looking soft and still peering at me, waiting patiently for my genuine truth. I tell her, "I have two brothers, Daniel and David. I'm in the middle and you've met David. Well, you're about to meet Daniel, and we are bringing in the drinks for his medical team."

"Oh," her expression wasn't one of pity, but more of concern, "Daniel is a patient here?"

"As of a couple of years ago, yes," I reply, "This is the answer as to why I acted the way I did when I saw Vince touching you."

Now her face shows the surprise of someone finding out the plot twist for the first time, someone who instead of sadness is staring into my eyes drawing up the angry storm that replicates my own, insight to my temper, my heart, my family, my past. She walks to me and reaches out to place her warm hand into my open palm, "I trust you, now let's go in before these drinks get too cold."

It was surreal to walk through these heavy familiar doors next to Alexis, the pungent smell of hospital cleaning supplies greeting us when we arrive to sign in, along with the sound of Sydney's near choke at the counter when she spots me bringing in a friend.

Placing the large bag in front of her, Sydney manages to free her sights from Alexis and lands them on me to greet us saying, "Good morning, Declan. You brought a friend?"

"Yeah, this is Alexis," I manage to say while I sign our names down on the clipboard for us, causing a flock of the usual women in scrubs to nose their way up front to also greet us. Alexis smiles and gives a small wave hello during these awkward stares she is getting from some of them now, the annoying blonde finding her drink while silently sizing Alexis up and down, only making me chuckle seeing how blatantly obvious it is how no other woman can even try to compare to my Siren.

Sydney kindly replies, "Welcome in, Alexis."

Placing my hand on the small of Alexis's back, I lead us to Daniel's room.

Chapter 25   Alexis

The art of explanation is learned within your life lessons and experiences throughout time, sifting through and picking out both the important pieces, and also mentioning those lost pieces that may not be so important, and how you choose to process the level of each piece's worth, plays a part on the end result.

Declan didn't waste my time with explaining pieces that didn't matter, he used his own brush to paint me into his world, both of us standing side by side peering over a ledge, that just broke off in front of us and tumbled down, taking our important parts with it.

I could feel his apprehension in his body language. He had a tightness in his jaw, one hand tossing through his hair while the other one kept a tight sweaty hold on mine while we were walking to Daniel's room. Even though everything surrounding this moment seems painful for him to deal with, he acts as though I am his biggest worry right now, focusing on me, looking down and waiting for my reaction while he reveals his painful parts of himself for me. It's like what he is giving to me in this moment matters more than anything in his world right now, like I matter.

The room was cool and dark, and I could hear the daunting sounds of beeps and silent creaks, but knew once we got close to the bed, there was going to be no other sounds. I decided to take the stress away from Declan, I let go of his hand without giving him a second glance or a reason to have to speak, and stepped beside the bed to see Daniel, an obvious genetic display of the eldest McQuade brother, and an obvious version of only a shell remaining in this lifeless body. He had an unshaven face, and I can't help but reach out and caress my fingertips against it in greeting.

"Hello," I whispered to him, fully aware of the energy exploding behind me while I begin to fall into the caretaker role I've been trained in throughout my life, squeezing in the small space I can fit in sitting crisscross position on his bed. I automatically start adjusting his arms to stretch across to alleviate his damned muscle stiffness and hold his hand on my leg to investigate his fingers and nails.

"It's the first time I've ever felt jealous of him in here," Declan speaks out from behind me as he finds a seat on a stool, and rolls over right next to me, reaching to lay his arms in a hold around my waist while he watches me hold his brother's hand. "I hope you don't hold every hand you meet for the first time."

"Only the warm ones," I reply back smiling, lightening up the mood with some of our banter as I continue, "Daniel, you have beautiful hands," laying his open palm out to place my small one on top, his much bigger.

Declan groans out, removing one of his arms to grab my wrist away and replacing Daniel's hand with his own then smiling at himself in a proud accomplishment, as we see how much smaller mine looks in his. Like a little boy taking claim on a toy with proving to have the bigger hand, teasing in front of his brother, making me melt all over again. Possession. One I can choose to take hold of me. One I may want, possessing the only hand I've ever wanted.

I ask Declan, "Can he hear us?"

"His body itself can hear us, and he might respond in a jerky movement or something," shaking his head he finishes saying, "but Daniel himself is gone. It's all because I beat Vince in a fight a couple of years ago. David, Dax, Ronnie, Daniel, we were all together. Daniel and this girl ended up in his truck to hook up and somehow got caught by Vince banging on his door. Turns out the girl was Vince's little sister who was only seventeen at the time."

My heart was sinking in my rage and sadness already invested in this story while he spoke. "I think I tried to help, but we were surrounded by a giant crowd of people witnessing everything happening..."

Declan's voice was calm when he sank into the past and told me his version of the night Daniel's brain injury occurred. Each word he spoke had a strength in its sound, pulling me in with him during his angry and terrifying moments and allowing me to hold his hand when he sinks into the familiar feelings of self-doubt with the memories of not being able to help, not being able to prevent the fight from happening in the first place. The reasoning of what sounded to be a consensual sexual activity turning into a girl's brother blowing someone else's choices up in front of spectators, a self-righteous move to make an egotistical claim just to benefit and prove himself, ending in an irreversible tragedy. Declan and I have both lost somebody, and he and I both have someone we blame, besides ourselves. Daniel was honorable, backed into a cage with a bully like there was no other choice in the matter. Now when you look at this young man that should have had so many more good years ahead of him, all you see on him that is growing into the future, are the whiskers on his face.

But Declan didn't stop there in revealing himself to me. He led me into the night we met at the Club and told me about his security team tracking Vince, who was there for the first time. The altercation now a sensible reason for the self-destruction Declan ended up in on Saturday. Leaving me with a bitter feeling about my gym harasser, and a charge for wanting to give Declan anything he desired to take away his pain, and that was hopefully hot sex.

It was horrible of my brain to even make the notation of how much I wanted Declan after his story. It was like needing angry sex and an explosive orgasm to alleviate the tension we have worked up. I think I was getting noticeably handsy on our ride back to my studio, because his motorcycle was speeding around the slow drivers faster than normal, blowing through a couple yellow lights, only when we arrive it's to a very different version of how we left it this morning, blowing any hopes about possibly getting laid. Recognizing Sabine's car in the parking lot, the front door is again littered with dozens of boxes stamped in SheerMe logo's, along with what looks like a storage unit placed on the side next to a giant aluminum trailer you would typically see or have at your high school used for an extra classroom, but bigger.

"What's this?" Declan questions to me.

"I have no idea, is that a Pod?"

"Looks like you might be needing it," he replies back, coming to a stop in front of what looks like fifty more boxes left outside.

"Lexi, oh my god, where have you been?" Squeals Sabine as she runs out to see us, slowing down and doing a quick wide eye glance at me once she noticed Declan next to my side, a different view than what she knew of last.

"Sabine, do you know what all these boxes are?"

Ugh! She cries out and directs her pointer finger at the boxes in front, "these were all dropped off before I got here, and I've looked in two and it's all lingerie, all in your size...which is also my size," she says with a gleam to her eye. Then, she continues pointing to the Pod to explain, "that is a storage unit that Marianna ordered for us to put all of this extra stuff in."

"Holy shit," Declan speaks out now as he listens to Sabine's breakdown for us, moving over to the boxes and starts to rip a couple open. I hadn't even blinked, that's how fast Declan was when he rolled out a loud groan, pulling out a red bodice and matching thong to hang on his finger.

His face turned a bit red as he throws the attire back in its box and begins to shuffle them to the side, "You two don't touch these boxes, I'll handle putting them away."
Sabine looks at me with a tight big fake smile pointing now to the trailer as she says, "Well it might be a good thing we have another extra helping hand around here since we have so much heavy lifting."
"What are you talking about?" I ask her now getting irritated at the whole mess.

Sabine replies, "That is our new trailer parked here to help when we need the extra space and also where your new bodyguard is staying."
My face falls, Sabine looks like she wants to puke, and Declan is first to spit out, "What?"
I shriek, "A bodyguard! Why would I need a bodyguard and why didn't we know about this?"

Sabine gives me a look and answers, "Turns out, that is something you are going to have to take up with Jameson."
This cannot be happening. Jameson being overprotective and hiring me security seems beyond out of control.
The door to the trailer opened and a large built man that looked to be around my own age steps out. Declan's facial expression turned murderous as the man starts walking over, he yells, "Over my Goddamn body!"
Seeing this new bodyguard up close with his casual jeans and muscle shirt, I can't help but also recognize the bearded man.

"You're not needed here, Pauley, so get your shit and leave," Declan calls out, as he steps out of the boxes and towards the man. "Declan, please," I call to him to allow me a second. He turned around and I saw his pupils dark and wide, softening just for me to shake his head and plead using his calmest voice, "This is Vince's cousin. There is no way I'm letting him be your motherfucking bodyguard."

"Declan man, this isn't personal," Pauley speaks out now, his genuine tone evident as he turns to me and sticks out his hand in greeting. I almost dive towards it, trying to block from Declan possibly pouncing on this man in my parking lot in broad daylight, and succeeding majorly at the block, maybe looking like a crazy sprinter, as Declan steps up slowly behind me, keeping his composure as he probably noticed my worry and his need to simmer down won over him, allowing me to speak to this man.
"Hi, Pauley, I'm so sorry about this, but there is no need for me to have a bodyguard."

Pauley smiles in a nice polite way and replies, "I have been told otherwise when I was hired privately to watch out for you, which is exactly what I intend to do."
"She said she doesn't need you," Declan pipes in from behind me, I back into him softly to try to help ease him and he takes that opportunity to curl his arm around me in a claim and lay his hand on my front stomach pulling me into him.

Pauley replies directing his attention towards me, "It's nothing invasive. I'm just here to keep an eye on the people coming in and out of here during your practices for the big dance you have coming up."

Clearly Jameson didn't disclose any details to Pauley about who I was or what I was really doing. Lying and saying I'm working on a dance, is exactly something Jameson would say because he keeps my safety seriously, but it's maddening when he does things like this without at least telling me first.

Until I speak to Jameson, I say to Pauley, "If you don't mind just staying in that trailer for now while I sort this out, maybe I'll be able to get some more details on all these new services."

Pauley obliges politely but before turning around he speaks out, "Look, I know there is some obvious personal tension here, but you should know that I am a professional. I will keep my personal affairs out of the way in order to keep you safe," then he turns around, not glancing at Declan again.

I turn to face his angry blues staring at the back of Pauley, taking his hand I tell him, "Come inside and I'll figure this out."

I was so thankful the pressure was taken off of us as soon as we walked back inside with Sabine immediately swooping in over us. She started showing us the new black leather couch that was delivered and placed in the corner of the main floor, along with a set of table and chairs in the kitchen area, something I wasn't planning on purchasing just yet, that was instead just purchased for me. Bringing out the food and drinks that were sent in, including a swanky charcuterie board, Sabine says, "Ms. Gueterra definitely has made sure we are prepared, even down to our meal preps."

"Snacks are always welcome. I wonder how long we have until we start getting cut off," I reply with grabbing a water and some grapes.

"I don't know, but we gotta be in tip top shape," chuckling and then while the three of us linger back to the main floor, the windows taunting us with the new metal placed in the parking lot, she reminds me in a smooth way, "don't forget we have that three hour introduction meeting at two today, so you only have an hour before that tech guy from SheerMe will be coming in. We'll have to get ready while he sets up the big screen in here. So, I'm going to run to the store to make sure my Papa has food in the house and some dinner tonight and then I'll be back for the beginning of all of this!"

Sabine set my mood much higher, she was right that it was an exciting victory to be chosen to work on such a profound project. There is a positive in our midst, even though sometimes everything seems so heavy. Declan and I stood beside each other in front of the windows and watched Sabine get into her car, Pauley outside his door keeping his own set of hired eyes on her.

Peering over, I noticed Declan's wary eyes, filled with tension and worry, a far different look in him than I was used to, and one that I hated to think had anything to do with me, but I knew differently. We hit a speed bump on Saturday night that pivoted us apart, and ever since Sunday came when he found me on the floor in heartache, he has tried everything in his power to nurse me back to health. Sacrificing one of his darkest secrets to me, laying it down in front of my feet in order to bring us back together. I knew completely then that these feelings weren't one sided. Now, even after the weekend and a morning of having to relive a terrible tragedy that lingers in his present, the only worry he seems to be occupied with, again, had

175

something to do with me, and I was ready to try to make it right, and I wanted to do it my way. I don't say anything, I just turn and start walking, and I'm trying not to laugh with my smile once he starts following me into the Mixx room and I close the door behind me.

I walk to grab my headphones and find the playlist I was wanting, while he just quietly watched and didn't ask questions. Stepping back up close to him, his hands center on my butt, while I tell him in a soft hum, "I want you to trust me now."

Arousal flickered in his eye and in his pants storming into me as I lead him to one of the chairs and sit him down. "I hope you like heavy metal," I gleam placing the headphones on his head. I find one of my favorite mixed works of popular rock and heavy metal that I created many years ago, looped with only the sound of the band but with no voice or singing, it was a good way to scream silently when I went to zone out. That is what I wanted to give Declan, a time to zone out.

I pressed play for him as he kept his eyes focused on watching me while I stood in front of him and took off my hoodie down to my bra. His lower body shifted off the seat a bit, the only sound he can hear is exploding rage while I step into his lap. His cock was hard underneath me as I grind myself down and start kissing on his neck, slow and steady, up a path and down his valleys in a long stroke with my tongue, working him into a panting animal before I had even begun. Keeping his focus on my seduction, his hands were getting friskier around my waist while I lift my bottom up to hover over top, making good usage out of all my Pilates while my fingertips unzip and push his pants down to his knees, springing free the King of me. Declan's mouth was parted while watching me, our eyes not leaving one another as he allows me to take the lead. Shifting in between him, I lower myself down until my takeover is a breath away.

He mumbles his bliss as I spit on the head of his dick and let it drip down, down, making his expression a priceless rapture watching as I go to catch it with my tongue and swirl it all around. I could taste his salty precum mixing in. Knowing that his senses were on overload with the sound of fast electric guitars roaring in his ears and watching me give him a blow job for one of our firsts, I took my time. Between my slow exploration with my mouth and my fingertips grazing his inner thighs, I was killing him with anticipation, working my way down to his shaft, trying to fill my mouth up with as much of him that could fit in my relaxed throat.

Watching every vein pulse and listening to his uncontrolled rhythm had me feeling like pleasuring him is all I am compelled to do. I have never willingly wanted to do this before, and it was empowering to watch and listen as he sang out to me his sexual praises.

"Ooo,"

"M'fhíorghrá,"

His mumbling sounds become my drug, motivating me for speed as I hold my ringed lips around him tight and start pumping my mouth around his cock, in and out, up and down, using my tongue action to lick circles down to his root, up and down, until the flood gates within him were set to release.

"I'm going to cum," he rasps out under his breath, giving me that extra power and plunging my mouth down on his massive cock to take all of him in, as much as I possibly could.

His Cobra sprang up in quick thrusts, beating the back of my throat as I pumped him and add in my own guttural vibrations that help tip him over the edge, a heavy load off the roaring beast.

His fingertips are lightly holding my hair while his orgasm spews long salty jets down my throat. I suck him up and don't pop off until my mission is complete, until I claim that last drop of him and his eyes slink to the back of his head, sated and leaning back in the chair, mumbling incoherently to himself.

Grabbing my hoodie to make better use of it as a towel to wipe my hands and face before I pull Declan's pants back up over him to climb back on top while he manages to toss the headphones off. He looks only half alive as I drag his lips to mine.

In between our kisses he says, "What you just did to me was so damn good, I can't think."

"Good. I don't want you thinking too much anymore, today," I said.

Sitting up and holding around me, he replies "All I know right now is that I'm not letting you go."

"I don't want you to."

He questions in a more serious voice, capturing me in another intimate moment for us, "Do you realize how much I needed to hear you say that?"

Using my thumb to stroke along his eyebrows, our hearts beating together, I respond saying, "Do you realize how much I need you to hold on?"

"You should know I'm known to have a tight grip," he says stealing my lips quickly to seal our truths for one another.

My wall I had put up for him has collapsed down making me both excited and also nervous. I have never stepped into a ride for two before, where my heart was involved so much so, that I have formed this craving and desire for him to keep needing me, in order to function properly anymore. Except, he was never just that mysterious man I ran into underneath the bridge, he has always been more, maybe even meant to be there, tuning us together.

However, accepting a commitment can also prove challenging. He is an owner of a Nightclub, now hosting the Live Lingerie Fashion Show, about to also find himself a new sense of popularity, and he already has girls falling all over him everywhere he goes. Even though he is mine for now, I can't forget about the possibility of getting my heart broken. He makes me feel so safe, and it wasn't a question about what I wanted, I wanted every second I could get with him while I could, no matter the cost.

He says, "Depending on what you thought, I was planning on running back to my place to pack a bag and come right back. I want to stay with you. I can just do some computer work from upstairs while you do your thing down here, what do you think about that?"

"Yes, that's what I want," I reply sounding a little desperate.

"Yeah?"

"Yeah, but you can work down here too if you want, I've got space in this room."

"You'll make space for me?" He asks with a playful smile, but his mask is looking more serious, searching for a deeper answer he wants to hear from me, space in my heart maybe? Willing to move forward but what does that mean for us? Shaking myself so I'm not so nervous, I reply, "Yes, I'll make space for you."

Chapter 26   Declan

I am beginning to feel like a new man proudly sporting my new collar. She ripped me from the lonely tunnel and started to give me the attention and care I needed to resuscitate me back to my good health. I have finally found someone who already knows how to harness all of my problems and suck them clean out of me, and I can taste the possibility of becoming united with this girl who is becoming the master of my heart.

After blowing me away, she led me back out to her studio dance floor and told me I needed some rest on the couch, shoving me down and rolling me on my side. Her commands were definite while she started floating around getting some things done and I watched and listened while zoning into my new beginning into how I thought.

There was a brighter picture than the one I had before, and I started reassessing the scene to pinpoint the new colors I needed to mix in, in order to illustrate a more objective vision I wanted to have for my future. I carried on this way, relaxed on the couch, even as Sabine returned, and the chatter around grew louder. I may have even dozed off, until I heard the deep voice that threw me out of my slumber, and I found myself standing straight again.

Finding my way back next to Alexis, Sabine, and the reminder of Pauley's inhabitance outside the front door, right as the man hired by SheerMe arrives to setup all the streaming meetings and practices that will take place in her studio. His name was Bruce, and he was a short, older gentleman, with a full head of salt and pepper hair, wearing a large suede satchel across his body and carrying multiple bags of his equipment. I keep my glare pinned on Pauley who avidly tries to avoid it, watching him as he steps in to help Bruce with his bags. I allow for him to do the heavy lifting in the reminder of his only reasoning for his existence here right now, to work. Deciding this is the best time for me to run some errands while Alexis gets busy with the beginning of this project, I say to her, "I'll sneak back in quietly when I return," rewarding me once again with her sparkling smile and a kiss. I guide her and Sabine back inside and then I turn to Pauley and tell him, "You and I need to have a talk," giving him a nod to go back outside, demanding a private conversation.

The girls proceed to get started with their work, Alexis giving me one more glance behind her shoulder to meet my eyes with a tender recognition, before I turned away and Pauley stepped up, following me from behind. Pauley was still attending high school when Vince moved in with him and I didn't know who he was before he started tagging along to all the matches to cheer in Vince's corner. All I really know of him is that he has kept by Vince's side throughout all the years I have known him, he was even there the night Daniel died, cheering Vince on.

I tried to keep my cool while starting a conversation, I ask, "Pauley, what the hell are you doing here?"

"I told you why I'm here, there isn't any more to it than that," Pauley replies, "listen, her other boyfriend is the one paying me to report to, not you. Funny, he didn't mention you."

This moment is proof of the truth in the magic of experiencing a mind-blowing blow job, it resets you, reinforcing stability to maintain your calm within, when you otherwise might have put somebody in a chokehold. I give him a stern warning, "I mean it, if you so much as touch one hair on her head, I will bury you alive."

Pauley starts shifting uncomfortably while he responds back, "I wouldn't fucking hurt her, that ain't me, I ain't like him!"

All I could see were our nonstop puffs of breath in the cold air while I reply, "Well, you sure as hell stick real close beside him, so that sums up about all I need to know about you."

"You know nothing about me!"

"I know who you have in your corner, Pauley. I swear to God if you or him get anywhere near her…"

Pauley bites in to cut me off with a stern tone, "I'm not going to let that happen. Whether you want to believe it or not, I have a code of honor to protect as well."

It's almost painful to breathe in while I say to him in my calmer voice, "That better be the only reason you are here, to keep your eye out for them. I don't want her to get involved with anything that has to do with our garbage, clear?"

Pauley looks in my eye and says, "You and I are on the same side with this."

"I guess we'll see about that," I replied, giving him a chin up in our momentary truce and walking to my bike. He seemed stoic and serious, and it feels hard not to believe he's being honest in what he says. I don't have really any idea why her male friend insists to have a sudden watch over her. It has me wondering what Jameson's intentions are with Alexis, seemingly not ever giving her choice and rather making big decisions for her. Now that I can connect him to the band MartaBeat, I'll be able to do some digging to find out information on him, and a better idea of the background between him and Alexis.

My phone rings right before I start my bike, and I see it's Dax, another call I was avoiding that I can't seem to do any longer. His voice is surprised when it picks up, "Look who is still alive."

"Yeah, I'm alive. I was just going to work from home today," I say trying to not bring up Alexis yet. Dax replies, "Okay well I was hoping you would swing in here for a bit today, there are lots of things we need to talk about."

Maybe I knew brainstorming with my friends on a Monday afternoon will at least help me get a better grasp on my situation with the SheerMe show and Alexis, maybe it's because I have a backup wardrobe that I keep there that will save me a trip to my condo, or maybe it's still the blowjob's magical effects causing me to say yes to things, because I found myself responding back, "I'll be there in an hour."

I swung into CeCe's parking lot to swap my bike for my truck that was parked there and left without going inside. Now that both parties have agreed to the fight, the manager bookie will gather the purse and send out the details of where and when it will take place. Until then, I'm still too angry and still too preoccupied with making up with Alexis and starting to work on plans for the show, I have decided I still can't dive into that matter of Vince and David's future fight right now.

My little brother has stayed out of the underground fighting scene since I disappeared from it after Daniel's accident and instead stuck to his path on running CeCe's Gym. There, he has been putting in just as much, if not more time, than I used to in the gym when the underground was my career life choice. Over the years, David has had multiple offers and call outs from heavy hitters and big betters to match him up on their rosters, but he has refused them all, creating some backlash in the underground fighting community who feel owed, like he should prove himself as my successor of sorts. I'm not sure he understands the sacrifices he just risked taking on this fight with Vince, sacrifices that I'm not willing for him to take.

Dax and Ronnie are both at their desks working, looking like they feel the same kind of tired as me and the humor on their faces were gone.

Dax is the first to speak, "So, did you talk to her? You look a lot better."
I quip back, "That's funny because I was just thinking about how you look worse."
"I feel worse. I've never felt like such an asshole before, it's just eating me alive. And then you walk in here all chippery and shit."
I laugh at him, my first smile in front of them since they sat here and watched me in my previous misery while Dax continues, "Well hopefully you have only good things to tell me to make me feel a bit better."

Ronnie adds, "Dax wants to know if she still hates us."
"I haven't had a chance to talk about either of you two, actually," I reply back as their eyes narrow in on me.

Dax groans, "You've been gone since last night, we thought you were with Alexis."
"I have been with Alexis," I say, "but we haven't quite gotten to speaking about the Show in working detail yet...thank God, because I have no idea anything about it!"
Ronnie sighs and asks, "Did you work things out with her, though?"
Hearing the question stung me. My buddies know my heart, but the three of us have not really gotten to the stage in our friendship where it includes serious women, until now. I'm the first one taking the dive into a relationship with a girl that commits me, and it comes with a gripping feeling they have no clue about.
"I think so," I answer honestly, "I took her to see Daniel."

"No shit." Ronnie says dryly, clearly shocked by my confession, as Dax shows the similar surprised reaction exhaling, with an 'oh' formed on his face. I get a nervousness to me as I continue talking about it saying, "it wasn't terrible, she acted surprisingly cool about it. We just sat with him, and I told her what happened."

Ronnie asks, "Did you tell David this?"
Shaking my head, I reply, "No, I don't want to talk to him right now. Especially because I got all this going on," I change the subject, "It turns out, Pauley is now her new private security detail, sent in by her friend back in Boston. The Jameson, guy."

"Are you kidding me right now, Declan?"
Dax questions looking like he is about to flip out, "You mean JamFresh is the same guy friend you knew about? Holy shit! How did you not see this!"

Ronnie pipes up trying to stick up for me, "I'm pretty sure all of us got duped by this chick, who by the way, doesn't exist online since I can't find out anything about her."
I get a chance to say, "I don't know the music scene like you guys do. I had nothing to go on beside the little bit she told me anyways, and now I know why. Turns out, she's a big deal, and I had no idea.

Dax already ahead of us, clicks on his keyboard to pull up a picture on his monitor. "Found her, 'JamFresh and friend,' is the caption posted on MartaBeat's Instagram page," he blows out a whistle and says, "Get out of here."

The three of us huddle in around the computer screen to see, there is no mistake who the girl is with those green eyes staring back at me, a younger version of my siren, with her arms around the notorious Jameson.

Ronnie states, "MartaBeat is performing in the SheerMe show, it's all in the contracts they sent over to us, but it doesn't list her name there either."

"Check the name Lexington," I say to him as I study the photo on the screen. Alexis and Jameson posing at a concert, and with his hands placed around her waist, he looks like a total problem for me. Jameson is a tall, medium built guy with brown skin, and although I thought I was familiar with the band, I've never seen his face before.

Ronnie immediately runs back to his desk to flip through paperwork and Dax started clicking around and ended up finding multiple pictures of Alexis posted under other people's profiles, but none tagging her name, and cutting her face out in some group photos.

Then there it was, I noticed before Dax did, it was obvious as soon as I saw her, pointing to the screen.

Dax reads the name out in another astonished voice, "Rachel Butler," who is standing in between Jameson and Alexis at a formal event.

Trusting Dax's instinct to know more about this than I do, I ask, "So why do you think he would hire a bodyguard for her?"

"I see they are close," I grumble out and proceed to my point, "but she leaves her names off the record on purpose. I'm not entirely sure why, but that's why I want to know why he would hire Pauley."

"That is really weird," Dax replies, clicking out and turning to me seriously, "I need to ask you a question, Declan. How serious is this thing you have going on with her?"

Ronnie steps over beside me with a packet in his hand giving me the same questioning look, I wasn't sure what they were trying to find, but I answer sincerely, "I'm thinking it's pretty serious."

Nodding, Dax replies, "That's what I thought, which is why Ronnie and I thought it might be best you step back from this project and let the two of us prepare for it."

Ronnie adds in, "You can be on scheduling duty instead, that way you can focus on David and your new girl more."

I was feeling both stunned and relieved at the same time, I say with a laugh, "Really, you two just don't want me to fuck this up for us."

"Yeah, pretty much," Ronnie says also chuckling.

Dax agrees with a nod while I shake my head in frustration. This proposal wasn't about business, we were partners and shared equal ownership no matter what, this was about my friends trying to help take some weight off of me.

"I still want to know what's going on," I say firmly.

"Here's your copy of all the details we got about it. You were right, there is a Lexington Paige listed in the Performing Acts with MartaBeat. All their time frames and minute details are in here but nothing else. She is like a ghost."

Dax answers, "Actually that is more than accurate, because I'm reading something..." he was looking down on his phone scrolling an article online, "... fans of MartaBeat specifically know her as the ghost band member, performing and always attending the shows, but never stepping in for press...when they are asked specific questions regarding the girl in interviews, all members, including Lead Vocalist JamFresh call her their 'ghost girl'..." he finishes reading and looks up to me saying, "I bet they've all signed NDA's to keep her privacy."

Ronnie adds in, "SheerMe had all of us sign NDA's yesterday regarding revealing any details of the show. So, because of those privacy rules, by law even now that we know what her name really is, we can't say anything. That includes not being able to say anything linking her name Alexis Andrews to the show in public to anyone, not without her consent anyway."

Dax says, "See, there you go, she gets to maintain her ghost status under a pseudo name."

Huffing a bit, I add my two cents in the matter, "She wants to keep her privacy, I respect that. I don't think that has anything to do with the band, I think it has a lot to do with Rachel Butler."

"That girl died a few months ago and they reported it as a drug overdose," Dax says using his entertainment encyclopedic brain. I wasn't going to divulge anything Alexis has told me about her friend, Rachel, even to my best friends, but I know for a fact Rachel set a timer for herself and died on her own watch. There was a very close relationship between she and Rachel that had Alexis hidden in the background for some reason, and it is that unknown reason that has me wondering if there is something that I should be concerned with regarding her safety.

I say again, "Back to my previous comment, Pauley is her bodyguard."

"How did we miss that?" Ronnie asks. It's Dax that gives me a limb to stand on when he says, "that doesn't surprise me since he's starting up that Security business. He isn't a bad guy, I don't think."

"So, do you think I can trust him?" I ask needing a direct response to ease my question about it. Instead, I get another flip of the coin as Dax responds, "If you are asking if I would trust him to do a good job keeping his eye out for the dancing babes, I'm pretty sure you have nothing to worry about. But if you're asking because you think somehow Pauley will lead Vince to her..." he pauses looking at me waiting for me to clue in. I respond, "yes, that's what I'm worried about."

Dax returns replying, "What difference does that make when he already knows that you are with her. That right there puts a bull's eye on her head if Vince wanted to fuck with you. Really though, I don't think he's going to do that. He just called out David for a fight, he isn't worried about who you're screwing."

"Maybe, but I don't want to take that chance, he will use anything he could think of that would throw David off."

Ronnie throws up his hand to make us stop so he can speak, and like that kinder dad heart he possesses, he turns to me and says, "I know this feels really personal to you, Declan. There are no words and no ways to make it right, because believe me I've tried to come up with thousands of possibilities, but there is nothing any of us can possibly do to fix what happened to Daniel. It was one of the worst nights of my life so I've never been able to imagine how terrible it must make you feel. His hands were holding tight on his hips when he shakes his head and says, "Then, two years later he comes in here to call out David in front of you on purpose! The fury I would be in if someone had the gall to do something like that to me is an unfathomable slap in the face, and you have every right to be pissed off. At the end of the day though Irish, forgive me when I say, I think this feels like it is more personal to you than it actually is to Vince. He wants to fight David in a grudge match because it puts his name on the fight that could possibly get him suited up in the bigger leagues, before he ages out and isn't worth a shit. It benefits him."

Dax's blonde hair skims his eyes while he adds, "Ronnie's got a point, being able to nail down a fight with David in the big leagues down under is probably his last shot at getting noticed. He has nothing else left in his life besides fighting, what else is he going to do for work?"

"We also thought I was going to be the one in that match against him, and we see how that is turning out. Vince has fought multiple competitors over the years that have ended up with battle scars from him, none as terrible as Daniel, but he's still known to go out of bounds. I have experience with him, I know how to beat him," I say ending in a deep sigh.

"David will beat him," Ronnie says, "I would bet all my money on him, even if I didn't love him as a brother."

I butt in, "But at what cost? Owning and running that gym is David's life and any unfair injury he may come out with after this literal revenge match, isn't worth his future."

"What about you?" Dax asks me, and then repeats himself for good measure, What were you going to say to Vince if he called you out on that fight?"

Raising my voice up a notch, I reply, "I would have locked that match down myself, and David wouldn't have to be in this position in the first place."

Dax replies, "Then you would have set yourself up for a disaster."

"What the hell do you mean by that? You don't think I could beat him if I challenged him again?"

He starts saying, "You could have skipped out on our deal in this Club because you had UFC in the bag. You already had the in, you just had to take it, but you didn't."

"Without even trying, you would destroy Vince Bordeaux in any ring, at any time, Declan. There is no question about that, but even if you beat his ass to a pulp and win, it doesn't change anything for you. You won't feel the high that you're used to when you win, and that will get in your head. I think you lose no matter what."

"I would still take it."

"Trust me, I know you would," Dax replies, "but as your friend, I can't say I'm not happy you didn't."

"I would have to agree," admits Ronnie.

Vince still currently ranks high maintaining his brute force status in fights, despite my record of previous wins against him.

He doesn't usually see losses. I give them a look and reply, "I just hope he goes far away when this fight is done with," I manage to say in my heavy thought, trying to listen to my friends and believe with my full heart that Vince wouldn't be capable of doing something else to hurt me on purpose, wishing it was that simple to convince this nag in my stomach to go away so I don't have to deal with this constant anguish revolving him anymore.

Ronnie gives a laugh and says, "you can't be mad at us about that either, we're already swimming in the asshole pool your girlfriend put us in," his grinning working to ease the tension from the discussion I was trying to avoid.

"Gah," a noise settles amongst Dax as he runs his hands over his face, probably suffering in memories of our past Saturday night when Alexis and Sabine pushed him in the asshole lane, rightly so. Ticking a noted reminder off my list when I remember to tell the guys, "Speaking of which, I have a way to help mend your Asshole cause."

Dax questions, "Did he just say, 'your cause?'"

"I believe that's exactly how I heard it too," Ronnie's brows furrow as he playfully asks, "What about you, Irish? How did you get left out of all of this groveling when this is mostly your fault?"

"Whoa, boys slow down," I say with an easy grin, "I can promise you, I have more groveling than I know what to do with."

Dax flusters with an impatient eye roll and screeches out, "Just tell us!"

"They haven't stopped receiving shipments from SheerMe, and they have too many boxes stacked up outside that need to be moved to their storage area."

"Manual labor?" Ronnie quirks in question right as Dax throws out his inked hand out to shut him up quickly and turns to me with a fire in his eyes confirming loudly, "We will do it!"

Laughing out, I took that time to gather up some items from my desk to take with me back to Alexis, with a plan in mind for Dax and Ronnie to swing by the studio later to help.

Chapter 27   Alexis

After another hour of intense power planning with the seventy-nine dancers that were watching in from in their small square pixel on the screen, we gathered a momentous plan of action with the team to knockout in the next few days.

I noticed Declan returning through the door while we were still in our two-hour introductions with Maya Gueterra, MartaBeat, and parts of the SheerMe team. He took his time to lay his sights on me to see what we are doing, sending me a wink before heading into the Mixx room. There was a large portable backdrop that Bruce had set up in front of the windows, allowing for Sabine and me to face the mirrored wall to reflect towards the camera, sporting our new SheerMe logo leotards that were so thin that they also showed off some fierce nipple action. Not even seventy-nine people tuning in could keep me from sneaking a peak at Declan again while he returned from a run with Luna, looking off the charts sexy in his matching black sweats and fussy hair.

It was late in the evening by the time Sabine, and I finished our work for the night. She went home while I snuck upstairs to shower and clean off before I found Declan sitting in the Mixx room working in his chair, using his laptop and old school manual calculator in front of him. He wiped his tired eyes away from the screen when he finally noticed me coming in.

"Are we going to your house or are we staying here?"

"Here tonight, home tomorrow," I reply back adding, "Margie and Estel's on Thursday night."

Declan starts shutting his computer down and gets up to walk over to me and asks,

"Did you eat? Are you tired and ready for bed?"

"Yes and yes. You?"

He lifts me up to our way and walks us upstairs, turning out the lights and tossing me on the bed. Then, snuggling in close with me, he says,

"My dad told me that Estel and Margie's daughter committed suicide."

"Laura?" I question in my stunned breath.

He pulls me in closer and responds, "Apparently the two of 'em showed up to drop off food and their condolences after Daniel's accident and told my dad their daughter committed suicide after she left for the city."

"How awful," I say, my heart pitting in my stomach, "that must be a terrible story they hold closely."

Another story about the loss of life on one's own terms, knowing all too well from Rachel's death what those of us that are left here shattered in mourning, possess. It's a different type of burden that the curse of death brings to the ones left behind suffering in sadness, which is also realizing the amount of turmoil our loved one must have been in during their last moments, before carrying out the forbidden act.

My phone started ringing from my bedside table, disrupting our conversation. I was in tired deep thought and too comfortable in Declan's arms to want to get it, saying to Declan, "I'm too tired, let's just ignore it."

He follows through, ignoring the phone and looking into my eyes, to instead asking me, "Are you angry with Rachel for killing herself?"

"Yes. I think I'm even more mad at her now that I know she planned it," I say above a whisper for him to hear over the ringer.

"Do you think you will ever, not be angry about it?"

"In a way, even though I know there was mental illness involved, I guess I still feel almost entitled to hold an angry grudge. Like she was mine enough to claim."

"I get that," he replies softly in his thought, "I think that's how I feel about this upcoming grudge fight between David and Vince. I am Vince's competitor, not David."

Holding me tight as we lay still listening to the phone, I was figuring by beginning of the third ring it was probably Jameson calling, but I wasn't wanting to answer to cut off Declan in the middle of opening up, since he doesn't often speak about his feelings with words.

His eyes flickered with emotion as he replies, "Everything about it pisses me off."

It was me pulling him in tighter during the pause of the fourth ring. I asked,

"But don't you think Vince automatically became a competitor for David the night he hurt Daniel?"

"I guess he did. But I wish he didn't, I don't want him to risk it like Daniel did."

"I know baby," I say stroking his cheek, "but he may have wanted to take the risk. And unlike, Daniel, David will be prepared."

I wasn't sure if I had said the wrong thing, watching Declan's eyes staring back into my own, until he let out a bit of a sigh and nodded to me. Meanwhile, the phone started ringing again, distracting both of us to have to break from our thoughts and acknowledge it.

I let him know sweetly, "Declan, that's Jameson calling me..."

Declan quick to say, "Oh good, you should answer it and find out if Pauley is staying the night or not."

"Pauley! I totally forgot!" I whip myself up and grab my phone to answer with a prompt, "Hello!"

"Hey. Are you there?" Jameson's voice sounds out on speaker while I'm stretching across with the phone to my ear.

"I'm here."

"Lexi, get the phone away from your ear, I'm talking on Facetime."

Shit

Flipping my phone to my face, I see Jameson laughing out now on the phone, shirtless in his bed. Super shit. Declan looked cool enough leaning back with his arms behind his head, so I just went back to snuggle where I was in Declan's chest, taking Jameson on the phone with me.

Luckily, Jameson gave me one of his quick looks only I could see, signaling his realization that I'm not alone, only my face showing up on the screen, and it doesn't stop him from still wanting to talk.

Jameson's sarcasm was thick when he states,

"Ooo, did I catch you at a bad time, Lex?"

"No, I was just about to call you about something too. And Declan's here with me," I reply back smiling while he kept quiet beside me. Jameson couldn't see his face in the picture, but Declan had the upper hand leaning down watching him.

"Alright, I'll listen to you first this time."

I find my flattest tone to say, "The security guard."

"You mean Pauley Zerziak," Jameson says with a sigh as he leans himself back to get comfortable.

It's like we are all here together, as I respond back, "Yes, Pauley. Why would you do something like that without telling me?"

"It crossed my mind that you were by yourself in that studio on a daily, and on a nightly, and I'm making sure you're safe."

Declan remained still with a normal heartbeat while I was revving up replying, "A trailer and a bodyguard is beyond ridiculous. Pay him whatever and tell him to be gone by tomorrow."

"Not happening," Jameson replies sternly with nothing else to give.

I argue back in question, "Why not?"

"Because I'm here, you're there, and this Show is going to start making headway through your area. This way, I can have an eye out for you, Pauley's hours are whatever your studio hours are."

"Studio hours or work hours?" I question as his he then starts giving me a glare through the screen like he's trying to reach my soul. I keep on saying, "It just seems a bit much."

"Ya, well, maybe I'm a bit much. And you're correct, guard hours are studio hours, whenever you're there, he's there." Jameson sits up straight in his bed while he says, "Lexi, you sleep there by yourself in an upstairs loft, in the middle of that far away, normally boring town. Don't think that isn't stupid shit."

"But, I have Luna here with me when I stay over...and now I have...you know...well I have Declan sometimes," I was beginning to feel like a teenager trying to convince her controlling father of something, stumbling around.

"Not a problem, Pauley knows to stay in the trailer at night, so he won't bother you. I even told him ha..." Jameson does a flip and starts chuckling, fist to his mouth to control himself like he's trying to hold the laughter in, but he can't.

"I told this security guy to try to stay inside the trailer at night because you have supersonic ears...and he agreed," Jameson visibly laughing harder now, as he can't believe Pauley's commitment level.

"I'll email you over all his information and contract details," finishing off like there was no other question, because he decided, causing Declan to give a half deep sigh, shaking it off in the middle.

I try to think about how to navigate this a little differently with Jameson, asking him, "You convince me to take on this job, then you think I'm putting myself at risk because of it? All of the sudden I need a Security Guard and I'm supposed to just accept it."

"Yes, please, just accept it."

"I don't think that's fair, Jameson. I need to know now if this SheerMe show will put me in harm's way for some reason?"

"It's not. The show is good for us, just drop it," his frustration was rising, but mine was a step ahead. I was angry he was being short with me, but I was more so embarrassed that Declan was having to witness this.

I try to put my foot down a bit gentler, "Please, you have to realize how crazy this is for you to do something like this about a show. One that I'm at lower risk for because they have the money to back up their privacy policies if needed."

He doesn't speak, he just goes from nodding his head to shaking his head, which isn't so much like him, causing me to push a little further adding, "What is it?"

When he remains silent, I begin to clue in. I peer up at Declan's face for the first time since the call started and he gives me a soft quick smile while looking into my eyes, and I can see the unease in him while he is trying not to speak up for me.

Turning back to my phone screen, I say, "Declan is fine. He can hear whatever it is you have to say."

Jameson snorted out a bit, saying, "I don't think so."

I took a deep breath, and spoke, "I'm telling you, I'm okay with it, whatever it is. I promise."

He says it fast, "Terrie's company is going bankrupt now that Rachel is officially off her client list. I guess there are more people that we know about that dislike the woman, because ever since Rachel died, she has been blasted with unfit parent headlines."

I shrug, "She was an unfit parent, if she's smart, she would really want to avoid me to keep me from talking."

"But she's not smart, and you disappeared with money she didn't realize wasn't going to be hers."

"So, she comes after me, she can't take anything away from me anymore."

Jameson explodes quickly, "And she's dating Thatcher Green again."

There was a catch in my breath at the name.

He proceeded to ask me, "Are you sure you want me to still continue?"

It was Declan's whisper I heard now, "You don't have to…" making me flinch my face up to interrupt him with a stern worry to my face, "you said you would hold on," causing his hooded eyes to lay in me to confirm his claim. I was scared when this unwelcomed name of my past was mentioned, and the last thing I wanted was for Declan to be left feeling unworthy of my trust, when right now he was the one I felt like I trusted the most.

Leaning back into Declan to peer back into the phone, I say, "Jameson, I have to move on. It was so long ago, that Thatcher Green probably has no memory left of my existence. I'm not going to worry about Terrie or her problems anymore."

Jameson responds, "Yeah, well I am. "Now this show is going to take place and I just don't want the two of them to figure out where you are in the middle of this already chaotic time for you."

It left me where it seems I was destined to always end up, on the side of caution. I blinked only once then I replied, "I didn't move here to run from Terrie. Pauley covering the Studio during the day is fine, up until this show is over. But that's it. I will not have him camping out here and watching my every move. If you don't tell him that, I will."

His eyes creased in irritation nodding back saying, "Got it tough guy, I'll call him tomorrow."

"Tonight," I said back, remaining in control while I had it, "Now tell me why you called me a million times."

Rolling his eyes, Jameson replies, "Because I was gonna ask what you thought about something. Like a spotlighted bar scene opening to our Shaggy?"

My excited eyes lit up with his as I shout, "YES!" "That used to be our favorite one back in the day!"

"Wasn't me," Jameson sings, "Alright well that's settled, I'll let you two get back to whatever. I'll talk to you tomorrow," giving me a grin and ending the call.

As soon as my phone was thrown back to the side, Declan whips around and pins himself over top of me, claiming me in a hold that has me pawing at is scent.

Close.
Intimate.
His.

"You're mine to protect now," he says, as he moves in to kiss me, sticking his tongue into my mouth to find mine, slowly devouring me in an electric tangle of fire. A fire that burns more and more in each breath of time we spend together.

"We can think more in the morning," Declan whispers over my mouth, his eyes still closed as he continues telling me, "But for now, I'm going to put you to bed," stealing my lips back in a soft thunder.

Feeling ready, I'm going to let him.

Chapter 28   Declan

She didn't beat me awake this morning. I'm not sure she had the chance, considering how stirred up I have been since she closed her eyes asleep. I studied her beautiful face in deep thought, feeling like a fool for not realizing she may hold her privacy close because she is still hiding from someone trying to hurt her. I woke up every hour on the hour, all I kept thinking about was how much I didn't know her like I feel like I should, and how much time I have spent worrying about my own problems and throwing her into them too, when really there is much more reasoning for her hiding in the bushes. Her history with Jameson and Rachel's mother that I didn't know about eating me alive.

He knows.

He protects her.

What money?

There was even a time in the night when I thought about getting up and knocking on the trailer door to question Pauley for things, he may even know about Alexis that I don't. I wasn't sure how long I was going to be able to keep looking over at my girl and feel like she is still not completely mine, without waking her up to tell me so and let me in. I'm engrossed by how she makes me feel and there was no way I am going to let anything get in my way of keeping her safe with me.

It was early morning beginning to see daylight when she slowly started waking up. Maybe she could feel my stirred up worries in my hands that held her in tightly because she arched her back to stretch, pinning her ass to my dick and allowing me to graze up to get a hand full of her tit and her nipple in between my fingers. Her body is hands down the sexiest, most tantalizing dream, I have ever seen on a woman, and I can't help that she makes me a mad man, touching and tasting every inch of her whenever I get the chance, like a drug I need to drink all the way down.

"I need you, baby," she whispers out to me while she rocks against my dick that had risen for her. She didn't need to say anything else as I become a rabid animal pulling down my pants and try sinking into her tight pussy laying from behind her.

"Feels so good," I pant, with just the tip in as I try to pump my length all the way inside of her, while she arches back clinging to me. Never have I ever felt this kind of sensation.

She started kissing the bottom of my scruffy chin causing even more sensational heat to rise within me, prompting me to grip her waist and lift her on all fours.

I knew I wasn't going to last long as she takes in each hard thrust my wrath of worries feeds her. She was there with me, moaning and screaming in pleasure, while I was watching her ass bounce gloriously into me.

Feeling her cumming on me finished me with a bang, stealing my breath and everything I had to give while I came. My body extremely sated, I lean over to plant kisses on her back while I pulsated still inside. My lips on her skin is almost a necessity, like a taste of what's yet to come. She started softly laughing when I pulled out of her, so I playfully spanked her and she laughed even louder, rolling over so I can help pull her back up.

"What is so funny?" I ask her, my smile just as wide as hers while I hold her face. Her emeralds sparkled with delight, answering, "I've never done that before!"

"What part?" I ask her back.

She replies with her cheeks blushing, "Any of it. You are way more experienced than me." I think my smile is bigger than hers now as I cannot believe it can get any better than this, and somehow it always does.

Picking her up to carry her to the shower, I reply, "I highly doubt that. I've woken up with you more times than anyone else."

Cringing to myself a bit embarrassed at my honesty on my dating life filled with one-night stands.

"Did you at least like it?"

Her eyes go wide as she responds, "I could do that every morning…I'll put that on your Alexis duty list!"

Yep, it can get better.

"I wouldn't consider that a duty, babe," I reply while turning on the shower, "but yes, I agree we should do that every day."

"I have to pee," she says to me jumping down and giving me a look. I tell her, "You better get used to peeing in front of me, because I'm not planning on leaving." I don't think there was anything this girl could do to bother me, and her sitting on a toilet to pee and drain my semen out of her is actually a rewarding sight for me.

When she steps in the shower, she says, "I had to check the time, it's 6am"

"Did you think you slept in?" I ask.

"I did sleep in, I am usually up by five."

"Sheesh," I reply, "I'm a night owl babe, I won't be able to leave work any time before midnight tonight to come over to your house."

"I'll leave the door unlocked," she says breezily as I watch in awe at the water dripping off her skin.

"You better not," I reply to her firmly, "I never thought I would actually have something I needed from Pauley."

"Oh, not you too," she groans while I embrace her, kissing the water off her shoulders while my hands graze her bottom, I bring it up, "I didn't know there was a reason."

Ugh

"It's not a fair reason," she starts saying as she scrubs soap on my chest, "Why do our showers always have to end up with me having to talk about my crazy?"

I could tell she was stalling and I wasn't sure why, so I said, "that's the last thing I think of remembering the last time we showered together," knowing if I make her feel more comfortable she will talk to me, and I wanted her to talk to me, so I kept my hands in motion when I add, "I'll get it out of you one way or another because I can't stop worrying about it."

"I don't think anything is wrong, Jameson is still worried about the past. It was a long five years being managed by Terrie and living with Rachel."

I couldn't help but blow out a frustrated sigh, causing her to peer up at me with wary eyes. I went to speak, but then I stopped myself. She was washing her hair underneath the water as I watched her, thinking about how I could tell her how I felt about wanting to know about all of her. I find my words and speak, "There is nothing you can say to me that will change how I feel for you. I wish you would tell me."

Looking at me with a scared look on her face, she tells me, "Thatcher Green was one of Rachel's psychiatrists when we were teenagers. He was hired by her mom to come to the house to meet with Rachel and prescribe her medicine for her depression and anxiety. He was always a hoax doctor, but Terrie was screwing him after the visits to make sure he prescribed her the oxy she fed on, so she didn't care if he wasn't giving Rachel proper care."

I was already cringing at the thought that it was a doctor that was the threat. Alexis kept speaking while we continued to get out of the shower and towel dry, the distraction making it easier for her to speak.

"We were sixteen and he had started making advances on Rachel during her appointments and she didn't tell me for a few months. He was always scheduled to see her during the middle of the day when I was still in school, so I didn't have any idea. He kissed her on the cheek and ended up kissing her on her lips one day and she confessed to her mom, but Terrie just flipped out on her instead. She started blaming Rachel for being a slut and of course never got rid of him. So, then Rachel asked me to start sitting in her sessions with her because she was afraid of him, and he started diagnosing her with paranoia."

The two of us were literally brushing our teeth and I couldn't believe what I was hearing. My mouth was full of soapy green spit, and after Alexis wiped off her face, she spoke to me so nonchalantly, like she didn't let the past bother her, continuing saying, "he had his own set of problems and ended up with this sick obsession with me and showed up at my apartment one night. It was really late, and I was sleeping, and he started casually knocking on my front door, which was locked by the way," she says to me smoothly sticking her index finger to my chest. I grab her finger and use my right hand to lift her up and then sit down on the edge of the bed, her facing me in my lap, in my arms as I ask, "Where were your parents?"

Focusing on a strand of my hair from my head in her fingertips, Alexis shrugs and replies, "Not around. I was home alone. He broke in and I locked myself in my bedroom. I didn't have a phone, but Jameson and I shared walkie talkies, so I screamed for him to come help me."

My eyebrows shoot up, and she smiles and says, "Yep, I told you, I didn't grow up with a phone."

"You were pretty vague. What happened?"

I'm feeling angry and appalled, and I can't move, and the only thing I can think of to do is curl my arms in tighter around her.

"Thatcher got nervous with my loud screaming and turned on his therapist voice outside my door, trying to convince me he wasn't going to hurt me and that he was just there to talk about my home life, but when I didn't stop screaming, he kicked the door in and wrestled with me. But Jameson and his older brother, Travis, came in and fought him off of me before he got my pants down."

"Jesus," I huff out managing to take a deep breath, "He was going to rape you?"

"Yea pretty much, but he didn't," she replies quietly like she's trying to comfort me from hearing this.

"Thatcher was probably in his late thirties at the time, and he was in good shape and too strong for me so he would have gotten what he came for if it hadn't been for Jameson. Anyways, Jameson's brother didn't let us call the cops. Travis is ten years older than us, and he was a part of some gang that was dealing drugs out of our apartment buildings, so he didn't want the 'unwanted attention.' But also, Thatcher had the upper hand when he left that night because he never had to admit what he did. He is a high-end concierge doctor who makes all this money from house calls for rich people and we were poor kids with no responsible parent avoiding being placed in foster care, so we left it."

Angry, I ask. "Is that the last time you saw this Thatcher fucker?"

Her eyes look into mine in her pause, shrugs and then she replies, "No, Terrie didn't stop screwing him. I didn't want to tell Terrie because it would have only hurt us, or more so Rachel, in the end. He was her doctor for another few months until he left for a few years, but they started dating again when we were twenty-two, and Terrie kicked us out for him to move in with her. She bought Rachel the condo in the city of Boston, where I just left from."
"So, for those few months of him still being Rachel's doctor, what did he do?"

Forcing a small smile for me she replies, "He acted like it never happened. Rachel and I had to still sit in a room with him on a monthly basis and pretend he didn't touch either of us, until he up and left one day and moved his practice to Atlanta a few months later. We thought Terrie had threatened him, but actually, within that time, both my parents overdosed on the couch. It was after that when Jameson and I found out through the word on the street that when Thatcher came looking for me that night, he ended up leaving striking a business deal with Travis. No ratting on anyone if Thatcher becomes the supplier."
The circle of her chaotic past is terrifying, and I had pulled us back to lay on the bed close to her to keep listening. She was tearing her wall down for me, and I was connecting all of her pieces.
I try to speak but I wasn't sure, "So the drugs your parents died from..."
She tells it to me straight, "Thatcher's drugs."
"Shit, Alexis!" I huff out in exasperation.
"I told you I'm complicated."
"Don't say that. I'm actually happy you are finally telling me all of this stuff, I reply. "So why would Jameson think Terrie and Thatcher may be a threat to you now?"
"Because when they dated a few years ago, when I was being managed by Kel and not Terrie, Thatcher started following me again. He stopped me one night while I was leaving my Condo and asked if I would have dinner with him."
"You're kidding me. He wanted you to date him?"
"Yes!" She says with a grin, "Can you believe that?"
I think for a second before I reply, "Baby, now that I think about it, it's not surprising you have stalkers. Look at you."

"Shush," she barks playfully then continues with her story, "Terrie allowed Rachel to pick out a new place to live within a certain vicinity to her office when we were twenty two and still under her control. That's when Rachel sought after her own plan and got in close with someone in the real estate business that gave her insight to upcoming lease terms for surrounding spaces, she picked out her condo and told Terrie to purchase it, and at the same time, Rachel took funds Terrie had put in an account for her for 'renovations' and instead gave it to me and Jameson to put a down payment on the two condos across the hall, that way we were together with her still and Terrie didn't know. Well, that meant, Thatcher didn't know, and when he came to my condo door one night and I saw through the peephole who it was, I called Jameson and he came out and beat the shit out of him in the hallway. I never saw him after that."

"So, now that Thatcher knows Jameson isn't around to protect you anymore, that's why he thinks Thatcher is capable of coming after you." It was clearer to me now why her friend felt so seriously about her protection.

I add, "I can't say I blame him for hiring Pauley, now that I know, but why would Terrie be looking for you?"

Alexis takes a deep sigh, places her hand on my cheek and answers replying, "When Rachel died, she left me all the money in her trust fund that B.B. had set up for her as a child to use when she turned 25, and Terrie was expecting to be able to access it since she always had a hand in Rachel's business. Now that Rachel is dead and left everything to me, and she's broke, she is desperate."

Shuffling up over her, I ask, "And you don't think that's something to be cautious about?"

Annoyed she replies, "No, I don't think I need to hire a bodyguard for the rest of my life."

"Well maybe just for as long as they are alive," I say to her then realizing maybe I shouldn't have when she bites back with another smart remark.

"That sounds like a great idea, why don't I go ahead and ask Pauley if he's up to make a deal." I don't let her speak anymore words as I plant an angry kiss on her lips, hoping to wipe the smirk off her face. She kisses me back then pulls away and asks, "Can we be done with this conversation now? I'm hungry and need to go to the gym before Sabine gets here."

"If you're talking about the same gym Vince goes to, I'd rather you not."

Huffing at me again she replies, "But that's my gym!"

"I happen to know another great gym in town," I say swooning.

"No way, my gym has cardio heaven in controlled temperatures. And there is no way I can lose my cardio in the middle of this dance."

"Let me come with you," I say before even thinking I might be pushing myself on her too far.

"You can come with me just this once so you can see for yourself there is no trouble, but you are not gym babysitting me, plus, I doubt you can keep up," she winks at me and then springs forward to go running down the stairs, with me behind trying to keep up.

Chapter 29   Alexis

It is Thursday afternoon, and Declan and I have dinner plans at Estel and Margie's tonight. I was feeling insecure about meeting up with Declan since I said goodbye to him from my house this morning. Last night, he had come over after his work around two in the morning, to stay with me, like he had said he would, right at the same time I was having one of my nightmares about Rachel. He looked quite pale once he woke me up out of my incoherent state and I found him over top of me. I think I must have just fallen back asleep, because the next thing I remember was waking up for my alarm in his arms this morning and leaving him asleep in my bedroom. I am embarrassed but also feeling nervous and in wonderment about how long it will take Declan to realize I'm a complete mess, and for him to decide he doesn't want me anymore. I thought I was making progress in my new normal, lately it seems like there has been nothing but backwards flips.

Already beginning to feel overworked in this project with it taking up all my time in practice, meetings, creating periods, workouts, sleepless nights, all of which have left me no time to stop and return to sorting Rachel's puzzle. I was finally turning off all of my equipment I've been using for the last three hours while locking myself in the Mixx room with my headphones to work. Stepping out, I find Sabine practicing on the dance floor in one of the lingerie bodices with thigh highs. She didn't see me, so I gave her a playful whistle.

She smiles wide and says, "I can't imagine how nervous you must feel doing this. I'm only a backup 'maybe' and I'm nervous!"

"You look great, and you are nobody's maybe. You are my first pick," I tell her as she gives me a glorious 'ya right' smile. I wasn't kidding, Sabine had big potential as a dancer if she wanted to devote her heart and time into it. She had the technical formations down and she landed most moves, she just needed to loosen up a bit, and it was nice to see her practicing when I wasn't working with her.

Continuing her moves and talking to me through the reflection of the mirror, she tells me, "You won't believe all the things that happened when you were in there today."

"Tell me all the things," I reply back, curious about how the world turned while I was in deep thought work mode.

She replies, "First off, our good buddies from Swollen showed up and started packing all of our boxes in the trailer. I didn't go outside to speak to them though, but I did see another priceless photo worthy face on that blonde hottie when Pauley came out to ask them what they were doing."

Laughing with her thinking about why they were here doing that in the first place, I ask.

"Is this them making it up to us?"

Laughing some more, she nods in between her steps then adds,

"Oh that's not even the best part of the day. That same girl came back again to ask for you and drop off her resume. I had to talk to her because of course she came when Pauley had left on his lunch break. She was snippy again and didn't leave me with anything but the dust from her shoes."

"How can someone be so stupid?" I ask.

Sabine replies, "I don't know, but the girl looks younger than me."

"I guess she will figure out she has no chance soon enough," I say walking up to the front to gather my things to take home with me. Looking out the window, I see the empty area and my front entrance clear from all of the boxes, in my mind I can't help but think Declan had something to do with the cleanup crew. Stepping outside, I walk over to the storage pod to peak inside since I hadn't yet looked at it up closely. There were racks filled and boxes stacked along the whole backside.

Suddenly a deep male voice speaks out, "Looks like a lot of stuff in there," scaring me while I'm stuck inside the enclosed unit, jumping back, and catching my back leg on a corner of a cardboard box, causing me to trip backwards over the box to land in arms.

"Shit! I didn't mean to scare you, I'm so sorry, are you okay?" It was David speaking to me as he tries standing me up straight. I wobbled a bit back to stand, but I could feel the blood behind my leg.

"You're bleeding," David says to me, now kneeling down staring eyes wide at my cut, "my brother is going to murder me."

I couldn't help but start laughing, and then I saw Pauley behind him with his arms crossed looking furious.

"I told you I was going inside to ask her if you were allowed in, now look what you've done. Alexis, I'm sorry."

"Stop it," I say with my hand out to Pauley, I could tell David had an edge to his normally easy-going demeanor, and I knew it had something to do with my new security guard who stopped him.

"This is not anyone's fault but my own, I'm super clumsy. Pauley, you don't need to stop and ask me about David, I'll write a list for you of those exceptions that are free and clear to pass you."

"Got it, ma'am," Pauley replies, nodding to me and avoiding David, turning back to go to the trailer, leaving me standing there with Declan's little brother, looking like a young ripped Sylvester Stallone, in his workout clothes.

"Hi, David!" I say excitedly to him, trying to ease the sore look on his face as he stares at my bloody leg that's starting to sting, "How did you get here?"

David brings his eyes back up to me, "I decided I needed a run, so I thought I'd pop in to see if my idiot brother has been here to beg for your forgiveness?"

"He has," I say causing him to laugh shortly and reply, "Well that's good to hear he isn't a complete fool after all, since I know how much he likes you. Which also means I'm a dead man if I don't fix you up immediately...am I allowed inside?"

I play smack him on the shoulder, leaning my weight on my slice free leg as I reply, "of course, sorry about Pauley, I'm not sure if you knew he was here."

The pain in my leg started stinging, and David steps over beside me to say, "Here, lean on me. We have to get you inside."

I do lean on him, still feeling a bit stunned about my injury now dripping off my foot. He speaks nervously, "I actually got a heads up about Pauley from Dax, so no big deal," about to take another step when we both hear the rumble and turn our heads.

"Shit, I'm a dead man," David grumbles out to me, following the sight of the unexpected arrival of Declan, seemingly revving the engine speeding around once he got closer.

I tell David as I keep leaning on him and walking forward, "Don't be so worried."

David turns to face me, looking paler than before and says, "They don't call him Irish for nothin' around here. You've seen just a taste of his Irish temper when it comes to protecting what's important to him. I not only made you bleed, now I'm touching you."

The engine turned off and David, who is towering two feet above me, whispers, "Can you walk faster?"

I giggle but get interrupted by a roar of curse words coming from Declan running towards us. Pauley was standing outside his trailer door watching the show with a wicked grin on his face.

"David!"

Before we could make it to open the front door, I see David's body lunge forward as Declan approaches my side, throwing his brother onto the ground.

"Declan!" I scream at him, "Why would you-

"What happened?" He asks me his face a rage, "Baby, you're bleeding, are yea okay?"

Before he lets me answer, Declan screams to David, "Open the door!"

Then he turns and picks me up, not our way though, I'm more like a baby in his arms, his blue eyes sear back into me. I guess he wants me to talk now that poor David has stumbled to open the door wide for us to walk in.

"It wasn't his fault, I tripped. It's just a small scratch."

"This is bloody all down your leg," his voice rising, "it's more than just a scratch."

I roll my eyes, as I am witnessing the Declan trying to keep his control in his moment of unnecessary panic, my panties are wet. Sabine hadn't noticed our abrupt arrival as she was still dancing in her skimpy outfit, and my smile couldn't be wider as I notice the pure shock on David who is staring at her. However, Declan disrupts my witnessing a man being stopped in his tracks by a woman, by running us up the stairs, with a scowl still upon his face, as he grumbles in question, "Do you have bandages up here?"

The wound started aching more, and I was starting to feel more thankful to be treated like a princess and being swept to safety, as Declan treats my stumble like a bigger deal than necessary. He lays me on the bed and turns towards the bathroom.

"Declan, I'm fine," I say as I sit up to inspect my leg. It's a long thin paper cut from the cardboard across the back of my shin. He comes back with a wet washcloth and starts cleaning me off.

"Ouchie," I squeal due to the sting from the cloth.

"What the heck happened?" He asked with a sweeter voice than before.

"I tripped over a box and landed on David."

"Why is David here?"

"Uh, I'm not sure actually," I tell him while he is seemingly not thrilled with my answer, so shaking my head I add, "you are so cute when you're mad. Broody, broody, broody," A smile comes out of him, making my nerdy comment worthwhile.

He replies, "well, it looks like it's going to be a big welt there. That won't be fun to practice on."

My laugh broke off into another yelp from the cloth wiping the blood off, Declan bandaged me up and carried me back downstairs to find a cuter sight of Sabine and David on the dance floor beside each other, him seemingly practicing her moves she is trying to teach him. They both stopped as soon as they noticed our return. I watch as Sabine starts walking to the back, and David's eyes track her, before bringing them back to Declan to say, "You look better than the last time I saw you."

Declan's unimpressed face fires back, "No thanks to you."

"You don't need to be moping around like a baby about it," David beefs back. I could feel the tension and wild tempers stirring between these two Irish brothers, both of their accents getting heavier in their bickering back and forth. Stretching this argument out longer than the time Declan and I have to make it to dinner to stay in Margie's good graces, so I interrupt the two of them before Declan rips his head off and say, "maybe we don't have to relive that night again for all of our sakes."

"I got the fight info," David says sternly, just as Sabine rejoins us from covering herself up with a t-shirt and shorts and steals his attention away for the second.

"When is it?" Declan asks immediately.

"Two weeks and there is a request waiting for you to sign off on, because they want to have it in the barn."

"I'm not approving anything about this. That's way too soon, you have no time to get properly prepared."

David ignores Declan's remark and proceeds with the rest of the information, "Brando Ford, the banker from Lake Champlain, was approached by Vince himself several months ago to see if he would consider me a profitable underdog in a match."

Declan replies, "He's had you scouted."

David responds with a nod and says with a teasing smile, "Apparently, I'm worth it. Even more so that now I switched it up."

"What do you mean?" Declan questions him immediately.

David keeps his grin when he says, "I made sure this was a grudge match. There is no way I'm fighting for money. I'm fighting for honoring Daniel, so I told Ford to take the winner's purse off the table. In Vince's response, he settled only if the fight could happen sooner."

I was trying to figure out how the betting works while Declan flusters around in his irritated noises. I looked over at my friend, Sabine, who had an even more confused look on her face than me, and I realized because she really has no idea what was going on, which was a whole other conversation about her crush I hadn't told her yet, I should give them space to talk. I say to Sabine, "Maybe we should go see if Pauley has any good snacks in his trailer."

She smiled and was about to agree but Declan stopped her with the movement of his body swiftly turning to face me and stating, "There's no reason to do that."

David also agrees with his brother quickly saying, "Yeah, please don't do that."

"A snack is pretty much the only reason we need," responds Sabine.

Declan screeches his eyes burning into me, "Well neither of you will be getting your snacks from Pauley for Christ sake!"

I snort out a laugh and cover my mouth to stop it, causing more noises of irritancies to come out of my broody man.

Declan's arms pull me into him as he says, "Baby, that idiot little brother of mine just took away probably the only thing that could have made this fight worthwhile for him."

"Cut it out, Declan!" David pipes back with anger in his voice, "Whether you like it or not, I am game on with going up against Bordeaux in the ring. This one's mine and I'm choosing to handle it my way."

"You shouldn't have to," Declan manages to reply.

But David's anger is already settled inside as he shakes his head and replies, "I'm not asking for your permission to fight. Ronnie and Dax have already agreed to authorize the use of the barn, so I don't need that from you either." Walking forward up to Declan's face, he continues, "Two weeks. And if you have that small of faith in me Declan, then do me a favor and stay out of my corner."

David marches out of the studio before any of us could say anymore, leaving us in his bitter dust.

Chapter 30   Declan

It was when my plate of Margie's food was being eaten up by my eyes more than my mouth when I realized how much David succeeded at hitting me hard, proving to be tampering with my good conscience by my lack of hunger tonight. Luckily, Alexis has been by my side, taking over conversation with Estel and Margie to help fill my gaps.

"Alexis," Estel says, "I hope you don't mind, but I ordered you a truckload of wood to be delivered next week."

Stunned, she questions him, "For me? Uh, what do I need that much wood for, exactly?"

Estel has a bite of food still stuck in his cheek when he quickly states, "Well, in case the power goes out in the winter, it's always good to have a pile handy. They will stack it just up on the side of your driveway, so it won't be in the way."

"Oh gosh, thank you, I hope that doesn't really happen. I have money, Estel. Let me pay you," she replies back frantically, looking like all she is thinking about is the sullen thought of being without a heater."

"No, you won't young lady, I'm happy to do it. I would have done it myself from a tree out back like I usually do, but I haven't gotten a chance to repair the ol' chainsaw yet this year."

Alexis asks. "You cut a big tree down by yourself every year?"

"Sure, I do. It's something I've done for years, Laura used to go out with me as my helper. We would pick out the best looking one that would give us enough wood to last us through the winter. Always say our thanks for its abundant supply and chop it down."

Margie adds in, "And in the Spring we would pay it forward and plant two more."

"Oh, my goodness!" Alexis squeals in excitement, "that sounds lovely. I've always chopped my own Christmas tree down. And when I was little, I would write the tree a thank you note and tell it how much I loved it and promised to make it beautiful," her reminiscing face a glow when she speaks about her Christmas memory.

One she didn't seem to have anyone else included in.

Estel chuckled and said, "Well dear, you moved to the right place. This year you will be pleased with your selection, Carl planted a small Christmas tree grove in your back corner many years ago and it's grown quite nicely."

Margie lays her hand on Alexis's and says, "I think you and I were meant to be."

"I think so, too!" Alexis replies to her.

I decide it's my time to pipe in sounding offended, "Hey!"

"Oh, you too, you pouty boy," Margie says to me looking bright, with her hair a fresh colored orange and bangs cut short across her face, "If my dinner can't perk you up, I'm running out of options since Alexis made me promise to skip the dessert."

Estel and I groan out our disappointment while Alexis puts on a sad face, making me quickly forget about the part about no dessert, only to scoot closer to her and place my hand on her thigh, saying out loud "I guess I'm still learning how to compromise."

"It's a lifetime journey, son," remarks Estel, as he hands me another beer.

Then continuing, "Speaking of compromise, I wanted to share something personal with you both. After our dinner the last time, Alexis, you had me thinking about that name of your friend's father, 'Butler.' I knew I had heard it before, and I finally went deeper into my thoughts, one of the ones you hold behind too many doors to try not to remember. And I found that memory his name was a part of."

Estel rocks on the back legs of his chair while continuing with his memory, "We were always very close to our daughter, and we always tried to keep an open mind about things, but when she finished high school and didn't want to go to college, it took a lot for me to wrap my head around understanding. She was eighteen and wanted to follow her dreams and be a singer instead. Margie and I sat down with her, and even though I had many differences, we all agreed Laura could take the year off and sort through some decisions for her future.

She was very smart and had done well, so if the time eventually came, and she had decided to go to college, all she had to do was pick somewhere and apply. Anyhow, it was over a year later, she was nineteen and all of us were butting heads a bit more about her dream of being a singer. I was still basically funding her aspiring career that she had chosen to work full time on, and she was becoming obsessed with getting out of this town. There was a talent audition for B.B. Butler Productions that she wanted to go to in Boston, but I told her I wasn't paying for it since she had no money and there was nobody traveling with her. She argued with me about it and ended up packing up and getting on a train and left without telling us in the middle of the night."

Alexis speaks, "Did she go to the audition?"

Margie answers for Estel, "She did go, but she didn't get the part. Although, she ended up meeting a friend during the audition instead, and that's who convinced her to stay in Boston."

Estel tells us, "She had come home and begged to move. That led to a discussion where we made a compromise that I would pay for her to go if she was attending college classes there, so that's what we settled on. She moved out a couple weeks later and Margie and I drove behind her to the University of Boston with her to set up her dorm room."

Margie looks at her husband and says, "That was such a long time ago, I can't believe you remembered it was B.B. Butler's audition."

He chuckles a laugh out and says, "I hadn't until Alexis reminded me of his name."

"Small world," I say.

Alexis had deep thought printed throughout her expression, quietly gathering her utensils to put on her plate, like she was trying to keep distracted, while she says, "That sounds like a time before Rachel was even born, when B.B. moved his office from New York to Boston. He was a true artist from what I have heard about him, he was probably a big deal for her to audition for, I couldn't imagine how nervous Laura must have been."

"Laura always thought he was a hunk. You know, she never spoke to us again about the audition once she said she didn't make it...," Margie takes a deep breath and wipes a tear from the corner of her eye when she proceeds to tell us, "Really, Laura didn't talk to us much about anything once she moved to Boston, because what she did tell us while she was there, turned out not to be the truth."

Alexis puts her hand on Margie's just as Margie does the same, a loving embrace. Margie tells her, "I know you told us about your Rachel, and I can tell she meant a lot to you. Unfortunately, Estel and I have had many years of grieving for Laura, who also took her own life, when she was only twenty."

Estel takes over to explain, "Laura committed suicide on the opposite end of Boston, far from the University...and when Margie and I went back to the school once we found out she died, they told us she never enrolled in any classes..."

Both Alexis and I share our sympathies, as Estel explains, "We didn't have cell phones to keep in touch like you can these days but looking back I can always come up with a bunch of things I should have done differently."

"Sounds familiar," I say unexpectedly, Estel gives me a smile and continues to say, "Well, I thought I would share with you, because not only do Margie and I really enjoy the company of you two young kids, and we know just by lookin' at ya, that you both have your own set of struggles going on. But we all have them, and it's how we pull through them that matters. And sometimes, it's nice to talk about it, and we are here for the both of you if you ever need that."

Maybe a dose of loving grandparent like affection can help soothe the soul no matter your age, because as solemn of a conversation we had tonight, Alexis and I both seemed to be in better spirits than the ones we came over here with by the end of the evening. Margie treated us to some of her homemade honey candies, a little sweet to make up for not having dessert. Alexis talked about her meeting she had with Maya Gueterra, and I discussed my part in ownership of Swollen. Both of us promising Estel and Margie tickets to the SheerMe Show, causing Margie's dark eyebrows to shoot up so high on her head in her excitement, they were almost hidden underneath her orange bangs. For it to be one of the first times Alexis and I have actually sat down together and discussed our work and business matters, having Estel and Margie there acting as our buffer, it didn't end up feeling weird at all. We were laughing, and I may have even made a move or two on Alexis below the table, giving away my not so innocent intentions I had with her.

Once we were stepping outside to leave, Margie asks Alexis, "Did you ever call Carl?"

Alexis looks over to me and says, "I think I'm going to try him when I get back home, hopefully it's not too late."

Estel touts back, "It's an hour earlier where he is in Florida, anyhow."

"Even better," I reply with a smile, knowing it was the right time since Alexis was feeling brave. While we were walking back to her house, I picked her up and carried her the rest of the way, blaming her hurt leg for my need to have her wrapped around me in our way. Pouring us some liquid courage once we got nestled inside, she tells me about the jewelry box and documents that Rachel left for her, making me even more invested in this hunt for Rachel's answers.

Alexis states, "I hate sounding awful, but I don't want to spend the rest of my life questioning and wondering about why Rachel did what she did, like Estel and Margie have to. Rachel at least gave me something to go off of to solve some of my questions, whereas Laura left them stranded without any reasons."

"You're right," I tell her, "One seems sudden and the other seems planned, but either way, I think I would have to reason with it somehow in order to move on."

Alexis dials Carl's number as we wait on speaker in anticipation.

The older voice gruffly answers the line and Alexis speaks, "I'm calling to ask if you would tell me about meeting Rachel Butler, who you sold your home to-"

"I'm not interested in talking to any tabloids!" Carl gruffs out with a stiff tone.

"Oh, no Carl, Rachel was my best friend. My name is Alexis Andrews. I'm the one who lives in your Paisley home now."

There was a silence on the line that felt intense until Carl replied more softly, "She died before she could even move in."

"Yes," Alexis replies softly, "A surprise to us all, she left the house to me. I was hoping you would have some insight to help me know why."

He says, "Alexis, I am not sure I can tell you anything that will help you."

Alexis looking into the phone with determination on her face replies, "Anything is better than nothing in determining Rachel's reasoning's that keep stopping me from being able to sleep here at night."

Carl gives an audible sigh and replies, "I found her sitting on the steps of my front porch. I thought she was lost at first, but then I saw her, and I knew exactly who she was. What is it that you want to know?"

Alexis looks at me for strength as she answers, "All of it."

Carl says, "I'm not sure there is much to tell. There are some things you will never be able to understand until it's looking right in front of you. When I saw those blue eyes, I knew it was my time to come be with my grandchildren here in Florida. That's all there was to it. She made me an offer on that porch, and I took it."

I knew Alexis felt disappointed after the phone call.

"It wasn't all a waste of time, he proved her actual existence in Paisley at some point. That helps with your timeline of things," I tell her as we lay in her bat cave bedroom, drunk and chatty.

"I suppose," she agrees unconvincingly.

Her small freckles that trail high along her cheeks were popping out of her alcohol flushed smile as I take advantage of our loose mouths and trail her with kisses while she let's me in.

"It bugs me because those weeks she wasn't with me this past Christmas, which was the longest I've been without seeing her since we met. I thought she was with Terrie at the beach house for the holidays, and she ended up here somehow. I can't stand that evil woman, I couldn't spend another day with her once I quit, but I feel bad because Rachel felt obligated to spend the time with Terrie still, but I was firm and didn't go with her last year."

"You fought through it because you knew it was for the right reasons, and I'm sure Rachel knew that too. When did you quit?"

Alexis sighs and replies, "I was twenty one when I figured out the reality of the amount of control Terrie had over me. Money, a bed, a job... it had me second guess the health of my relationship with Rachel too. I needed Rachel, but sometimes I think she needed me more."

"She was sick babe, who took care of her if her mother didn't?" I asked, already knowing the answer.

"I did. I gave everything I had to her for all those years when she was really sick. We spent weeks of nonstop work for Terrie and then we would go straight to bed, because she never felt good enough to go out. It started wearing on me, and one night, Jameson called me up to tell me MartaBeat's tour dates, and I flipped out in excitement, but Rachel just laid in her bed and smiled. It made me so angry at her and I think that's when I began to realize how deep I was in the Butler world and if I wanted to keep my own sanity, I needed to find myself again. So, as hard as it was to explain to Rachel some of the things her mom did to me over the years... that I couldn't excuse the way she could anymore, I felt like it was my most vulnerable moment when I packed up and I had nowhere to go that I belonged."

"Your parents didn't leave you anything?"

Alexis laughs and pokes the tip of my nose with her finger playfully as she replies,

"Besides ruined credit and shit loads of debt, they gave me nothing. Jameson offered me to stay with him, but he was also playing shows and partying every night then, in and out screwing different girls each night, so I instead moved in with Kel and her husband for a couple of months until Rachel came through with the condo. I made the move for myself for once, but I still needed her to save me, financially, until I made it on my own enough to pay her back. The day I told Terrie I quit, Rachel tried to be strong for me... but I think she felt like I quit on her a bit too. I never wanted to have to see Terrie again and that meant refusing to accompany Rachel to the holiday festivities her mom held that she had to still attend."

I reply, "Hell no you didn't want to do that."

"No, I didn't, but that space gave her the time to buy a house in this town, transfer all of her things to me, and purposely drink down a bottle of pills Thatcher prescribed to her."

Writhing, rolling, throat on fire
A can of waste
A can to taste

My heart pitted in my stomach, "Rachel wrote that in her poem."

Her astonished eyes open wide and a serious look spread across her face, as she says, "Declan, you're so right. That's what those words meant. She planned how she was going to do it too."

I needed to take back control of our moods, so I kissed her lips, again, and again, until I knew I distracted her well enough to tell her,

"Alexis, I think it's time I tell you about my plans I have for you for the rest of the night."

"Please have good plans," she whines into kissing my mouth, stroking her tongue on mine.

Screwed. I was actually making lots of plans with her in that moment. I was feeling like she was finally becoming mine.

I tell her as I start taking off her clothes, "Only good plans from now on, baby."

Chapter 31   Alexis

Declan decided that I needed a redo at meeting Dax and Ronnie sometime this week, while also letting me know that they will be the ones to work with me through this SheerMe project. Declan made sure to convince me that his role is the most important, making sure he keeps me satisfied each night and morning, and in between, to keep me charged and ready. It shouldn't be hard for him, or it always is, depending on how you look at it. Declan has no problem fully satisfying me. We spent the weekend in tortuous pleasure in between work and play, giving away our hearts with each minute that ticked by. There was no simple answer to what was happening between us. I've even started expecting him to be with me when he's not working, making this relationship seem much more serious than I ever could have imagined in such a short amount of time.

Like a gift, he was so happy with himself when he played me this video on his phone that he recorded for me. It was of himself touring through his condo, walking in room to room, and even opening his empty fridge, to prove to me he has a home, and he lives alone, somewhere I've never seen before. Of course, it was the cutest thing ever and I appreciated his thought, but I almost didn't want him to go back to his condo. I like having him stay with me, I sleep better with less nightmares, and I'm getting used to having him beside me.

Super shit.
Stay Cautious.
My heart is involved now, I hear it thumping for him even when he isn't around, and it's becoming a steady rhythm.
 He had gone to stay on the couch at David's on Sunday night, and I knew his routine when Monday rolled around, he told me about his visit with Daniel when I talked to him one of the several times. Declan called me almost every hour on the hour yesterday until I think I convinced him he needed to go check on David, where he stayed over last night. I worked by myself all day since Sabine was off taking her last set of final exams, and when I finished I thought it was best to run through my thoughts in my cardio heaven. Until I wasn't alone and once again, I had a badgering neighbor.
"Don't you know better when to leave things alone?" I question looking over to Vince, shirtless with his chest and head looking bigger than ever, like I could just take a needle and pop him so he can deflate back to normal.

"I've never been one to listen," he replies arrogantly as he starts his treadmill up to my same speed.
This was a different feeling coming over me than the last time I saw him, maybe because I hated him more.

He speaks, "Seems we have that in common, since I'm sure you were told not to come here again by a certain someone. Breaking his rules, tisk tisk."

He was pushing the conversation to Declan already, and even though he was right about Declan feeling wary of me coming to this gym once he knew Vince's past aggressions towards me, he still has never told me I can't be here, like Vince is implying.
"We have nothing in common," I tell him looking straight ahead.

"Well, we certainly have this gym in common. Not to mention the matching physique. I mean damn girl...I will give you everything you will ever need."

He was ruthless.
And ugly.
But they were only words he spoke.
"It seems late for you to be here. Don't you have anything better to do?" I say sounding bored, trying to divert this awkward situation from any possibility of a relationship.
He laughs and side eyes me replying, "I can think of a few things, but, as the curse of Irish luck still has it, you are denying yourself the opportunity to know what true passion can give you."
I can't help but laugh at him now, adamant about standing my ground this time and not being the one to run off. In my most sarcastic tone I reply, "Oh how ever will I survive?"
He answers, "It's not a problem, I know Irish can't handle such a delicate flower, but I know how to make you blossom when you realize the error of your ways. When you come looking for me, I'll be right here."
"It's actually times like these when I come at odd hours to avoid you."
"Then maybe I'll come looking for you. It won't matter the hours sweetheart, once I succeed at kicking your lover boy's other brother's ass, you'll be looking at the new owner of this place."
I take back my stance on trying to not sway from what I was doing once I heard him say it, a permanent position here in Paisley, slowing down my pace pressing the minus sign as hard as I could a few times, I look over at Vince, fair skin and a fresh buzz cut looking delighted with himself.
"And when you don't win, what then?"
His laugh made me cringe, Vince replies, "I'll tear all three of those McQuade's down one by one, just you wait."
"Why would you even care to do that?" I asked.
I know I shouldn't be getting myself involved in this but what he just told me was on purpose, and it pissed me off. He knew he was succeeding at getting under my skin, as he replies back, "Besides them always getting in my way, I don't care at all for them, doll, I'm just going to go ahead and finish them off because I can." I blinked twice to make sure I wasn't hearing or seeing things, as he then slowed down and jumped off the treadmill.
Meeting my eyes with a smile, he says, "I'm glad you moved here, Feisty. You put a little spice in this town it needed, and I want it. I'm sure I'll be seeing you around." Vince gets one last eyeful, then turns away, leaving me alone to my walking pace on the treadmill with unease stirring in my gut. I tried not to let him get to me, this was what he was, a bully, that Declan warned me about.
I spent another hour working off my irritation, and after I was cleaned up and walking out to my car, I heard the music blaring before looking up to see Vince through his windshield in the parking spot next to mine.
He keeps the car running with the old Aerosmith blasting, as he walks around to my driver's side next to me and says, "Have you decided to give me a turn, yet?"
He was closer than necessary, and with his music blasting, it covered our words.
Unfortunately, I've had my fair share of situations like these, but I always usually had a buddy

with me. Now, without Jameson, the only one I know to call would be Declan. And I want to try to get out of this before it comes to that. I'm calm and stern when I reply to Vince stating, "Get out of my way."

He grabs my ass in a quick lunge with a vicious laugh, as he sneers in my ear, "Nobody gets in my way, especially not Irish Fucking McQuade," his breath spitting on me as he lets go and struts back to his car. I yelled through the music as he pulled away, my fire was burning, and I was as angry as ever when I got in my car.

I took my time driving back to my studio. I was alone again, and all stirred up even after a shower. I was feeling guilty, and I knew this wasn't something I wanted to tell Declan about since it would only make him more vulnerable during this time when he was just coming around to the idea of David's fight. I hated that maybe I put myself in this position, maybe I should have stayed away from that gym and none of this would have been put on my shoulders. I was knocking before I knew what I was going to say, but I know there is something to those confidentiality papers Jameson made him sign, and right now, I needed to voice out my concerns to someone.

Pauley answers the door like there was a fire. "Alexis! You brought dinner?"

"I brought you a good dinner while, unfortunately what I picked up for myself is like a snack portion I have to spread out as my dinner because of this show coming up."

"Come on in, sorry, I wasn't expecting company."

It was spatial for it being a trailer, with a secluded area for sleeping quarters and a full bathroom. It still felt stuffy and wasn't too clean since only Pauley was occupying it.

There was a security desk that had the monitor showing of the outside of my studio's parking lot and front door, which made me feel a bit creeped out, but I couldn't go there at this point. I pulled out our food and we ate on the small round kitchen table with the takeout utensils. Without small talk, Pauley knew me better than I knew him, so I decided I should just ask, "Do you trust Vince Bordeaux since he's your cousin?"

His face tensed for a second and I could tell he was debating what to say. Pauley replies, "I don't think it's a good idea for me and you to have this conversation."

"Why not," I ask. I know I didn't put him in the easiest position, but his answer is important to me, and I wanted him to carry this conversation further.

He says, "Because you're Irish's girlfriend. And my answer about Vince doesn't mean anything when it comes to your safety."

"I'm not going to feel safe if I can't trust you, Pauley. Listen, consider this conversation confidential for my security."

Pauley winces before he answers, "That trust goes both ways when you're asking me something personal."

It was understandable for him to keep a guard up, and I didn't want him feeling uncomfortable, so I decided to try to a different tactic by asking him the question differently.

"What if Vince were to come to this studio today and knock on my door. That's what I want to know, what would you do?"

Pauley doesn't hesitate when he replies, "I would get him the hell away from here. Even have to call the police if I had to."

The moment reminded me of the time when Maya got an answer from me without me knowing.

"He is that dangerous that you would assume he was here for trouble?"

He shifts in his seat and replies, "Because again, you're Irish's girlfriend."
I ask. "So, if I wasn't Declan's girlfriend, Vince wouldn't be a threat to me, right?" He paused and knew at that point where I was going with this, trying to breakthrough.

Straight faced with eyes staring back into mine, he says, "Regardless, I would get him out of here."
"He was at the gym when I went today, and he purposely tried talking to me again." I tell him, giving something back as we begin to learn to trust one another.

Pauley sends out a line of curse words before he asks me. "Did he hurt you?"
I fib a bit of the truth when I tell him, "He just made some rude comments, but I haven't told Declan. I thought you could help talk with me about it first."
"He will lose his shit, but you need to tell him." Pauley says immediately back.
"Do you still talk to Vince?" I ask.

"Vince is my cousin, and for many years, because of that, I had no other choice than to support him. I haven't seen or spoken to him since he has come back. We had a falling out. I wouldn't trust him around you. Irish has a right to be worried about him being a loose cannon." The rumble took us both by surprise, shaking the trailer upon Declan's arrival. My gut felt heavy, but I shook myself off while we both then just looked at one another, a silent nod communicating our new understanding. Then we both giggled watching Declan through the monitor, as he walked inside the studio then came right back out in a huff, straight to the trailer door. I heard the pounding only once as Pauley was right there to let Declan step in. Turning, he then notices me sitting here at the table smiling at him, until I realize he has a bruised eye and fat lip, forcing me to get up and quickly go over to him.

"Hey, what are you doing in here?" He asks as he reaches around my waist.
All I can say is, "You're hurt."

"This is just from practicing, I'm good. What are you doing in here?" he asks me again with his hand nudging at my waist, and I see Pauley roll his eyes while I answer, "I just picked us up some dinner, we just finished."
If I knew anything about my man, his jealousy was bubbling right now just because I'm in here alone with Pauley, my Security Guard. I needed to think about how to talk to him about today. I walked back over to the table to cleanup my containers and throw them away, slowly. Then returned back to Declan's side, his eyes searing into me in his silence, even his one that's going to be black in the morning, then he led me out of the trailer by the small of my back.
"Baby," he starts with me, most likely whining about finding me there, as we begin walking, and I knew where he was going before he said it. Regardless of how ridiculous it may be, his quick Irish temper always turns me on.
I speak before he can say anything else, "I missed you."

Finally, our way in one swift movement, hungry when we attach, but before our lips reunite, Declan whispers back to me, "I missed you so much."
My fingers were splayed in his hair pulling him in and I could taste his blood as I kissed him wildly while he carried me inside, straight upstairs.

Standing before the bed, "You know I'm a jealous man," he says to me in between kisses, still bothered by finding me in the trailer with Pauley. I use a move I learned from him, and instead of speaking, just sending my hand down his pants to find what I was looking for, and straight-faced start stroking him. The corner of his mouth was his first to twitch, giving away that he was slowly, with every stroke, losing his sense of control.

"All I want is right here," I tell him as I start feeling precum draining from his tip, a sure sign he wants me too. He jerks his head back and gives me a deep groan of appreciation, sending out a massive tingling wave down through my vagina. He grabs my arm to stop it from moving while he manages to find his voice, looking into me and rasping out, "You're mine."

"I'm yours," I say back, appeasing him to pull us on the bed, swipe me around, and lay me on my back. He takes over the little control I had, tossing my shirt off and looking down lusting overtop of me, taking all of me in when he sees my sexy purple bra.

He grunts.

I tell him, "I didn't want you to go over there and get all beat up," as I reach up to feel his swollen skin. He kisses the inside of my wrist while I graze over his wounds with my fingertips. "Nobody beats me up but you, baby," he whispers softly, "I only let David get a couple good rounds in on me when I was distracted about thinking of you, of this," he mutters on his way down, kissing the tops of my breasts, he continues saying, "You're all I think about."

It's one of those things in this new relationship, it seems that neither of us wants to admit to the other how much we want and need, so we try to give space and only suffer through it wishing we were together. I was glad he took over the control because I was also distracted now, by the thought of deciding whether or not I should tell Declan about the incident at the gym today. Now that he is with me again, it made me forget about the fear Vince set in me, because I felt safer than I ever could in Declan's arms, my fiercest protector.

Knowing it had to be later if ever, I tried putting that memory to the side, while I enjoyed the touch of the one person that can make me throw all my worries away.

Chapter 32   Declan

There never seemed to be enough time in my days anymore, since it was all taken up between thoughts of my girl and preparing David for this Grudge match. I wasn't going to let my stubbornness mess with my loyalty. David and I have always had respect for one another, but it's the deep love I hold closely for my brother, which ached hard enough inside, that it made me toss my pride away, and show up at CeCe's the other night, allowing him a few free blows to make up for my shitty behavior.

So, when another evening quickly rolled around, I told Alexis to get ready for a night out, and I drove us to Swollen together. This time I held her hand while I walked us in, setting forth to the bar where Ronnie and Dax should be, since I arranged for them to meet us here for drinks, and to hopefully smooth over the tension that came about on Ladies night. She has become a part of me now, and the time has come to make sure it was known to all. She wore her hair braided down to the side and a metallic blue dress that hugs her just right, that I've already ripped off her once before we left. She is perfection walking beside me.

Mine.

"I don't deserve you," I tell her, as we walk in through the back entrance.

She squeezes my hand tightly and replies, "I'm sort of nervous they already don't like me."

I stopped us and told her plainly, "That's not true, they do like you, and I'm one hundred and twenty percent certain Dax, is the one who's the most nervous. Plus, I'm going to let you know now, there is nobody going through me to get to you tonight, so don't worry."

"You're the only one worrying about that," she replies.

She was right, I suppose, I wanted to keep a tighter hold. My nerves were a bit off balance too, but it has nothing to do with her meeting up with my friends and has more to do with bringing her back to the same place we fell apart the last time, my work, my bar, and hoping this isn't problematic for either of us. I begin to plan on this night being pretty quick, already not being able to keep my hands off of her.

There was a Gin and Tonic the way she likes it, with lime, ready for Alexis when we joined Dax and Ronnie, with Brady bartending. My friends swarmed her with their apologies as soon as they saw her, like a couple of chicks flocking towards their mother's nest. She of course hugged them both and pretended like nothing happened. Ronnie shook his head in disbelief secretly to me, which began to bug me after the third shake. I tried to make them all know it too, sitting on the chair with her standing in between my legs, and keeping my arm around her front at all times, not trusting anyone.

Dax and Brady were fan Girling her, discussing names of bands and players I wasn't sure existed.

Dax takes the time to ask, "Who's your favorite band of all time?"

Alexis replies cocking her head playfully, "MartaBeat, obviously."

Brady swoons, unaware of anything about the SheerMe show or Alexis's involvement, to say, "Oh my God are you serious? I did not think we would have the same taste in music! And such a unique group from Boston!"

Dax and Ronnie look uncomfortable, not certain what to say so we allow the girls to take away this conversation.

Alexis sparkling as she replies, "Now you have to tell me what kind of music you thought I listened to?"

Brady's smile stretched wide with her matching purple lipstick while she cries out, "Well mainstream Pop, of course!"

Alexis shakes her head back and forth and answers, "I actually love anything with a good beat."

"Touché!" Brady replies, handing another drink down to her, then asking, "What's your favorite MartaBeat song?"

Alexis bends back and whispers to me, "she doesn't know?" I nod her my negative, and she smiles in understanding to perk back up and answers Brady, "I'm partial to them all."

"Is there a reason for that?" Brady asks, and Alexis replies, "there is, but I want to know your favorite song before I tell you," Giving her a smug smile and sipping her drink. Brady looked at her skeptically but went along with it and responded, "La La Lexington. What gives?"

I felt Alexis stiffen, and I knew when I heard the name what that meant. A song about Alexis, and one I don't know. Alexis plays her cool and replies, "Good pick. I'm a personal friend of the band, JamFresh is my bestie."

"No way!" Shrieks Brady, right as Dax takes a drink down now that he can move. Then she adds, "Does that mean you can introduce me to JamFresh?"

"I'm sure he will be here introducing himself soon enough." Brady cheers then runs to the other end of the bar for another order.

Dax says to me, "David told me the barn went through." I had also heard that information since I was with David when they got the call confirming the fight being held in our ring behind Swollen. Nodding to Dax I reply, "He's getting ready, working hard."

Ronnie speaks, "David was telling me you gave it hard to Clay the other night."

"I might have knocked him around a bit more than he's used to, nothing tragic, David was our referee," I reply while giving a sly smile to Ronnie. I didn't forget about Clay swooning over my girl, and all I did was made sure he knew she was mine, and he wasn't going to comment on her ever again. Speaking of my girl, she's been slowly shifting in closer to me after every drink, and now a few drinks in and her cheeks are rosy up next to mine, as I take this as my cue. I order us a ride back to her house on my phone and stand up. "Alright guys, we're out of here. I'll see ya tomorrow."

"Boo," calls Dax who is also looking drunk. Ronnie gives Alexis a hug and tells her, "I guess you're a good change for him, he's been sacking it early ever since he met you."

Dax interrupts, "We all know Irish's motto, 'the better you feel, the better you perform.'"

Ronnie says, "I thought it was, 'to learn you must listen.'"

Dax adds, "'Work hard and never play for you must live like Gremlin's prey'," all of us laughing as Dax then says to Alexis, "your boyfriend is a walking inspirational quote when you need him, he used to say that one to us all the time when we were training."

My phone pings and I take her away from them before they divulge all the embarrassing information about me. Brady comes around from the bar to give her a proper hug goodbye before we start walking out, or stumbling rather, all the way to the curb to meet our driver when I heard Al's voice call out for me.

"Do you have a second, Boss?"

Closing in on Alexis and me, with a smile shining through his hairy beard on his face, he adds, "Well, who do we have here? Hello Darlin'."

"You better make it quick before I fire you," I tell him playfully, making him chuckle then give me a look and say, "I' ya...I heard somethin' and wanted to let you know about it, but uh..."

Al pauses and places his hands on his large hips and finishes, "I'll call you later and we'll talk, you two go have fun."

I stop him before he goes and reply, "Al, just tell me what it is."

"I got some information on our friend..." he replies vaguely.

Confident, I ask. "Vince, what about him?"

Al smiles and gives Alexis a look, then back to me he responds, "turns out he got a record while he's been gone. Booked for another 'domestic violence' while he was in Canada last summer, maybe even got kicked outta the country."

"I knew I loved Canada. Those Canadian's probably saved the poor girl!" I tell him with a slap on the shoulder, "Thanks, Al. I hope you have a good night."

I knew Vince wasn't a sharp-edged sword the way he always struts around. He hasn't been seen around here since he left after Daniel's accident, knowledge for myself maybe, but knowing the Vince I'm dealing with while he is back here, gives me insight for both myself and protecting the ones I care about, including Alexis. She already has enough on her plate to worry about, so I'm hoping she doesn't think too much about what Al just told us.

Back in the car, her face is serious while I pull her on top of me while the driver rolls us away.

"I already told you, he isn't going to get close," I tell her lips.

"I trust you," she replies, only to make out with me until we made it back to her house in Paisley.

Chapter 33   Alexis

We had woken up to a blanket of white across the ground, another beautiful morning in my bat cave of Paisley, next to my Declan. I wasn't sure how I got so lucky, not only from the four orgasms he gave to me last night, but the happiness I feel with him is like waking up anew each morning.

Mine.

Happy.

My world was becoming my own.

We both heard the knocking on the front door, and let out our audible sighs, before our eyes even met each other's, because we already knew who that could be.

Margie stood in safety getup, with a see-through plastic bubble around her head, showing off her big smiling face, while she exclaimed, "Come on, I'm about to feed my bees some honey!" Declan and I suited up with the extra bubble tops she had for us, and walking through the side of their home, she and Estel showed us all around her backyard. Her garden was a magnificent sight of fresh vegetables and ferns, along to her flower beds tattooed with homemade painted rocks, gorgeously maintained with her hives standing tall like a set of drawers on wooden legs. Margie explains while she lifts up the top of one of the hives, "The bees all swarm around the Queen in the wintertime to keep her warm and safe. I store about two gallons a year of their honey and then feed it back to them to keep them all fueled. If I don't have enough of their own honey, I bake some sugar fondant and they just love that too."

Declan still rocking this space suit, is closer to the bees than where I have decided to stand, he's seemingly all into this as Margie lets him pour the honey on the place in the box. I took out my phone to snap a few pictures of them as they concentrated hard on their job. Margie states, "You see they are all interconnected in their relationships, just like people." Backing up next to Estel, I noticed a bee stuck in the snow near my feet, "Oh no little guy," I say looking down at it.

"That's just a part of it," Estel says to me as he kneels down to pick up the dead bee bringing it up, displaying it out for me, laying small and still in his palm.

Margie says, "Oh yes, you may find quite a few dead ones around, that's natural. Laura used to bury them all underneath her painted rocks in the garden."

I take a brave deep breath and give Estel a knowing look while cupping my gloved hands out for him. He smiles and places the bee in, silly of me to be so scared of such a little thing. It had the tiniest little hairs that coated it, with wet wings looking of lace, which draped across the bottom. Feeling sad for the dead bee, a short life of working hard to keep someone else alive, left out in the cold, all I want to do is give it a nice spot to rest. I graze around the garden and find my favorite rock, the picture of the yellow sun sporting black sunglasses and a wide 'U' of a smile painted across the face. Estel gives me a big laugh when I tip the rock over and throw the bee under quickly with a jump, not expecting the extra creepy crawlers to come out from underneath. Estel says through his chuckle, "She painted that one when she was fourteen, I've been recoating them with urethane every year to keep them from fading."

A reminder sound pinged in my brain, and I tell Estel, "That was how old Rachel, and I were when we met for the first time, at the same dance class. I was only six weeks older than her." Estel asks, "What year were you two born?"

"Nineteen ninety-five."

"Good heavens," Margie bursts out, "that was the same year Laura died."

Hesitant to make this a sad situation, I was glad when Estel saves me, looking lovingly at his wife, he says, "Well it just reminds us how old we are dear, Declan what year were you born?" Declan replies brightly, "Nineteen ninety-three," causing Estel to laugh again, as he starts to lead us back to the front, minus the bubble hats. Declan told me all about the beehive I missed out on seeing and I showed him the pictures I took of him looking hot even in his bee protection gear.

Declan asks with wide eccentric eyes and a grin, "Babe, do you think we could start doing that in your back yard?"

"Yeah right!" I exclaim, "Luna and I aren't going to die from killer bees."

"Don't you know you're my Queen, I won't let you die," he says pulling me in while we stomp our boots back on my front porch.

Tingling.

It's a warm tingling feeling, and it makes me shutter when he gives me these beautiful words that I can always hear the truth in.

I reply, "I like the sound of that, but what about Luna?"

"I'll build her a fence," he replies with a smile and adds, "She's a tough dog."

"As long as you build the fence first, you can have the bees," I say laughing and running inside.

The days leading into David and Vince's Grudge match were here, and now it's the Eve of the fight. It's been a long week with a heavy workload with only small, scattered time spent with Declan since he has been spending most of his time training next to David, preparing.

I hadn't ever spoken to Declan about what happened at the gym with Vince, and I hadn't been back there since, either. There was just no way with his nerves already panicked that I wanted him to worry about something he doesn't need to spend anytime focusing on. I feel like I've also put a heavy bet down, counting on David's win to take away the possibility of Vince purchasing the athletic gym in town.

I was beginning to feel nervous about the idea of the fight. David has become like a little brother to me too since I get to hear about him through Declan's stories, and not only does the idea of him getting hurt make my anxiety rise, but it's all knowing how anxious and scared Declan is going to be feeling that seems to worry me most. I have never actually seen a boxing match or fight in a ring before, but I was told by Declan that he needed me to be present during it, that way he knows where I'll be. So, I've also recruited Sabine to be by my side, while he remains in David's corner. Sabine wasn't too thrilled about the idea either, but a different feeling since she was crushing harder than ever on David.

With Declan staying over at CeCe's tonight, Jameson finally caught me at a good time to have me listen to videos of the drummer he was interested in taking over for the band, while I stir in my cozy bed with Luna.

Afterwards, Jameson gleamed at me through the screen when I agreed that Austin is great. But his face turned its expression to a sullener look when he squinted his eyes more curiously at me.

Changing the subject, he asks, "How are you holding up, lately?"

He always somehow knows. I tell him the truth he wants, "She's on my mind every day."

"Mine too. But hey, I was thinking about your house situation a bit more," he said then paused. I ask. "And?"

Jameson replies, "Rachel didn't go with Terrie to the beach house during her holidays," stunning the breath out of me. He quickly continues to throw the rest of his confession out saying, "it was only the first week that she stayed with me in my condo but she didn't want you to know because she was feeling low, and it was Christmas, and she didn't want you to feel sorry for her."

Heat flared through my cheeks, and even though I was feeling double crossed, I knew that we all had our secrets, so I hummed for a second to calm myself down.

"I'm sorry, I was put in a pretty difficult position."

Gathering my composure, I ask, "Do you know about her being in Paisley?"

Jameson replies frantically, "I swear I don't know anything about your house or your town. Listen, she left on the 27th and she told me she was going to visit an old caretaker of hers in New York."

"Vienna?" I question, putting together the timeline in my mind and linking Vienna to the jewelry box.

"Yes, that's right. Do you know her? Good, I thought for a long time she wasn't real since I found out when you got the house deed that she didn't tell me the truth and went to Paisley instead."

I could understand his predicament, but I still couldn't help but feel a bit betrayed. I tell him, "I get it, but I still don't like that you guys did that. I think she was the one who duped the both of us, Jameson. I don't want to tell you this," I took a deep breath, and I knew I had to let it out, so I did, saying, "I'm pretty sure she planned her suicide for a long time, and I think she started planning during the holidays."

The air felt lighter when I let it out since I was needing him to come to me to talk about her.

Jameson huffs back stating, "I figured that."

I felt so relieved, but I still wasn't sure about letting him know about the scavenger hunt she left me. He just gave me a beginning piece without knowing, like setting up the corners, and I was beginning to see things differently.

"How did she get away without going to the Hamptons?" I asked.

"She waited for Terrie to be on the airplane before she called her and told her she had the flu and wasn't going to make it. I don't know how, but it worked, and I think it's because Thatcher was in the Hamptons with Terrie."

I reply, "The possibility sounds plausible, but how did she get away with visiting New York? And buying the house?"

"She borrowed cash from me for her travelling. She didn't want to use her card because it would let Terrie know her location. And she also left her cell phone in her condo during her trip, so she wasn't reachable. She must have driven through Paisley on her way to see Vienna or something."

His idea didn't seem likely since she wrote about this town in such a way that she connected to it more than just a pass through. But he was right, if it wasn't a town Rachel just passed through, then what was it about Paisley that spoke to her?

Sour, I reply, "Maybe Vienna knows everything and me and you are just the fools."

"I was a fool for not telling you about that, I just felt like I was protecting you in some way."

Taking a deep breath, I said, "I like chocolate."

My conscience was slowly eating at me. We protected each other. It was his time to let me in, but I still didn't feel ready enough to tell him, so I didn't. Two men in my life who do all they can to protect me and two secrets I must hold to protect each of them. Separate curses. And we are all just trying to find the light.

Chapter 34   Declan

Do you believe in Déjà vu?

If you do believe, and you find yourself stuck inside that moment of it, where you actually feel like you remember having that dream you're currently floating in, following it through in slow motion, but you can't break free. Already, you know how it ends but can't quite spit it out, only causing what you remember of the déjà vu to be cut short and you're left in its midst. You start thinking you are the smartest person in the world because you feel like you beat the illusion at its own game, practically cheering for yourself.

What happens next? Since somehow you feel like you were exposed to the memory before, did you just save yourself from the evil that was coming for you, because you feel like you remembered the ultimate déjà vu moment?

You're just part of the trick of it all. Suckered into the panic doom of a fake memory to make your reality stop time for the few minutes you sort out your puzzle.

It's the morning of David and Vince's fight, and I have found myself in a possible déjà vu moment, hugging the toilet. I never thought it would come to this, being so sick over a worry. A worry of being alone and losing both of my brothers. A worry of doom hovering over me.

Maybe if I stay in here, this day will go away, pass like the grudge match never existed in the first place so we can all move on, except for Daniel, who can never move on since he is doomed either way.

Similar to any run of the mill, casual morning, David struts into the bathroom to brush his teeth, looking like an underwear model in only his boxer briefs, like it's no big deal I'm currently hovering in here as he just starts brushing.

"Blow me brother, this is your fault," I say to him shamefully while he simultaneously shakes his head at me, disappointed like, and replies. "Ye have little faith. And you need to brush your teeth."

I groan, "I will when you're done."

David's toothbrush is sticking out of his mouth while he looks around and asks, "Where's your toothbrush?"

Considering I've been bunking at CeCe's almost all week, I reply half-heartedly, "In your mouth."

"Dude, that's gross."

"Well, it would be more gross if I didn't brush my teeth all week."

David rinsing says, "It's almost like I've been swapping spit with Alexis."

I yell to him, "Get out! And leave your toothbrush here!"

The feeling of throwing up never subsided, and as much as I didn't want reality to bite, I had to eventually shower and exit the bathroom. Making my way downstairs to the bustling morning gym, I found Xander in the ring already working with David on some moves, while I find coffee.

Xander calls out to me and remarks, "You don't look so good, Irish. Maybe you need to visit your girlfriend to make you feel better."

David busts out a laugh and says, "If only it were that easy."

I didn't answer since I wasn't sure if I could say on the grounds of this gym in front of all these guys that it practically was that easy. If only they knew how hard it's been on me to maintain my focus on training with David and to pretend like not being able to see her hasn't messed with me. All that girl needs to do is look my way and I feel better. After this fight is over, I don't plan on looking away ever again.

David asks. "Will Pauley be at the barn tonight?"

"All I know is that Alexis gave him the night off since she'll be with me."

David sarcastically replies, "Nice of you to share with him, big brother. He seems to be getting cozy over there from what I can tell."

I ask. "What would you know about that?"

"Just the last time I was there, instead of the trailer they had him inside holding flash cards out for Sabine to study like they were all friends."

He was still in the ring throwing some punches at Xander who was blocking for him and I couldn't help but take a sip of my coffee and give back the smug to reply, "That sounds like a you problem, and since you're stuck with me for the rest of your long annoying life you get to keep with tonight when you blow off Bordeaux's head, you're just going to have to learn about women from me too."

"Not likely," David brutes out. But I've seen my brother looking at Sabine, similar to the way I look at Alexis, and just as shocked since he's never had any type of serious relationship himself to know what to do with a girl like that. A girl you know is not going to be a toss away. A girl that makes you do dumb things like take runs through town just so you can pass by her work. To give myself an extra pat on the back for the morning, I reply to David saying, "I'll take a run by there in a bit to check things out."

He misses his throw to Xander while he shouts, "I'll come with!"

David practically sprinted like this wasn't one of the most important days in his life, hours away from fighting Vince who will be surrounded by his group of supporters, where there will be no upper hand but the skill he possesses. I see Alexis and Sabine dancing through the windows, and once they see us, Alexis darts out in her bare feet as I run to scoop her up. Our Way.

Too excited and not able to keep from telling me, Alexis blurts, "It was like Christmas yesterday since all that wood Estel ordered me was delivered and all our fencing items I ordered came, and when I went to the hardware store, I ended up with all the chainsaws and items Estel and I need for when we cut down trees," her smile brighter than a perfect spring day as she finally is able to breathe after getting it all out at once.

Now it was my turn to leap as I reply, "You ordered everything for our bees?"

Her face quickly went sour as she said, "No. Fence first, remember?"

Before I can respond, David chirps in, reminding me we aren't alone as he says, "Oh my God, what's going on with you guys? Are you becoming Axmen or something?"

Sabine replies, "Beekeepers."

Alexis retorts with a wide smile, "No bees until the fence is built," then asks David, "Are you ready for your victory dance tonight, Rocky?"

His face lights up as mine is probably looking how I feel, which is questionable.

David replies, "Hell yeah I am, whatever that is."

I squeezed her tighter in my arms as she laughs and says, "You know, after your victory, because you're such a strong tough winner, the night usually ends with a naked lap dance or something. Doesn't that happen after your fights?"

My mouth went dry as David's eyes could have said it before he did, "Huh. I think you're right about them dances, but I will have to receive one of those tonight to remind me…from not you, obviously," David stutters around looking at the girls. Alexis makes life easier when she laughs and replies, "How about if you do the work and win. I'll do the work and find you a dancer."

"Deal!" He shouts in conclusion all while Sabine and I look nauseous.

I tell her, "The fight starts at midnight, it's loud and disgusting but you two will be standing behind the roped off area with Ronnie and Dax. I've got a car picking you up here at the Studio no later than eleven."

Giving me a kiss, she says, "We won't be late. I promise!"

Although I wanted to spend more time with her, we had no time left to get more seriously prepared for tonight, so we left them to finish their work. I think David and I both forgot for a few hours that it was supposed to be one of the biggest fights of his life.

Chapter 35   Alexis

Later in the night, after the darker skies rolled in, Sabine and I were picked up by Declan's ride he sent for us and rolling out. Sabine was still mad at me for telling David to expect a victory dance from someone, obviously her, so I made sure to let her borrow my best pair of stilettos. I think I won her back over, maybe even helped convince her to be brave enough to follow through with said dance. I wore a forest green one-piece jumpsuit, partial to Ireland. Open on the sides with a silver tube top underneath, showing some skin until I throw a fur coat over top, I was styled and ready to step into a world of seeing what it's like meeting Irish McQuade.

The barn was down a side dirt road from Swollen, a bumpy ride like going off roading until we got out at a pasture that acted as its parking lot. In the cold, we followed the crowds of mostly men inside and found Ronnie who quickly swooped us over to our area. The dark wooded barn was just that, freezing cold with bodies filling in around the boxing ring lit up under LED lights. There weren't many faces that I recognized. Besides Dax and Ronnie, these were different people than the ones from the Club. Standing on dirt and hay, Sabine was biting her nails she was so nervous for David. I'm not sure what has me feeling so revved up, but I feel a wildfire blowing through me that somehow connects to David. Maybe I just truly believed in him to win, or maybe I'm just so terrified of the other options. Avoiding getting hurt, and winning this quickly, were my only options for David, and how I was going to end this night. I wanted to see him show everyone what true, honest grit can do to wipe out the opposite of him, the filth of Vince Bordeaux.

Ronnie let us know Declan, David, and Xander are waiting inside the office until it's time to come out. It was getting louder as the minutes passed, cheers and yells were heard all around while they held their arms up, holding and trading slips and money, setting different bets and wagers with one another. Dax joined in with us right when the loud hoots and roaring started, sounding out the strong support for tonight's underdog arriving into the ring, David McQuade. I couldn't see over the heads above me, but I was trying to be the loudest one there. The friction started rubbing off in the room, shooting sparks of anger upon heads causing chaos to ensue with some pushing and shoving within the crowd. Sabine and I had our arms intertwined, we were in this together, swaying and stepping back and forth, keeping close to the mass bulk surrounding us. Vince entered the barn and I looked in the opposite direction, finding my blues of solid ice centering in on me along the way. Declan stood with malice across his body, currently being tormented on the inside by a recurring nightmare, but he found me in the sea of it, and stilled. It doesn't make sense how much I wandered but somehow, I've been on my way to him the entire time. A rare connection creating its own storm wherever it lands.

It Landed.

I think this is love.

I know this is love, and I don't know what to do with it.

I fell in too deep.

Bells ring

Trying to focus, even is the designated area, the crowding was insane. I had to crane my neck far back to be able to see the opponents in the ring staring one another down. David barely tops Vince in height, but it's downright scary how much more mass Vince carries in his body than David.

Sabine stands straight, with a single tear rolling down her face, and all I can do is pull her tighter.

Bare knuckled, the fight rules are discussed how they declare the winner, starting with three, four minute rounds, ending once one of them either taps out in submission, or gets knocked out. My heart started beating out of my chest when it began.

Vince throws out the first punch, but David cranes his neck and dodges it.

Whack

Whack

There was already blood spraying, but the two were grabbing hold to one another like a twisted pretzel that I couldn't see who's blood it likely was. Their feet stepped quickly around, and I caught sight of the side of Declan's cherry red face in belligerent rage screaming out from his place closest to them. It made me just want to do the same thing, scream profanities loud and zone out into my world of sound that can give me pause while we cheered for David.

Sabine a stoic steel with her arms crossed in front while she stared, the only nerves now that show, come from her biting her bottom lip. Dax was on the other side of me with both arms high in the air.

Getting the upper hand, Vince lands three quick blows to David's ribs on his side, causing David to bend lower and put more weight on his legs, using them for his power he pushes Vince back. It looks like Vince was going to fall back, only he maintained his balance and straightened himself forward for just a second before he takes another lunge at David.

David holds his ground with his knees bent, while throwing solid punches on the side of Vince's face.

They were both still standing by the end of the first round as both men sauntered over to their corners after the bell. No time to waste as Xander was quickly beside David helping wipe off the blood and sweat from his face while also pouring water down his throat. Declan had his arms waving when he spoke to David, pumping him up with words of wisdom.

The intensity of the second round had betters going wild with both fighters starting off landing serious blows to each other's faces. If I had my switchboard, I'd be zapping those punch noises loud like the old school batman.

The tango on their toes had them swirling around. David seemed quicker, throwing sharp jabs while they danced.

Maybe that quick lesson with Sabine was worth it after all.

A direct hit Vince took to his shoulder knocked him backwards causing him to lose his ground and fumble for his balance. Shifting his weight forward, Vince lunges back at David before he was grounded again.

Impatient.

And too damn arrogant.

And it may have been Vince's worst move. He didn't give that extra second he needed to be balanced enough to withstand the second wave of force David threw at him, taking another misstep, Vince fell to the floor with David landing on top.

There was a bustle of panic around, including the one busting from my own chest, but Sabine and I were the weaker ones in the force being pushed around and again having trouble seeing. Since I was in Declan's world, I was losing my temper and I needed to know what was going on. I shook Dax's arm next to me and shouted, "Pick me up! I can't see!"

With our surroundings the way they are, I cannot believe he still looked at me like he was next to die if he touched me, which made me angrier.

Gesturing with my meanest expression Dax knows from experience, he bends down, and I quickly hop on his shoulders, just as Sabine jumps on Ronnie's.

Finally, like little girls on daddy's shoulders watching the show, we screamed our heads off.   ,

Both Vince and David growling like lions, sporting mouthfuls of blood in their teeth as they spar. Like a lioness, Sabine's sudden bout of shouts are closest too me to hear, "Rip his filthy head off!"

Still wrestling on the ground, David was using his strength from his legs to straddle Vince and keep him pinned down, and for the first time in this struggle, it looked like David had the control of the fight.

Sitting higher up on shoulders gave me a better view of the entire barn. Looking over at Declan, I notice him squeezing his fists together showing off forearms of muscled madness, almost leaping over the rope spitting his screaming rant. Giant meatheads along with their arm candy stand in Vince's corner yelling and badgering him to get back up, but I don't notice Pauley anywhere in the crowd.

There was only another minute left in this second round, and the pressure was explosive, and David had his back to us, but was still on top.

David was able to crank his arm back fully, and like a slingshot, landed a punch to Vince's nose. Rebounding with another.

And another.

Vince's sneer is still on his ravaged face when his head rolls back, long enough to be considered out.

David wins.

Screaming and crying, Sabine and I were absolute crazy people, but it was the hype happening in front of me that had me exploding in crazy joy. Vince sat sulking in his corner while his team worked on sewing his ugly face up. I hope he was wide awake when they raised David's arm, I wouldn't know since I was too busy watching Declan fall to his knees on the ground when they declared David's victory.

Like playing chicken in the pool, Sabine and I were still balancing upon Dax and Ronnie's shoulders being weaved in closer to the winner's corner, and my heart melted once I saw David crouching overtop, holding Declan in an embrace that holds a meaning only those two will ever understand, for Daniel. It was beautiful in the middle of people scattering every which way trying to get out of here.

Dax calls out from underneath me, "I'm gonna put you down up here where there isn't so many people."

A voice sounded out loudly behind us, "Dax, if you don't give me my bloody girl-"
Without use of my legs, I depended on Dax to twirl us around, and in one flawless switch, I was back in the right arms again. Declan's grin was insane joy telling me, "He did it! He's okay, baby."

"I'm so happy," I tell him.

"Me too," he replies while grabbing my lips for a kiss. Then he says, "We're celebrating at CeCe's tonight, need you to meet us there. I've just got to help David drive his truck back home and patch him back together when we get there."

Nodding my head and kissing him, he pulls back and adds, "And Alexis, I'm expecting one of those victory dances tonight."

Teasing him, I reply,

"Baby, you have to earn the victory dance, I'm not quite sure you can claim this win."
We blended in with the carloads of people going in and out of Swollen once we got on our way towards CeCe's Gym. Sabine and I were entertained by a cab driver named, Willy, who chatted with us the entire way back into the familiar streets of Paisley. Main street was shut down in the middle of the dark night, quiet and lightly lit, and when we didn't see any of the cars back at the gym yet, we decided to go for fashionably late. I paid the cab driver extra to keep driving to my house, so I could let Luna outside to go to the bathroom. Willy waited in my driveway while Sabine and I freshened up inside and of course let the dog out.

There was something new I was feeling tonight. Content. There were roots starting to grow inside my new normal in Paisley, life was looking up from where I was prior to here. I didn't realize how too perfect my new normal was coming together until we were on our way back and the cab driver, Willy, said something that reminded me how I ended up here in the first place.

"You live across from the buzzing bee lady."
My head quirked and so did my photographic memory when I replied, "Come again?"

"I went to school with a girl that used to live in that house across from yours. Her mom was a teacher, and she was obsessed with bees, like the bug, she would always wear the different bee pins," Willy gives a chuckle and continues his story saying, "We always called her mom the 'buzzing bee lady,' and Laura used to hate it."

My curiosity perked while Sabine could care less while she scrolls through her phone for lap dance moves, I meet Willy's eyes in the rearview mirror and bluntly ask,
"You knew the same Laura that used to live here over twenty years ago?"

"Sure did, we were in chorus together, she had a really nice voice. I remember going to her funeral too, her poor parents were a wreck. But wouldn't you know it, her mom wore a Queen Bee pin by her heart on her black dress that day."
"The Queen Bee..." I feel like I've already stepped outside of my body, looking from above to process what is piecing together in my brain.

Coincidence in those words and the same ones I have behind glass in purple? Paisley. A connection. But how can that be? I was saying Rachel's words repeatedly, trying to listen. We were pulling up in front of the Gym, Sabine opens her door to get out and I continue to sit still, because I'm paralyzed in a different world right now.

I think I may have the answer, and there was no way I was coming down from this hovering over until I see for myself.

I tell Sabine, "I wanted to check something at the Studio really quick. Will you tell Declan and I'll be right back?"

She wasn't too thrilled to walk in by herself, but she saw there was something on my mind, so she shut the door and let Willy drive me up the street. I tipped him a lot of cash, all of it in my wallet and told him to go. I wasn't wanting someone waiting for me outside if what I'm about to see matches what I think may have been in Rachel's words.

Right in front of me.

I was reaching far with this one, but Rachel and I were far from having anything easy, so the possibility for this to somehow be the troubling answer, the answer that tipped her over the edge.

My new normal.

I was trying to concentrate with my heart thudding out of my chest while walking through the dark to find where I put Wings of Paisley last. Straight up the stairs, I kneel down to pull it out from underneath my bed and skim over her words again with help from the bathroom light left on.

A sight to see
A buzzing bee
My only truth lives in Paisley

Stopping myself once I'm interrupted by the noise of whispers and footsteps sounding like they are coming from downstairs. Thinking Sabine has come back for me, I grab hold of my frame and walk down to the bottom step before I stiffen at the eerie silence. I could see through the windows that the parking lot was still empty, and there was no sign of anyone here. Despite the weirdness, I gathered the courage to tell myself I'm too in my head again, picked up my feet and decided to finish what I came here for and go get the speaker safe out of my Mixx room. Only, I wasn't in my head.

Swirls of long hair whip around me from out of the dark, and I'm hit with a strong force across my face, knocking me on the ground.

Crawling to look up, all I can see is the color red.

Chapter 36 Declan

It was more than bitter, and it was more than sweet. I didn't realize how thirsty I was for this fight until it was over. Once the relief of David's win came over me, I could remember that sense you can find in between your body and your soul when your blood is pumping and your adrenaline is hyped, like parasailing over lava, what I used to feel when I was that close to sinking my teeth in a ring, before Daniel's accident. Although it wasn't me like I would have wanted, the feeling of pride swept over me when they raised my little brother's hand up. Not only did David prove himself and his strength to me and everyone else but watching him gave me the sense that I'm capable of moving forward. I need to be strong like David and have a willingness to remember that David and I still have a future together, even though the shame and guilt of not having Daniel a part of these things can be bitter, time has changed and there are new memories being created. Good stories coming out of the tragic ones. I'm making plans for my future now.

Clay and my dad setup the gym with tables and booze, and the after party had begun at CeCe's as soon as we walked through the door. Xander and I immediately sat David down in a chair like a king, with a full bottle of whiskey, and stitched him up. Word of a party got out, and flocks of friends and friends of friends we knew started showing up. I was trying to be patient waiting on Alexis to arrive while celebrating with David and our friends, but once we got bombarded with some boxing bunnies trying to chat us up, I couldn't just stand around anymore. This fight was over, Vince can leave town again, and instead of worrying about what happens next, I know there is only one other thing I need to do. To make tonight the reason it's all worth it, I need to find my girl and tell her how I feel, then go to bed with her tonight, and wake up with her tomorrow.

"You made sure to tell them to meet us here, right?" David asks me when he notices my eyes flickering around looking for her.

I spot Sabine looking puzzled standing with Clay, and I'm about to lose my shit but someone else beat me to it, David huffing from behind me and making his way to her in a faster stride. Sabine's face lights up and she throws herself at David in a hug, making my brother act like he needs more attention and sneakily pushes me out of his way during the hug. Cock blocking was not my intention, but my own cock had his own plan made up, and we were trying to hunt for Alexis.

I ask Sabine simply. "Where is she?"

"She should be back here soon, she told me to tell you she just ran back to her studio for something. That was like, less than 10 minutes ago."

I ask. "For what?"

My brother's face looked like he would have punched me if there weren't a bunch of people around while I kept Sabine's attention with my line of questioning.

Her face sank as she replies, "Honestly, I don't really know."

I took a deep breath and settled myself a bit with a drink. But everything changed a few minutes later when Pauley walks in the door with a freshly beaten face. Strutting only a few steps past the gawking eyes, he lands his swollen sights on the three of us. Like walking into enemy territory, he didn't get too far without being stopped and swarmed by our muscle, but he was on a mission.

Pauley calls out, "Irish, I need a word."

With most people here unaware of my dealings with Pauley from the dance studio, he is being pushed out of the door by the time I get closer to him. "Let me through," I growl as I push through, pulling Pauley with me to stand outside. David and Sabine also joined us in following us out, being it is David's voice speaking out from behind me first,
"You're face looks like your cousin's, but it's your legs that are about to have a problem walking in here like that."

"Congratulations on your win tonight, although I wish you would have done something about his legs because then he wouldn't have been able to sneak up on me to do this," Pauley replies pointing to his face and continues, "I was on my way here to night to apologize to you. I've tried to separate myself from Vince since the night he went off the rails and fought your brother. If I could take it all back, I would. And maybe I should have told you that a long time ago, but it never felt right, until Alexis asked me which made me think about it more."

"You talked to Alexis about this?" I question now beefing up and getting boiled. Pauley looks puffy when he replies, "Not really, only when she asked me about him and what I would do if he came near the studio, you know, it was that same night she brought me dinner and she had that run in with Vince at the gym."
No, I don't know. Uneasiness started coming over me, and with everything in me already set on overdrive, I couldn't go another minute. I started running. Trusting my instincts has never felt this scary, but there was something telling me she was in trouble.

There was another emotion involved in my heart that had me picking up my speed.
Love.
I have never been so certain in my entire life, and tonight I'm trusting my instincts, that connection, that force of nature that led me to her in the first place.

When I smelled the smoke halfway there, Sabine's screams behind me tore me into a madman while I sprinted as fast as I could towards the fire.
Coming up to it, a ferocious blaze engulfed the trailer Pauley worked in, right outside the studio, with flames working their way towards the pod. Shielding my face with my arm from the heat, my sight on a body coming out through the front door. Running closer squinting, I see who it is, Vince Bordeaux. He doesn't get a chance to see me as I pounce on him, roaring and throwing thunderous strikes as we roll, and I wrestle him into the ground, pressing his face into the concrete. I knew I didn't have much time.

"Where is she?" I bellow out, pushing him down harder.
Another voice speaks out to give me my answer, a high shriek coming from the doorway, "She's in here!"

David appears by my side yelling, "GO!"

Taking over my grounding of Vince, I stand up to see a familiar redhead.

Whiplash

As I run past her while she shouts, "In her media room!"

The flames were about to engulf the entire studio, and there were only minutes left to find her and get her out of here. Taking the familiar path to the Mixx room, the black leather couch is placed in front of the closed door. If I had the time, I would have murdered Vince right then, but I didn't have the time. Maya Gueterra ordering only heavy luxurious leather, I push it out of the way and kick down the locked door to find Alexis breathing. She was actually scrambling around with papers in her hands when I found her in one piece. Her big fearful eyes see me once I run to her, she cries, "Declan!" "Rachel's things, I can't lose these things!" I could tell she was frantic and looking closer there was a red mark down the side of her face, causing my rage to explode and swoop my girl, and all Rachel's things, up into my arms at once. She adjusted to our way, holding around my neck with just one arm, and she crouches her body and other arm around tightly gripping the items.

I ask her loudly, "Are you good?"

Looking at me she replies, "Yes, now I am."

The smoke was darkening around the doorway once we stepped onto the dance floor on our way out, I couldn't tell if it was smoke from the other buildings or if it was from the one we were in. Her head rested on my chest in complete silence when I guided us out the rest of the way

I catch my breath once I get us through to the outside where there were crowds of people forming, some still running up to the lot. I see my group of friends I know well in the distance, hovering together tight. I'm assuming they dragged whatever is left of Vince over there to get away from the fire. We were a safe enough distance away from the fire ourselves, but I purposely ran Alexis and I to the side, avoiding everyone for now to be able to assess her without anyone there getting in my way. As much as I would like to go over there and end Vince, the most important thing is right here with me, in my arms. And I need to make sure she is okay before I do anything else.

Glancing down and stroking my hand down the side of her cheek, I'm about to ask but I don't get a chance to speak, because Alexis beats me to it, shifting to my eyelevel as she lays her palm on my cheek and says, "I am fine. You saved me. You're always saving me."

I blame the smoke for the tears that formed in my eyes when I reply "Baby, it's been you saving me this entire time… but your studio…," pausing in a deep sigh.

I wasn't even proud of myself like she was trying to praise me for, feeling the opposite since it's the devil from my life who did this to her, going after the best thing that's ever happened to me.

He got close enough she almost got killed, mimicking the last time tragedy struck during celebrating a win against Vince.

The sirens were wailing on the way towards us as we watched the side of the studio start catching on fire.

Sabine runs over and almost jumps onto Alexis's back crying in fear. Alexis shakes her head and says, "It doesn't matter right now, did that other girl get out?"

Sabine cries out,

"Yes! It's that girl, Lexi! The same one that's been asking for you about a job! The guys are holding them down waiting for the police to get here."

Alexis looks horrified as she cries out, "No, they need to let go of her, she tried to stop him for me."

I yell out, "Talk to me, tell me what happened."

Scrambling, Alexis gives Sabine the few items of Rachel's that she spared from the burning building. Police have started swarming right as we get closer to the scene where David likely dragged Vince. David jumps off and police takeover, while his sister surrendered to another officer next to Dax, Ronnie, and Xander.

Before we approach, Alexis tells me, "I came here because I think I figured something out about why Rachel picked this place. And thanks to you for saving me, we still might be able to figure it out now since we still have her things!"

Alexis almost looked joyous while she gives me a quick kiss on my lips and continues saying, "I was upstairs when I heard something and when I went downstairs, I ran into the two of them. But I think I surprised them too because they didn't seem to know I was there. Vince slapped me across the face."

My teeth clenched trying to hold in my rage. I could see the memory in her eyes when she spoke, "they were arguing about what he was doing, and she was trying to stop him. She kept screaming, 'you told me she wasn't here, this has gone too far,' and he ended up smacking her too. He was raging, that's when he dragged me to my Mixx room and shut the door to lock me in. I think I'm lucky that's all he did. Then they left, and that's when he must have set the trailer on fire, because she came right back in to try to move the couch and screamed to tell me that I needed to get out. So, I panicked and tried to gather things, I think he came back in to get her, but then you got here. How did you get here so fast?"

We were interrupted by police needing statements, but Alexis instead pointed towards Vince's redheaded sister and screams out, "STOP, LEAVE HER!"

My eyes finally land on the same redhead that changed Daniel's fate on the night he went braindead. She was handcuffed beside a police cruiser, standing with her head down staring at her feet.

David steps up beside me to put his hand on my shoulder, pointing to Vince's sister as he says, "That's a blast from the past, now isn't it."

"Sure is," I agree.

There was a lot going on for us when Alexis was explaining the situation to the officers. When they spoke to her about pressing charges, she agreed to do so for only Vince, leaving his sister out of it legally, assuring the police that she already had the best lawyer that was going to have to help her deal with it. Vince is being booked into jail tonight, regardless. We all had to give statements, which at least distracted us from having to watch the firefighters start hosing down the studio, whereas the trailer and pod were already total crumbs.

As for Vince's sister, Sonia, she claims that Vince has been abusive towards her for many years, even sending him to jail over claims, but apparently the parents used their high military rank and money every time to cover for his actions over the many years. I thought I heard it all when she made the statement about tonight to the police, claiming Vince forced her into trying to befriend Alexis, hence why she tried getting a job. Until Sonia dropped another bomb on me tonight when they were taking her off for questioning.

She turned to me and David when she told us, "That was the worst day of my entire life. I'm so sorry, I would take it all back if I could, I didn't know when he sent me to the bar that night, that he would do that to Daniel."

I choke out, "What did you just say?"

She starts crying, tears running down her freckled cheeks when she replies, "He was so mad that he lost, just like tonight. He freaked and made me come to that bar that night. He told me to find you, but Daniel found me beforehand, and I ended up really hitting it off with him. So, I ignored whatever Vince told me to do. But my brother tracked me down on purpose and figured out a way to get back at you. I'm so sorry, Daniel was sweet."

I don't know what came over me when I blurt out in response to her,

"You picked the better man. He was sweet."

I give Sonia a nod, as she then turns around and follows the officers.

My eyes searing into Alexis's greens, as I take a deep breath after that encounter. I'm still holding her our way, not letting her go.

The medical teams were checking the both of us out and practically had to force me into making me sit Alexis down in the back of the ambulance, to make sure to get the correct blood pressure readings. I had actually ignored them when they first asked me, or maybe I ignored them more than once. Either way, the EMS tried to convince me it was for the best I let her down but had to eventually get David to come over to help coax me to do it. Alexis didn't make a peep regarding those encounters either, she instead just silently waited for me to sort it out on my own with her arms around my neck...or with the help of David pulling my arm back. Then once they started checking her with medical instruments it made me start panicking about the possibility that she was hurt...so, then I made all four of the EMS workers on that ambulance recheck her to be completely certain everyone got the same normal numbers.

It was early morning hours when she and I both got the green light to go home. And by home, I mean back to her house in Paisley, since I was literally just paying rent on my empty condo lately. Sabine's father picked her up to take her back to their house but promised to first drop off all the saved items of Rachel's at Alexis's house for her. David gave me one last hug before he joined the large group walking back to CeCe's, to send the party home and go rest himself. Breaking off the group by himself in the distance is Pauley. I shout out his name loud and clear, and with everyone pretending not to watch as I walk with Alexis up to him, I hold out my hand. "Thank you," I told him clearly. He winced and replies, "No thanks to me, it's my fault he came here tonight in the first place."

"If there is any blame to be held it lies on me. I'm the one he wanted to ultimately hurt."

Alexis speaks up for the first time since having to tell her side of the story too many times to the police. "Neither of you are to blame. Vince would have done something to me regardless, he has problems..." she glances up at me and lays on her sweetness thick while she explains, "Vince already got to me at the gym the other day when I was running on the treadmill again. He told me he was purchasing that gym once he won the fight against David, but he had this sick way about him, wanting to make sure he saw all of your family go down. I thought he was still harassing me on purpose to stir you up. So, I didn't tell you. I didn't want to mess with the fight."

"But Alexis, you told Pauley?" I ask trying not to throw my unjust anger onto her, but I felt betrayed.

Pauley throws out his two cents stating, "She most certainly did not tell me about Vince buying that gym."

"No, Declan, I didn't tell Pauley," Alexis says, eyes still focused solely on me, "Vince must have already had his sights set on me, since he sent his sister over multiple times to try and get a job. But...also...he may have kinda..."

She was hesitating before she completed her sentence, "...cornered me in the parking lot afterwards and grabbed my butt."

Yeah, my fire from the backburner was bursting out in front of me now, I shuffle quick on my feet, almost hopping, and have to step away from her and Pauley for a second to catch my breath. He touched her twice. Not just the cowardly slap across her face he took tonight, like I thought. If he wasn't already getting booked in jail, Vince could have ultimately succeeded on ending me if I had known. If only he was still around for me to lay my hands on, because I would have gotten life in prison.

Instead, trying to gather my cool, hands on my hips. I turn to see my girl standing still, looking nervously at me. He isn't taking her away from me. I strut back to Alexis, grab her butt to lift her our way, to tell her, "Let me take you home."

Chapter 37   Alexis

Aftershock.

It was the first shower we had together where we didn't speak, just took our sweet time sudsing each other up and washing the night off from us. Declan wrapped me in a towel and curled up on the couch with me while we fell asleep.

The only thing that was gone for good was my studio, but I think I've been through so many losses in my life to guard my heart, I can't even feel the sadness for losing it yet. As terrifying of a night it was, it ended with me wrapped up in the strong warm arms of the man who saved my life. A man who holds a breath of life for me that I need in order to survive.

A few hours later, we were woken up by Luna's barking at the door, but Declan squeezed me tighter.

"Don't you move," he said, "Let me go see."

But Declan didn't get the time, because the front door was already being unlocked from the outside and busting in through is Jameson.

"Alexis!" Jameson shouts, while strutting in like he owns the place, throwing his backpack on the floor and petting Luna in a hello.

Scrambling to my feet in just my towel, Declan's surprised stricken eyes leap up over me while he stands to cover me with his large bulk frame.

Shit

I squeal in delight, "Jameson, I'm here but I'm naked! Close your eyes so I can run and get on some clothes!"

My heart is happy when I see my best friend in the entryway now, in person and not on a screen, stopping suddenly and turning, with his fingers in the corner of his eyes when he replies, "seriously! Fuck, hurry up!"

Giving Declan my most convincing this is all going to be alright kind of look, I dart to my room to get changed while I hear Declan introducing himself. I was almost relieved I didn't have to actually witness that moment, these two strong willed men trying their hardest for me to be polite to one another. Declan is the love of my life, which he doesn't even know yet, but regardless, I plan on keeping Declan. However, I am also going to count on Jameson for the rest of my life too, so Declan is also going to have to come to terms with that, and an understanding regarding our friendship. Since they live in two different states, I'm not too concerned they will have any problems. This is something I've already decided in my head. I am choosing what Rachel gave to me.

A new normal.

Once I skip out and find Jameson and Declan in the Kitchen, parted by the Island counter, I hear Jameson's angry voice. "He blocked her in with the couch! The fucking couch!"

He screams at Declan, "What kind of crazy person did you get her involved with?"

Holding his hand up and his jaw solid straight, Declan retorts, "You're right, I shouldn't have let him near her again."

"Again!" Jameson howls, just when I come up from behind him and wrap my arms around his middle in a tight squeeze.

"Shut up, Jameson, I'm alive because of Declan. Now turn around and give me a hug hello!" Dressed in dark skinny jeans and a cotton tee fitting around his tall slim body frame, Jameson's chestnut eyes look glossy and tired when he looks at me for the first time.

"I can't believe it," he says to me in a throaty whisper. "When Sabine called me, I got the first flight out," grabbing me and pulling me in for a hug. Tight and familiar, but a grip that spoke volumes.

It was warm and much needed since it's been too long, but Declan was there watching me looking sullen, so I blew him a kiss from behind Jameson's back.

"I see you've met Declan, and you have already come up with quick conclusions, but you're wrong to be blaming him."

Jameson blatantly rolls his eyes in front of the both of us, causing Declan to smirk.

Jameson replies sharply, "You almost died!"

"But I didn't die!" I tell him.

He gives me a look and takes a deep breath as he says plainly giving up, "There are several things of food sitting on your front porch, and I've had a long night traveling, so I'm hungry. Feed me Seymour."

Declan almost looked grumpier when he responds pointing at Jameson saying, "If that's Margie's food, this is the last thing I'm going to share with you."

Margie's food always brings people together, and once we all had full stomachs from the multiple quiches and casseroles, she had left for us, egos in the room simmered down low, as we all felt defeated.

But it also helped clear my smoke-filled head and reminded me that my time was up in hiding Rachel's secrets.

Chapter 38   Alexis

A cry passed along

With both Jameson and Declan here in my Paisley home, I decided to take the lead into how I wanted today to go, with sitting them both down back on the couch and bringing over the bag filled with all Rachel's items. Each of them on opposite corners, I walk over to hand Jameson the frame that holds Rachel's, Wings of Paisley song, then turn to snuggle in Declan's arms for strength as I wait for Jameson to read it silently to himself.

I was crying while I watched his eyes flutter over her words in troubled pain, as Declan quietly held me tight. This was a big moment for me and Jameson, Declan felt it, we all felt it. The three of us connected to this grieving journey together, somehow all arranged with one another to help bring the pieces all together. Like Rachel would have wanted.

"She wrote this for you when she came here the first time…" Jameson states as a rhetorical question out loud to himself as he adds, "why would she write this?"

Sticking up for me like a true man of honor, Declan tells Jameson, "Alexis wasn't sure, she wanted to understand before she told you."

I give a chuckle at Jameson's not impressed face, and reply with the only curious question on my mind, "What do you hear, Jameson? What is Rachel saying do you think?"

Declan's body tenses behind me, just as I watch Jameson's relax while reading Wings of Paisley over again, and then answering, "I don't know, that Paisley made her want to kill herself?"

"Maybe or something in Paisley triggered her," I say. Like a smart ass, Jameson retorts dryly, "Yes, she spent too much money on this house obviously, 'a deal at a cost, she took, and she lost.'"

Grr

Declan couldn't hide his snort out in amusement, giving Jameson the slightest corner grin. Standing myself up quickly, I move them, having to be pretty bossy, out of their comfy spots on the couch to the outside front porch. Freezing cold but my adrenaline pumping, I tell Jameson firmly, "This is where Rachel wrote it. Now sit down here and read the last paragraph again, out loud."

With the smoothest voice of an angel, he read;

A sight to see

A buzzing bee

My only truth lives in Paisley

Fishing for the strength to come across

But the shadows from my dark

May make them fall apart

Not in on the secret, I don't want to bring you pain

So, I was happy to be a fly on the wall in Paisley

I found my wings in Paisley

When he finishes, Jameson squints at me to ask, "What's going on here, Lex?"

Declan looks at me with more questions in his eyes, so I ignore Jameson and instead smile at Declan, exclaiming, "Yes, baby. I think she literally put me right in front of where she wanted me to be. Will you go get the bag with the other things for me, while I speak to Jameson for just a second?"

He steals a kiss from me first, then politely nods while passing Jameson through the doorway, back to the inside.

Sitting down on the steps next to Jameson, I give him a loving nudge. He smells of his familiar coconut scent from his hair mousse, while he runs his thumb over the words.

He says quietly, "So, this is why you're so adamant about being here then? She left this mystery song for you."

"She left this for me along with the deed to the house."

Jameson asks, "Why didn't you tell me?"

"I was mad, thinking she wrote me a song about her misery as a parting gift, so I didn't want to add that on you, because like you, when I read it and with everything I know about Rachel, it doesn't make sense that there is any actual truth. But, I don't think it could have ever started to make sense until I actually lived here."

Declan comes back out with the bag in hand, as I keep talking, "I hear the words in my sleep, I've examined them to try to figure it out, but I wasn't getting anywhere. Declan read it and made me think, okay, what if Rachel did have some sort of story here in Paisley.

"It doesn't make sense," Jameson answers shaking his head adding, "none of this makes any sense."

I reply, "Well, then my neighbors, Estel and Margie," I point across the street and make sure both of them follow my direction when I proceed, "told me over dinner that the man who used to own this house was convinced by Rachel to move but when we called him, he said she gave him an offer and he knew taking it was the right thing to do."

Jameson's eyebrows furrow, as he turns to face my house as he exclaims, "during her drive through?"

Then he shifts, "Wait! I'm sitting out here in the freezing ass cold, and you have no point?"

Declan says, "I don't think she would be out here if she doesn't have a point."

I proceed to say, "I do think I have a point, but I actually do need to warm up too, so you're going to have to be nice because I want you to meet Estel and Margie."

Declan speaks, "you had a long night, maybe we should just go lay back down."

Jameson agrees, "I could sink back into that couch."

"I almost died for this. No more secrets. Come on!" I tell them both hastily, with Declan grabbing my hand quickly and tugging me in while Jameson saunters behind us.

I probably just endured one of the most horrific nights of my life, but after Declan getting to me in time and being able to save Rachel's things and a night in his arms, a morning wakeup call from my best friend showing up in Paisley for the first time, and a new sense of reality in my new normal, prepared by Rachel, that this hovering out of body experience is in complete control of me, flying me through these moments with a higher energy. If my hunch is right, it comes with many questions along with opening old wounds, the old wounds Rachel wasn't strong enough to face. And I was hoping it wouldn't drop me in the middle of this.

The front door of Estel and Margie's house was flung open the moment we crossed the street, passing the bass fish mailbox, and onto their freshly shoveled driveway. Margie's eyes darted straight to Jameson once she stepped out onto her porch.

Estel shouts out, "my poor girl, we are so sorry about the fire. Thank God you're alright."

I yell back to them, "Declan saved me again!" We step up to the porch, giving them big hugs and introducing them to Jameson. I could tell Declan had a lighter mood once he entered Estel and Margie's house, like a familiar family home that takes away some stress from you just by stepping inside. Declan was still holding the bag Sabine put my things in, and I asked them to all sit down with me. I was feeling brave, out of this world brave and I wasn't even sure what I was doing. Declan smiled at me the whole time, I don't think he had any idea what I was doing here either, but he was just happy to be able to sit beside me under a table again. Dirty man.

I start my formal sit down with a deep breath as I begin to tell them what I think Rachel is telling me. Turning to Estel and Margie, I start to tell them, "Rachel, Jameson, and I were three very close friends growing up in Boston, and we all had some very tough times. But one thing none of us could ever understand, was how horrible Rachel's mother, Terrie, was as a person let alone a mother."

Jameson interrupts, "Lex, what are you doing?"

"I beg him, "Please just trust me. I think it matters."

Jameson looks away in irritation and takes a stretch back on his seat while Margie places a comforting hand on his shoulder and I'm being commanded to steer forward on this cloud, so I add, "Rachel lived across the hall from us in our Condo building, and prior to that while growing up, I lived with her and her mom since I was seventeen. We were with her every single day, so that's why it confuses us why she did all of this."

Jameson chimes in. "And let's just say she was not the type of person that would go randomly buy a house."

"Right," I agree and continue with everyone's full attention, "but nevertheless, bought this house in the very beginning of January this year from Carl, that's when we know she was here. And then, when she came back to Boston, she started taking legal counsel to write out a will, planning for her death, forcing her mother out of everything, and leaving me with things like, the house, a bank account, and this." I pull out the frame the place it on the table and continue to say, "But we don't know why. And I'm asking why, because what Rachel left for me was almost a cry for help when I realized she had planned her suicide all along."

I hand over the Wings of Paisley to Jameson and again tell him, "Will you read it out loud for us. I want Estel and Margie to hear this."

Jameson obliges, probably because he still had Margie close beside him giving him her warm comforting care and he doesn't have the heart to misbehave.

Once he finishes reading, I let them all in on my secrets, "I started asking questions to figure out what may have led Rachel to purchase the house and our friend Kel told me about a conversation Rachel had with her prior to the holidays about Rachel applying for a passport since she didn't have one, and that she apparently told Kel she stored her documents in my safe."

Shaking my head while I'm reminding my own self about the time I already had the answers to it all right in front of me, but I didn't look twice at the birth certificate because I was too consumed with the music box.

I continue explaining, "the safe is something Rachel bought for me as a gift for my birthday a long time ago, and it looks like a speaker. It was brought in with the movers, just like the rest of my things, placed inside my Mixx room..." pausing with the sudden sad reminder of the fire taking the Mixx room away from me, I look to my blues to help comfort me. Zapping me, I keep talking, "So, when I did indeed find my speaker safe, I also found another little something she left for me inside," eyeing Estel and Margie, I say, "when Declan and I called Carl, he told us he knew who Rachel was as soon as he saw her blue eyes, and it just made him decide right then on that porch to sell to her, and that's what made him move to Florida."

I've stunned Margie to silence, and Estel scratches his head.

Jameson is the one to speak, "Yeah, well maybe he felt compelled to sell since she was famous or something."

Declan pipes in, "Carl also said you wouldn't understand until it was right in front of you," giving me a quick glance and smile, making me feel like he may have caught on to where I may be leading this.

Shaking my head, I reply looking at Jameson, "I know it sounds crazy, but doesn't it sound like Estel, and Margie may have something to do with why she bought that house?"

I tell him, "One thing you should know before I keep going, is that Estel and Margie have told us about their daughter, Laura. Who, like Rachel, also committed suicide, but back in 1995 while she was in Boston?"

Declan's hand gropes my thigh while I keep the nerve to explain, "Last night, before the fire, Sabine and I were on our way to meet Declan at CeCe's gym. We had a cab driver stop here first so I could let Luna out, and when he pulled out on our way," I give the gentlest smile while I look at Margie and Estel and tell them, "The cab driver told me about remembering your daughter, Laura from school and he had made a comment about Margie being called the 'buzzing bee lady.'"

I'm getting really nervous, and maybe it's the smoke finally coming up and bugging me in my cloud, or maybe it's because I am going to feel like a fool if I saw it wrong in my scramble last night.

Declan finds my eyes, sees my worry and smiles, pulling up the bag on his lap and looking inside, to pull out the papers. I see his eyes roaming across, while Jameson looks like he is going to pounce on him. Declan looks at me, then hands it to Jameson.

I see Jameson reading the paper and gives a loud, "Oh shit!" Then he looks at me in horror, only to take one for the team, and bending his head down to his side, Margie was looking sick with her eyes all over the place, trying to figure out what is going on, just as Jameson slides the birth certificate over in front of her on the table.

I take a deep hard swallow. The tears are out before Margie has time to cover her mouth with her hands in her shock, as Estel looks down over his reading glasses in still form. Laura is listed as Rachel's birth mother on her original birth certificate from the state of Massachusetts, not New York where Terrie claimed she had the baby. B.B. Butler is her father.

"How can this be!" Margie screams, looking terrified at Estel while she screams again in a higher shriek, "How can this be, Estel?"

"Her birthday," Jameson says looking frantic, "That wasn't Rachel's birthday, Rachel was born in April, not March."

My mind raced and my eyes leaped to the dates printed in ink on Rachel's Massachusetts birth certificate. The birthday Rachel had always known when she was alive was April, 7, 1995. And sure enough, the birth certificate claims she was born March 21, 1995.

But she ended her life a week before her birthday this year. Which had me thinking out loud, "So she turned twenty-five in March, which means..."

I pause to look up to Jameson with his eyes wide and his hands on his hips, "She was already twenty-five."

"Lexi," Jameson shouted my name like I was doing something wrong in class and continued, "Please fucking tell me you have actually looked at that trust fund account to see if there were any previous transactions before you got a hold of it...like for your house!"

I hadn't. And with the look on my face, everyone knew. Declan started laughing. Laughing. Jameson huffs out in more irritation and hands out his hand for me to give him my phone, I do, and

I say, "But she wouldn't have had access in January."

Jameson speaks, "Lexi, you haven't even created an account. You have millions of dollars in here with no profile created. Really?" He doesn't even wait for my rebut since he snaps his head back down and starts typing fast, most likely creating me a profile.

As we all wait for Jameson to find whatever he's looking for on my phone,

Declan states still in his laughter, "I knew she had no idea about money when she swiped over a thousand bucks at the hardware store," then he squeezes me as I nuzzle embarrassed in his neck.

Jameson states, "Yep, Carl got his money in March. Which means Rachel knew about this birth certificate in January."

Declan states with more laughter, "I bet she made a deal with Carl to transfer it since he knew who she was."

Margie huffs out, "Carl knew who Rachel was?"

Declan jerks but says, "I think we actually all may owe Carl a thank you. He said he knew those blue eyes, well turns out, Margie and Laura have those too!"

Margie stiffens.

Jameson excused himself from the table, to go stand out on the front porch to catch his stunned breath. I figure this time was as good as any when I pull out the jewelry box.

I had that thought, that this was the moment it's all about to blow up in my face by having to witness their reaction to the sight of the box, obviously recognizable, both looking like they were doubling over in heart attacks right in front of Declan and me.

Declan's sweet Irish voice rang out, "there, there, you mustn't cry for the angels now, they both found their wings and they're together again."

"Oh, sweet boy you are," Margie squeals through her tears. Sniffling, Estel picks up the knowing box and opens it wide, and as the music starts, they both give a smile.

Margie dives in for the pins and her smile grows wider as she said, "I cannot believe it. She always seemed so ashamed of my quirkiness as she got older, I thought she threw these away."

Estel holds the jewelry box when he quietly gets up out of his chair and walks away, only returning a couple minutes later with a small silver key in his other hand when he pulls another chair up close next to me and says,

"When we returned to her apartment where she lived to gather her things, this box was missing, and it was ultimately the one item Laura had that was important to her, and to us, so it was always an added struggle to the entirety of it all. I made this box for Laura when she was a young girl."

Jameson walks back inside right as Estel opens the box again, this time with a large smile on his face when seeing the dancer spin around in her queen bee costume. Declan picks up the last note Rachel left me inside, with her purple scroll, just as Estel gives a soft look to Margie and continues to tell, "All these years, and I've kept this key thinking I was a fool for ever believing I would get a chance to do this again one day."

Estel sticks the little key in the hidden hole underneath the inside of the lid, right where Rachel originally placed that note for me, and turns it to open up a hidden compartment.

Stuffed inside is a an old worn white envelope, torn open neatly from the top, with browner in the worn spots looking like it's been stuffed in this box for the time it's been sitting.

"What do we have here," quirks Estel in his surprise. He pulls out the stashed envelope, only to have a photograph fall from underneath his fingertips onto the kitchen table.

I may have fainted. I thought Rachel was crazy when I found out she left me this house. Then I realized she may have wanted me to know what made her fall apart so much, and after Laura's reveal I thought I knew. I was certain I had only a few pieces left to solve Rachel's puzzle and they must come from Laura's past, and then I could assume Rachel's reasoning for it all and I could move on in this new normal.

"Alexis," Declan shakes me while I sit next to him in my comatose state I felt like I was in.

I hear Jameson give another loud grumble of curse words just as Declan has pulled me onto his lap now while I stare at the picture in complete shock.

"This is Laura," Estel points to the blonde-haired, blue-eyed girl who looks identical to Rachel, sitting with a baby on her lap. He continues telling me in his own exasperation, "that was her roommate we had only met once, she had an accent, and obviously a baby too."

Both women sit side by side holding their babies in the photograph, Rachel looking days fresh.

"Tereza," I speak my mother's name quietly out loud, while pointing to the friend next to Laura in the photograph, the roommate, the one she met at B.B.'s audition, holding a baby only looking older. I managed to say through my confusion, "that's my mother, and that's me."

"Well, this just got weird," Jameson says sternly with his hands on his hips, "Did Rachel see this picture? She would have had to know this was you and your mom, Lex, I mean it looks like you, holding a baby," he gives out an audible sigh of disbelief as he continues to mutter, "If I saw this picture at a random setting, I would bet money that this woman is you, because the memory I have of what your mom looked like, was not this. It's a true shame of what drugs can do to you."

Estel was still looking at the picture like he was silently asking his daughter a million questions. There was a silence across us all, until Declan holds out his hand to the picture and asks Estel, "May I?"

Holding the photograph up to the light, Declan's husky voice calls out, "Hot mamas," giving us all a chuckle amid our shock and pulling me from my own stupor. He pulls out the letter and unfolds the paper looking like it was ripped out of a journal and starts skimming it privately. It looks short, but Estel stays stoic as he gets through it.

Maybe finally, after all these years, they can get answers they looked for.

My Dearest Bumble Bee,

Take good care of her for me. And when she is old enough, tell her how much her mother loved her. I am sorry if I hurt you, but your wife is right, I have nothing to offer this child, and she will do much better than I ever could in your arms with the person you are meant to be with.
Like a fly on the wall, I will always be watching over the both of you.

Love, Your Queen Bee

There was a gut-wrenching truth that has come out, Terrie's words manipulating a young mother, scared and alone, into letting her baby go. Preying on Postpartum depression. And, yet somehow now my mother is involved, making me realize we have only cracked open the can, and there are some hard truths still waiting to come out. But for now, this was hard enough for us all to take in. We all needed time to heal, time helps heal, we can ask more questions tomorrow.

Chapter 39   Declan

When Vince decides to strike me when I least expect it, like the Devil, all he ever leaves in his path is ash and rubble. Cold, dark, smelly crumbs and bits of ash blow in the wind around us. Deciding it was best for Alexis to get some rest while Jameson and I try to play nice to one another and have come to scour the premises of what is left of her studio. Sometimes I'm wrong, and sometimes I'm blindsided, but all those times don't carry any importance if that one time, I was right when it mattered. I don't want to imagine what this day would feel like if I didn't listen to my instincts last night, but I'll be damned if Jameson is going to let me get away with not thinking about it.

He asks, "So, why was Pauley not on guard last night?"

"There was no reason for him to be here, since Alexis wasn't working."

Jameson throws a smart remark, "but, she was here. That's exactly why I hired him for an around the clock gig and then he coulda just lived in the trailer. I had already paid him, it was a done deal, before you two called him off."

I reply with an even tone, "That was between you and Alex-"

"Don't feed me that shit!" Jameson interrupts, "You were sitting right there in that conversation, you knew I had reasons I hired security for her."

"Yes, but the reasons being something that had nothing to even do with what happened last night."

"I guess maybe if I had known that her new boyfriend has a lineup history of trouble, I would have put an extra guard on her. Instead, she made me put my trust in you," he shouts, a deep scowl on his light brown face showing his anger. Fighting words, fighting about keeping the one we love safe.

Who is better at taking care of her?

I am, obviously.

I raise my voice, "I didn't want Pauley here to begin with because he is Vince's cousin. That's who he went after first last night, before he even got here, to Alexis. Even torched his trailer first..." I point to the dust on the ground where the trailer used to stand, "Pauley's trailer you put right there."

"It's funny, I don't see the fucking thing now do I? But if Pauley were here..."

I laugh interrupting him now, "You obviously haven't seen Pauley's face. He wouldn't have been able to hold him off. And you know what, I don't give a shit 'bout that because lemme' tell you something,"

I walk closer to where Jameson stands, "The only thing I give a shit about, is that she is safe, and alive, and breathing."

"Yeah, well you and me both. Because if you had let my best friend burn to death because she was stuck behind a leather couch, in this fuckin' town!" He takes a deep breath, never backing down from me, yet he finishes more coolly, "I would have lost my shit if you hadn't of been there in time."

Why are people from Boston confusing?

"Wait," I pause with a sly grin, "Is that a city 'thank you?'"

"Hell, no it's not," Jameson replies, "it just means she's going to have two guards on her now, because I'm not leaving until after this show."

I was halfway shocked at the mercy he was laying on me after all of that, but I was more shocked that he just said he wasn't leaving, so I figure no time like the present when I start off strong.

"Where do you plan on staying?"

"What the fuck is that supposed to mean? You worried I might sneak into Lexi's room at night and bang her?"

My blood was more than boiled, but he wasn't avoiding the conversation we needed to ultimately have.

"I'm not worried, because there won't be any possibility you'll get through me to try."

Ha

Jameson laughs out, and it's the first time I've actually seen him without a scowl on his face.

"Listen. I know she's into you, and I'm not tryin' to step in the way with you guys' business, but she is important to me too, and I intend to take care of her the same way I have for the last fifteen years. So, if she is someone who only matters to you because of what you got going on in between the sheets, I'm going to ask you to step off."

"I'm not going anywhere," I say with no second thought, "Trust me, you better believe I'm staying in the house and in the sheets."

"I'm here to take care of her now," I tell it firmly, more like a done deal but also a plea to him. But I won't ever be done, without this deal.

An awkward pause goes by before Jameson gives a smile, and then it scarily gets wider, and he holds his arms out wide on his sides and replies to me, "Guess this makes us roommates, dawg!"

I guess that was our moment of truce for now. The fact that he isn't going away brings a bit of a damper on things for me. I've watched him closely since he stepped inside today, making sure where his hands landed during their embrace, seeing how he interacts with her is important for me to find out. And it seems that is something I am going to have to start getting used to keeping my eye on, but so far, he doesn't seem to have that romantic vibe with her. When we got back to Alexis's house, Jameson took off to the guest room to makes some calls while I hunted for Alexis. There were stacks of home cooked meals scattered along the countertops and stacked up in the fridge, varieties of different dishes made by all local families around our congenial community, trying to send their sentiments regarding the fire.

"There is so much food, I could feed an army, and it just keeps coming," Alexis tells me when I found her in a seemingly more energetic mood since I last saw her, while also squirming around in the kitchen in total disarray, looking hot in sweat pants and a tight tank top that shows her cleavage.

I'm feeling more than hungry.

Starved.

"One lady said I'm on some type of food chain!"

My food chain.

I show her how delicious I think she is when I come up behind her and tug her into me, as I'm sure she can feel ever so slightly just how wild she makes me when talking about feeding.

Bringing her arm up to touch the side of my face she turns her head to kiss me softly then says, "I hope you're hungry."

I growl in her ear while she giggles, making even my quick minute of hope worth it.

She says softly, "I see you brought Jameson back in one piece."

"Only thanks to you," I tell her in good humor.

Her smile fades away from the side of her face I'm studying as she says, "He told me about staying here until the show is over, and I said he could for now, but I also told him to go ahead and find a rental since the whole band will all be here by the end of the week," she turns around to face me, hands on my cheeks as her emeralds gleam and she asks, "Is that ok that I did that?"

The worry in her face planted worry in mine. "Wha-..." I stop myself abruptly to blink.

There was no more waiting, I tell her, "Jump up."

She does, our way, and I speak, "When I was waiting for you at the gym last night...well pretty much that's all I was doing...but when you didn't show up..." leaning my forehead onto hers, I tried to continue, but I couldn't.

I did watch her close her green eyes to kiss me softly. Her top lip has this salacious fullness to it that I love to suck on in between our kisses.

When we get heavier, giving me her mouth with tongue, tasting of sweetness, I pull back and tell her in a clear voice, "I love you."

My heart was tricked by my voice box, now thudding frantically as it caught up to the words that I just spoke out to a girl for the first time in my life, while I stand here with her in the kitchen. Words that didn't describe the love I felt. Maybe I could have thought out something a bit more romantic, but I've never practiced this. She was already mine, I just needed to tell her. Surely, I didn't do too bad, because I was rewarded some noises she squeaked out after I said it. But then she asks, "Are you sure?"

Maybe I miserably failed. I aim for the second best try, "I am sure I love you. I am sure of it with every breath in my lungs. I love you, Alexis."

Her eyes getting wetter by the second, she replies, "I love you, Declan. But I'm really scared I'm going to lose you, too."

"You're not going to lose me," I tell her trying to calm her fear we both seem to have in common, "I'm tougher than I look."

"Just give me fair warning," she says.

Being playful I get close to her ear and whisper, "Nothing is fair. But believe me, when I promise to love you, I don't break my promise. And I promise to love you as hard as I can."

"I'm going to test that theory," she says to me, but seductively, as she trails her fingers down my abdomen like she isn't doing a thing, "I'm pretty sure I owe you that Victory dance."

Testing in Session.

Alexis is my victory.

Chapter 40   Alexis

I have not seen or heard anything from Estel and Margie since we last spoke over three weeks ago, but she keeps leaving boxes of food for me at my front door, stress cooking, I suppose. Twenty-five years may sound like a lot of time gone by to some, but to Estel and Margie, Laura didn't leave them with time, the only thing she left them was heartbroken, doomed to find their way back to a new normal with her still there, just not in reach. And then this happens, ultimately revealing to them that Rachel Butler was their granddaughter, their blood, their only truth who also took her life. They will choose when they are ready to return to the table and help me solve the rest of the puzzle.

With Laura listed as the birth mother, it was still B.B. Butler's name listed under the father, apparently nicknamed Bumblebee, which brings us all to the conclusion to an affair of some sort. One may even wonder if the making of Rachel happened the weekend Laura went to Boston for the audition. Either way, it gives insight into why Terrie always treated Rachel like a secondhand toy, still to blame, why Rachel never connected with Terrie, why she was never given the chance, why Rachel still left.

For Rachel, even after figuring it all out, it was still not worth her breaths, for she decided it was wings that she had to have instead.

But that was Rachel, if that was something she had decided, and it was a decision she could make on her own, regardless of what we all think she coulda, shoulda done, that was her choice for herself. Although, it's my choice that I can still throw my middle finger up to the sky to let her know how I feel about it, sometimes.

Sabine has been close to my side as well, like a fourth roommate who has been working with Jameson and I on SheerMe stuff in the living room, mostly Jameson, while I work on Declan in the bedroom.

A few days after the fire, when it actually dawned on me that it will probably take another six months before I can have my studio back, I started sulking more, feeling all that independence I just had was way too brief, and the last thing I wanted to do, was have Jameson bossing me around in my living room.

I had come up with the best plan ever to make me feel better, so I had Sabine sneak most of Margie's dinners over to CeCe's gym for David and Len, without Declan or Jameson finding out. Working like a charm, throwing Sabine into the ring with David, bringing food no man would be stupid enough to turn down.

David is definitely not stupid.

Even so, with food still exploding from my kitchen, Declan thought he had the best idea ever when he decided we needed to host a party on Jameson's last day bunking with me, us, and also since the entire band had arrived in Paisley.

So, with a group of giant muscles from Paisley eating and drinking and laughing with a group of band nerds from Boston, my old came together with my new, making it all mine.

Until it wasn't just all mine anymore.

It was the night before the SheerMe show, and Maya Gueterra had our week lined up hour by hour, minute by minute, literally scheduling us around the clock with work so tightly, that we had dedicated times for our bathroom breaks. Since practice was at Swollen, my pee breaks usually ended up with Declan and I sneaking around in the club, trying to spend every second we had together. Claiming he never wanted to watch during our practice sets, trying to just wait for the night of to be surprised, tonight being the eve of, Declan seems overwhelmed with anxiety in anticipation for the show and my Live performance, maybe shaking my behind with Jameson and the other dancers has gotten him extra wound up. I'm finding my own self feeling more wound up than my usual right now, while trying on this piece of lingerie in my bedroom. Meanwhile, Declan huffs outside the door waiting to see what I have on, his first look at what I have to wear.

Strapped in white lace, I step out a few minutes later, out to find Declan pacing in front of the stone fireplace he had burning with the wood logs crackling.

"Baby," he halfway says it, jaw dropped to the floor, and I could tell in his eyes, almost looking high in his lust, that those sparks were beyond anything explainable, something maybe only the tunnel knows, or maybe Daniel or Rachel.

Growling his steps up to me slowly rasping out,

"Breathtaking, Just my luck, they have you lookin like an angel and a siren all in one," taking hold of me finally, lifting me up but slower than usual, taking the time watching my legs spread for him, giving him a show since I'm practically naked in this getup.

Wrapped around him in our way, there was something important on my mind and I had to ask him,

"After this show is over, do you think we can go chop our Christmas tree down?"

Our Christmas tree, I was making plans for us, because he was a part of me now.

"My answer is yes, since you bought every chainsaw, handsaw, and axe that store in town had available, we are all ready to go. But.." he paused while looking at me with such seriousness in his eyes, bringing me worry.

I ask. "Are you okay?"

He smiles, wide, then wider until I have the most beautiful face of a man in front of me when he replies, "No baby," he says still smiling and chuckling, "I'm not okay."

Amused but confused, I scoot my lower half tighter to him. Rushing back to a serious face when he responds, "Whoa, hold on beautiful, I'm about to make it all okay."

Kissing and moving at the same time, Declan grabs a wrapped medium box he had hidden underneath a pillow, next to Luna, and brings it up to me.

Stern look on my face, I tell him, "I don't need prezzies to make anything okay, Declan! I'm happy."

He gives me a sterner look back and pulls the gift away from me to hold it behind his back, and replies, "Not me. I won't be completely happy without you having this. But if you're choosing to not want my gift, I'll take it back."

My heart can't take it, exploding since he is so annoyingly cute sometimes, I laugh and reply, "Not fair!"

While flailing my arms around behind him in response, to then say, "okay fine, I'll never be okay until I see what's inside that box."

Declan grins, spinning the box back to me as I grab it out of his hands to rip it open.

"A teddy in a teddy!" I scream out in pure delight at the sight of my little brown bear with a purple threaded nose and a black teddy dress.

I kiss Teddy repeatedly, over, and over, and then I kiss Declan too, until he stops me and shakes his head to say,

"No, Alexis, I'm still not okay."

Confused, even more so when he puts me down, leaving me standing and not our way, Declan in front of me by the fire. With a brightness in his blue eyes, only blue skies when he is with me, he asks, "What good is a Teddy without a heart?"

I stared, flying in his skies for a few seconds until he threw out a quick signal, gesturing for me to look back down to my teddy in my hand. I do, I gleam at my sweet teddy and realize there is something under the dress by its heart. Declan states, "up through the skirt'll do," as he bends down on one knee in front of me. Up the skirt I go to find the hole in the heart, with a real prize inside. I pull out a solitaire diamond ring, a huge rock, but it's the tiny purple diamonds circling around my huge rock that makes this explosion of a feeling so charged.

A feeling I never knew existed, a feeling that I have been chosen, a feeling of love I've been waiting for.

My eyes blurred with happy tears, Declan stoic as a still Lion when he starts speaking to me,

"Alexis Paige Andrews, I will never be okay without you. I will never be okay until you become mine in every way I can think possible. I want my own new normal, with you. My choice was made the moment I found you in your moo moo in that tunnel, and you stole my heart. It's yours and I don't ever want to let you go. And I'll beg you forever to keep me. Will you marry me? Please."

"Yes!"

"Yes, Yes!" I scream my answer so quick to then jump on top of him in my excitement. All I ever needed was always here in Paisley.

Happy.
Content.
But more than that. It's the love that matters.

Chapter 41   Declan

My lungs should be on a poster, strong and in the best breathing shape of their respiratory lives, the both of them free from any waste. She said 'yes' to me. Me. Mine. I wanted every single round I had left in me to be spent with Alexis, the new fight of my life, a priceless one. The night of the SheerMe show has come, in full swing as Dax and Ronnie keep busy throwing their hands up with Maya Gueterra's demands, while I'm taking my 'off the clock' seriously, and instead I've been doting on my soon to be wife with anything and everything she needed prior, like waiting for her in the dressing room. One day, maybe my two buddies will find their person, and understand what it's like having your heart and your fate sealed in a swirl as one. The biggest punch of my life.

MartaBeat and Alexis have finished their final check, and the show was to start within the hour. The wait for Alexis to come out of the bathroom got heavier when Sabine and Jameson came running in screaming and singing, both on cloud nine, in extreme excitement ready for action. A shirtless Jameson in bright red boxer briefs had his guitar in hand while he bangs his fist on her door and yells, "Are you ready to shake that ass, girl?"

My annoyance rumbles as Alexis laughs from the other side of the door and replies back, "I'll be out in a minute."

"What about you," he asks gleaming at me, sarcastically taunting, "Are you going to be able to handle watching your soon to be wife dancing her luscious ass all over my ---"

I stood up quick, only to see Jameson jerk back in fear. I got him for the first time, and there was so much laughter rolling out of the both of us now. The two of us have come to a mutual understanding, and after I got his permission to ask Alexis to marry me, his smile hasn't moved from his face, or mine, and I guess I'd have to also admit that I have grown to like the guy.

Sabine in full display like an underwear model, says, "Will you two settle down, and will someone help me tighten this strap since Lexi is taking forever in there?"

She is turned around with her back to us, fiddling with her lack thereof lingerie, as Jameson took that as his cue to leave, darting out the door in one leap. Irish luck has it, when my brother, David arrived right in time. With a more serious look as he walks in, passing and ignoring me, while stepping behind an unaware Sabine and laying his fingers on her shoulders to the strap, causing her to flinch backwards towards him, just handing him the move. I don't know what has taken him so long, but judging by his look, he's about to shit his pants.

Thinking about nerves, the door to the bathroom finally opens, and I see Alexis standing in all her SheerMe glory, while giving me a weak smile. Within an instant, I'm closing us in the bathroom together. I ask while cupping her flawless face, "What's wrong?"

"Maybe it's my nerves. I don't know, Declan," shaking her head going down her rabbit hole of fear, "what if I can't do this?"

Standing there over her, I tell her,

"You've already done everything. The only thing you have to do now is press play."

Nodding in her understanding, but worry highlighting her face, she speaks as soft as a mouse when she replies,

"Well, what if that play button is pressed before we are ready?"

Commotion outside the room disturbs us as I hear Margie's voice, but I try my hardest to keep focused on her greens. I say, "then we catch up, just like we always do."

I don't know why I added myself into her equation, it just felt right I suppose. Then, I started to worry she was getting second thoughts about marrying me, and my heart sank when I try to choke out, "We can wait until you're ready if -"

Interrupting me, she shouts, "No!"

"That's not what I want." She says it, but doesn't have anymore time to explain in questions, because Sabine has opened the door with eyes large, while she says,

"Your neighbors are here."

Alexis lightly presses her hand on my arm to step around me and hold her bare arms out to a formally dressed Margie, wearing her Queen Bee pin, just as I feel a large cold hand grip my forearm and pull me out of the bathroom, only to have Estel throw his suited arms around me in a big hug.

Alexis speaks out, "Wow, you came! Did you find your seats? We put you next to Declan's family." Margie answers still holding Alexis but with tears in her eyes, "We're so sorry we didn't call, please forgive us, it won't happen ever again. Estel and I don't want to miss out on anything else, and you belong to us now."

I take this as my time to pipe in, "Well, actually," Alexis holds her hand up to show off her engagement ring to Estel and Margie, and the two both started crying like babies, but in happiness. Jumping up and down and giving us more hugs and loving words. Estel, always a pal, says to me, "Declan, we knew you weren't going anywhere. You know our table is always set for four."

Alexis throws her hand up to cover her mouth just as Jameson steps back in and stumbles with his words. "Oh, shhi'yaa...hi'ya ...Margie, Estel," also fumbling with his indecencies as he steps in, looking at Lexi in worry.

All of us in the room watching as Jameson stands in front of her and says, "Lexi, do you remember the last time you got the flu?"

Shaking her head, furrowing her eyebrows, she replies in question, "No?"

"Exactly." He states. "Now you decide to get the flu? We go on in twenty minutes."

I step over to her, caring much less about the show and more about my girl as I ask, "Are you feeling that sick?"

Her hesitation telling me she is most definitely feeling sick.

A very high pitch squeal comes from the corner as we all look over at a shell-shocked Sabine, just as she says,

"She doesn't have the flu, people! Look at her, she looks fantastic to me! And it's almost time, maybe everyone should be moving along," her hands waving us all off with her chest pumping so fast.

I almost laughed as I tell her, "You look mighty fine tonight, Sabine."

David barks out at me like we are not in a room with people, "Zip it!" I am laughing now as he turns a pink on his fair cheeks that stick out with his thick dark hair, trying to recover from his sudden outburst. Turning to Sabine and backtracking, "You do look mighty fine, but he's not allowed to say that."

She asks him why, right as I hear a beep, to turn and realize Jameson has a thermometer in Alexis's ear.

"97.7, you good," he says brightly.

"No, I'm not good," Alexis replies, making me also blurt out back to Jameson, "nope, you better find yourself another ass," and pulling her into me so I can study her more.

"Is this a joke? Because it's not funny!" Sabine screams in her panic, while Jameson just stands there in disbelief looking at the ground, and then there's David, still looking like he's about to shit his pants. All of us in this room together as the idea of Alexis not performing has entered the conversation.

Alexis looks like she is in pain when she apologizes and says, "This is what was meant to be, we have gone over everything you need to know a million times, you will perform this better than I ever could. It was always meant to be you up there."

Jameson is about to speak but gets distracted by Alexis running back to the bathroom and slamming the door behind her. Turning his head to Sabine, he states in a serious tone, "This is one of those times where you either hop on or get out."

Strutting up to Jameson, Sabine looks straighter when she replies, "I'm just about to enjoy the ride."

Grinning, Jameson laughs out and then runs out of the room to inform the director of the switch. Estel and Margie also start walking out to get to their seats, but not before Margie calls out, "Declan!"

Turning toward her, she smiles and says to me, "I keep the extra leaf for the table in the garage."

Totally confused at what is going on, I'm left with just Sabine and David in the room. Time is running out, but before Sabine does, she turns to my baby brother and says, "Will you wait for me when the show is over?"

My brother finally makes his move, grabbing Sabine by her lower back and pulling her in for a kiss. Smiling but concerned, I don't hesitate when I barge into the bathroom to find Alexis standing over the sink looking pale.

"Talk to me, what's wrong," I say pulling her hair out of her face.

Alexis says, "Will you hold me."

No more questions as I pull her up into me, our way, and the concern in my face should be blatantly obvious by now. She strokes my cheek and looks at me with doe eyes while she says, "Remember when my studio burned down, and so did all of my things?"

"Yes, of course. Is it something you're missing that you're thinking about that's got you feeling like this?"

"Well actually, yes. So, it turns out, that great little birth control pill I took daily at work, went down in flames with the building."

All I can do is stare at her.

Rolling in her greens.

Biting her fingernails, she starts to cry, "I am such an idiot, I didn't even think to..."

"Shh," I blurt out, cutting her off.

A few seconds of looking into her, things got blurry, and she quietly whispers, "Declan, are those sad tears or happy tears?"

"Happy tears," I manage to say, pulling those lips into mine because they were made just for me, mine, and I couldn't be happier to have our new surprise.

"Only happy tears from now on," I say to her now smiling face, while I'm crying, feeling like a baby, because we're going to have a baby.

"This is how it's meant to be, and I couldn't be happier. I love you, Alexis," I tell her through my blubber.

She wipes my tears when she softly replies, "I love you more, Declan. You are my only truth, forever."

End

For all those struggling with mental health, you are not alone. Stay strong and keep stepping forward.
#YOUMATTER

Made in the USA
Columbia, SC
07 March 2023

13340352R00150